BEHOLD THE GRAIL—

"Chalice of Tears, or I Didn't Want that Damned Grail Anyway" by Marion Zimmer Bradley—Whether she wished it or not, Lythande had been cursed with a mission and a gift, and until she fulfilled this quest, she would be deprived of spellcraft while magic ran wild throughout the land.

"The Cup and the Cauldron" by Mercedes Lackey—Elfrida was a follower of the Goddess, Leonie a believer in the White Christ, yet each had been gifted with a vision and a quest.

"That Which Overfloweth" by Andre Norton—The invaders had come, those bringers of death and stealers of treasure, but would they overlook the greatest treasure of all?

These are just a few of the spellbinding, original tales that await you in a volume as full of magic's promise as that most wondrous and legendary chalice itself—

GRAILS: QUESTS OF THE DAWN

GRAILS

Quests of the Dawn

Edited by Richard Gilliam, Martin H. Greenberg, and Edward E. Kramer

ROC
Published by the Penguin Group
Penguin Books USA Inc., 375 Hudson Street, New York, New York 10014, U.S.A.
Penguin Books Ltd, 27 Wrights Lane, London W8 5TZ, England
Penguin Books Australia Ltd, Ringwood, Victoria, Australia
Penguin Books Canada Ltd, 10 Alcorn Avenue, Toronto, Ontario, Canada M4V 3B2
Penguin Books (N.Z.) Ltd, 182–190 Wairau Road, Auckland 10, New Zealand

Penguin Books Ltd, Registered Offices: Harmondsworth, Middlesex, England

Published by Roc, an imprint of Dutton Signet, a division of Penguin Books USA Inc.
First appeared as a portion of *Grails: Quests, Visitations, and Other Occurrences,* published in a limited edition by Unnameable Press.

First Roc Printing, March, 1994
10 9 8 7 6 5 4 3 2 1

LIBRARY OF CONGRESS CATALOGING IN PUBLICATION DATA:
Grails : quests of the dawn, visitations, and other occurrences / edited by Richard Gilliam, Martin H. Greenberg, and Edward E. Kramer.
    p. cm.
"A Roc book."
ISBN 0-451-45303-4
1. Grail—Literary collections. 2. Quests—Literaryy collections. 3. Fantastic literature,

(The following page constitutes an extension of this copyright page.)

American. 4. Christian literature, American. I. Gilliam, Richard. II. Greenberg, Martin
H. III. Kramer, Edward E.
PS509.G68G73   1994
813'.0876608—dc20

93-11965
CIP

Printed in the United States of America

This book is dedicated to Fritz Leiber,
whose literary works have inspired us all.

The editors would like to thank Susan Barrows,
Paul Cashman, Robert A. Costner, Pamela Lloyd, Susan Phillips,
Ellénina Riley, James A. Riley, Elizabeth A. Saunders, Lamar
Waldron, and Caran Wilbanks for their assistance
in preparing the manuscripts for this tome.

Contents

———— ✠ ————

ix

GRAILS

Quests of the Dawn

The Question of the Grail

✠

Jane Yolen

Answer: Christ's vessel.
What is the question?

We could argue ships, the weight
of boats upon the Galilee,
the width and breadth of arks,
the wooden scow scurrying between
Avalon and eternity.

We could argue cups, the weight
of jewels in the ham-fist of kings,
the belching cauldron of Annwyn,
a simple Semitic glass
holding incarnate blood.

But I rather argue a woman's weight,
the bowls of my breasts, my cup-like womb,
the mounds fitted for blood,
for salt in equal measure,
for the treasuring of life,
for divine revelation,
for the granting of it—
bowls, cups, mounds—
and the pattern of the maze.

1

The Cup and the Cauldron

✠

Mercedes Lackey

Rain leaked through the thatch of the hen-house; the same dank, cold rain that had been falling for weeks, ever since the snow melted. It dripped on the back of her neck and down under her smock. Though it was nearly dusk, Elfrida checked the nests one more time, hoping that one of the scrawny, ill-tempered hens might have been persuaded, by a miracle or sheer perversity, to drop an egg. But as she had expected, the nests were empty, and the hens resisted with nasty jabs of their beaks her attempts at investigation. They'd gotten quite adept at fighting, competing with and chasing away the crows who came to steal their scant feed over the winter. She came away from the hen-house with an empty apron and scratched and bleeding hands.

Nor was there remedy waiting for her in the cottage, even for that. The little salve they had must be hoarded against greater need than hers.

Old Mag, the village healer and Elfrida's teacher, looked up from the tiny fire burning in the pit in the center of the dirt-floored cottage's single room. At least the thatch here was sound, though rain dripped in through the smoke-hole, and the fire didn't seem to be warming the place any. Elfrida coughed on the smoke, which persisted in staying inside, rather than rising through the smoke-hole as it should.

Mag's eyes had gotten worse over the winter, and the cottage was very dark with the shutters closed. "No eggs?" she asked, peering across the room, as Elfrida let the cowhide down across the cottage door.

"None," Elfrida replied, sighing. "This spring—if it's this bad now, what will summer be like?"

She squatted down beside Mag, and took the share of barley-bread the old woman offered, with a crude wooden cup of bitter-tasting herb tea dipped out of the kettle beside the fire.

"I don't know," Mag replied, rubbing her eyes—Mag, who had been tall and straight with health last summer, who was now bent and aching, with swollen joints and rheumy eyes. Neither willow-bark nor eyebright helped her much. "Lady bless, darling, I don't know. First that killing frost, then nothing but rain—seems like what seedlings the frost didn't get, must've rotted in the fields by now. Hens aren't laying, lambs are born dead, pigs lay on their own young . . . what we're going to do for food come winter, I've no notion."

When Mag said "we," she meant the whole village. She was not only their healer, but their priestess of the Old Way. Garth might be hetman, but she was the village's heart and soul—as Elfrida expected to be one day. This was something she had chosen, knowing the work and self-sacrifice involved, knowing that the enmity of the priests of the White Christ might fall upon her. But not for a long time—Lady grant.

That was what she had always thought, but now the heart and soul of the village was sickening, as the village around her sickened. But why?

"We made the proper sacrifices," Elfrida said finally. "Didn't we? What've we done or not done that the land turns against us?"

Mag didn't answer, but there was a quality in her silence that made Elfrida think that the old woman knew something—something important. Something that she hadn't yet told her pupil.

Finally, as darkness fell, and the fire burned down to coals, Mag spoke.

"We made the sacrifices," she said. "But there was one—who didn't."

"Who?" Elfrida asked, surprised. The entire village followed the Old Way—never mind the High King and his religion of the White Christ. That was for knights and nobles and suchlike. Her people stuck by what they knew best, the turning of the seasons, the dance of the Maiden, Mother and Crone, the rule of the Horned Lord. And if anyone in the village had neglected their sacrifices, surely she or Mag would have known!

"It isn't just our village that's sickening," Mag said, her voice a hoarse, harsh whisper out of the dark. "Nor the county alone. I've talked to the other Wise Ones, to the peddlers—I talked to the crows and the owls and ravens. It's the whole land that's sickening, failing—and there's only one sacrifice can save the land."

Elfrida felt her mouth go dry, and took a sip of her cold, bitter tea to wet it. "The blood of the High King," she whispered.

"Which he will not shed, come as he is to the feet of the White Christ." Mag shook her head. "My dear, my darling girl, I'd hoped the Lady wouldn't lay this on us . . . I'd prayed she wouldn't punish us for his neglect. But 'tisn't punishment, not really, and I should've known better than to hope it wouldn't come. Whether he believes it or not, the High King is tied to the land, and Arthur is old and failing. As he fails, the land fails."

"But—surely there's something we can do?" Elfrida said timidly into the darkness.

Mag stirred. "If there is, I haven't been granted the answer," she said, pausing as she spoke. "But perhaps—you've had Lady-dreams before, 'twas what led you to me. . . ."

"You want me to try for a vision?" Elfrida's mouth dried again, but this time no amount of tea would soothe it, for it was dry from fear. For all that she had true visions, when she sought them, the experience frightened her. And no amount of soothing on Mag's part, or encouragement that the—things—she saw in the dark waiting for her soul's protection to waver could not touch her, could ever ease that fear.

But weighed against her fear was the very real possibility that the village might not survive the next winter. If she was worthy to be Mag's successor, she must dare her fear, and dare the dreams, and see if the Lady had an answer for them since High King Arthur did not. The land and the people needed her and she must answer that need.

"I'll try," she whispered, and Mag touched her lightly on the arm.

"That's my good and brave girl," she said. "I knew you wouldn't fail us." Something on Mag's side of the fire rustled, and she handed Elfrida a folded leaf full of dried herbs.

They weren't what the ignorant thought; herbs to bring visions. The visions came when Elfrida asked for them—these were to strengthen and guard her while her spirit rode the night winds, in search of answers. Foxglove to strengthen her heart, moly to shield her soul, a dozen others, a scant pinch of each.

Obediently, she placed them under her tongue, and while Mag chanted the names of the Goddess, Elfrida closed her eyes, and released her all-too-fragile hold on her body.

The convent garden was sodden, the ground turning to mush, and unless someone did something about it, there would be nothing to eat this summer but what the tithes brought and the King's Grace granted them. Outside the convent walls, the fields were just as sodden; so, as the Mother Superior said, "A tithe of nothing is still nothing, and we must prepare to feed ourselves." Leonie sighed, and leaned a little harder on the spade, being careful where she put each spadeful of earth. Behind the spade, the drainage trench she was digging between each row of drooping pea-seedlings filled with water. Hopefully, this would be enough to keep them from rotting. Hopefully, there would be enough to share. Already the eyes of the children stared at her from faces pinched and hungry when they came to the convent for Mass, and she hid the bread that was half her meal to give to them.

Her gown was as sodden as the ground; cold and heavy with water, and only the fact that it was made of good wool kept it from chilling her. Her bare feet, ankle-deep in mud, felt like blocks of stone, they were so cold. She had kirtled her gown high to keep the hem from getting muddied, but that only let the wind get at her legs. Her hair was so soaked that she had not even bothered with the linen veil of a novice; it would only have flapped around without protecting her head and neck any. Her hands hurt; she wasn't used to this.

The other novices, gently-born and not, were desperately doing the same in other parts of the garden. Those that could, rather; some of the gently-born were too ill to come out into the soaking, cold rain. The sisters, as many as were able, were outside the walls, helping a few of the local peasants dig a larger ditch down to the swollen stream. The trenches in the convent garden would lead to it—and so would the trenches being dug in the peasants' gardens, on the other side of the high stone wall.

"We must work together," Mother Superior had said firmly, and so here they were, knight's daughter and villain's son, robes and tunics kirtled up above the knee, wielding shovels with a will. Leonie had never thought to see it.

But the threat of hunger made strange bedfellows. Already the convent had turned out to help the villagers trench their kitchen gardens. Leonie wondered what the village folk would do about the fields too large to trench, or fields of hay. It would be a cold summer, and a lean winter.

What had gone wrong with the land? It was said that the weather had been unseasonable and miserable all over the kingdom. Nor was the weather all that had gone wrong; it was said there was quarreling at High King Arthur's court; that the knights were moved to fighting for its own sake, and had brought their leman openly to many court gatherings, to the shame of the ladies. It was said that the Queen herself—

But Leonie did not want to hear such things, or even think of them. It was all of a piece, anyway; the knights fighting among themselves, the killing frosts and rain that wouldn't end, the threat of war at the borders, raiders and bandits within, and the starvation and plague hovering over all.

Something was deeply, terribly wrong.

She considered that, as she dug her little trenches, as she returned to the convent to wash her dirty hands and feet and change into a drier gown, as she nibbled her meager supper, trying to make it last, and as she went in to Vespers with the rest.

Something was terribly, deeply wrong.

When Mother Superior approached her after Vespers, she somehow knew that her feelings of *wrongness* and what the head of the convent was about to ask were linked.

"Leonie," Mother Superior said, once the other novices had filed away, back to their beds, "when your family sent you here, they told me it was because you had visions."

Leonie ducked her head and stared at her sandals. "Yes, Mother Magdalene."

"And I asked you not to talk about those visions in any way," the nun persisted. "Not to any of the other novices, not to any of the sisters, not to Father Peregrine."

"Yes, Mother Magdalene—I mean, no Mother Magdalene." Leonie looked up, flushing with anger. "I mean, I haven't."

She knew why the nun had ordered her to keep silence on the subject; she'd heard the lecture to her parents through the door. The Mother Superior didn't believe in Leonie's visions—or rather, she was not convinced that they were really visions. "This could simply be a young woman's hysteria," she'd said sternly, "Or an attempt to get attention. If the former, the peace of the convent and the meditation and prayer will cure her quickly enough—if the latter, well, she'll lose such notions of self-importance when she has no one to prate to."

"I know you haven't, child," Mother Magdalene said wearily, and Leonie saw how the nun's hands were blistered from the spade she herself had wielded today, how her knuckles were swollen, and her cheekbones cast into a prominence that had nothing to do with the dim lighting in the chapel. "I wanted to know if you still have them."

"Sometimes," Leonie said hesitantly. "That was how—I mean, that was why I woke last winter, when Sister Maria was elf-shot—"

"Sister Maria was not elf-shot," Mother Magdalene said automatically. "Elves could do no harm to one who trusts in God. It was simply something that happens to the very old, now and again, it is a kind of sudden brain-fever. But that isn't the point. You're still having the visions—but can you still see things that you want to see?"

"Sometimes," Leonie said cautiously. "If God and the Blessed Virgin permit."

"Well, if God is ever going to permit it, I suspect He'd do so during Holy Week," Mother Magdalene sighed. "Leonie, I am going to ask you a favor. I'd like you to make a vigil tonight."

"And ask for a vision?" Leonie said, raising her head in sudden interest.

"Precisely." The nun shook her head, and picked up her beads, telling them through her fingers as she often did when nervous. "There is something wrong with us, with the land, with the kingdom—I want you to see if God will grant you a vision of *what*." As Leonie felt a sudden upsurge of pride, Mother Magdalene added hastily, "You aren't the only one being asked to do this—every order from one end of the kingdom to the other has been asked for visions from their members. I thought long and hard about asking this. But you are the only one in my convent who has ever had a tendency to visions."

The Mother Superior had been about to say something else, Leonie was sure, for the practical and pragmatic Mother Magdalene had made her feelings on the subject of mysticism quite clear over the years. But that didn't matter—what did matter was that she was finally going to be able to release that pent-up power again, to soar on the angels' wings. Never mind that there were as many devils "out there" as angels; her angels would protect her, for they always had, and always would.

Without another word, she knelt on the cold stone before the altar, fixed her eyes on the bright little gilded cross above it, and released her soul's hold on her body.

"What did you see?" Mag asked, as Elfrida came back, shivering and spent, to consciousness. Her body was lying on the ground beside the fire, and it felt too tight, like a garment that didn't fit anymore—but she was glad enough to be in it again, for there had been *thousands* of those evil creatures waiting for her, trying to prevent her from reaching. . . .

"The Cauldron," she murmured, sitting up slowly, one hand on her aching head. "There was a Cauldron. . . ."

"Of course!" Mag breathed. "The Cauldron of the Goddess! But—" It was too dark for Elfrida to see Mag, other than as a shadow in the darkness, but she somehow felt Mag's searching eyes. "What about the Cauldron? When is it coming back? Who's to have it? Not the High King, surely—"

"I'm—supposed to go look for it," Elfrida said, vaguely. "That's what They said—I'm supposed to go look for it."

Mag's sharp intake of breath told her of Mag's shock. "But—no, I know you, when you come out of this," she muttered, almost as if to herself. "You can't lie. If you say They said for you to go, then go you must."

Elfrida wanted to say something else, to ask what it all meant, but she couldn't. The vision had taken too much out of her, and she was whirled away a second time, but this time it was not on the winds of vision, but into the arms of exhausted sleep.

"What did you see?" Mother Superior asked urgently.

Leonie found herself lying on the cold stone before the altar, wrapped in someone's cloak, with something pillowed under her head. She felt very peaceful, as she always did when the visions released her, and very, very tired. There had been many demons out there, but as always, her angels had protected her. Still, she was glad to be back. There had never been quite so many of the evil things there before, and they had frightened her.

She had to blink a few times, as she gathered her memories and tried to make sense of them. "A cup," she said, hesitantly—then her eyes fell upon the Communion chalice on the altar, and they widened as she realized just what she truly had seen. "No—not *a* cup, *the* Cup! We're to seek the Grail! That's what They told me!"

"The Grail?" Mother Magdalene's eyes widened a little herself, and she crossed herself hastily. "Just before you—you dropped over, you reached out. I thought I saw—I thought I saw something faint, like a ghost of a glowing cup in your hands."

Leonie nodded, her cheek against the rough homespun of the habit bundled under her head. "They said that to save the kingdom, we have to seek the Grail."

"We?" Mother Magdalene said, doubtfully. "Surely you don't mean—"

"The High King's knights and squires, some clergy and—me—" Leonie's voice trailed off, as she realized what she was saying. "They said the knights will know already and that when you hear about it from Camelot, you'll know I was speaking the truth. But I don't *want* to go!" she wailed. "I don't! I—"

"I'm convinced of the truth now," the nun said. "Just by the fact that you don't want to go. If this had been a sham, to get attention, you'd have demanded special treatment, to be cosseted and made much of, not to be sent off on your own."

"But—" Leonie protested frantically, trying to hold off unconsciousness long enough to save herself from this exile.

"Never mind," the Mother Superior said firmly. "We'll wait for word from Camelot. When we hear it, then you'll go."

Leonie would have protested further, but Mother Magdalene laid a cool hand across her hot eyes, and sleep came up and took her.

Elfrida had never been this far from her home village before. The great forest through which she had been walking for most of the day did not look in the least familiar. In fact, it did not look like anything anyone from the village had ever described.

And why hadn't Mag brought her here to gather healing herbs and mushrooms? The answer seemed clear enough; she was no longer in lands Mag or any of the villagers had ever seen.

She had not known which way to go, so she had followed the raven she saw flying away from the village. The raven had led her to the edge of the woods, which at the time had seemed quite ordinary. But the oaks and beeches had turned to a thick growth of fir; the deeper she went, the older the trees became, until at last she was walking on a tiny path between huge trunks that rose far over her head before properly branching out. Beneath those spreading branches, thin, twiggy growth reached out skeletal fingers like blackened bones, while the upper branches cut off most of the light, leaving the trail beneath shrouded in a twilight gloom, though it was midday.

Though she was on a quest of sorts, that did not mean she had left her good sense behind. While she was within the beech and oak forest, she had gleaned what she could on either side of the track. Her pack now held two double-handfuls each of acorns and beechnuts, still sound, and a few mushrooms. Two here, three and four there, they added up.

It was just as well, for the meager supply of journey-bread she had with her had been all given away by the end of the first day of her quest. A piece at a time, to a child here, a nursing mother there . . . but she had the freedom of the road and the forest; the people she encountered were tied to their land and could not leave it. Not while there was any chance they might coax a crop from it.

They feared the forest, though they could not tell Elfrida why. They would only enter the fringes of it, to feed their pigs on acorns, to pick up deadfall. Further than that, they would not go.

Elfrida had known for a long time that she was not as magical as Mag. She had her visions, but that was all; she could not see the power rising in the circles, although she knew it was there, and could sometimes feel it. She could not see the halos of light around people that told Mag if they were sick or well. She had no knowledge of the future outside of her visions, and could not talk to the birds and animals as Mag could.

So she was not in the least surprised to find that she could sense nothing about the forest that indicated either good or ill. If there was something here, she could not sense it. Of course, the gloom of the fir-forest was more than enough to frighten anyone with any imagination. And while nobles often claimed peasants had no more imagination than a block of wood—well, Elfrida often thought that nobles had no more sense than one of their high-bred, high-strung horses, that would break legs, shying at shadows. Witless, useless—and irresponsible. How many of them were on their lands, helping their liegemen and peasants to save their crops? Few enough; most were idling their time away at the High King's Court, gambling, drinking, wenching, playing at tourneys and other useless pastimes. And she would wager that the High King's table was not empty; that the nobles' children were not going pinch-faced and hungry to bed. The religion of the White Christ had divorced master from man, noble from villager, making the former into a master in truth, and the latter into an income-producing slave. The villager was told by his priest to trust in God and receive his reward in heaven. The lord need feel no responsibility for any evils he did or caused, for once they had been confessed and paid for—usually by a generous gift to the priest—his God counted them as erased. The balance of duty and responsibility between the vassal and his lord was gone.

She shook off her bitter thoughts as nightfall approached. Without Mag's extra abilities Elfrida knew she would have to be twice as careful about spending the night in this place. If there were supernatural terrors about, she would never know until they were on her. So when she made her little camp, she cast circles around her with salt and iron, betony and rue, writing the runes as clear as she could, before she lit her fire to roast her nuts.

But in the end, when terror came upon her, it was of a perfectly natural sort.

Leonie cowered, and tried to hide in the folds of her robe. Her bruised face ached, and her bound wrists were cut and swollen around the thin twine the man who had caught her had used to bind her.

She had not gotten more than two days away from the convent—distributing most of her food to children and the sick as she walked—when she had reached the edge of the forest, and her vague visions had directed her to follow the path through it. She had seen no signs of people, nor had she sensed anything about the place that would have caused folk to avoid it. That had puzzled her, so she had dropped into a walking trance to try and sort out what kind of a place the forest was.

That was when someone had come up behind her and hit her on the head.

Now she knew why ordinary folk avoided the forest; it was the home of bandits. And she knew what her fate was going to be. Only the strength of the hold the chieftain had over his men had kept her from that fate until now. He had decreed that they would wait until all the men were back from their errands—and then they would draw lots for their turns at her. . . .

Leonie was so terrified that she was beyond thought; she huddled like a witless rabbit inside her robe and prayed for death.

"What's *this*?" the bandit chief said, loudly, startling her so that she raised her head out of the folds of her sleeves. She saw nothing at first; only the dark bulking shapes of men against the fire in their midst. He laughed, long and hard, as another of his men entered their little clearing, shoving someone in front of him. "By Satan's arse! The woods are sprouting wenches!"

Elfrida caught her breath at the curse; so, these men were not "just" bandits—they were the worst kind of bandit, nobles gone beyond the law. Only one who was once a follower of the White Christ would have used his adversary's name as an exclamation. No follower of the Old Way, either Moon or Blood-path would have done so.

The brigand who had captured her shoved her over to land beside another girl—and once again she caught her breath, as her talisman-bag swung loose on its cord, and the other girl shrunk away, revealing the wooden beads and cross at the rope that served her as a belt. Worse and worse—the girl wore the robes of one who had vowed herself to the White Christ! There would be no help there . . . if she were not witless before she had been caught, she was probably frightened witless now. Even if she would accept help from the hands of a "pagan."

Leonie tried not to show her hope. Another girl! Perhaps between the two of them, they could manage to win free!

But as the girl was shoved forward, to drop to the needles beside Leonie, something swung free of her robe to dangle over her chest. It was a little bag, on a rawhide thong.

And the bandit chief roared again, this time with disapproval, seizing the bag and breaking the thong with a single, cruelly hard tug of his hand. He tossed it out into the darkness and backhanded the outlaw who had brought the girl in.

"You witless bastard!" he roared. "You brought in a witch!"

A *witch*?

Leonie shrunk away from her fellow captive. A witch? Blessed Jesu—this young woman would be just as pleased to see Leonie raped to death! She would probably call up one of her demons to help!

As the brigand who had been struck shouted and went for his chief's throat, and the others gathered around, yelling encouragement and placing bets, she closed her eyes, bowed her head, and prayed. *Blessed Mother of God, hear me. Angels of grace, defend us. Make them forget us for just a moment. . . .*

As the brainless child started in fear, then pulled away, bowed her head, and began praying, Elfrida kept a heavy hand on her temper. Bad enough that she was going to die—and in a particularly horrible way—but to have to do it in such company!

But—suddenly the outlaws were fighting. One of them appeared to be the chief; the other the one who had caught her. And they were ignoring the two girls as if they had somehow forgotten their existence. . . .

Blessed Mother, hear me. Make it so.

The man had only tied her with a bit of leather, no stronger than the thong that had held her herb-bag. If she wriggled just right, bracing her tied hands against her feet, she could probably snap it.

She prayed, and pulled. And was rewarded with the welcome release of pressure as the thong snapped.

She brought her hands in front of her, hiding them in her tunic, and looked up quickly; the fight had involved a couple more of the bandits. She and the other girl were in the shadows now, for the fire had been obscured by the men standing or scuffling around it. If she crept away quickly and quietly—

No sooner thought than done. She started to crawl away, got as far as the edge of the firelight, then looked back.

The other girl was still huddled where she had been left, eyes closed. Too stupid or too frightened to take advantage of the opportunity to escape.

If Elfrida left her there, they probably wouldn't try to recapture her. They'd have one girl still, and wouldn't go hunting in the dark for the one that had gotten away. . . .

Elfrida muttered an oath, and crawled back.

Leonie huddled with the witch-girl under the shelter of a fallen tree, and they listened for the sounds of pursuit. She had been praying as hard as she could, eyes closed, when a painful tug on the twine binding her wrists had made her open her eyes.

"Well, come on!" the girl had said, tugging again. Leonie had not bothered to think about what the girl might be pulling her into, she had simply followed, crawling as best she could with her hands tied, then getting up and running when the girl did.

They had splashed through a stream, running along a moonlit path, until Leonie's side ached. Finally the girl had pulled her off the path and shoved her under the bulk of a fallen tree, into a little dug-out den she would never have guessed was there. From the musky smell, it had probably been made by a fox or badger. Leonie huddled in the dark, trying not to sob, concentrating on the pain in her side and not on the various fates the witch-girl could have planned for her.

Before too long, they heard shouts in the distance, but they never came very close. Leonie strained her ears, holding her breath, to try and judge how close their pursuers were, and jumped when the witch-girl put a hand on her.

"Don't," the girl whispered sharply. "You won't be going far with your hands tied like that. Hold still! I'm not going to hurt you."

Leonie stuttered something about demons, without thinking. The girl laughed.

"If I had a demon to come when I called, do you think I would have let a bastard like that lay hands on me?" Since there was no logical answer to that question, Leonie wisely kept quiet. The girl touched her hands, and then seized them; Leonie kept herself from pulling away, and a moment later, felt the girl sawing at her bonds with a bit of sharp rock. Every so often the rock cut into Leonie instead of the twine, but she bit her lip and kept quiet, gratitude increasing as each strand parted. "What were you doing out here, anyway?" the girl asked. "I thought they kept your kind mewed up like prize lambs."

"I had a vision," Leonie began, wondering if by her words and the retelling of her holy revelation, the witch-girl might actually be converted to Christianity. It happened that way all the time in the tales of the saints, after all. . . .

So while the girl sawed patiently at the bonds with the sharp end of the rock, Leonie told her everything, from the time she realized that something was wrong, to the moment the bandit took her captive. The girl stayed silent through all of it, and Leonie began to hope that she *might* bring the witch-girl to the Light and Life of Christ.

The girl waited until she had obviously come to the end, then laughed, unpleasantly. "Suppose, just suppose," she said, "I were to tell you that the *exact same* vision was given to me? Only it isn't some mystical cup that this land needs, it's the Cauldron of Cerridwen, the ever-renewing, for the High King refuses to sacrifice himself to save his kingdom as the Holy Bargain demands and only the Cauldron can give the land the blessing of the Goddess."

The last of the twine snapped as she finished, and Leonie pulled her hands away. "Then I would say that your vision is wrong, evil," she retorted. "There is no goddess, only the Blessed Virgin—"

"Who is one face of the Goddess, who is Maiden, Mother and Wise One," the girl interrupted, her words dripping acid. "Only a fool would fail to see that. And your White Christ is no more than the Sacrificed One in one of *His* many guises—it is the Cauldron the land needs, not your apocryphal Cup—"

"Your cauldron is some demon-thing," Leonie replied, angrily. "Only the Grail—"

Whatever else she was going to say was lost, as the tree-trunk above them was riven into splinters by a bolt of lightning that blinded and deafened them both for a moment.

When they looked up, tears streaming from their eyes, it was to see something they both recognized as The Enemy.

Standing over them was a shape, outlined in a glow of its own. It was three times the height of a man, black and hairy like a bear, with the tips of its outstretched claws etched in fire. But it was not a bear, for it wore a leather corselet, and its head had the horns of a bull, the snout and tusks of a boar, dripping foam and saliva, and its eyes, glowing an evil red, were slitted like a goat's.

Leonie screamed and froze. The witch-girl seized her bloody wrist, hauled her to her feet, and ran with her stumbling along behind.

The beast roared and followed after. They had not gotten more than forty paces down the road, when the witch-girl fell to the ground with a cry of pain, her hand slipping from Leonie's wrist.

Her ankle—Leonie thought, but no more, for the beast was shambling towards them. She grabbed the girl's arm and hauled her to her feet; draped her arm over her own shoulders, and dragged her erect. Up ahead there was moonlight shining down on something—perhaps a clearing, and perhaps the beast might fear the light—

She half-dragged, half-guided the witch-girl towards that promise of light, with the beast bellowing behind them. The thought crossed her mind that if she dropped the girl and left her, the beast would probably be content with the witch and would not chase after Leonie. . . .

No, she told herself, and stumbled onward.

They broke into the light, and Leonie looked up—

And sank to her knees in wonder.

* * *

Elfrida fell beside the other girl, half blinded by tears of pain, and tried to get to her feet. The beast—she had to help Leonie up, they had to run. . . .

Then she looked up.

And fell again to her knees, this time stricken not with pain, but with awe. And though she had never felt power before, she felt it now; humming through her, blood and bone, saw it in the vibration of the air, in the purity of the light streaming from the Cup.

The Cup held in the hand of a man, whose gentle, sad eyes told of the pain, not only of His own, but of the world's, that for the sake of the world, He carried on His own shoulders.

Leonie wept, tears of mingled joy and fear—joy to be in the Presence of One who was all of Light and Love, and fear, that this One was She and not He—and the thing that she held, spilling over the Light of Love and Healing was Cauldron and not Cup.

I was wrong—she thought, helplessly.

Wrong? said a loving, laughing Voice. *Or simply—limited in vision?*

And in that moment, the Cauldron became a Cup, and the Lady became the Lord, Jesu—then changed again, to a man of strange, draped robes and slanted eyes, who held neither Cup nor Cauldron, but a cup-shaped Flower with a jeweled heart—a hawk-headed creature with a glowing stone in His hand—a black-skinned Woman with a bright Bird—

And then to another shape, and another, until her eyes were dazzled and her spirit dizzied, and she looked away, into the eyes of Elfrida. The witch-girl—*Wise Girl,* whispered the Voice in her mind, *and Quest-Companion*—looked similarly dazzled, but the joy in her face must surely mirror Leonie's. The girl offered her hand, and Leonie took it, and they turned again to face—

A Being of light, neither male nor female, and a dazzling Cup as large as a Cauldron, the veil covering it barely dimming its brilliance.

Come, the Being said, *you have proved yourself worthy.*

Hand in hand, the two newest Grail Maidens rose, and followed the shining beacon into the Light.

That Which Overfloweth

———————— ✠ ————————

Andre Norton

There are many tales, legends, stories misshapened by years of mistelling, generations of adding to—or subtracting from. Once there was a man who fled with a handful of followers overseas to the farthermost known portion of the great empire. He took with him, it is said, two things of Power, a staff and another possession which he guarded so jealously that even those who shared his exile seldom saw it.

In the far country he set the staff into the ground in a place which was already known to Power, where older Presences than those the voyager worshiped, had long held steady. And that staff, cut and dried for years, rooted and brought forth blossom so that the man believed he had found that place where the seeds he and his carried with them could flourish. But his other treasure was hidden away—though in plain sight—and so remained through the rise and fall of kings and empires and the passing of uncounted centuries, even into the last years when the world itself grew sick, promising death's coming.

They came in just after dawn, the dire wolves. Since Jan had broken his leg there was no trained sentry on the High Hill. Guran was very young but he had the horn, and he sounded it, before he was picked off by a sky bolt. Thus he bought those at the shrine village a small measure of time.

Not enough.

She Who Spoke had already reached the inner shrine when the alarm sounded. For a single breath she stood tense and still and then she beckoned to those two who had lingered by the entrance in awe of this sacred place.

"There." She pointed to the dressed stone on which stood the unlit candles of sheep fat, alongside the faded flowers of yesterday's offering. Then, in demonstration of what must be done, she set her hands to the edge of the stone, feeling frantically for what was a key.

There were screams from beyond now, the cries of a village put to pillage. Death cries. Cassia, as she stooped to obey the Voice, shuddered. She heaved with all her strength as Lana was doing to match her at the other end of the stone. Reluctantly it began to move.

"In with you," the Voice's fingers bit painfully at Cassia's shoulder as she pushed the girl-child toward the black hole they had half uncovered. There was no way to protest that order. Terrified, not only of the dark gap before her but at the sounds which reached them, she pushed into that opening, and, a moment later, felt Lana's weight shoving her yet farther in and down. Then, before she could protest, the stone was swinging back, to leave their thin childish bodies pressed tightly together.

"Lana." There was no answer from the other—she was only a heavy weight against Cassia's shoulder and arm. "Lana? Voice?" she whimpered once again and then was silent.

Her sight adjusted a little. There was a measure of light here, cramped as their quarters were. Now the sounds from outside. . . . Cassia cowered and tried to put her hands over her ears to blot out those cries and yet could not because of Lana's weight.

"Voice?" her lips shaped a whisper, "Voice?"

She scrunched herself forward and found that she could look out—but only at the level of the rough flooring. The edge of a dull green robe swung, blinding her peephole. She could guess that the Voice had not tried to run any more than she had tried to squeeze into this too small place, but was standing at the altar, even as when she called upon the High One.

Lana stirred now, and then shrilled a cry which nearby Cassia viciously stifled, finding the other girl's mouth quickly enough to muffle that. She bumped her head against Lana's and whispered fiercely:

"Be quiet!"

The outside clamor was growing stronger and there was a last piercing scream from just without the shrine. Then they came—Cassia could only see boots cobbled from badly dried skins, the point of a stained blade which still dribbled thick red drops to the pavement.

"Calling down your Word-Wrath, slut?" That voice spoke words so oddly accented that Cassia found them hard to understand. She felt Lana strain and jerk beside her.

"You have come to *her,* what would you?" That was the Voice and she spoke with such calm that Cassia could almost believe the woman's wits had been rift from her and she did not see these crowding in—three of them, counting by the boots she could see.

"In that, Spar. They keep their goodies in that!" A different voice, puzzling because Cassia had heard it before—when? Who could be evil enough to betray the secrets of the shrine?

"Goodies, eh? Well, let us see these goodies you would guard, slut. We've found precious little worth the taking elsewhere in this swine's pen."

"Spar, the slut's got a knife." There was a roil of movement among those tramping feet, the green robe edge swirled away, freeing Cassia's line of vision the more. There was a choking cry, a hand slipped slowly down over the peephole and was gone.

"Get that ring from her, Harve. You say their stuff's in here?"

Cassia shuddered and Lana twisted in her hold as there came a blow which vibrated through the altar stone above them.

"Oh, so you weren't talking out of the wrong side of your jaw after all, Vacom. Well, well. And here we were thinking that all the good stuff had been combed out of these pens long ago. Black, yes, but that's silver. And this is something better!"

Cassia could understand now what was happening. They had opened the box top of the altar stone and were dragging out those very precious things which only the Voice might touch, and then only after purification. Vacom? Her lips formed a vixen's rage snarl—that trader whose ship had come to grief on the outer reef a season ago and who had been given refuge in the village afterwards until he could join with a band of traders who had come through in the fall. He had been here at Midsummer.

Again Cassia snarled. So that was how he knew about the Precious Things! Sneaking spy—Let the High One smite him with the sloughing of skin and the blindness of eye so that he would take a long time in dying!

"Old," that was the first voice, "this is damn old. And I'd wager on it that those are real stones! We've more'n enough paid for this raid!"

"Hey—you broke it!" There was a sharp protest.

"No. It just comes apart. What's this inside? Some stinking clay pot thing—we can do without that."

It struck the floor straight in the line of Cassia's sight, a round brown cup just such a one as Farllen the potter made and fired from riverbank clay. Oddly enough, the rough handling it received did not break it; through all her fear Cassia wondered at that.

"That's it. Get this slut's cloak and bag it up." The one who gave orders was already turning away from the altar. He toed the cup and it spun around, out of Cassia's sight.

Cassia waited, her ears straining for the slightest sound. All screams and cries had ceased, the feet she had watched had tramped out. Still . . .

"Voice?" she whispered through dry lips and knew somehow she could expect no answer to that call.

Lana squirmed around against her. Their heads were now so close she could feel the younger girl's fast puff of breath against her cheek.

"Wait." Cassia dared to whisper again, this time to her fellow prisoner.

How long did they wait? Cassia felt the sore cramp beginning in her arms and legs. If they did not move soon they might be too stiff to try at all. She loosened a hand and groped into the dark over her head, feeling along the inner side of the altar. She found that deep groove she sought and settled her fingers well in.

"Lana," she breathed, "find the other turn point."

"They will kill," the other girl protested.

"They must be gone—at least from the shrine." Cassia held onto her patience. "We cannot stay here any longer." Though, of course, Lana might also be right and they would be simply betraying themselves. However, there was little choice.

She felt the movements of the other girl, knew that she was indeed in search of that second hold which would give them a door to freedom.

"Ready? Then move." Cassia felt her nails break, the skin of her fingertips abrade, as she obeyed her own order. Slowly the stone walling them in answered and there was enough light to set them blinking.

Cassia squeezed through that opening. She pulled herself up by a grip on the altar itself and nearly lost her hold when there came a faint moaning from very near at hand. Then she was out, to crouch by the Voice. The woman's robe was rent at the breast and over that she was pressing tight her hands, as if she could so stem the blood which oozed between her fingers. Her eyes were open and she looked at Cassia with understanding and knowledge.

"Voice—let me see!" The girl tried to pull away those binding hands.

The woman opened her mouth and a trickle of blood rilled down her chin.

"This is an end blow, my daughter-in-light. There is no healcraft which will answer."

Lana had crept to her other side, shaking, white faced. "Voice—Voice, what—what shall we do?"

"That which is willed for you. First," she turned her eyes, not her head, as if all the strength she had left would not allow more, to Cassia, "give—give me to drink—from the Blessed pool."

Cassia scrambled on hands and knees toward the entrance to the shrine. In going, her hand struck against something which rattled across the floor, and, catching at it, she found what she held was that earthen cup. Clutching it, she moved out. There was the stench of death here. Already carrion birds dropped out of the sky, their blackness an offense in the daylight. Cassia tried not to look at the two hacked bodies which lay most plainly in sight. Old Kazar, who had lost an arm three seasons ago yet must have come to the shrine's defense, sprawled half into the pool. The red from the gash, which had hewn him near in two, swirling out in the once clean, sweet water.

Cassia stood helplessly looking at the befoulment, the cup in her shaking hand. She could not dip out—that. . . .

She edged about the basin in the opposite direction from that body, seeking some place which was still clear. There was nothing—and farther on. . . . She caught her lower lip between her teeth to cut back a scream. A child, Rowna's babe, staring sightlessly upward.

Cassia broke and ran back towards the shrine. Alive—why was she alive when all else were dead, dead befouled—lost.

As she entered the shrine she strove for control. She was a Chosen—she must remember that always.

"Voice," she knelt beside the woman whose head Lana now supported against her own thin shoulder. "The water—it cannot . . ."

"Dip the cup, daughter-in-service, and bring it to me!"

All the old command was in the Voice's words. Cassia could only obey. She returned, found a place at the pool farthest from these two bodies, dipped her cup into the water which was ever thickening with the red stain. She filled it near to the brim and started back, nursing the cup against her breast lest she spill some of its contents. But as she moved—surely that could not be true! The water was clearing with each step she took. As she reached the door of the shrine she might be bearing such an offering as was always brought in all purity to the High One.

"Voice," she cried breathlessly, "the water—it holds no more the stain of death—it is pure."

Swiftly she put it to those lips between which blood still welled a little. The Voice drank.

"How ... ?" Cassia marveled.

"Drink," commanded the Voice. And Cassia, raising the cup carefully with both her hands, took a mouthful. Not just pure water—this had the richness of the first fruits—she could feel the warmth of it in her throat, and then through her, driving out the death chill, the ragged tatters of fear which had been a binding on her.

"Lana," commanded the Voice for a second time, "drink also!" Cassia passed the cup to the younger girl and watched her drink. Yet when Lana handed back that small rough bowl it was as full as it had been after the dipping at the spring.

"The cup that overfloweth," the woman's voice was thinner, as if she tired after some great task. "It cleanses evil—brings fresh life again. Things of power exist for our comfort, my daughters. Such may be lost from time, yet always they rise again. This much is true, that those who serve are themselves served in a different way. Now. . . ."

She closed her eyes for a moment and when she opened them again they seemed to Cassia to be seeking, as if they could no longer find her face.

"My time has passed, daughters-of-the-heart. Take you that which is of Power and go forth from this place of death to find what may be healed or cherished under the wide arms of the High One. You shall be led, and when you find the place meant for you there shall be a sign. For a thing of Power knows well where it must shelter. Go with the blessing of sun and moon, earth and sky, fire and water, all that sustains life."

There had been a feast long ago, in a far county. And a cup passed which held the promise of life. Things of Power are never lost though they may pass from the sight of men for a time—yet always they shall come again.

Chalice of Tears, or I Didn't Want that Damned Grail Anyway

✜

Marion Zimmer Bradley

A long time ago, Lythande had had a sharp lesson in the fact that the first law in Magic is to mind your own business, in a world where the penalty for entangling yourself in someone else's magic can be severe. But that didn't occur to her when she saw the old man lying in the road. He looked as if he were choking to death; and with her Healer's instincts, which could always override common sense, she could not have kept herself from kneeling at his side and asking what ailed him.

"Nothing," the old man murmured weakly. "My day is done. I have lived too many years." And indeed it seemed that he might well be the age of Lythande's grandsire—and yet Lythande had lived the span of four or five ordinary lifetimes.

"You should not say so," rebuked Lythande, whose training led her always to deny death in her patient's thoughts. But secretly she thought he might very well be right. Never had she seen any man—not even the immortal magicians of her own Order—quite so bent and stooped with age.

Lythande lifted his head gently. "The first thing is to get you out of the very middle of the road; night has begun to fall, and there will be rain before morning."

"No." The old man struggled away from her hands when Lythande would have raised him up. "I must make disposition of what I bear; I am sworn." He fumbled among his ancient and tattered robes, gray more with age than dirt.

What he brought out was a thing of beauty. At first it seemed to be a chalice of silver; but as Lythande looked more carefully, she could see that it was fashioned of birchwood, pale grey, and beautifully turned, and set into a silver frame. The wood was so pale and smooth that the whole thing looked as if it were fashioned of silver.

Lythande drew back. "I beg you, grandfather, do not bestow it upon me."

"I cannot, and I would not if I could," replied the old man, testily. "The Grail chooses its own Guardian. It is for you to seek out that Guardian, under the geas I now lay upon you."

Lythande jerked back in alarm; but before she could set the spell which would render the air around her void of magic, there was a brief, lightning-like flash.

"Behold the Chalice of Tears," whispered the old man. Under his ancient, grey gaze, the Grail seemed to shimmer with a strange luminescence, a sort of underwater radiance. Lythande did not want to behold, much less touch, the magical object: but almost of their own volition—or was it the spell laid upon the chalice?—her fingers closed about it. Resigned, she looked down again at the old man to ask him where she should seek the ordained Guardian of this Grail; but his face had gone slack and he had ceased to breathe.

Lythande sighed and drew the tattered grey robes over the old Guardian's dead face. She would have spoken a spell to rid herself of the outworn shell of his body, but the spell died unspoken. The chalice seemed to cast a faint shimmer in the air about her, and Lythande guessed that it was the sort of magical artifact that could endure the presence of no magic but its own. As she knelt in the road holding the chalice, the worn form of the Guardian began to vibrate, then to fade. Soon nothing real remained but a little greyish dust stirred by the invisible winds; and then it vanished.

"So," Lythande said aloud, "At least the Guardian of the Grail has saved me the trouble of burying him. Now what must I do? Guide me, I pray, ancient father."

Shorn for the moment of her magic, Lythande felt as helpless and vulnerable as a declawed cat. Goblet in hand, she withdrew to a hollow in the trees, aware that she must rely on her skill in divination.

She rummaged in her pack for the worn cards she kept there, took them out of their frayed silk shielding, and spread them before her. She had no especial faith in the cards, but with none of her own spells at her command, their wisdom was all she had to guide her. Her own magic would not serve to give her some hint of where she should seek this guardian.

She looked carefully at the cards spread before her, fascinated as always by their mysterious designs. These cards had been a gift from an ancient wisewoman, who had said that any given reading would be relevant only to Lythande's own immediate situation. As she might have suspected, the first card was the Ace of Cups; immediately at its right lay the shrouded and enthroned form of the Priestess.

"Bother," thought Lythande. "That is the selfsame chalice which has been bestowed upon me, which tells me nothing." Again she cast the cards, and again the Grail, the Ace of Cups, not even a significator. This time she shuffled the cards for a long time before she set them out; and once again she beheld the Grail. One of the laws by which such as Lythande lived was *Seek for that which repeats*. So she knew that somehow the cards had laid themselves out to guide her—if not by their own magic, then perchance by that of the Grail itself.

Next to the Grail she beheld the form of the Hermit, seeking forever a light which burned like a star within his own lantern.

"That is the Guardian of the Grail," said Lythande aloud. "Tell me something I don't know, O cards, I entreat you."

Again she cast the cards; but this time she made very sure to thrust the Ace of Cups well within the pack. But, when she turned the first card, behold! There again was the Ace of Cups, and next to it, again the High Priestess. Lythande could not help smiling to herself.

"So," Lythande thought. "The Guardian of the Grail is a woman? O cards, tell me now, where dwells this sorceress? The old man has made it clear this quest is not for me." Nor did she want it, though she felt a little miffed that she should be thought unfit. But then, perhaps the Sorceress card kept coming up because the chalice was in fact in the hands of a woman, though Lythande might never be known by any man to be a woman—the destiny placed upon her by the master of the Order of Adepts of the Blue Star.

Lythande continued to cast the cards; but cast as she would, nothing came up but disasters—flood, fire, and earthquake. And at last she thrust the cards back within their silk wrappings, thinking that if all these disasters were meant for the possessor of the Grail, she must make haste to get the thing into the hands of its ordained Guardian. But like the old man, the cards had given her no clue about where to begin looking.

Lythande wrapped herself in her grey mage-robe, placed the Grail carefully within her sack, and laid herself down to sleep. Perhaps she could find a clue in her dreams. . . .

Her sleep was restless, and when she woke, a thin fine rain was drizzling down from a grey, occluded sky.

"So," Lythande said to herself, "the Chalice of Tears begins to make its influence felt; even the sky weeps. Guide me, I pray, Master."

When she had eaten a little of the bread and fruit she kept within her pack, she settled down to wait. Since the Grail had assumed mastery of her steps, she would await its guidance. If the Grail would choose its own Guardian, then it must give direction to her steps.

As she waited, letting her thoughts wander, she heard from afar the sound of a choric hymn. The singing grew gradually louder, and soon a group of pilgrims emerged from the streets, singing as they walked. At their head was a woman, tall and strong, swathed in a grey veil somewhat like Lythande's own mage-robe.

"I greet you, master musician," she called out cheerfully at sight of the lute strung over Lythande's shoulder. "Whither away?"

Lythande drew herself to her feet. "I am a minstrel," she said. "I have a quest which has been laid upon me."

"Will you tell me of your quest?" asked the woman gaily. "Perhaps one of us can lighten your load?"

"I think not," said Lythande arrogantly. She had never had a very high opinion of women, and did not believe that the magical thing she carried would bestow itself upon this coarse, jolly woman, red-handed and vulgar. Surely this could be only some fortuitous guidance on the steps of her quest, to indicate the direction she should take—no more. "Yet, if you will have it so, I will travel in your company."

"Be it so," said the woman. "All are welcome to share our road; and it may be that the Gods have sent us your way. Who knows? We may even have some part in your quest. Nothing is accidental, brother of magic."

"Indeed," Lythande said politely, but secretly she was not pleased to think that she had anything much in common with this sorceress. Those great red hands could hardly be given to the uses of the High magic; they were only fit to such hedge-magic as souring a farm wife's milk within the churn. Such a one to put herself on a footing with an Adept of the Blue Star? Lythande gave a secret shudder and resolved that she would stay in the company of these pilgrims not an instant longer than necessary.

"Let us be off, then," she said. It might be that in their holy city they would encounter a great Sorceress fit to become the custodian of the Chalice of Tears—which after all had chosen Lythande herself as its temporary Guardian. Surely she must not bestow it upon any lesser than herself.

The fine misting rain had turned into a steady downpour. Lythande was not too much troubled, for the grey mage-robe was almost impervious to weather; but the women in the procession looked like so many wet cats. The woman leading the pilgrims grunted dolefully.

"You bring us ill fortune, magician. Will you not tell us of your quest?"

"I think not, at least not at present," said Lythande, thinking that this downpour might be the element of water telling her she was on the right track—surely no more than that. "Let us press on. For my quest has to do with the very elements themselves."

"So be it, my brother, if you say so," answered the woman, looking wistfully at the shape of the lute beneath Lythande's robes. "While this weather continues, we can have no music; for the rain would damage your instrument."

"That it might," said Lythande, wondering crossly how long she would be marooned in this company. "Let us onward."

They slogged through rain for most of the day. Dusk had fallen when at last they came to an inn. Its sign bore the device of a brush of painted thistles and the words, *The House of Necessity.*

"This is surely a sign to me," Lythande thought, "for I am driven by necessity."

"I think we must halt here," said the woman at the head of the pilgrims, "for our company numbers three dozen or more, and there is no other shelter for many miles on this rain-blighted moor. And its name is a sign to us, for surely we have been brought here by necessity."

"Quite," thought Lythande, certain than the sign had been for her. Indeed, how could it be otherwise? She gladly entered the welcoming inn, and took off her robes. She ate a hearty meal, for there were only women within the company; the geas which forbade Lythande to eat or drink in sight of any living man was completely literal, and did not forbid her to satisfy her hunger and thirst in the sight of any number of women. After her meal, and weary with walking, she began to prepare herself for sleep; but before she settled into her mage-robe, the women's leader asked, "Will you not give us a song, minstrel?"

"Gladly," replied Lythande, not sorry to have a good excuse for displaying her talents in this company. She sang a song of sorrowing quest which sounded like the wild stormy sea off her native coast.

"Such a song of woe," commented the group's leader. "If there is such a sadness in your heart, minstrel, may I, Manuela, not share your burden? For I can see that it is heavy, minstrel, and it has been laid on us that we should share one another's burdens and sorrows."

"It is not time," said Lythande. She did not think this commoner sorceress could be of any help to her in much of anything, let alone her quest; nor had she any love for being called *brother* and so put upon an equal footing with this hedge-witch Manuela. But she said nothing more, and went to sleep in one of the smaller rooms, for she would not share a common chamber with the pilgrims.

When she woke, the sun was streaming through the windows, but that was not what had wakened her. It was a cry of consternation from the room in which the pilgrims had slept.

"Alas! We are marooned!" Lythande sprang to the window. During the night, a dam had burst, and the inn was completely surrounded by water. Fortunately, the inn was on a small rise, or they might have been washed away and drowned.

"Bother," thought Lythande. "Now I can neither pursue my quest nor rid myself of these women; for good or ill, the Fates have cast me into their company."

Manuela echoed her thoughts as she came into the room. "Alas, my brother," she cried, "the Fates have abandoned you, for how can you fulfill your quest now? It is worse for you than for us; since we are pilgrims through life, our quest may be fulfilled wherever the Fates choose to send us, but I can tell it is not so with you."

"It is not," said Lythande. "But as the Fates send me, so I must abide."

Manuela said hesitantly, "Are you sure I cannot be of any aid in your quest, brother magician? For it seems to me that there is something more than coincidence in our meeting. You are, I am sure, a great and powerful magician; but if I can serve you in anything—"

"I think not," said Lythande. "Yet I thank you for your good will, Manuela."

The water did not go down that day. Just before evening, the women were gathered in the main room of the inn, where Lythande was diverting herself by playing on the lute. Suddenly, there was a great rumbling noise, and the floor seemed to shake itself and rock. The women clung together in fright, crying out.

"What was that? Brother magician, what was that?"

"Only an earthquake," murmured Lythande, shaken. Again the ground shook, and then settled; floods, and then earthquake! She must make haste; for if this were the Grail ruling the elements, first the element of water, signifying flood, and then the earthquake—the element of earth—what could have gone so amiss? She must make haste with her quest, or worse might follow. Yet marooned in this inn, alone with these women, how could she continue the search for the Guardian of the Grail?

She could not cross the barrier of waters unless they went down substantially. Could it be that the Guardian was here—either among the pilgrims, or perhaps the keeper of the inn herself?

Lythande sought out the innkeeper. She was a big woman, and looked like any of a hundred women, wrapped in her great apron. Lythande's heart sank, but she felt compelled to ask.

"Mistress Innkeeper, are there other guests at the inn? Other magicians, mayhap, who did not join with us in the common room last night? Those, perhaps, who bade you to keep their presence a secret?"

"No, my lord Magician. Only yourselves, and the pilgrim women. But did you not know that the leader of your company, one Manuela, is a great magician? Perhaps it is of her that you speak."

"I am sure that it is not," said Lythande. "I am only by chance in her company." It vexed her that the innkeeper should compare these hedge-witches with an Adept of the Blue Star. But for the moment she was marooned in their company; she must even bide with them until the Keeper of the Grail should see fit to come to her.

Dismissing her worries, Lythande went to their room and lay down. Soon she fell asleep. Just before sunrise, she was jolted out of sleep by an earthquake, this one considerably more violent than the others.

"Look for that which repeats," thought Lythande. "What a donkey I am, to be sure! Perhaps her Goddess thought I needed a lesson in humility."

She sought out the common room where the pilgrims, clustered about Manuela, were kneeling and praying that the elements might turn away their wrath. Far out in the water surrounding them, Lythande could see an ominous bubble of fire—a volcano! The element of fire was about to join its fellow elements. Lythande knelt hastily beside Manuela, who broke off in her prayers.

"Yes, my brother magician?"

Lythande knelt and drew forth from the mage-robe the silks concealing the Grail. "I think I am guided to bear this to you," said Lythande. "It may be that the Gods who own this thing think I need a lesson in humility." And suddenly Lythande felt long unaccustomed tears blurring her eyes.

Manuela rose to her feet. Her round, good-natured face seemed to glow; she held out her hand and said, "My brother—no, my sister—I wondered how long it would take you to get around to telling me about it. For when the waters rose, I guessed; and when the earthquakes shook us, I was nearly certain."

Her drably-draped form seemed to take on height and power; she raised the Grail above her, in a ritual gesture older than time.

Beyond the window, the waters were receding in the dim light of early dawn. "You can be on your way, magician," said Manuela, smiling. "I will care for the Grail. And you, be not too quick to judge your fellow man—or woman. Oh, and forget not to break your fast before you go," she added, with homely sternness.

"So it is ordained," Lythande replied, and went to speak to the innkeeper about breakfast. Having surrendered the Chalice of Tears, she no longer felt like weeping. In fact, Manuela was right; she was hungry.

The Feast of the Fisher King

A Masque in Verse
(with narrative inclusions)

Diana L. Paxson

A storm drives rain across a land of tangled woods and blasted mountainsides. Tree-limbs thrash as it batters the forest; wind howls across weed-choked fields. Lightning slashes the sky. You see, first, a riven oak, stark against the stormy sky. You see a tumble of stones that once were a homestead, but this land is barren now. You see, finally, a castle, its stone flanks gleaming in the lightning's flare. Long has it stood there, and withstood worse storms than this one. Once it was a fair and gracious adornment to the mountainside. But now it appears a fortress, battered and grim. Only in the highest tower does one lit window glow like a captured star.

A single rider forces his horse through the storm.

SCENE I: GATEHOUSE, THE CASTLE OF THE GRAIL

Enter Perceval, shaking rain from his cloak and peering about him. He knocks heavily on the door with the pommel of his sword.

Perceval: Doorkeeper, ho!

On the other side of the door, the Doorkeeper makes her way slowly down the stairs, a lighted candle flickering in her hand. She

seems a comfortable, comforting old soul, but there is at times a
disquieting wisdom in her eyes.

Doorkeeper: *(muttering)* Whoever can that be?
   The door is barred and darkness rules the world . . .

Perceval: *(knocks once more)* Ho—let me in—the night
   grows cold!

Doorkeeper: 'Tis cold?
   Perhaps, but I am old—old bones go slow,
   and I've a weary walk to let you in.
   The stairs are steep and perilous with years;
   the passageways are chill, and grim the gate
   that opens on the wasteland of the world.
(Perceval knocks again)
   Be patient, you—I'll come, hard though it is
   to brave the dark outside that gracious hall
   where my dear lord sits throned. . . .

Perceval: *(batters furiously)* In God's name, come!
   The sun's long set; I would not linger here
   where evil voices whisper on the wind.
   Cold as the nether depths of Hell it blows,
   now here, now there, now countering itself
   as if it wished to blow the world away.
   But I have battled 'till I reached your gate—
   unbar the door before I break it down!

Doorkeeper: *(stops, shaking her head)* Here is one
   unversed in courtesy!
   How comes he here? Did I not know that none
   may find this place except by my lord's will.
   I'd think this churl a hapless wayfarer
   indeed. But my lord's ways are not for me
   to question—

(Perceval kicks at the door)
>   All these years my lord has lain
>   so patient in his pain ... be patient now
(hurries to the door)
>   and I will let you in!

(The Doorkeeper opens the door and Perceval bursts through as if propelled by the wind. He shakes himself and stares around him. He is sturdy in build, with a mop of fair hair, and when he throws back his hood it is clear that he is very young.)

Perceval: So—here you are!
>   I feared this place abandoned, and the light
>   that burns in yonder tower some elvish trick.
>   I fear no man—but I have seen no man
>   since noonday, at the river's edge. A man
>   sat fishing in a rowboat there. He said
>   I'd find a castle if I came this way....
>   From day to darkness I have wandered here,
>   wondering if that counsel was deceit
>   to lose me. Vagrant lightnings lit my way,
>   rain lashed the rocks, the stunted trees, and me,
>   and all the world except the barren ground.
>   Through this I struggled, 'till I glimpsed these towers.
>   Whose keep is this? What Lord would care to dwell
>   where brute beasts lair, and other things less ... kind?

Doorkeeper: Pay them no mind—no evil enters here,
>   though all the elements may be at war,
>   though creatures never blessed by God—cold trolls
>   and loathly worms, or wolves that are no wolves
>   may nightly through these deserts make their way;
>   though souls of men forever shut from grace
>   wail round our walls; they may not come within.

This balance my lord's power has maintained.
(sighs) And yet I fear we'll be beleaguered here
until God's Judgment Day—or else until
the destined hero comes. Long ago
this land was fair, they say . . . the sun shone warm
and rain fell gently from the brimming skies,
borne by the welcome winds. Man tilled the earth
and praised Earth's Lord . . . But you're safe now—
as for my lord, soon you may question him. . . .

*(Perceval has taken off his helm, and now he loosens his cloak.
The Doorkeeper lifts the candle and looks him up and down,
ogling him.)*

You'll break no mirrors, lad! Such shoulders, too—
as fair a form indeed as ever God
filled with the breath of life and said, " 'Tis good!"
But you're wet through, and chilled, too, I would
guess.
Take off that cloak and doff your arms as well—
such grim gear's no fit raiment for this Hall!

(Doorkeeper helps Perceval off with his cloak and mail)

Perceval: God's blessing on your hospitality!
I lay last night upon the earthen floor
of some poor peasant's cottage. It's been long
indeed since I saw courtly folk—I hope
you can forgive my battering at your door?
I am but newly trained to courtesy. . . .

Doorkeeper: Be easy, lad—'tis true the night was fell.
Forgiveness asked is always granted here.

(Perceval looks at his garments with some embarrassment)

Perceval: I fear this tunic's all I have to wear . . .
if your lord keeps high state, I would be shamed
to go before him so.

Doorkeeper: No need to fear—
    We will not be behind in courtesy!
    There is a proper garment for each feast—
    put on this robe—I see it fits you well!

(The Doorkeeper helps Perceval to put on a robe of white samite, and the boy stretches out his arms, admiring it.)

Perceval: In such garb I could stand in God's own Hall!

Doorkeeper: You will find my lord's Hall near as fair.
    Follow me. You are awaited there. . . .

The Doorkeeper lights another candle, gives it to Perceval and leads him up the stairs and through several passageways until they arrive at the Great Hall. The music of a fair and stately dance can be heard. At one end of the Hall is a dais, and there one may see the Fisher King huddled in his carven chair before a long table. His hair is white, his face gaunt, but there is still fire in his eyes. What age and pain have done to his body are hidden by the folds of a purple cloak. But only two places are laid. As the Doorkeeper brings Perceval to the arched doorway, the music grows softer and fades.

SCENE II: THE FISHER KING'S HALL

Perceval: What is it that I see—this kingly Hall,
    all luminous with candles? Golden light
    gleams on its ordered pillars, and its floor
    is polished porphyry. . . .

Doorkeeper: There you must go—
    That is the feasting chamber of my lord.

Perceval: No, not so soon! Within, I will not dare
           to question.... Tell me of the tapestries
           whose jewel tones and rich and cunning work
           so tease the eye one thinks the figures move—
           what story do they tell?

Doorkeeper: They tell the tale
           of Joseph, a great lord in Palestine,
           who laid the shattered body of Our Lord
           in his own stone-built tomb, and when Christ rose
           in glory, worshipped Him. But evil men
           pursued him for his faith. Thus, with his sons
           he fled, his ship borne by the wind of God,
           across the azure waves to Logres, where
           lay sanctuary for the Holy Things.

Perceval: And who is that great lord who sits enthroned,
           surrounded by so fair a company,
           like saints around the throne of God?

Doorkeeper: My lord
           that is, whom some men call the Fisher King.

Perceval: Is he indeed the one I met this noon?
           How still he sits—still as a hidden pool
           that no wind ruffles. How much majesty
           shines through the lines of suffering in his face.
           Untutored as I am, how can I go
           before *him*? Come with me!

Doorkeeper: No, I must stay,
           content, to do the task to which I'm called.
           But *you* are called to enter here, so go!

(The Doorkeeper pushes Perceval forward, and he slowly moves through the dancers toward the Fisher King.)

       Indeed, I am content, though I remain
       forever on the threshold into bliss.
       I am a child of earth, but I have known
       the taste of glory now and then. I sit
       and hear the singing of this company
       (angels sing less sweet) and see them dance
       through all the starry figures of the skies,
       and nightly I look on my dear lord's face,
       and nightly my eyes see the things of God. . . .

(The Doorkeeper sinks down on a bench by the doorway and remains there as Perceval approaches the dais and the King turns to look down at him. He makes an awkward bow.)

Fisher King: Fair sir, be seated. You are welcome here.
       I grieve I cannot rise to greet you—please
       believe I mean you no discourtesy.
(Perceval mumbles an apology, and takes the empty place beside him. A silent servant brings him a plate of food.)
       I may eat nothing but a little bread,
       and for my drink sip only at red wine,
       but here are noble meats, and honey mead—
       be you at rest—now eat and drink your fill. . . .
(Perceval drinks deeply from the goblet and picks nervously at his food.)
       And if you will, tell us what name you bear?

Perceval: Sir Perceval of Galles, good my lord.

Fisher King: Ah—you must be son to Gahmuret
       and Lady Herzeloide—

Perceval: I do not know,
       so long I've wandered since I left my home.

Fisher King: You've been blown far afield indeed.
        In truth,
        we who are rooted here would gladly have the tale of your
        adventures—

Perceval: Oh, my lord,
        I cannot think this noble company
        would care to hear such things as I can tell.

Fisher King: Yet 'tis not so. What know you of your
        worth?
        Speak as the spirit moves you—you may find
        such virtues as you never had in mind. . . .

SCENE III: THE PAST REMEMBERED

Perceval: My lords and ladies, they say that I was born
        deep in an ancient forest, where I knew
        none but my mother, and those faithful few,
        her servants, who refused to leave her there.
        But neither court nor castle did I know,
        nor use of arms, nor name of chivalry.

Fisher King: Your brothers both were slain in Arthur's
        wars; your father died of sorrow when they fell.
        No wonder if your mother feared for you . . .

Perceval: She feared for me? But why? No matter why—
        I played alone. I carved me javelins,
        and ran the wild beasts down. But a day came
        when I lay resting in the forest gloom,
        and heard a sound like thunder, though no cloud
        was in the sky, and then a clattering,

and clang and clink and jangle, and I thought—
'My mother says the devils sound like this!
I'll wait and fight and see how fierce they are!'
And so I crouched, spear ready. . . . Then I glimpsed
above the thicket, something fluttering,
bright as a flock of birds. I rose and saw
them come . . . Good Masters, I had never known
a sight so fair. They glistened like the sun,
and where they did not glitter, color glowed
as if a rainbow wrapped them. Then I thought,
'These must be angels, for my mother says
they walk in beauty—I will worship them . . .'

Fisher King: *(aside)* Thus may the darkness be
transformed to light
when understanding grows. The pure in heart
has eyes to see it.
Is this then the one?
(to Perceval) But lad, you must not worship mortal men—

Perceval: I know that, *now.* They told me they were
knights,
and Arthur makes men knights in Caerleon.
To Arthur I would go. My mother wept
of course—she did not understand, but still
she gave me her advice:
　　　　"All ladies serve for honor's sake—
　　　　may kiss or ring be all you take;
　　　　learn names of those with whom you ride,
　　　　let noble counsel be your guide;
　　　　and when a church lies on your way,
　　　　I bid you enter it and pray . . ."
　　　　　　　　　　　I listened well,
but I could stay no longer at her side.

Fisher King: Alas, had you no pity for her tears?
I fear the wind has borne them all away
and turned to dust the eyes from which they fell.

Perceval: Through the green woods I rode, and soon
I found a fair pavilion in a field,
striped gold and crimson, and a lady there.
Mindful of my mother's word, I passed
within and bid her give me kiss and ring,
(though she protested, had I not as guide
my mother's counsel?). And a cake or two
I also took to still my hunger; then
I trotted on.

Doorkeeper: *(aside)* What shame to treat her so!
Had she a lord? And when she told her tale
did he believe her?

Perceval: The forest left behind,
I saw next day the towers of Caerleon
rise pale as clouds upon the eastern hills.
I came to Arthur's gate that afternoon.

Fisher King: Great is the presence hall of Caerleon
where from his high seat Britain's noble king
gives laws. A hundred heroes sit around
his table—none do worldly deeds so well.
How fared you there?

Perceval: I fared both well and ill,
for as I passed the gate, I saw a knight
dressed in red armor pacing up and down.
A cup of gold he tossed from hand to hand,
and laughed. And when I came into the court
I saw them all afraid, because the cup
was taken from the queen. But I cared not—

I asked for arms and knighthood. Then Sir Kay
said Arthur gave the Red Knight's arms to me.
So I went out to take them. The silly man
did not at first believe me, but at last
he raised his lance, and I my javelin—
Lord save us. I could hardly miss a mark
so close as that! And so the Red Knight fell.

Fisher King: The flames may blaze on high when wind
meets fire,
but they cannot consume what whips them! So—
you had your arms. Tell us what happened then?

Perceval: *(embarrassed)* I did not know how arms are
fastened on,
and could not get them off . . . I thought perhaps
armed knights like crayfish open to the fire,
and so I lit one . . .

Doorkeeper: *(aside)* Did he *burn* the man?
Is this the newest use of chivalry?

Perceval: Just then a knight of Arthur's court came out
and taught me better. He would have me go
back with him to the king. But Kay had laughed
at me. I turned and took the road once more.

Doorkeeper: *(aside)* He's well begun, but even
heroes born must master chivalry—

Perceval: My horse was good,
The sky shone blue, my shield cast back the sun,
my ring mail made sweet music as I rode.
In joy I traveled through a goodly land
and came at last up to a castle tall
where two squires played at battle while their lord

stood by. I paused to watch; he asked if I
wished to know how to use the arms I bore....

Fisher King: What was the name borne by this kindly
lord?

Perceval: Gornemant, he said. I never saw
a nobler man.

Fisher King: Nor will you, though you fare
ten times the leagues you've come. He is my brother, and
all worldly knights he leads in grace ...

Perceval: In faith, his face was gracious towards me—
Gladly he showed me all the skills of arms:
blade flickered brightly as he struck and swayed
as though he moved to music, to the beat
of blow denied by parrying sword or shield;
and spear he lifted lightly; heavy mace
let fall; the subtle dagger; arrow swift;
all these he taught, with every law that makes
a stage for honor of the battlefield.

Doorkeeper: *(aside)* I think the crimson color of his arms
must suit this hothead well indeed!

Perceval: I stayed
with him a month. Before the moment came
for my departure, clothing fit for prince,
and knighthood's stainless order, he bestowed,
and with it, counsel:
        "Kill not him who will mercy pray,
        the helpless help in every way;
        go to the minster when you can,
        pray God to keep you Christian man—"
                        Thus had my mother bid

as well. I told him so, and he replied,
"If you continue saying, 'Mother said,'
you will but look a fool. If you must quote,
say you were told thus by the lord who made
you knight . . ." And last he said:
> "When you can, go silently,
> for too much speech a sin may be. . . ."
> And sir, indeed,
I have talked long tonight. 'Tis time I ceased!

Doorkeeper: *(aside)* My faith, he speaks truth there!
Midnight comes on,
and yet, so strange a tale's not often heard.
But is there purpose in his wandering?
This Perceval's a very Will'o th' wisp . . .
what blew him to our door? We question him—
he answers well, but will he ask again
when our turn comes for marvels? We shall see. . . .

Fisher King: Ah, lad—there are some times when one
should speak. . . .
But tell us what chanced when you left the hold
of Gornemant—this is your host's command!

Perceval: There's little more, in truth. For several days
my way lay through a land that once was fair,
but had been burnt and battered: smoke rose still
where farms had been, and carcasses of beasts
cut down in wantonness lay here and there.
And yet the castle's flag still bravely flew,
although a hostile army hedged it round.
The invaders let me gain the castle gate
(thinking, no doubt, a single man no threat)
and the defenders gracious welcome gave
although we dined on but one skinny fowl
and loaf of bread for twenty hungry men.

Fisher King: What castle was this then, and why besieged?
                      What lord was he who warded it so well?

Perceval: They called it Belrepaire, though scarce it
                      seemed
               so then! No lord ruled there. It was a maid
               who was both the commander and the prize
               for which two armies fought. She was Blancheflor ...
               Once, wandering in winter woods, I saw
               three drops of blood from some poor stricken beast
               lie on the snow. Just so in Blancheflor's cheek
               does the bright color flow, so fair is she,
               and like a plaited sunbeam shines her hair,
               and like the stars of heaven shine her eyes ...

Doorkeeper: *(aside)* A very paragon! With such a love,
                      whatever does he here? The youth is mad!

Perceval: That night she crept unasked into my room,
               and weeping, told me how her enemy
               had sworn to have her, willingly or no.
               My mother and my lord both bid me serve
               all ladies, but I would have championed
               Blancheflor unbid, so gracious and so fair
               was she, and so I told her, and we lay,
               exchanging comfort, 'till the new day dawned.
               I vanquished first the mighty seneschal,
               and then his master, presumptuous Clamadeu,
               and since they begged for mercy, sent them both
               to yield them prisoner at King Arthur's hall, but I stayed
               well-content at Belrepaire....

Fisher King: And yet you left at last—

Perceval: My mother's face,
               all wet with tears as I had seen it last,

intruded on my joy. I wished to have
her blessing on my wedding day. I ride
with her face and my lady's in my heart . . .
For many days my search has led me on
through wilderness, until this eve I came
to your high hall. And that is all my tale.

Fisher King: God grant your mother's tears have been a
rain that may wash all your sins away. I think
it is from Heaven's Halls of Light that now
your mother prays for you. . . .

Perceval: My mother dead?
What then is left to look for?

Fisher King: That one thing
which every man must seek. . . . Do not forget
your mother's face, or pity, or the love
that leads to wisdom. These will guide your quest.
Now eat and drink—your portion is untouched,
for we have so constrained you to your tale
you've had no time! Such courtesy but ill
befits my hall. Be comforted therefore,
and eat your fill.

SCENE IV: THE FIRE SWORD

*The musicians resume their playing as Perceval applies himself to
his food with full concentration.*

Doorkeeper: *(aside)*   Indeed, my hope
is equal with my lord's that this young man
will see and say what must be seen and said.
And yet I fear all his adventuring
has not taught wisdom. Lord, why must your great

nobility, or else the High God's law,
forbid plain speech about the Mysteries?

Fisher King: *(aside)* Ah, Lord God, see how the sleeping
world turns underneath its coverlet of stars
until the pattern shows that warns the hour
is near ... Now, soon, the Hallows will appear.
And this time will my healing come as well?
The years flow past. No longer do I know
how long I have stagnated here—not lord
in full, not fully free. I, who before,
was Lord of all Earth's Powers, now scarce hold
one, and all my virtue slowly seeps away.
What bread can truly nourish such as I?
What friendly fire warm me, what wind inspire,
what living water wash away my pain?
And yet, this holy company calls me
their lord. From this flawed vessel draw they grace,
which I draw from the Hallows, and to them
it comes from Thee, my Lord ... In Thine own time
Thou wilt deliver me and this poor land
I know. And yet, my life ebbs fast from shores
of polished bone. Oh, send Thy Chosen soon!

(The fire in the hearth leaps up suddenly, sending a flicker of ruddy light across the Hall.)

Perceval: My thanks to you, my lord. I have dined
well. . . .

Fisher King: And finished in good time . . . but who comes now?

(As if the fire has taken the form of a woman, a maiden with a tangle of fiery hair, and a gown all embroidered with a pattern like darting tongues of flame, comes into the Hall. She is carrying a sheathed sword.)

Perceval: *(aside)* Of all the wonders I have seen this night
        she is the fairest—hair like living flame,
        a face as bright as any burnished blade,
        and eyes as keen ... I cannot meet her gaze!

Maiden: Now grace be to this house, and to its lord,
        And unto all within—

Fisher King: Fair niece, be welcome.

Maiden: My lord, I may not sit and take my ease
        until the task to which I have been bound
        is done. For as I lay upon my bed
        my heart burned within me. Then I knew
        the time appointed for my task was come.

Doorkeeper: *(aside)* More wonders than our own are here
        tonight;
     - it has been long since this bright maid came here.
        But what's the fate that drives her hither now?

Maiden: *(holds high the sheathed sword)* .
        Behold the greatest treasure of my House,
        the mighty sword once smithed by Trebuchet!
(She draws the blade and turns it to catch the light of the candle flames.)
        See how the candle flame ignites
        the gems that form its hilt—no elven lord
        bore ever sword so rich. See how the blade
        seems made of living light, which, as I turn
        it, flickers crimson as a tongue of flame,
        thrice-forged it was in heaven's holy fire. . . .
(The sword flares crimson, then the color fades.)
        With such a brand a warrior might strike down
        a thousand foes and never quench its zeal;

and 'tis so balanced, in a righteous cause,
a thousand blows would never weary him!

Perceval: Truly, I have never seen its like—
it outshines her who holds it. My right arm
yearns for its weight as once my limbs desired
to clasp Blancheflor. . . .

Fisher King: But he who grasps this sword
must know what foe to strike. Why do you bring
this blade to me?

Maiden: So that you may bestow it.
You will know to whom it should belong—
Give it to him who'll wield it worthily!

Fisher King: *(aside)* Do I know him, then? How sure she
seems,
and how her eyes burn on young Perceval. . . .
(aloud) If 'tis your will, I will you give this blade
to that knight who now sits by my side.

Maiden: To you, fair sir, I do present this sword—
Strike always for the right! If you betray
our trust, and fight in anger, pride, or fear,
it will betray you in your hour of need!

*(The maiden gives the sword to Perceval. He takes it reverently,
then rises, steps aside and tries it, wielding it like an extension of
his arm.)*

Doorkeeper: *(aside)* Does it begin? This has not chanced
before—
he has the sword, the other Hallows come . . .
Will Perceval then know what must be done,
and then will my dear lord be freed at last?

Perceval: *(sheathing the sword and turning to the Maiden)*
Lady, such a gift is more than I
deserve, yet I swear I'll try to make
the measure of its worth . . .

Maiden: You swear to try?
That is too dim a word! Nay, rather strive
to strike from your intention such a fire
as will consume all doubt!

Perceval: Stay, you are
too hot for me. But I'll do what I may . . .
This adventure's surely the most strange
of all I've known, and this place full of wonders!

Maiden: Wait—there may be greater wonders still . . .

Perceval: I will wait, and watch, and listen too,
as he who gave me knighthood bid. I would
not burst the frail sphere of this miracle
with speech . . . I know not if I wake or sleep!

Fisher King: Wake now, and watch, and may our Lord
you keep. . . .

SCENE V: INTERLUDE OUT OF TIME, THE HALLOWS APPEAR

Silence . . . a stillness that spreads as the musician puts down his instrument, and the dancer pauses in the midst of the dance. The Fisher King sits poised in an agony of anticipation more compelling than any motion. Perceval watches him, but the others are looking—where? At the candles, which are flickering wildly though there is no wind? At the darkness that pools and gathers in the corners of the room? The air throbs as if it had become too dense for

*human breathing. Then a glow appears in the farther doorway, and
pent breath is released in a communal sigh.*

*Two lads enter, dressed in white and holding candles thick as
their own wrists, that burn with a steady glow. Eyes rapt with concentration, they pace through the Hall. A moment passes, then an
older youth follows them, with a man's growth but not yet a man's
strength or passions. He holds a lance of ancient Roman make, its
wooden haft polished with handling, its head corroded with age.
He moves with an awkward grace, seeming not to see where his
feet lead him, for his eyes are fixed on the lancehead, whence a
drop of blood is rolling down. He, too, passes through the Hall,
and Perceval's eyes widen, but he says no word.*

*And now there comes a maiden whose white gown gleams
through the veiling of her dark hair like the moon through clouds.
She moves as to a music that only she can hear, cradling the silver
platter with the bread upon it, newly baked, leaving its own incense
in the room. There is a sweetness in her smile that eases the spirit,
and yet the tension in the Hall grows greater still. Perceval shifts
on his bench, seeking to see where they are going; wondering what
they are waiting for. But he says no word.*

*And then . . . the radiance increases, but this is no lamp or can-
dle, neither sun nor moon. A woman's form appears within it, but
already the brightness is too great to tell if she is beautiful. But her
walk is music, and where she passes comes a sweet shimmering of
bells. Yet no man in all that company looks at her, but only at the
thing she carries, at the Grail. . . .*

*What do they see? Look at the light within you—what do you
see there? For one it is a cauldron edged with moonstones, filled
with the water of immortality; another sees a clay cup lined with
gold that once held holy blood; for one it is a glowing green stone;
another sees only the woman's body there. Silver or gold, jeweled
or plain, it is the vessel of life that she bears through the Hall. And
each one, seeing, perceives that thing above all most desired, and
is content to behold the Mystery.*

*But Perceval sees only a beautiful woman carrying a chalice.
To him the sight seems both fair and strange, but who is he to*

question? And the day has been long—his eyelids grow heavy. As the Grailbearer passes out of the Hall, he rests his head upon his arms and lets his eyes close.

With the Grail, all light goes out of the world. The Hall is in darkness, its people only silhouettes against the glow of the dying fire. Out of that darkness comes the cry of the king—

Fisher King: Bear me away! The Holy Things are gone—
the Feast is over, and I am betrayed!
This dolt, who could have healed me with a word,
lies wrapped in stupid slumber. Bear me hence!
For I must set myself to bear my pain
for yet awhile, until the Lord Christ please
to send him who will set me free again....

Doorkeeper: *(lights a candle, and lifts it to reveal Perceval asleep with his head on the table)*
Alas, my lord speaks true—see how he sleeps,
worn out with wonders ... This lad could have been
the master of such powers as would restore
to harmony the jangled elements
of nature and of man. But he would not
his own self master even to stave off sleep!
Ah, one must know what questions should be asked
to get the answers that give mastery.
Well, fool—sleep in your innocence! The dawn
comes soon, and you will go your heedless way ...
(The Doorkeeper extinguishes her candle.)

SCENE VI: THE WASTELAND

Day is dawning in the forest. Water drips from broken branches and stands in muddy pools. The ravages of the storm can be seen clearly, but there is no sign of a Castle near. Only the faintest of trackways suggests men have ever passed this way. Perceval's horse noses at the sodden grass. Perceval himself, clad once more in his armor, is lying nearby. Muttering, he stirs—

Perceval: The sword . . . the spear . . . the dish . . . the Grail . . .
       the Grail! Heaven's Hallows pass before my eyes—
       what does it mean? I dare not ask my lord
       the Fisher King—I'll ask the Doorkeeper
       when morning comes . . .
(His head drops back and he sleeps once more, then murmurs—)
                   The Grail . . . how fair it is. . . .
       It blazes with such light! *(he opens his eyes)*
       What did I dream?
       Sunlight burns my eyes—the day has come!
(He sits up, looking around him.)
       But where am I? Surely a moment since,
       I sat within the Fisher King's fair Hall
       beside him at his table, and I saw . . .
       can I believe the sights I thought I saw?
       And then I fell asleep to such a song
       as sing the morning stars, and yet I wake
       to find myself alone in this green glade.
       There is no sign of Hall or Castle here,
       nor any Christian soul. Was it a dream,
       or some fair vision such as saints are given?
(He stands up, looking about him in confusion, and sees the sword at his feet.)
       But no—look here! I do not dream this sword!
       Then it *was* true, and I have been cast out
       into the empty morning of the world. . . .
       How can I live without some shred of hope
       that I will find the Hallows once again!
       I would pledge all I have or hope to win
       to know a day will come when I return. . . .
(He sinks down, despairing, then reaches out to grasp the sword.)

And yet I have this sword. Have I then hope?
I swore to use it worthily ... I will,
and pledge I will not cease from wandering
until the Castle stands revealed once more,
and once more I feast with the Fisher King.
Then will I ask the meaning and the use of
Grail and platter, of the spear and sword.
Let me but come again—I will not fail
this time to ask the meaning of the Grail!

Perceval raises the sword on high in witness, sheathes it, and wraps his cloak around him. Mounting his horse, he sets off along the trackway, and soon his figure is hidden by the tangle of trees.

In the empty glade a bird begins singing, and sunlight, shafting through the trees into a pool of standing water, is reflected back in a dazzle of brightness that holds for a moment the image of the Grail. . . .

* * *

Author's note: I first encountered the Grail dramatically at a performance of Wagner's *Parsifal,* and academically in a graduate seminar at the University of California. My fascination has continued. This masque, based on the earliest (surviving) account of Perceval's visit to the Grail Castle, as told by Chrétien de Troyes, was first created for performance at Mythcon XII in 1981. The reading version with narrative insertions has been prepared for this volume.

Given the liberties that some of the medieval authors took with the story, I feel no need to apologize for my changes, including the restoration to the other objects in the Grail procession of an importance which the medieval authors glossed over. In identifying the four hallows with the four elements I am following in the footsteps of W. B. Yeats and Charles Williams.

Those who care for such things are welcome to interpret this text on any level they like—psychological, spiritual, symbolic, or allegorical. I see no reason why any number of readings, like the many versions of the Grail story itself, cannot be equally "true."

May you, the reader, find what you seek here. . . .

The Gift of Gilthaliad

Brad Strickland

In the days when the Fair Folk shared the world with the sons of men, it chanced that a young prince of the Elven Court of Silandrior grew to be friends with a Human prince. The Elf, Gilthaliad, son of Alendar, spent much time with his young Human, Prince Davel of the Grey Mountains. Gilthaliad wished to understand the ways of Humans, and he studied their customs and their beliefs. Upon the occasion of Davel's betrothal, Gilthaliad determined that he would follow custom and present his Human friend with a gift.

However, Gilthaliad would not offer such a gift as the Fair Folk usually bestowed to Humans or to each other. He would not give long life, haleness of limb, or keenness of eye, nor a blessing upon the issue of the marriage, nor even luck. Instead, Gilthaliad decided to create a work of art with his own hands, in the way of the Human smiths and artisans. This gift he would present to his friend. Long and secretly he labored before producing a wondrous creation: a chalice, wrought of gold and silver curiously intermingled, set about with precious stones, and of a surpassing, eerie loveliness.

When Gilthaliad had finished, he showed the chalice to his elders, who disdained it. "I find no enchantment in this," Gilthaliad's father, Alendar, pronounced. "My son, why do you imitate the Dwarves and the Humans, and soil your hands with base metals, when you might with a thought produce a work of magic?"

Vainly did Gilthaliad try to explain his reasons. Neither Alendar nor any of his people believed that the chalice was other than a toy, a piece of childish vanity not becoming one of Gilthaliad's lineage, station, and age. With bitterness in his heart, the tall young prince took the chalice to the wedding, where with few words he presented it to his Human friend.

However common the chalice appeared to the Fair Folk, it stunned the Humans at the wedding. Davel's dark eyes filled with tears at the mere sight of it, and the whole court gasped in admiration—and envy.

Years passed, as years will, and a curious change crept over the court of the King of the Grey Mountains. Davel's father, Tarkes the Protector, grew aged and feeble, and at last died, and so Davel ascended the throne before he was quite thirty summers old. Sadly, the strongly built, dark young man ruled negligently, careless of his duties. He reigned in a time of uneasy peace, when frontier skirmishes with restless northern barbarians flared all too often. Those who dwelled on the borders of his land first turned to him for aid, and when that did not come, they turned toward him to curse his name. The court became decadent and improvident, and yet Davel failed to bestir himself to any praiseworthy action.

His wife, too, a woman of great beauty named Ninuel, grew restless and dissatisfied, and the court whispered that she took lovers. All of this was the fault of the wondrous chalice wrought by Gilthaliad. For King Davel was so jealous of it, so enraptured by it, that he kept it in a secret room that only he could enter. At all hours of the day or night he would steal away to this chamber to regard the beautiful work of Elven hands. He lost himself in contemplating the uncanny complexity of line, the rich sheen of the metals, and the cunning setting of the stones. Loveliest of all was the multicolored dazzle of the gems themselves: ruby, orphischel, emerald, chalcenite, sunstone, diamante, none duplicated, all beautiful to behold. The chalice enraptured the eye, gladdened the heart, and made all mundane cares recede to unimportance in Davel's mind.

Now, it happened that one of the Queen's lovers was an adventurer from the outlandish countries bordering the Eastern Sea, a sinewy, blond man with cold blue eyes. Indeed, his eyes seemed older than the rest of him, for he was five years younger than the King. He stole his pleasures with Queen Ninuel in such places and at such times as he could. They trysted when she went forth to the hawks, or when she went to bathe in the Goddess Glade forbidden to all but women of the blood royal, or in the evenings when the court lay asleep and the King was rapt in contemplation of his chalice.

On one of the latter occasions, when they lay together in the state bed in Ninuel's room, she whispered of the chalice in tones of jealousy and bitterness. She sounded like a woman envious of a rival.

Koron, her lover, chuckled deep in his throat. "What should it matter, if Davel is fool enough to prefer cold metal and stones to hot, lusty flesh?" he asked, laying a warm hand on Ninuel's bare stomach. With a teasing forefinger he circled her navel, causing the skin to quiver. "The better for us, who know what to value and what to spurn."

Still, the Queen's partial description of the chalice intrigued Koron. She had spoken in angry, bitter tones, but the grail she described had to be a creation of marvelous beauty. All that night, and then all the days later, Koron thought to himself that he would mightily savor a vision of the wonder. After all, it had stolen King Davel's affection from a woman who was a better than fair lover.

And so, not many days later, Koron began to ask Ninuel to filch for him the key to the strongroom where Davel kept his treasure of treasures. "It is a terrible difficulty," she complained. She explained that Davel always wore the brass key on a golden chain around his neck. Ever and anon his hand would steal to the place where it hung against his chest, beneath his tunic, and he would reassure himself by touch that the key was safe.

When Ninuel objected, Koron made light of the trouble and

danger. At last he persuaded Ninuel to describe for him the key, which was small but cunningly wrought by Hirik-kirril, the Dwarven smith whose skill at locks and mechanical contrivances surpassed all others. Koron knew that any lock fashioned by such a master would be impossible for anyone to open without the genuine key. Dwarf-locks brook no lockpicks, they say, and this one would be even more craftily wrought than most.

But Ninuel's description of the key gave an inspiration to Koron. He went to a brass-smith in another town a day's ride from the castle, and he had the man make up for him a lock and a key to fit it. The key was of the same general appearance and size as the one to the strong-room. Koron threw away the lock, but with the key he returned to the castle, and into Ninuel's hand he surrendered the small piece of brass, and into Ninuel's ear he delivered his instructions about what to do.

More days passed, until finally a court day arrived. Although he hated the bother of sitting in judgment of matters he considered trivial, Davel had the responsibility of hearing the complaints and requests for boons of all the nobles. So with a sigh and a curse he rose on that morning. Ninuel offered to help him dress, an office which she had not performed in several years, and Davel, somewhat flattered, consented.

The king bathed and made himself fresh, and Ninuel and her maids dried him with thick towels. While so doing, Ninuel cleverly took the real key from its chain and replaced it with the false. Davel had not long sat upon his throne, delivering his begrudged judgments, when the true key to his strongroom rested in the hand of Koron.

The foreigner stole to the strongroom and opened the door. He lifted the lantern he bore and caught his breath. In the first moment of his seeing it, he lusted for the chalice, and that morning he left with it concealed in his saddlebag. He rode hard and long, until his horse staggered beneath him, and then he bought another horse, and used it in similar fashion. Koron galloped madly east, passing beyond the borders of the Kingdom of the Grey Mountains, then along the King's Road through the valley of the River Vale, and so, after many days, to the sea.

On the court day, though, Davel left his throne at sunset and hastened to his treasure room, but the key would not turn in the lock. The king then noticed the key's strange feel beneath his fingers, and he cried out in rage. He bethought himself and quickly saw that Ninuel must be the traitor. Davel went to her and demanded the truth. She swore she knew nothing of the key. In his anger, Davel struck her. She, angry in turn, screamed that she would never tell him her secrets. He stopped at nothing, not even the cruelest of tortures. His will proved the stronger. Ere she died, Ninuel confessed all and cursed the faithless gender of men for their coldness and their unnatural lust for the chalice.

All this time, Gilthaliad had continued in his friendship for Davel, though their meetings had grown rare. That friendship ended when Davel began to muster a warlike army. The Elves, troubled by these events, sent Gilthaliad as an emissary to the court of the King of the Grey Mountains. The haughty monarch told Gilthaliad that he planned to march through the lands of the Mountain Elves to reach the haven whither had fled the traitor who had seduced Ninuel. Davel's shame at losing the chalice was so great that he did not mention that loss, and in the despair of the time, Gilthaliad quite forgot about the wedding gift he had made with his own hands. The Elven prince warned Davel that the Fair Folk would not permit a march of so many men across their domain. "Then woe to the Fair Folk," Davel said with a dark oath. "For revenged I shall be, and they lie in my way."

Thus began the bitter war of the Mountain Elves and the Kingdom of the Grey Mountains, a war that lasted three summers. The Elves, never many, dwindled in battle and lost their king. Their counselors realized the Fair Folk had to retreat or perish, and at last they withdrew from their pleasant glades in the foothills of the mountains. Gilthaliad left with the other survivors, grieving in his heart. The Fair Folk regarded him bitterly, for still Gilthaliad spoke warmly of Davel. Gilthaliad knew that he would face ages of trial and struggle before he could claim kingship over the Exiles of Silandrior, as the Elves now called themselves. Still, he did not blame Davel, for Gilthaliad thought that the king must have loved his queen dearly and that he had been maddened by her unfaithfulness.

Davel stood in high esteem after the victory. Men now called Davel "King One-Eye," for he had lost his left eye in the same battle in which Gilthaliad's father, Alendar, fell. Davel One-Eye gathered his forces, added to them, and swept eastward, capturing all the cities of the River Vale, as far as the coast itself. There he learned that Koron now reigned over the Isle of Mists, many leagues to the east in the midst of the Sea of Storms. Accordingly, Davel built a fleet and pursued him.

Koron's people were a seagoing race, with a formidable fleet of their own. For several years they held off Davel's repeated attempts to invade their land, with each side growing weaker. Then at last the Turingien hordes from the bitter north swept down into the Grey Mountains and overthrew Davel's army, enfeebled by years of warfare. Koron's stronghold, too, suffered, and events forced him to sue for peace. At last, middle-aged and broken in spirit, Koron offered his most priceless possession, the chalice, to the barbarian leader. The man accepted that as ransom and agreed to let Koron live.

Sad to say, he was no longer in his right wits, for parting with the wonderful chalice so grieved him that he became broken in mind. He wandered for many summers, a ragged, dirty, babbling man who muttered darkly of gold, silver, and jewels. At last, when the frost of age was beginning to come upon the brain-broken Koron, the witling stumbled into a southern inn. There he begged for drink and told mostly unintelligible tales of himself, his days of glory, and of the wondrous cup. A man came shouldering through the crowd, as filthy as Koron, and as poor: a man whose left eye was missing, whose face a cruel scar pulled horribly awry. The man's one remaining eye burned dark and bright with hatred. With a hoarse scream, old Davel fell upon Koron, his dagger drawn. The two rolled upon the floor, and when the drinkers separated them, Koron lay dead, a dagger thrust through his heart. Old Davel One-Eye, his chest heaving, drooled a few words about the chalice. Then he, too, died, his heart burst.

The kingdoms of the South united to fight the barbarians who had swept as far southward as the River Vale. The barbarians, in their way, fell to quarreling among themselves over the spoils of their conquest, and before long the chalice had passed from vanquished to victor many times over. A nameless churl bore it for his warlord in the Battle of the Black Pools, where the Southrons broke the power of the Turingiens at last. The victorious armies drove the barbarians far back up into the wilds of the north.

The people of the Grey Mountains and the valleys rejoiced at the overthrow of the Turingiens, who had enforced their harsh rule for a century. The Kingdom of the Grey Mountains was no more, but parts of it fell into the hands of the conquering Southern rulers. Among them was an older, more solemn Gilthaliad, now the king of his Elven court. The winning of rule had hardened him and had worn away much of his youth, and yet inwardly he had not altered very much. One of his first actions upon assuming the New Kingdom was to erect a black stone monument, a graceful spire graven with the name of his ancient friend. His people, who had come to respect him as a leader, tolerated this gesture, though as often as not they mocked the stone monolith whenever they chanced to pass it.

Now, after that last battle, the churl who protected the chalice fled from the strife and passed northward all alone. He stole from farms he passed or waylaid travelers to live. On a winter's morning he tried to cross the High Pass of the Waste Mountains, only to fall back in the teeth of blinding snow and screaming winds. Numb with cold, the man crept into a cavern to find shelter, and with trembling hands he gathered enough dry twigs to build a mean fire. He hunched over this, warming himself, and he took from its pouch the wonderful chalice, feasting his eyes, though his belly clenched with hunger.

He did not see or hear the stealthy dragon that crept from the inky depths of the cavern. He probably felt nothing at his death, for the beast bit his head off cleanly. The reptile then made a slow feast of the body, and at the end it spied the jeweled cup. Picking it up carefully in its teeth, the dragon returned the chalice through tortuous ways to its hoard, a thigh-deep mound of gold and jewels. The chalice occupied a place of honor, the summit of the mound, and when the dragon curled for sleep, it wound its sinuous body around this greatest of treasures.

And there the chalice rested for many generations of men. The dragon grew older, and more cunning, and more voracious. It left its cavern rarely: once every seventy years to mate, and three or four times a year to feed, and other than that it dozed and dreamed of its treasures. Then as it aged, the dragon began to range closer to its cavern, for to fly long distances was tedious. So the people of the High Dales began to suffer sorely from the dragon's raids, in which the ravenous beast slaughtered eight or ten sheep at a time. Sometimes the dragon took shepherds, too, and as it grew older, its taste for manflesh grew keener. At last the people of the High Dales called for a hero to slay the creature.

Such a one was Belvenor, a young knight and a free lance. In the peaceful latter days of the South Kingdoms, Belvenor craved adventure. When none offered itself, no wars, no crusades, no tournaments worthy of the name, he became a wandering knight. So he wandered at last to the High Dales. There he heard the tale of the dragon, and there he swore he would champion the cause of the people against the ravening brute. The young women sighed, for he was tall, strong, and well-made, and he bore himself like a man of courage. The farmers told him stories of the dragon and of its habits, and in the end Belvenor settled for a while in the village. He visited himself to the priest once a day for purification, and he tracked through the high mountains all through the daylight hours, seeking some sign of the beast.

Dreary weeks passed, the days cold and bitter—for it was

again winter—and Belvenor found nothing. As spring began to open the tight buds of the high country, another stranger came to the village, a wandering magician, bitter of countenance, tall, thin, and stooped. Boys danced after him as he walked the streets of the village, the mountain winds whipping his ragged cloak about him. The cloak was the color of stormcloud, and when the children annoyed the wizard too much, he would lift his staff and lightning would flash. The boys tumbled away as fast as they could run when the thunder slammed against their ears. In short space, the magician heard of Belvenor's quest. Soon he made the young knight's acquaintance. Before long they sat at the same table, and at the table in the inn one evening the magician spoke to the knight: "Quests may end when you find a friend. You may find the beast when you expect it least. I counsel you, and what I speak is true."

With a forebearing smile, Belvenor replied, "Old man, riddle me no riddles. Weary I am of this quest, yet I must see it through. If you would help me, then say so in plain language, nor offer me thy conundrums and thy quiddities."

"And what will ye give me, Sir Knight, should I find the dragon for you?"

"Why, what would you have?"

The hard old eyes twinkled. "Say, the pick of the dragon's hoard, one piece, one bonny token, from the bed of the worm, no more than that. All the rest may be yours, and the farmers', so that I may choose just one small boon for my delight and my treasure. Say yes to that, and with my magic I will trace for you the crafty pathway trodden by the cunning foe."

"So said, so done," Belvenor said, his smile indulgent. "Yet I think you will find it passing hard to turn this boast to action."

The magician clapped his hands together. "A bargain made, a bargain sealed! A worm ye'll find, for woe or weal!" And he rose from his place and left the inn, leaning on his stick.

That night the magician's tent on the edge of the village was alight with strange fires and glows, and all the next day the magician did not appear. When he did show himself again, he looked haggard and worn, even older and more a scarecrow than he had looked at first. That evening he again sat with Belvenor in the inn, and the two of them talked long and earnestly. At last the towns-folk saw them clasp hands. The wizard passed to the knight a rolled sheet of parchment, and they parted company.

On the morrow after that, Belvenor was gone, together with his steed and his arms. The magician remained in town, working spells of healing and removing curses. Some days passed, and when the magician's tent began to out-draw the temple, the priest grew con-cerned and ordered the old man out. The magician grumbled, but he packed his tent and his tools. "I will be back," he promised. "For in a fortnight I have an appointment with a certain adventur-ous young knight." The ragged old man left that evening riding an ass, one of the sure-footed mountain breed.

Unfortunately for them both, the spring thaw had come to the heights. The magician was not a league south of town when he heard a world-shaking roar. He looked up into the darkness, and he tried to shout out a spell of protection, but the avalanche was upon him. Man and beast tumbled down, down, down, in a jumble of uprooted trees, flying boulders, and cascading ice. Both perished in the fall. Tons of mud, stone, and broken trees buried their bro-ken bodies, and no one ever found their bones.

And far to the north, Belvenor followed the parchment map over trails he had searched before. This time, though, he found the cavern opening, overgrown and hidden, and crept inside. He re-called the magician's advice and followed every article, and at last he emerged in the dragon's cavern. The beast, sleeping lightly, curled twice around the hoard it guarded, instantly wakened and reared, breathing fire. Belvenor hid himself behind his shield, though the heat scorched his skin and made him cry out, and he charged forward. The dragon struck, feinted, and struck again. Belvenor hacked at it with his sword, spilling steaming-hot blood but delivering no mortal blow. The combatants staggered in the piles of gold, slipped on coins, skidded on jewels. Belvenor fought in gasping silence, the stench of sulfur strong in his nose, and the dragon hissed and snarled.

When at last the dragon snapped its jaws at him, Belvenor stumbled back, and he fell beside the chalice, his sword flying from his grasp. The dragon roared and reared. It arched its neck to plunge its fangs down and into Belvenor's body.

Belvenor, desperate, clutched something and threw it. It was the chalice. The dragon's red eyes followed the arc, and the beast shot out its neck as it tried to catch the chalice before harm could befall it. Belvenor recovered his sword and charged, ripping a deep wound in the hollow of the dragon's throat, where the neck joined the trunk.

The dragon screamed through clenched teeth. Acidic blood gushed out, boiling and steaming, and Belvenor, gore-blinded, fell back. He had fatally wounded the beast. The dragon collapsed, half-rose, coughed a fiery gout of thick black blood, and died.

The young knight bore hurts in half a dozen places, his skin blistered and blackened. He rested awhile and then went to cut off the dragon's head, as proof that he had fulfilled his quest. Then he saw what the beast had clenched in its jaws: the wonderful chalice. He pried it loose and sat staring at it, and in his heart a bleak bitterness rose. For this, of course, was what the rogue of a magician would claim, he was sure of it. More, the young knight suspected that the mendacious old wizard had somehow known about the magnificent chalice, and that he, Belvenor, had been merely a pawn in some game the old man played with the dragon.

Still, honor dictated his return and his granting the choice of the hoard to the magician. There was that—but then the dragon had given him grievous injuries. Belvenor reasoned to himself that he needed rest and healing before he ventured back to the village. He had food enough for a week, and in the tunnels springs of water were everywhere, and so he remained in the cavern, near the festering body of the dead dragon. The longer he stayed, the more loath he was to return to the village, and the greater the hold the chalice had upon him.

So long did he remain that his food ran out, and he hacked pieces of the dragon's flesh to eat. His torches burned out, one after the other, until the last had gone. All grew dark in the cavern, save only the chalice, which appeared to him to have a light of its own. And so he stayed, and ate the strange flesh, and never noticed that the air was becoming more and more foul, until one morning he stirred no more. In his dead grasp he clutched the chalice, and so it passed beyond the knowledge of men.

A time of intense cold came, and it lasted for many ages of men. Ice crept slowly down from the north, grinding all before it. It wore away the mountain in which the chalice rested, stone by stone, year after weary year. The bones of the dragon and of the young knight alike the ice crushed to powder. The chalice alone of all the hoard remained intact, locked in the cold heart of a glacier. Each year, inch by inch, it made its way back to the south, following the tortuous ways of the valleys.

And then the age of cold was over, and the ice sheets began to retreat. This was a time when no men walked the lands of the northern mountains, for Humans had fallen into other concerns and had moved to other countries. But the Fair Folk yet lingered, in small numbers and in scattered settlements, beneath the eaves of the ancient forest.

So it was that two Elven children, playing in the chill waters of a mountain stream, saw something glimmer. When they lifted it, they gasped, for it was a chalice of surpassing beauty. They examined it, and inside the lip they saw the runes of Gilthaliad, their own great-great-grandfather. The two took the chalice home to their parents, and their parents journeyed with them to Elvenkeep, where the aged Gilthaliad still reigned. Toward evening on a day in spring, the two children found the old Elf resting alone on a stone bench in a wild orchard. He leaned against a tall spire of ebony blackstone, into which someone had carved runes long ago. Time had all but erased the graven word, and the letters were unreadable now. The two brothers approached Gilthaliad shyly.

He welcomed them with a smile. He had changed much from the young Elf that he had been, for the slow ages put care and lines upon even the faces of the Fair. Men say that a century of theirs is but a day to the Elves, but many centuries indeed had passed, each wearing away Gilthaliad's youth as the ice had worn away the mountains. The old king's hair was a pure silver, his form somewhat stooped and gaunt, and his steps slow. The old among the Elves thought that it would not be long before Gilthaliad would undertake the voyage to the Lands of the Ancestors, and some had begun to speculate about whom he might name as successor.

Still, in the friendly orchard, this and other cares lay far away. "And what do you bring, young kinsmen?" Gilthaliad asked the children kindly, though in truth he had forgotten their names.

They offered him the idlewood box they bore. "We found this," one of them said in an abashed whisper.

"It bears your mark," the other added, his voice no louder than his brother's.

Gilthaliad opened the box and took the chalice from its depths. He turned it this way and that in the sunlight, and a faint regretful smile played across his face. "Yes," he said at last. "Yes, I remember this. I made it long, long ago, when I was not much older than you. It was a gift for a friend."

"Will your friend be glad to have it back?"

Gilthaliad shook his head. "Alas, he was of the race of men, and died ages ago. Strange how clearly I remember him even now, a strong young man with laughing eyes and the fire of love in his heart. It is too bad that men are so brief upon the world, for he was a good friend to me. I recall a day when he told me of the woman he loved, and I determined to give him a gift in gladness. Indeed, I remember that day more clearly than yesterday's meetings. I must be growing old."

One of the children nodded, and the other shook his head. Gilthaliad laughed at the contradiction.

"If your friend is dead, are you glad to have the cup back?" the second child, the more venturesome, asked.

Gilthaliad sighed. He gave the matter the merest thought, and the wonderful chalice dissolved to golden mist. "It was but a toy," Gilthaliad said. "No enchantment went into it, and it had no importance. Now, my good kinsmen, to matters of real concern: let us go in to dinner."

The old Elf and the two children made their way into the court, and behind them the golden mist shimmered for a while in the long sunlight of afternoon, and thinned, and then was gone.

Curse of the Romany

─────────── ✠ ───────────

Ilona Ouspenskaya

I, Darla, tell this tale. No other.

I am the daughter of Boltac, Chief of the Rusk, and, O my brothers, you may remember the mighty tales which are told of the Rusk, not only around the campfires of the twelve valleys, but throughout all Dacia itself. It is said fear of the Rusk extends even to our distant cousins of far Iberia, and that is why they so seldom bring their wagons eastward to threaten us.

As the daughter of a chief, it is expected I will marry the son of a chief, and it is here the woe of my tale begins, for I was betrothed of Garvus, son of Jassy, the Chief of the Buchar, with whom we had fought for more passings of the moon than there are leaves on a tree. Garvus was the strongest among all the tribes of the Romany, and unequaled as a hunter. Armed only with his whip, stalked he the wolves, who were so constant a threat to our camp and to our lives.

Garvus was handsome, and not so cruel with his women as are many of our race, which is to say that there was not a chieftain's daughter within a hundred leagues who did not hope to acquire him as a mate. None, that is, save me, for I was beloved of Sven, a man of my tribe, the son of Terak, himself a simple trinket maker, and a person of little credentials, though honorable his craft truly was.

I was favored of my father, and thus had the family of Terak brought to our wagon only last moon. This patronage stood me well, for Terak had proved an earnest worker, but labor, no matter how sincere, cannot remove a low birth for either the father or the son. I was hopeful of placing Sven as an apprentice to our wagon master, and thus elevate his family, though hardly to the level needed to marry the daughter of a chief.

We had come to the valley Runyon, long kept safe for all the tribes. Our wagons stood tended in the clearing, the wheels braked and blocked, and the flaps vented to let in the clean, crisp air. Though I have seen it many times, yet always will I thrill to the sight of our brightly colored wagons basking in the silver light of the night-time sky.

Nearby gathered we Rusk to celebrate our treaty with the Buchar.

In the fullness of the moon I danced around the campfire while my brothers and my cousins sang and passed several goatskins of wine between them. My hair shone in ebony glory as I tossed my hands about my head in time to the rhythms of the chant. Wild are the days as the winter solstice nears, and I enjoyed the dance knowing that I pleased those who watched.

As tradition required, first I danced the dance of the hunt, to honor those who risked themselves to bring us food, and then the dance of the Cup, to honor the forgiveness that must be given to all who ask. The honor of the final dance was, of course, performed in the name of our guests, and in particular for Garvus, himself.

Sven was seated at the western end of the circle, noting both his low standing and unproven merit as a provider. As you may suspect, I lingered as I wove my dance near Sven, making sure to draw my bodice taut, giving to Sven a silhouette of my fine, firm figure which I so longingly wished to give to him in marriage. His eyes, soft and brown, met mine each time I passed, and in this way we silently told each other of our love.

These provocations were not lost upon Garvus, who was seated by Boltac at the head of the circle. I held no quarrel with Garvus, who I admired for his many qualities. Alas, admiration is not love, and it was for Sven which my heart did beat.

The dance ended to a lusty cheer and Garvus stood, raising the largest of the goatskins to his face. "What ho, O my brothers!" he said, the wine dripping from his strong lips. "Long have the Rusk and the Buchar fought many a noble fight. Many have our wagons fallen, their wheels never again to travel. From tonight forward may we fight, but as friends, against those who would challenge our common interests. Seven campfires ago I was welcomed among you and shortly I shall leave, our tribes to be united one moon hence. May long we prosper!"

A great roar arose, for much beloved had Garvus become among our tribe. I took my place by him, as was my duty. My heart knew not how to hate him, for Garvus was as much trapped by his birth as I mine. There was a girl of his tribe for which he held affection, and whom he would choose were he free to do so. I had heard news of this whispered around the cooking pots, a place where reliable information can frequently be obtained.

"Darling." I turned to my betrothed. "My head is light from this dance and I would take a walk now to clear it."

"Now, woman?" Garvus grinned. "Surely not now. Even hunters do not walk alone at night in these woods."

"I need to be by myself, dearest. Soon I will leave these hills to journey with you to your tribe and their camp. May I not enjoy a moment of solitude among the woods of my people?"

"Woods of your people! Ha! You Rusk are known to frequent many woods along the twelve valleys. Yet I will not order you to remain, if you will promise me not to stray farther than the light of this fire, by which you danced so enticingly tonight."

"Agreed, O my husband to be, but you must not follow me, nor watch, for we shall be together enough years yet."

"As you will, woman," said Garvus, his patience extended. "But keep safe from the night and those who live in it. I have seen spoor today, from those who must hunt when the time of the snows approach."

I turned and strode away from him, heading for the small creek which ran some spans behind our wagons. I knew of a large rock, slightly upstream, where I might sit and consider.

No flame of the fire was to be seen as I reached my appointed place, though the glow of the smoke drifted into the sky above, and thus my word to Garvus was kept. I sat upon the bank, my back resting against the stone, softened by the moss of the creek. In the water I cooled my feet, lest I acquire soreness from my dancing.

Even though I have not trained as a hunter, I should have heard the footsteps which were approaching, for such are the skills of the Rusk. But lost in my thoughts was I so much that startled I was when Sven stepped through the glade.

"Sven!" I gasped. "You should not have followed me."

"Would you deny the invitation of your dance tonight?"

"O Sven. I love you, but this must not be, for it would mean many more deaths among our brothers were I not to marry Garvus."

"Let us then run away, to the old places beyond the twelve valleys. Far away from Garvus and his kin."

"No, dear one. Though my heart is yours, my body and my duty must belong to Garvus."

"I won't let—YOW!!!"

Crack! The sound of a whip split the silence of the night. As my beloved fell, I looked to the rear of him and saw Garvus standing, smiling over the carcass of a wolf.

"A good thing I followed this pup." Garvus beamed while unwrapping the cord of the whip from the broken neck of his prey. "I thought he might be hunting tonight."

"Sven!" I screamed, kneeling by him. "The wolf has struck you!"

"It is only a scratch, woman. His shoulder will be sore, nothing more," Garvus asserted.

Still dazed, Sven rose to his haunches. "Garvus, I thank you for my life and for that of this woman. The wolf is a silent hunter. I was foolish to follow Darla."

"Not so foolish as Darla to venture away from the camp. Woman, you promised not to leave the light of the campfire," said Garvus.

"Look at the light of the smoke, O my betrothed. Did I not keep my word?"

"Nay, woman. You know your deceit. Words are easy to twist. We both understood what was meant."

"And did you not also break your word, Garvus? Did you not follow me here?" I asked defiantly.

"Be civil to me who has done you no wrong. I merely followed this trinket maker's son, whom you so brazenly enticed this evening. I will hold it not against you this time, O Darla, but watch you well from now onwards. Come, we must carry the boy back to camp and treat his wounds."

"I can walk," gritted Sven. "I need you not to carry me."

"As you will, son of the maker of trinkets, but know this. Our tribes will gather here one moon hence, and you will watch me take my bride. Take care you tempt not her honor."

Silently we walked Sven to the wagon of Scopa, the healer of our tribe. There we sent for Anna, sister of Sven, who bound and dressed his wounds. Sven rested well, and I returned with Garvus to my father's wagon, where he and Boltac haggled over my dowry until the dawn, upon which Garvus was off.

On Boltac's order, we, too, left the valley later that day. To our friends, the wagons of the Rusk are the most welcome of all sights of the road. So powerful are we Rusk, that there are few who profess not their friendship. There were thirty wagons in our caravan at present, and seven more which were away on trading missions. No other tribe could claim half so many.

Once on the road, I knew I would hear no more of Sven until we reached the next village. I watched the wagon of Scopa as it trailed the others, with five of my father's finest guardsmen riding alongside, protecting the rear. Prudent is the tribe whose ill and wounded are sheltered from danger. I saw not Terak. It was said my father had sent him ahead by fast rider, to preview our wares to those of the next town.

When we reached the village Bowsk, I was at last allowed to leave my quarters, and then only to entertain the townsfolk at the square. I saw Sven's father seated among those gathered to watch, but no glimpse of my beloved did I find. I danced, following the rhythms of the balalaika, oblivious to all but my thoughts of seeing Sven. Fortunately, Bowsk was a prosperous village, and our take was good. As the night approached, I knew our men would retire to the local tavern for a long evening of revelry.

Though it was we who pitied those people fixed to one place, so strong was their prejudice against our tribes that never were we allowed to camp inside a town. Despite the stories you may have heard, our men are seldom thieves and our women are even less often harlots. The field in which we secured our wagons was separated from the town by a large grove, so much the better, since by the sounds of the birds therein I would know in time were our men to return early. Good fortune smiled, as Scopa's wagon was placed next to that of my Uncle Tosh, who as Master of the Hunt, always camped next to the wagon of the Chief.

I waited until full dark to sneak my way. Outside, Anna tended the fires. She looked up as I entered Scopa's wagon, but made no effort to stop me. Sven lay inside, on a cot to the rear. With horror I gazed on his comatose form. Blood oozed from his festered wound onto the blankets wrapped around him.

"He has worsened every day." It was Anna, who had entered behind me.

As I burst into tears, Anna held me, comforting me as well as she could. "Stop crying if you would help Sven," said Anna. "He needs you, for your father has said it would be best if Sven stays ill until after you and Garvus are married."

"There is an apothecary in the town," I said. "I noticed it today while dancing."

"Darla, no. You mustn't even be here," said Anna. "I'll try to go there for you."

"There is little danger," I replied. "The building is on this edge of the town. We must take Sven there at once. You might misdescribe the wound and cause the apothecary to give incorrect treatment."

And so we did. We carried Sven across the grove and into the town. I could hear the voices of our kinsmen in the nearby tavern as I knocked on the door of a small, one-story stone structure.

"Who is it?" came the firm, but not gruff voice from inside.

"It is Darla, who danced for you today, with one of our tribe in need of your care." I was expecting to hear the voice tell us to come back in the morning, but surprisingly the door opened and we were allowed in.

An elderly white-haired man squinted at us. Anna and I took the still-unconscious Sven to a nearby table and laid him face down upon the sheets. I watched intently while the learned man examined my beloved. Yet even so, I had time to notice the many shelves which lined the available space on each wall, and the jars and boxes which lined the shelves. The light of the candles, though faint, still sufficed to show the grievousness of the wound. "What was it that struck him?" asked the apothecary.

"A wolf," I replied, telling the story.

"He must be treated at once," the old man said, and went about his word, busily moving from jar to jar, medicating a compress to attach to the wound. Despite what you have heard of persons of his profession, never once did he ask of payment of his fee, nor did he grumble about being roused from his sleep.

In a few minutes, the poultice was finished. "Here, this should cleanse the cuts," he said as he laid the preparations upon Sven's shoulder.

Smoke arose instantly, and the bandage burst into flame upon the back of my beloved. Sven arose, for the first time in days, grabbing at his back until the offending cloth was thrown to the floor. A desperate howl came from deep within Sven, as the agony of his pain worsened. He bolted for the door, hurling Anna aside, and, before any of us could react, had disappeared into the darkness.

"Sven!" I screamed, "O my Sven! Return to me! Return to me!" Alas, I did so to no avail.

Our noise did serve to call attention to ourselves, and several townspeople rushed toward us, while a few others chased after Sven as he disappeared into the night. I recall little of the next few moments, so dazed was I to have lost him who I held most dear.

There is one sight, however, which I will never forget, though

I wish I could. Cowered in a corner was the apothecary, his eyes showing the fear within him. "Silver," he muttered. "The potion contained silver. Silver," he said, over and over, until finally I understood.

We were driven that night from the town. Tosh's wagon was lost, overturned by the angry mob. Only when my father ordered three wagons set afire in a narrow pass, did we escape our pursuers. By fortune, none of my tribe was killed, though more than twenty were wounded, several of them severely. Each of the surviving wagons bore many more than customary, and tempers flared among the crowded.

Perhaps you do not know the sadness that accompanies the loss of a wagon. I had seen it only twice in my life, both times in warfare. The wagons are our homes, and when a wagon is lost, the property of the family is lost as well. Worse yet, the loss had occurred at the start of winter. Construction could not begin on replacements until spring, and it would be mid-summer next before the work was completed.

For my father's part, he was not angry with me, as I had thought that he should be. He remained quiet and morose, in a way that I had not seen him since the death of my mother, some seven years prior. Not until her passing had I first come to notice Sven, for it was his mother, Janna, who saw to the womanly side of my raising afterwards. But alas, Janna too did depart this earth two winters hence, victimed by a spreading chill which affected most of us and took five of our tribe to the caravan that lies beyond.

I thought on these matters as we traveled. Already two nearby towns had refused to allow us to trade. Without trade we would starve, even if winter were not approaching. We had but a few goats among the wagons, and little food stores among us. We are not farmers and herdsmen, O we who travel the roads, and while our hunting prowess is strong, we had come to that time of year when the game of the woods begin their long and restful slumbers, deep hidden in their lairs.

We were traveling away from Sven, lost somewhere in the

woods, with only the drive of his curse to help him make his way. I knew not whether to fear his death, or to fear that he lived, hunted and shunned by other men. With little else to do, we settled at the glen of my betrothment and awaited the return of my affianced.

It was not Garvus, but his courier who arrived first. "Fear not," the message began, "I have heard of your troubles and my people stand with you."

This gave me strength, for I knew that only an overwhelming sense of duty could bring Garvus to join himself to a woman who had so unjustly shamed him. Such served to again increase my admiration for him, though this did in no way weaken my love for Sven.

I watched each night as the cycle of the sky changed, knowing that soon the wagons of the Buchar would be arriving. And as appointed, so they did, camping down the stream a little ways, so as not to overcrowd the meadow.

We of the Romany are not like those of the city, to whom idleness is common. The demands of the road are harsh, and we Romany must take only that time to do a thing which it takes to do.

The campfire had been prepared and I joined Garvus there along with each of our fathers. Many a time had the hand of Boltac held an axe against the Buchar, but now this hand took mine and joined it to the son of Jassy.

I was comforted to see that the priest who faced us was Father Philip, traveled to this place from the Abbey Annat, where I had first taken the sacrament of the Cup. His kindly smile served as a comfort in this, my time of troubles. The unruly crowd quieted as he removed his cowl from his head and rested it on the back of his neck, this being the traditional indication the ceremony was to begin.

The proceedings were brief, to have taken longer would have delayed the celebration, the anticipation of which was the true reason those gathered were in such good cheer. We were pronounced wed, and I must admit I felt a womanly tingle as Garvus cast his arms around me and placed his lips on mine.

For once I did not dance, that honor falling to a younger cousin of mine. To tell the truth, I think my kinsmen welcomed this new face, for there was little surprise left in my performance so many times had it been seen. Certainly well was she greeted by those of the Buchar, and I could see several of their warriors eying her as would they eye a potential mate.

We reveled with our friends and my spirits were strong, so happy were those around me. But soon Garvus turned and said, "Come," and I knew it was time for my duties as a wife to begin.

His wagon was not placed with either camp, but privately at the edge of the forest. As we left the campfire, I saw the lusty sneers on the faces of many, and I felt degraded into something that was less than I had been. No longer would I dance for my kinsmen. No longer would I so closely feel the rhythms of the music that I loved. My duty now was to live among strangers and to bear children, to prepare food for Garvus, and to mend and wash his clothing. By the time we reached his wagon, tears welled to my face despite my fight against them.

"What, woman?" said my husband. "Will you cry and spoil my wedding night?" Full tears now streamed down my face. I reached my hand to steady myself as I placed my foot on the small ladder that led into the wagon's cabin.

I saw Garvus scowl, and then I saw his hand, palm open, approaching my face. The initial sting dazed, but did not hurt. I fell, and he raised his arm again, but this time it did not strike.

A taloned paw grabbed the neck of Garvus, jerking him away. I saw the head of the beast—not quite a wolf or a man—clamp its maw onto the jugular of its victim. The creature released his grasp, his prey slumping to the ground. Blood spurted onto my bodice. Beside my feet lay Garvus, mortally wounded.

The soft brown eyes of the creature met mine, and in a moment more than words passed. Isolation and loneliness overwhelmed the message of love I wanted to find in his gaze. Though I could bear to look no longer, intently did I hold my sight. It was he who broke the trance, for by now we had attracted the attention of those around the campfire. The mob was running toward us and my rescuer fled as unseen as he had arrived.

Garvus moaned and I took him into my arms to comfort him. Though he had struck me, I still felt no hate for him, for I had been as wrong as he. What does it matter to hate, when death nears, as to all of us it someday must?

The mob had split, about half giving chase into the night, the others gathered around us.

There are many tales of the strength of Garvus told, but I think this was his greatest. Brushing aside my arms, he raised himself to his feet, bracing against the steps at his back. He stood, blood draining from his neck, and the murmur of the crowd changed to a deathly silence.

"Avenge me, O my brothers! Avenge me well!" he shouted to them, and then he fell, never to rise again.

Before the dawn I was on my way to the Abbey Annat, escorted by six of my kinsmen, and an equal number of the Buchar. We traveled in a cart drawn by mules, alongside of which the guardsmen walked. Father Philip was nominally in charge of the procession, though all knew the way and the purpose of the journey. I was kept secluded. I knew not the driver, he was a Buchar. Unlike any male I had met before, he responded not to my most comely greetings. We arrived at the abbey two days hence, and I was silently taken to a windowless room and left.

How long I waited I cannot say. No food was brought, and from my hunger my wait must have been longer than a day. I slept not at first, so turmoiled were my thoughts. Not only for Sven did I cry, but for Garvus, too, and for all of both our tribes on whom I had brought this sorrow. Only when there were no tears left in my body did I sleep.

I knew not the woman who awakened me. Her habit marked her as a member of the sisterhood, though there were no convents that were less than a full day's travel. She, too, did not speak, motioning for me to follow.

Though I knew the public part of the abbey well, soon were we deep in its reaches. Through two sets of doors we passed, each locked from the outside and manned by a member of the brethren. There was little light, so widely spaced were the torches along the way. I could see moist spots along the stone walls, and I assumed us to be below ground, somewhere beneath the keep of the abbey. The sound of water dripping into unseen pools accompanied our footsteps, as did the vermin that scuttled in the places where the light did not reach. There were many passageways off to the sides, some of which we took. I followed the Sister, obediently.

The hallway we were traveling seemed to descend slightly, but to this I could not swear. Finally we came to a large oaken door, without either a lock or a guard. The Sister opened it and stood back, so as to let me enter, which I did.

There was but a single candle on the small, circular table in the room's center, and I could see the outline of a cowled figure seated there. I shuddered as I heard the door close, its creaking much more noticeable than when I had stood with the Sister in the hallway. She had not entered.

A hand came forth from within the robe, extended in my direction, its thin, leathery forefinger crooked as if to bid me forward. "Be seated, child," came the weak, raspy voice. Though the candle rested before him, the precipice of his hood shadowed his face.

I moved as if in a dream, oblivious to all but the flow of the moment. There was but one place for me to sit, a wooden chair which stood next to my host.

As I neared, I could see the glow of his eyes reflect the light of the candle. He clearly did not relish the light, keeping his body turned, so as to minimize its effect. His eyes glowed a color red I had never before seen. Brighter and darker than the soft pink with which we women dress, but not red either, glinting like fresh blood on a sword. I sat facing him, not the table.

"I have been brought up to this place to tell you a story," he began. His plain brown robe moved noticeably as he labored with his breath. "Let me tell it quickly and return, for it pains me to be this near to the world of the sun. Great forces are at work, in ways you would not suspect. The curse of the Romany is upon your tribe, and only a maiden such as yourself may lift the curse without causing the death of the accursed innocent."

"Tell me what I must do, Father."

"Arghh," he cried weakly, cringing his unseen neck into his shoulders. "Do not call me that! Can you not see I no longer wear the crucifix about my neck?"

"A thousand pardons, sir. I meant not disrespect. What shall I call you then?"

"It matters not. Just listen, girl."

"But what of the Cup? The sacrament we are taught that washes away all? Will it not help?"

A look of tiredness came into his eyes. "The sacrament is unimportant, and only the True Cup, long hidden in the old places, could cleanse an evil this strong. There is an easier way."

"Yes?" I replied.

"When next the moon is full, you must return to the stream where the tragedy first began, to the very spot where the curse was struck, and there you must give yourself to the creature while he is in his feral form."

"Give myself? Give my life?" Fear dashed through me.

"No, child, give yourself as a woman, as you would have given yourself to your husband, had he not been killed. Only a maiden pure in body may lift the curse upon one she loves. But be careful. Your kinsmen think you sent to cloister. They hunt to kill, and with proper weapons, too. The arrows of their bows bear silver tips, and their traps are clever and many. The wagons of many tribes have joined the hunt. The creature has killed across the countryside, and will kill again before the moon is properly phased."

"Why do you not want my kinsmen to kill him?"

"That would not end the curse. It would merely destroy the innocent upon whom the curse has manifested itself. Another would follow, maybe not for several generations, but it would follow."

"And if I succeed?"

"Then the innocent will be restored, recalling nothing."

"And this will rid the world of these creatures, for all time," I replied.

"Alas, no," he said, his voice almost a whisper. "Tell me. When you destroy one wild dog, does the whole pack vanish?"

"No, of course not."

"But you do have one less wild dog with which to deal. And so you see. The sons of this abomination are few. One less will be of benefit to all. Now go, and do this thing, and free your beloved from this curse."

I did not count the days I remained in the depths of the abbey, seeing only my keepers and the good Sister who tended to me. I discovered her name to be Marcia, a woman perhaps twice my age. She was of great comfort to me as I waited for my appointed time, thrilling me with stories of the old places which lay far beyond Dacia.

We left the abbey at night. The cold was grim, and I could see where early snow had fallen. I wore the habit of a nun, so as to disguise myself. Two of the most trusted of the brethren served as drivers of our cart. Father Philip traveled with us, Marcia remaining at the abbey. The moon was four days from its fullness, the extra travel time being allowed for the priests to perform sacraments for the townspeople along the way. This was the custom of all priests who traveled, and to have done otherwise would have been to call attention to ourselves. We stopped frequently, gathering such information as we were able. Even so, we arrived at the stream a full day early, but stayed well into the woods, lest we be seen.

The rumors we heard in the towns verified what I had been told in the abbey. The killings formed a pattern, shaped like a long circle, with the most recent ones heading directly for the valley Runyon. This had not been lost on the hunters tracking the creature, but fortunately the closest group was rumored to be the Buchar, who were not so familiar with the area as were we Rusk.

From the back of our cart, I watched the sun set over the hills. What few clouds there were lay low, illuminated in a golden haze. I feared not the touch of a man, but to be taken by an animal was a different matter. I had seen his talons rip into flesh, and his teeth chew the life from the neck of Garvus. Who knew what might be done to me by a beast in passion, even one who had been, and still remained, my beloved? The stories of the villagers all had one common thread. The creature had become more savage with the passing of each night.

I gathered my courage, and set forth for the stream. I was no longer disguised, having dressed in less confining garb more suited for my task. The rock was still there, though the harsh cold had lessened the moss it bore. I considered disrobing immediately, but a sharp gust of wind convinced me otherwise. My wait was not long.

He stood before me, his approach again unheard. I reached to my waist strap, and stepped out of my tunic, my flesh bare to both the wind and his eyes. Their kindness was gone. No longer could I see my beloved looking through that hideous visage.

He came at me at once, his hairy member quickly penetrating the softness between my thighs. "Sven! I love you, Sven!" I shouted, as pain throbbed within me. His fierce growls drowned my sobbing, as his teeth nipped petulantly at my face.

Harder and harder he took me, thrusting deeper with each plunge, until I became aware of approaching torches, and those who bore them. The creature gave a piercing howl, neck arched to the sky, and then slumped over, as if in a deep sleep.

I was grabbed and pulled from under my consort. "Kill the beast!" came the shout from many in the crowd. "And then the girl!" added several more.

The mob quieted, and I knew not why until I saw Father Philip step from the trees.

"Holy Father, give us your blessing to destroy this abomination," demanded the leader of the mob, who only now did I recognize as Jassy.

"What abomination?" responded the good Father. "True, we have found these two children fornicating under the devil's moon, but the punishment for that is thrashing, not death." He gestured with his arm toward the rock. Sven lay there, unclothed to be sure, but Sven, and not the creature to whom I had given myself.

Jassy was sullen, but could do no more. Revenge still lay within him, but to commit murder when ordered otherwise by a priest is a certain route to hell. He turned and left, his mob with him.

Eight more times I have seen the moon full, and each time Sven has remained unaffected. Soon we will reach the old places and begin our search for the Cup. I bear Sven's child, the product of our first joining. It is a restless child, for eight times I have felt its fingers sharpen, and eight times I have bled, each time worse than before. I have told no one. I fear I shall not be delivered before the moon rises full again. I have no purity left to give.

Only the One True Cup can lift the curse of the Romany. . . .

Dagda

— ✠ —

James S. Dorr

We all have our searches, mine,
for the restoration of that which was once mine,
the green glades of Ireland, the mist of her sky,
the foam of her Western Sea, the dappled sunlight
that plays on a Beltine dawn in her forests,
the company of brothers I left behind—
the vessel of plenty. The Cauldron of Ireland.

I?

I am the fat one. The spinner of star-trails who
wears peasant clothing, a hood, a short tunic—
ass bare to the wind—sandals made from raw leather.
I am the Dagda, and these things I carry:
a club so heavy, of straight-grained ash,
that eight men must lift it on wheels when they fetch it,
so huge I kill nine with one blow of its round tip
then breathe life back to their armored corpses
by striking a second time with its grip-portion,
so burdensome that when I drag it behind me
dikes spring in its wake to form walls to defend from;
a harp, of living oak, so finely tuned
that birds of the morning learn their songs from it,
so measured in rhythm that crickets and frogs find
the music of nightfall within its tones,
so sweet in its playing that when,

drunk with beer, I pluck and sing to it
the seasons themselves—Samhain and autumn,
Imbole, Beltine's spring, August and Lugnasad—
come forth in order;
                    the Cauldron of all good from which,
to each man by his measure of virtue,
flows porridge and honey, meat and strong wine,
flow blessings of sunshine and earth-seeding moisture,
flow growth and, yes, dying too, that which is needed
so all in its own season new life may follow.
These things I take with me, lashed to my back,
bouncing and jangling, mocking the flesh-quiver
of my wide buttocks, the jounce of my belly
as I wander, seeking.
                  I am the Grail bringer.

I am Dagda,
father of Danu who bore the Tuatha,
of Brigit, of Bobd the Red,
Ceacht and Midir,
of Ogma and Oengus, who later betrayed me;
the lover of Boann,
bed-mate of Morrigan;
friend and companion of Lug, the spear caster,
of swordsman Nuada, who lost his hand in the fight at Mag
    Tuireadh,
of Fal, with his stone slab that cried out only
when trod upon by Ireland's true king.

I was a king, too, but only after.

I was a soldier, at first with the others opposing the Fir Bolg,
then later an engineer, a builder, against the attacks
of Fomorian pirates.
              I built Ireland's castles:
her stone-faced earthworks, her ditches, her berms,

her white, round-topped towers that glint in the sea sun,
her caltrops and shingles, I built these and more;
and one castle also—that, also, later,
when Ireland had fallen beneath the Milesians,
and I to my kingship—I built not of earth and rock
nor wood and metal, but glass and crystal
with walls so transparent that air loomed more darkly,
with towers so high that they reached to the moon,
and I set it spinning, beneath the moon's turning.
I lived in this tower.
I fished in its moat, fish I cooked in my Cauldron.
I hung on its wall the great spear of Lug,
the sword of Nuada,
and, within its floor, set the smooth stone of Fal.
I lived in this tower; through the walls of my castle
I saw the affairs of men, sons of Milesians,
as they coursed the wide earth.
I saw the Grail-Cauldron when it was not with me,
a plate stained with drops of blood from a man's body
that hung from a cross;
a bowl set for begging;
I saw a man, cross-legged, who sat on a deerskin,
another who rode an ox,
one torn by animals;
I saw men's battles with weapons more fearful
than any I dreamed of,
ships screaming through air, fire and earth springing skyward;
I saw oceans dark with blood,
seas choked with excrement,
rivers made sluggish;
I saw forests leveled.
I saw a king, also, across the Giants' Causeway,
to east of my island, draw others around him.
I saw him building, much like I—
slim, though, not fat-bellied, never enjoying
quite fully the things he should—

gathering heroes, much like my brothers,
sending them forth from him.
I saw him doomed, later—for now I saw his knights
fan out across the land, some crossing oceans,
seeking my Cauldron.

One I let find it, a peasant-knight, Perceval;
through my glass walls, I guided his travels.
We had much in common.
At last when he came inside, unlike the others
polite in the ways of court, he blurted words out
in peasant fashion:
*   "Where is the Grail?" he asked,*
that and no other words, when with a clatter
the spear of Lug fell from the wall where it hung;
the sword of Nuada shivered and glowed;
but the floor remained silent.
*   The land bloomed, somewhat,*
as I gave my answer. A hand gesture only.
The Cauldron appeared, its pearl-crusted sides
frothing over with brown ale, its lip pouring usque-beagh—
"water of life"—as I held out our flagons.
I bade him drink deeply and, belching, I drank too,
refilling our vessels as soon as each emptied.
We drank wine and brandy, to each as he wished it, and,
mellowing, I took my harp and tuned it.
I sang him a story, of times long ago, when I and my brothers
were captured by pirates, the corsairs of Fomor.
I told—this is true—of the pit the Fomorians
dug in the green earth to rival my Cauldron.
They hollowed the planet.
They filled it with porridge boiled out of meal
from all corners of Ireland, the west and the east,
mixed with milk from her cattle,
then turned to where I stood, waiting and watching,
my club taken from me, my arms tied behind me,

and said, "If you indeed claim to be Dagda,
Eochaid Ollathair, Raud Ro-fhessa—
the 'father of all' and 'lord of all knowledge'—
then surely you will not refuse this, our supper."
I nodded and motioned my bonds to be loosened;
I knelt by the pit, refusing their spoon.
I crouched and I ate until I had licked it dry,
washing it down with the foam of the ocean, and,
when I had drained that too, I stood and farted,
leveling villages,
then took and lay with a princess of Fomor,
herself on top of me, of course, so I would not crush. . . .

Sir Perceval reddened. "Enough!" he shouted.
The holy Perceval fled from my castle,
its stone floor still silent;
the Grail-Cauldron shimmered.
It faded to dark as I plucked from my harp's strings
the music of Samhain's Eve, when all time stops,
so my guest could find his way back to the evening
he entered my tower.

                    Assured of his safety,
I watched as the spirits of Ireland assembled:
first beauteous Cessair, who died in the Flooding;
then those, the twice-twelve couples under Partholon,
who tilled the plains and brewed Ireland's first beer;
then the people of Nemed, who fought four great battles,
but in the end were defeated by Fomor;
then the Fir Bolg and the Fir Gaileoin and the Fir Domnann who,
in their turn, battled against the Tuatha De Danann,
my own daughter's progeny;
leastly the Sons of Mil.
                    That was my kingship,
to dwell in my glass fort, the last of my people

who had not fled under the land or the ocean,
to watch the sun set, the fields harrowed and wasted.

To watch as the final riders approached me,
some, as the peasant-knight, seeking my Cauldron,
others, less fortunate, lost in their wanderings.
One died in my castle.
To wait.
To cast myself, harp and weapons,
castle and Cauldron, west, into the star-fields,
west of the ocean, west of the moon and sun,
west into blackness sprinkled in brilliance,
fire-points as thick as sand—

                           We all have searches, mine,
only for that which was mine once already,
the green glades of Ireland: a land unspoiled.
The wind of a new sea.
The mist of a sky and the foam of its sunlight,
dappled in forests,
so others, the Grail-seekers, might yet come after.

The Sailor Who Sailed After the Sun

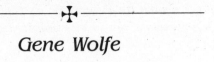

Gene Wolfe

But if the great sun move not of himself;
but is an errand boy in heaven. . . .
—Melville

In the good days now lost, when cranky, old-fashioned people still wore three-cornered hats and knee breeches, a lanky farm boy with hair like tow walked to New Bedford with all his possessions tied up in a red-and-white kerchief. Reuben was his name. He gawked at the high wooden houses so close together (for he had never seen the like), at the horses and the wagons, and at all the people— hundreds of men and dozens of women all shoulder-to-shoulder and pushing one another up and down the streets. Most of all, he gawked at the towering ships in the harbor; and when, after an hour or so, a big man with a bushy black beard asked whether he was looking for work, he nodded readily, and followed the big man (who was the chief mate) aboard, and signed a paper.

Next morning the third mate, a man no older than Reuben himself, escorted Reuben to a chandler's, where he bought two pairs of white duck trousers, three striped shirts, a hammock, a pea-jacket, a seabag, and some other things, the cost of everything to be deducted from his pay. And on the day after that, the ship set sail.

Of its passage 'round the Horn to the great whaling grounds of the Southeast Pacific, I shall say little, save that it was very hard indeed. There were storms and more storms; nor were they the right sort of storms, which blow one in the direction in which one wishes to go. These were emphatically storms of the wrong sort. They blew the ship back into the Atlantic time after time; and Reuben believed that was what made them storms of the wrong sort until one blew the man who slung his hammock aft of Reuben's own from the mizzen yard and into the churning waters of the West Scotia Basin. The man who had slung his hammock aft of Reuben's had been the only man aboard with whom Reuben had forged the beginnings of a friendship, and the emptiness of that hammock, as it swung back and forth with the labored pitching of the ship, weighed heavily against him until it was taken down.

At last the storms relented. From open boats tossed and rolled in frigid seas, they took two right whales (which are whales of the right sort) and one sperm whale (which is not). There is no more onerous work done at sea than the butchering and rendering of whales. It is without danger and thus without excitement; nor does it involve monotony of the sort that frees the sailor's mind to go elsewhere. It means working twelve hours a day in a cold, cramped, and reeking factory in which one also lives, and every-thing—men, clothes, hammocks, blankets, decks, bulkheads, masts, spars, rigging, and sails—gets intolerably greasy.

One dark day when the ice wind from the south punished the ship worse even than usual, and patches of freezing fog raced like great cold ghosts across the black swell, and the old, gray-bearded captain rubbed his greasy eyeglasses upon the sleeve of his greasy blue greatcoat and cursed, and five minutes afterward rubbed them there again, and cursed again, they were stove by a great sperm whale the color of coffee rich with cream. For a moment only they saw him, his great head dashing aside the waves, and the wrecks of two harpoons behind his eye, and the round, pale scars (like so many bubbles in the coffee) two feet across left by the suckers of giant squid.

He vanished and struck. The whole ship shivered and rolled.

In an instant everything seemed to have gone wrong.

In the next it appeared that everything was as right as it had ever been, four-square and shipshape, after all; and that the crash and shock and splintered planks had been an evil dream.

Yet they were stove, nevertheless. The ship was taking green water forward, and all the pumps together could not keep pace with it. They plugged the hole as well as they could with caps and coats and an old foresail, and when, after three days that even the big, black-bearded mate called hellish, they reached calmer waters, they passed lines under the bow, and hauled into place (there in the darkness below the waterline) a great square of doubled sailcloth like a bandage.

After that they sailed for nearly a month with the pumps going night and day, through waters ever bluer and warmer, until they reached a green island with a white, sloping beach. Whether it lay among those lands first explored by Captain Cook, or on the edge of the Indies, or somewhere east of Africa, Reuben did not know and could not discover. Some mentioned the Friendly Islands; some spoke of the Cocos, some of the Maldives, and still others of Ile de France or Madagascar. It is probable, indeed, that no one knew except the captain, and perhaps even he did not know.

Wherever it was, it seemed a kindly sort of place to poor Reuben. There, through long, sunny days and moonlit nights, they lightened the ship as much as possible, until it rode as high in the water as a puffin, and at high tide warped it as near the beach as they could get it, and at low tide rolled it on its side to get at the stove-in planking.

One day, when the work was nearly done and his watch dismissed, Reuben wandered farther inland than he usually ventured. There was a spring there, he knew, for he had fetched water from it; he thought that he recalled the way, and he longed for a drink from its cool, clear, up-welling pool. But most of all (if the truth be told) he wished to become lost—to be lost and left behind on that island, which was the finest place that he had ever known save his mother's lap.

And so of course he *was* lost, for people who wish to be lost always get their way. He found a spring that might (or might not) have been the one he recalled. He drank from it, and lay down beside it and slept; and when he woke, a large gray monkey had climbed down out of a banyan tree and thrust a long, careful gray hand into his pocket, and was looking at his clasp knife.

"That's mine," Reuben said, sitting up.

The monkey nodded solemnly, and as much as said, "I know."

But here I have to explain all the ways in which this monkey talked, because you think that monkeys do not often do it. Mostly, at first, he talked with his face and eyes and head, looking away or looking up, grinning or pulling down the corners of his mouth. Later he talked with his hands as well, just as I do. And subsequently he came to make actual sounds, grunting like the mate or sighing like the captain, and pushing his lips in or out. All this until eventually—and long before he had finished talking with Reuben—he spoke at least as well as most of the crew and better than some of them.

"Give it back," Reuben said.

"Wait a bit," replied the monkey, opening and closing the marlin spike, and testing the point with his finger. "That may not be necessary. How much will you take for it? I offer fifteen round, ripe coconuts, delivered here to you immediately upon your agreement."

"Don't want coconuts." Reuben held out his hand.

The monkey raised his shoulders and let them fall. "I don't blame you. Neither do I." Regretfully, he returned the knife to Reuben. "You're from that big ship in the lagoon, aren't you? And you'll be going away in a day or two."

"I wish," Reuben told the monkey, "that I didn't have to go away."

The monkey scratched his head with his left hand, then with his right. His gray arms were long and thin, but very muscular. "Your mother would miss you."

"My mother's dead," Reuben confessed sadly. "My father too."

"Your sisters and brothers, then."

"I have only one brother," Reuben explained. "While my father was alive, my brother and I helped on the farm. But when my father died, my brother got it and I had to leave."

"Your troop, on the ship. Unless you had someone to take your place."

"No one would do that," Reuben said.

"Don't be too sure," the monkey told him. "I would trade this island for your clasp knife, those trousers, your striped shirt, your cap, and your place on the ship."

Reuben shook his head in wonder. "This beautiful island is worth a great deal more than our whole ship."

"Not to me," said the monkey. "You see, I have owned this island ever since I was born, and have never seen any other place."

Reuben nodded. "That was the way our farm was. When I could live there I didn't really care about it, so that when my brother told me I had to go, I felt that I'd just as soon do it, because I didn't want to work for him. But now it seems the dearest spot in all the world, next to this one."

Thus it was arranged. The monkey dressed himself in Reuben's clothes, putting his beautiful, curled tail down the left leg of Reuben's white duck trousers and the clasp knife into the pocket. And Reuben dressed himself in the monkey's (who had none). And when they heard some of the crew coming, he hid behind the banyan tree.

It was a watering party with buckets, for the ship had been mended, and refloated again, and they had come to refill its barrels and butts. Each sailor had two buckets, and when one set a full bucket down to fill another, the monkey picked it up and waited for him to object. He did not, and the monkey became quite friendly with him by the time that they had carried their buckets back to the ship.

The mates were not fooled. Let me say that at the outset, neither the bushy-black-bearded chief mate, nor the youthful third mate, nor the sleepy-eyed second mate, who never even appears in this story. All three knew perfectly well that the monkey was not Reuben; and if they did not imagine that he was a monkey, they must nonetheless have suspected that he was something not quite human and perhaps of the ape kind. This is shown clearly by the name they gave him, which was Jacko. But since Jacko was a better sailor than Reuben had ever been, and a prankish, lively fellow as well, they did not say a great deal about it.

As for the captain, his eyeglasses were so greasy that Jacko in Reuben's shirt looked the very image of Reuben to him. Once, it is true, the chief mate mentioned the matter to him, saying, "There's somethin' perqu'ler about one of our topmen, Capt'n."

"And what is that, Mr. Blackmire?" the captain had replied, looking at the chief mate over his eyeglasses in order to see him.

"Well, Capt'n, he's shorter than all the rest. And he's hairy, sir. Terribly hairy. Gray hair."

Scratching his own greasy gray beard with the point of his pen, the captain had inquired, "A disciplinary problem, Mr. Blackmire?"

"No, sir."

"Does his work?"

"Yes sir." The chief mate had taken a step backward as he spoke, having divined whither their talk was bound.

"Keep an eye on him, Mr. Blackmire. Just keep an eye on him."

That was the end of it; and indeed, Jacko soon became such a valuable member of the crew that the chief mate was sorry he had brought the matter up.

But to explain to you how that was, I am going to have to explain first how whaling was carried on in those days, before the invention of the modern harpoon gun, and the equally modern explosive harpoon, and all the rest of the improvements and astonishing devices that have made whaling so easy and pleasant for everyone except the whales.

Those old harpoons, you see, hardly ever killed the whale—they did not penetrate deeply enough for that. The old harpoons were, in fact, really no more than big spears with barbed heads to which a long rope was attached as a sort of fishing line.

When the harpooner, standing in the bow of his whaleboat (you have seen pictures of Washington crossing the Delaware doing this), had thrown his harpoon, and it had gone a foot or two into the hump, as it usually was, of the poor whale, the whalers had only hooked their catch, not landed it. They had to play it, and when it was so tired that it could hardly swim and could not dive, though its life depended on it, they had to pull their boat alongside it and kill it with their whale lances, either by stabbing it from the boat, or actually springing out of the boat and onto the whale. And to say that all this was a difficult and a very dangerous business is like saying that learning to ride a tiger requires tenacity and a scratch-proof surface far above the common.

For a whale is as much bigger than the biggest tiger as the planet Jupiter is bigger than the big globe in a country school, and it is as much stronger than the strongest tiger as a full, round bumper of nitroglycerin is stronger than a cup of tea. And though it is not as savage as a tiger, the whale is fighting for its life.

Which Jacko, as I have implied, became very skilled in taking. No sailor on the ship was bolder than he with the whaling lance, none more ready to spring from the whaleboat onto the great, dark, slippery back, or to plunge the razor-sharp steel lancehead between his own feet, and raise the lance, and plunge it again and again till the whale's bright blood gushed forth not like a spring but like a full-grown river, and the whole of the sea for a mile around was dyed scarlet by it—just as certain rivers we have, that are bleeding their continents to death, dye the very oceans themselves for whole leagues beyond land with red or yellow mud that they have stolen away.

A day arrived (and in part it came as quickly as it did as a result of Jacko's efforts, let there be no doubt of that) when the great tuns in the ship's hold were nearly full. Then the captain, and the crew as well, calculated that one more whale would fill them to the brim. It was a pleasant prospect. Already the captain was thinking of his high white house in New Bedford and his grandchildren; and the sailors of weeks and even months ashore, of living well in an inn, and eating and drinking whenever they wished and never working, of farms and cottages and village girls, and stories around the fire.

Jacko was in the fo'c'sle that day, enlightening a few select friends as to the way the chief mate walked, and the way the captain lit his pipe, and the way in which a clever fellow may look between his own legs and see the world new, and other such things, when they heard the thrilling cry of "There ... there ... *thar* she blows!" from the maintop.

Three whales!

Jacko was the first on deck, the first at the davits, and the first into the first of the half-dozen whaleboats they launched. No oarsman pulled harder than he, his thin, gray back straining against Reuben's second-best striped shirt; and not a man on board cheered more heartily than he when Savannah Jefferson, the big brown harpooner with arms thicker than most men's thighs and a child's soft, sweet voice, cast his harpoon up and out, rising, bending, and falling like lightning to strike deep into the whale's back a boat's length behind the tail.

What a ride that whale gave them! There is nothing like it now, nothing at all. Mile after mile, as fast as the fastest speedboat, through mist and fog and floating ice. They could not slow or steer, and they would not cut free. At one moment they were sitting in water and bailing like so many madmen, nine-tenths swamped. At the next the whale was sounding, and like to pull them down with it. Long, long before it stopped and they were able to draw their boat up to it, they had lost sight of their ship.

But stop it did, eventually, and lie on the rough and heaving swell like the black keel of a capsized hulk, with its breath smoking in the air, and the long summer day (it was the twenty-first of December), like the whale, nearly spent.

"Lances!" bellowed the chief mate from his place in the stern.

Jacko was the first with his lance; nor did he content himself, as many another would have, with a mere jab at the whale from the boat. No, not he! As in times past he had leaped from the top of one tall palm to another, now he sprang from the gunnel of the whaleboat onto the whale's broad back.

And as he did, the whale, with one powerful blow of its tail, upset the whaleboat and tossed the crew, oars, lances, and spare harpoons into the freezing water.

A hand reached up—one lone hand, and that only for a moment—as though to grasp the top of a small wave. Jacko extended the shaft of his lance toward it, but the shaft was not long enough, nor Jacko quick enough, quick though he was. The hand vanished below the wave it had tried to grasp and never reappeared.

Then Jacko looked at the whale, or rather, as I should say, at the little round eye of it; and the whale at Jacko; and Jacko saw the whale for what it was, and himself for what *he* was, too. He took off Reuben's cap then and threw it into the sea, where it floated. Reuben's second-best shirt followed it, and floated too. Reuben's white duck trousers followed them both; but those trousers did not float like a duck or like anything else, for the weight of Reuben's clasp knife in the pocket sunk them.

"I am an animal like you," Jacko told the whale. "Not really like you, because you're very big, while I'm very small. And you're where you belong, while I'm thousands and thousands of miles from where I belong. But we're both animals—that's all I meant to say. If I don't molest you any more, ever again, will you let me right the boat, and bail it, and live on this terrible sea if I can?"

To which the whale said, "I will."

Then Jacko cut the harpoon line with the head of his lance, and let it slide into the sea. It is hard, very hard, to pull out a harpoon, because of the big, swiveling barbs on the head that open out and resist the pull. But Jacko worked the head back and forth with his long, gray, clever fingers, and cut when he had to with the head of the lance (those lance heads look very much like the blades of daggers), and eventually he got it out, and threw it into the sea, and the lance after it.

By that time it was nearly dark—so dark that he could hardly make out the upturned bottom of the whaleboat; but the whale knew where it was, and swam over to it until it bumped against its side. Jacko braced his long monkey-feet against the whale, grasped the gunnel through the freezing waves, and by heaving till it seemed his arms must break righted the whaleboat again, although it was still half full of seawater.

He leaped in with a loud splash, and the whale slid, silently and with hardly a ripple, beneath the dark sea.

Jacko bailed with his hands all that night, scooping out the cold seawater and throwing it over the side; and it is a good thing he did, for he would certainly have frozen to death otherwise. His thoughts were freed, as I have explained, and he thought about a great many things—about the beautiful island he had left behind, and how the sun had joined him there every morning in the top of his tall banyan tree; about finding bright shells and things to eat on the beach, and how he had scolded, sometimes, certain friendly little waves that came up to play with his toes.

All of which was pleasant enough. But again and again he thought of the ship, and wondered whether he would see it in the morning. He did not want to go back to it. In fact, he discovered that he hated the very thought of it, and its greasy smoke, and its cold, and the brutal treatment that he and others had received there, and the more brutal hunting of the peaceable whales. Yet he felt that if he did not see the ship in the morning he would certainly die.

Nor was that the worst of that terrible night, for he found himself haunted by the men who had been his companions in the whaleboat. When he went to the bow, it seemed to him that he could make out the shadowy form of Mr. Blackmire, the chief mate, seated in the stern with his hand upon the tiller. When he went to the stern, there was no one there; yet it seemed to him that he could make out the dark, dim shape of Savannah Jefferson in the bow, crouched and ready, grasping a harpoon.

Worst of all, he sometimes glimpsed the faces of the drowned sailors floating just beneath the waves, and he could not be certain that they were mere shenanigans of his imagination; their still lips seemed to ask him, silently and patiently, how it was that he deserved to live and they to die. At times he talked to them as he had when they were alive, and he found he had no answer to give them, save that it might be that he was only destined to die more slowly and more miserably. When he spoke to them in this way, he felt sure that the night would never end.

But that night, which seemed so very long to him, was actually quite short as measured by your clock. Our winter, in this northern hemisphere, is summer in the southern, so that at the same time that we have our longest winter night they have their shortest summer one. Morning came, and the water in the bottom of the whaleboat was no deeper than his ankles, but the ship was nowhere in sight.

Morning came, I said. But there was more to it than that, and it was far more beautiful than those plain words imply. Night faded—that was how it began. The stars winked out, one by one at first, and then by whole dozens and scores. A beautiful rosy flush touched the horizon, deepened, strengthened, and drove the night away before it as ten thousand angels with swords and bows and rods of power fanned out across the sky, more beautiful than birds and more terrible than the wildest storm. Jacko waved and called out to them, but if they heard him or saw him they gave no sign of it.

Soon the sun revealed its face, in the beginning no more than a sliver of golden light but rounded and lovely just the same, peeping above clouds in the northeast. Then the whole sun itself, warm and dazzling, and its friendly beams showed Jacko a little pole mast and a toylike boom, wrapped in a sail and lashed beneath the seats.

He set up the mast and climbed to the top (at which the whaleboat rolled alarmingly), but no ship could he see.

When he had climbed down again, he gave his head a good scratching, something that always seemed to help his thought processes. Since the ship was not here, it was clear to him that it was very likely somewhere else. And if that was the case, there seemed no point at all in his remaining where he was.

So he fitted the boom, which was not much thicker than a broomstick, to his little mast, and bent the small, three-cornered sail, and steered for the sun.

That was a very foolish thing to do, to be sure. The sun was in the northeast when it rose, but in the north at noon, and in the northwest as the long afternoon wore on, so that if you were to plot Jacko's course you would find that it looked rather like a banana, generally northward, but inclined to the east in the morning and rather favoring the west toward afternoon. But while Jacko did not know much about navigation (which he had always left to the captain), it was comforting to feel himself drawing ever nearer to the sun, and if the truth be told it was probably as good a course for looking for the ship as any of the other incorrect ones.

That day, which was in fact long, as I have tried to explain, seemed terribly short to poor Jacko. Soon evening came, the angels streamed back to the sun, night rose from the sea and spread her black wings, and Jacko was left alone, cold, hungry, and thirsty. He climbed his mast again so that he could keep the vanishing sun in sight as long as possible; and when it was gone, he dropped down into the bilges of the whaleboat and wept. In those days there were no laboratories, and so we may be fairly sure that he was the most miserable monkey in the world.

Still, it was not until the tenth hour of the night, when the new dawn was almost upon him, that his heart broke. When that happened, something that had always lived there, something that was very like Jacko himself, yet not at all like a monkey, went out from him. It left his broken heart, and left his skin as well, and left the whaleboat, and shot like an arrow over the dark sea, northeast after the sun. Jacko could not see it, but he knew that it was gone and that he was more alone now than he had ever been.

At which point a very strange thing happened. Among the many, many stars that had kindled in the northeast when the last light of the sun had gone, a new star rose (or so it seemed) and flew toward him—a star no different from countless others, but different indeed because it left its place in the heavens and approached him, nearer and nearer, until it hung just above his head.

"You mistake me," said the star.

"I don't even know you," replied Jacko, "but can you help me? Oh, please, help me if you can."

"You have seen me every day, throughout your entire life," replied the star. "I have always helped all of you, and I will help you again. But first you must tell me your story, so that I will know how to proceed."

And so Jacko told, more or less as you have heard it here, but in many more words, and with a wealth of gesture and expression which I should strive in vain to reproduce. It took quite a long time, as you have already seen. And during that long time the star said nothing, but floated above his head, a minute pinpoint of light; so that when he had finished at last Jacko said, "Are you really a star, and not a firefly?"

"I am a star," the star answered. If a small silver bell could form words when it spoke, it would no doubt sound very much like that star. "And this is my true appearance—or at least, it is as near my true appearance as you are able to comprehend. I am the star you call the sun, the star you pursued all day."

Jacko's mouth opened and shut. Then it opened and shut again—all this without saying one word.

"You think me large and very strong," the star said, "but there are many stars that are far larger and stronger than I. It is only because you stand so close to me that you think me a giant. Thus I show myself to you now as I really am, among my peers: a small-ish, quite common and ordinary-looking star."

Jacko, who did not understand in the least, but who had been taught manners by the chief mate, said, "It's very kind of you to show yourself to me at all, sir."

"I do it every day," the star reminded him.

Jacko nodded humbly.

"Here is how I judge your case," the star continued. "Please interrupt if you feel that I am mistaken in anything that I say."

Jacko nodded, resolving not to object (as he too often had in the fo'c'sle) about trifles.

"You do not desire to be where you are."

Jacko nodded again, emphatically, both his hands across his mouth.

"You would prefer some me-warmed place, where fruiting trees were plentiful and men treated monkeys with great kindness. A place where there are wonderful things to see and climb on, of the sort you imagined when you left your island—monuments, and the like."

Jacko nodded a third time, more enthusiastically than ever, his hands still tight across his mouth.

"And yet you believe that you could be happy now, if only you might return to the island that was yours." The star sighed. "In that you are mistaken. Your island—it is no longer yours in any event—is visited from time to time by the ships of men. The first man, as you know, has already made his home there, and more will be moving in soon. This age is not a good one for monkeys, and the age to come will be far worse."

At these words, Jacko felt his heart sink within him; it was only then that he realized it was whole once more—that the part of himself which had run away from him when his heart had broken had returned to him.

"Steer as I tell you," said the star, "and do not be afraid."

So poor Jacko took the tiller again, and trimmed their little sail; and it was a good thing he did, for the wind was rising and seemed almost to blow the star as though it were a firefly after all. For a few minutes he could still see it bright against the sail. By degrees it appeared to climb the mast, and for a long while it remained there, as if the whaleboat had hoisted a lantern with a little candle in it. But at last it blew forward and dropped lower, until it was hidden by the sail.

"Are you still there?" Jacko called.

"I am sitting in the bow," the star replied.

But while that was happening, far stranger things were taking place outside the boat. Night had backed away, and twilight come again. A fiery arch, like a burning rainbow, stretched clear across the sky. Ships came into view, only to vanish before Jacko could hail them; and very strange ships they were—a towering junk, like a pagoda afloat; a stately galleon with a big cross upon its crimson foresail; and at last an odd, beaked craft, so long and narrow that it seemed almost a lance put to sea, that flew over the water on three pairs of wings.

"A point to starboard, helmsman," called the star. As it spoke, the twilight vanished. The shadow of their sail fell upon the water as sharp and black as that of the gnomon of a sundial, and around it every little wave sparkled and danced in the sunlight. Jacko steered a point to starboard, as he had been told, then turned his face toward the sun, grinned with happiness, and shut his eyes for a moment.

The sound of many voices made him open them again. A river's mouth was swallowing their whaleboat between sandy lips, and both those lips were black with people, thousands upon thousands of them, chanting and shouting.

"Where are we?" Jacko asked.

"This is Now." The star's clear voice came from the other side of the sail. "It is always Now, wherever I am." Beneath the lower edge of the sail, Jacko could see a man's bare, brown feet.

"Here and Now is your new home," the star continued.

"They will treat you well—better than you deserve—because you have come with me. But you must watch out for crocodiles."

"I will," Jacko promised.

"Then let down the sail so that they can see you. Our way will carry us as near the shore as we wish to go."

So Jacko freed the halyard, letting the little sail slip down the mast, and bounced up onto the tiller.

"Come here," said the star, "and sit upon my shoulder." Which now made perfect sense, because the star had become a tall, slender, brown man. Jacko leaped from the tiller to the mast, and from the mast onto the star's shoulder just as he had been told, though the great gold disc of the star's headdress was so bright it nearly blinded him. And at that a great cheer went up from all those thousands of people.

"Ra!" they shouted. "Ra, Ra, *Ra!*," so that Jacko might have thought they were watching a game, if he had known more about games. But some shouted, "Thoth!" as well.

"Ra is the name by which I am known Now," explained the star. "Do you see that old man with the necklace? He is my chief mistaker in this place. When I give the word, you must jump to him and take his hand. It will seem very far, but you must jump anyway. Do you understand?"

Jacko nodded. "I hope I don't fall in the water."

"You have my promise," the star said. "You will not fall in the water."

As he spoke, the whaleboat soared upward. It seemed to Jacko that some new kind of water, water so clear it could not be seen, must have been raining down on them, creating a new sea above the sea and leaving the river's mouth and all of its thousands of bowing people on the bottom.

Then the star said, "Go!" and he leaped over the side and seemed almost to fly.

If you that love books should ever come across *The Book of That Which Is in Tuat,* which is one of the very oldest books we have, I hope that you will look carefully at the picture called "The Tenth Hour of the Night." There you will see, marching to the right of Ra's glorious sun-boat, twelve men holding paddles. These are the twelve hours of the day. Beyond them march twelve women, all holding one long cord; these twelve women are the twelve hours of the night. Beyond even them—and thus almost at the head of this lengthy procession—are four gods, two with the heads of men and two with the heads of animals. Their names are Bant, Seshsha, Ka-Ament, and Renen-sebu.

And in front of *them,* standing upon the tiller of a boat, is one monkey.

It seems strange, to be sure, to find a monkey in such a procession as Ra's, but there is something about this particular monkey that is stranger still. Unlike the four gods, and the twelve women with the cord, and the twelve men with paddles, this monkey is actually looking back at Ra in his glorious sun-boat. And waving. Above this monkey's head, I should add, floats something that you will not find anywhere else in the whole of *The Book of That Which Is in Tuat.* It is a smallish, quite common and ordinary-looking, five-pointed star.

Water

—✛—

Lee Hoffman

Something moved on the ridge. A horse. A mare from the shape of her, as white as the full moon overhead. In that light, she looked as if she were made of the same stuff as the moon. As if she were aglow.

She stood gazing into the arroyo, scenting the night, then gave her head a sudden toss that fanned her mane out in the moonlight. It seemed to Evan as if she had looked straight at him, and he thought she was going to bolt. But she began to pick her way slowly down the slope.

If he could catch her, he thought, he'd get away and get to help. Then he admitted to himself that there was no way in hell he was going to catch a wild horse now. The wound in his leg was burning like a fever. He'd had to crawl on his belly to get hid in the rocks, and he was a lot weaker now. He'd never be able to make it out at all.

Dammit, it wasn't right he should die like this and nobody ever claim justice for Hank. Likely nobody'd even find out how Hank had been shot down—and him, too—them being drifters in strange country when it happened. He watched the horse, wondering if she were only a dream. She reached the shadows in the arroyo and disappeared.

He let his eyes close, holding the image of the mare in his mind. Properly broke to saddle, she'd fetch a fancy price from some fine lady. Only he wasn't sure if he owned anything that beautiful he'd be willing to sell it at any price.

Something moved close by. He jerked open his eyes, and was looking into the face of a woman. A young face framed by hair as pale as the mare's mane. Astonished, he blinked. And it wasn't the face of a woman at all, but the white mare, just inches away. She didn't look scared of him. Just curious. Cautiously, he lifted a hand toward her.

The mare stood. She let him touch his fingertips to her neck. Maybe she didn't need to be saddle-broke. Maybe she was a runaway. Some lady's pet. Maybe he could find the strength to get onto her back. He edged his hand up and wrapped his fingers in her lush mane. As if it were a signal, she began raising her head, helping him lift himself.

The wounded leg wouldn't take weight at all. By clinging to the mare, he got himself up on the other leg. But no further. The world was spinning around him. He leaned his face into her neck, smelling the sweet warm horse scent of her, thinking it was good to have her company, even if she couldn't help him. Thinking it was better than dying alone.

Darkness.

There seemed to be an old woman poulticing his wound. He thought it was his grandmother. If anyone could help, he figured it was Granny. She was half Mandan and knew Indian medicines and prayers. She'd pulled him through some kind of serious illness when he was a knee-high tad. He slept easy, certain she was taking good care of him.

The warmth on his face was the morning sunlight. It glowed through his closed eyelids. He brought a hand up to shield his eyes, and opened them. Glaring blue sky. Barren gray rock. A few shriveled sprigs of brittle straw that had once been living plants.

He was still lying among the rocks in the arroyo. Granny had only been a dream, he thought. But he didn't feel close to death, the way he had during the night. The pain in his leg was no longer a raging fire. It felt like it was healing. He wondered if maybe he could survive after all.

But to live, a man had to have water, and there didn't seem to be one damned water hole in this territory that hadn't dried up.

That was what caused the trouble in the first place. Water. For days, he and Hank had ridden through land where the water holes were fast drying up, and the grass turning brown under the hooves of their mounts. In time, there'd been no water at all. No grass left. More dead carcasses than living critters on the range. They'd been travelling with dry canteens when they came to the barren creek bed and began to follow it, hoping somewhere upstream it'd still hold water.

The horses got eager, as if there were a scent of water in the air. By the time they'd come to a fence, Evan and Hank could smell it themselves and were as eager as the horses. So they'd cut the wire.

The shots seemed to come out of nowhere. The first one went into Hank's back, slamming him face down into the dirt. The second caught Evan in the leg as he was throwing himself onto his horse, meaning to hightail for cover.

There'd been more shots. He didn't know which had hit his horse. He hadn't even known it was hit, until it began to falter and then fell. He'd been riding for his life. Whoever'd done the shooting wasn't satisfied with just running him off. The shooter'd lit out after him.

Wasn't right there'd been no warning. Wasn't right there'd be no justice for the dead.

A sound. Hooves on rock. A jangle of bit chain and a creak of saddle leather. A ridden horse. He drew breath and held it, listening intently. Two horses. A small breeze brought him in the scent of them. Horse sweat, oiled leather and man sweat.

One of the riders spoke. "He's got to be around here somewheres."

"You sure you hit him, Hode?" the other asked.

"Damn sure, Boss" the one called Hode said. "He couldn'ta got far once his horse went down."

They were the same ones, Evan thought. The ones who'd killed Hank and damn near killed him. And they were close. His hand traced down the empty holster at his side. If only he hadn't dropped his Colt when the horse collapsed, at least he'd be able to take one or both with him when they got him.

"Hey, looka that!" Hode shouted.

Evan could hear the boss draw a sharp startled breath.

"That's the purtiest thing I ever seen," Hode said.

"I'm gonna have her!"

"But that trespasser...."

"We can finish him later. I want that mare!"

The sound of a horse galloping off. And the other following close behind.

Cautiously, Evan lifted himself onto one elbow and peered over the rocks that had shielded him from their view. He saw the white mare on a rise, and the two riders racing toward her. She was drawing them away from him.

It was the first good look he'd had at the men who wanted to kill him. One was stubby and broad through the shoulders, mounted on a red roan. The other, on a leggy bay, was tall and lean and appeared to have a scruff of dark beard.

The mare stood watching the riders for a moment, then trotted off along the rise, as if taunting them. Then suddenly she wheeled and disappeared down the backside of the rise, leaving only a plume of dust to mark her going.

Moments later, the riders were gone over the rise.

That didn't mean they'd never come back. Evan surveyed his situation. From the floor of the arroyo, the rocks hid him, but from above on that ridge where the white mare had stood, he'd be clearly visible. He turned onto his belly, dug in his elbows and began to drag himself in search of a better hiding place.

Then he saw the hole. One big boulder resting on a couple of smaller ones, with a space between them. It looked about shoulder-wide, and high enough for a man to squirm into. He pulled himself toward it.

At the hole, the air had a clean cool damp scent, like a cave where the hanging rock might drip with water and little streams run in the crevices. But that wasn't the only smell. A rattler leaves its own peculiar odor in its den. This was strong enough he figured the rattler was still there. Maybe more than one. Maybe a whole snarl of them, sleeping in the darkness.

But if there was any water at all in the arroyo, it was likely down that hole. And a man had to have water to live.

All the stirring around roused the pain in his leg. He lay still, letting it ease while he thought about rattlers.

Their bite could kill, but a man could eat their flesh. The trick was to strike first. Or make the rattler strike elsewheres.

He considered that a while, then got himself sitting up. His leg went to hurting again. Determined against the pain, he stripped off his leather vest. Then he flung a fist-sized rock into the hole.

It landed with a *thunk*. A harsh rattling answered. Left-handed, hanging onto an edge, he tossed the vest into the hole. From the sound, the rattler struck at it. Instantly, he jerked it back. He could feel the tug of the snake's fangs.

As he dragged it out, the snake came with it, striking again and again, pumping its venom at the leather.

As soon as its huge head was visible, Evan lunged. Even as he dragged the lure with his left hand, he slammed his right down just behind the snake's head, pinning it to the ground.

It exploded in his grip, writhing and thrashing. Its monstrous mouth was wide open, the long fangs dripping. For a moment, he was afraid he wasn't strong enough to hold it. With a twist of his arm, he snapped the vest around over the ugly head. Letting go the vest, he grabbed up another rock. He slammed it down on the leather-wrapped head and felt something break under it. Again and again and again.

The sinuous body kept convulsing. It was said that even if you cut a snake's head off completely, the body didn't die until sundown. Once he was convinced that, despite its twitchings, this one would never strike again, he stopped the pounding.

When he let up his grip on the snake and sat back, he felt the pain in his leg again. It swept through him, as if only his concentration on the rattler had held it at bay. For a moment, he was dizzy with it, and afraid the world around him was going black.

When finally he felt able to move without passing out, he began tossing more rocks into the snake's den. They returned only echoes. No more startled rattles. He wrapped the remains of the snake in his vest and dragged it along as he pulled himself inside.

Within the hollow, he fingered the Barlow knife from his pocket. Moving slowly so as not to start up the pain again, he began cutting at the body of the snake.

Raw meat was better than no meat. The moisture of it helped his thirst. He figured it would keep him alive a while longer.

All the exertion had exhausted him. Despite his intentions, he fell into sleep.

He dreamed of the old woman again, only this time he wasn't so sure it was his half-Mandan grandmother. But she was surely somebody's granny. In the dream she had someone with her. A stocky middle-aged woman who gave him food and drink and somehow kept getting mixed up with the snake. In the dream, it seemed a friendly snake, offering itself to be eaten, the way a mother offered her milk to her babe. At the same time, it was the woman, offering him a marvelous cup that stayed full, no matter how much he drank from it.

He woke feeling a lot stronger for having eaten and slept. But he was still thirsty. The damp scent of the air said there must be water around somewheres. Groping, he located the entrance to the cave. It felt plenty big enough to crawl into, and the bottom was as smooth as if someone had packed the earth for a floor. But it was blacker than inside a cow's belly. Using his hands, he explored the area ahead of him as he worked his way in.

Suddenly the smoothed-out floor ended. And the smell of water was strong in his face.

He had a flint in his pocket, and the steel blade of his Barlow knife, but no tinder. He'd already used his bandanna to bind up the wound on his leg. He tore off a piece of his shirttail and frayed it by feel, then struck sparks until an edge finally caught. The scrap of cloth burned just long enough for him to have a good look around.

In front of him was the bed of an underground river that had stopped running not long ago. There were a few thin puddles in the hollows at its bottom. Indians had used the place at some time in the past. On the river bank, there were several old pots and baskets, and a stone circle filled with ashes. That accounted for the packed-earth floor. He got himself aimed at the relics before his light went out, then found them with his hands.

A basket went to pieces in his grip. The dried-out bits made tinder for another fire, and by its flare, he could see a heap of firewood near the stone circle. He felt like he ought to be singing thanks to some Indian spirit as he stacked wood in the circle and got it burning.

With the luxury of light, he saw the Indians had left a weapon as well. A lance with a fine flaked stone point lashed to it. The shaft was broken, but the wood hadn't rotted. It felt oak-strong in his hands. The broken ends fit together perfectly.

He ate some of the rattler's flesh, then used his Barlow knife to cut a thong from its hide. With it, he bound together the broken pieces of the lance. The raw skin would shrink as it dried and turn hard as iron.

He had no idea whether it was night or day, only that he was very tired. He slept again, and when he woke he built another fire and roasted snake meat over it on the tip of the lance. The hide patch had worked well. The repaired joint felt as strong as if it had never been broken.

With effort, he worked his way down to the puddles. The water was cool and sweet, with a taste as pure as moonlight.

In the cave, time lost meaning. Twice he slept without dreaming. The third time, three women came to him.

The granny and the middle-aged one had a young one with them. He recognized her. Hers was the face he'd seen for an instant when the white mare came nuzzling him, back in the arroyo. She was carrying branches with the fresh green leaves of spring on them. Holding the branches as if they were a torch to light the way, she led him through long winding tunnels and out into the bright sunlight.

He woke with only a dim memory of the dream, but with a strong notion it was time to leave the cavern.

He realized the darkness in the cavern was not total. A ways down the dry riverbed, he could make out a smudge of gray. He puzzled over it, wondering why he hadn't noticed it before. Likely it meant there was light reflecting from some place around a bend, where it spilled through a hole in the cavern wall. If there was another way out of the cave, he wanted to know about it. A smart prairie dog always had a back door to its burrow. Those two who wanted to kill him knew the area where he'd gone to ground. He wanted to see them again, but on his own terms. If they were back in the arroyo waiting for him with guns in their hands, he'd just as soon get out somewhere else.

His leg was healed enough for him to get around on it, using the mended lance for support. With a piece of firewood for a torch, he made his way along the riverbed. Past the bend, at a fork, he could see the source of the light. It was coming through a fissure down the right branch. Crawling over a jumble of water-worn rock, he reached the opening.

He found himself looking down at the dried cracked bottom of what had once been a large pond at the foot of rough rock face. On the bank across from him was a stand of trees that still held some of the greenness of life. And in their shade, a pole cabin, outbuildings and corrals. A woman was sitting on a bench by the cabin door, shucking corn, flipping an occasional grain to the chickens that clustered near her feet. A thin twist of smoke curled from the cabin chimney.

Suddenly the stones he rested on were sliding from under him. And he was sliding with them, tumbling down the rock face. He heard someone holler as he slammed into the ground.

Half-stunned, he struggled to get his breath and focus his eyes. The fall had hurt, but it didn't feel like it had injured him. The lance was still in his hand. He braced himself against it for a try at standing up.

A man's voice growled, "Keep still and let go that gun."

Evan froze. Very slowly, he turned his head. The man was

standing to his left, on the rim of the dry pond. An old feller with a full gray beard, but the hand that held a revolver pointed at Evan looked steady enough to use it.

Evan figured the Graybeard mistook the lance for the barrel of a long gun. He called out, "It ain't a gun. It's a stick. I got a bad leg."

Someone was coming from the direction of the cabin, carrying a rifle. A smooth-faced boy, maybe fifteen or sixteen. He halted on the rim of the dry pond and peered at Evan, then shouted, "It's a spear, Gran!"

Evan moved his hand slowly away from the lance. Lifting himself on one elbow, he looked up at the boy. "I been using it for a stick. I got a bad leg."

"Keep him covered," Gran told the boy. Still holding the revolver leveled, he headed downslope toward Evan. As he came near, he asked suspiciously, "You one of Redmor's hands?"

"I don't even know nobody name of Redmor," Evan told him.

"Then what the hell you up to? What were you doing up there?" He gave a nod toward the peak of the rock face, as if he thought Evan had slid all the way from the top. "Spying on me?"

The woman had followed the boy from the cabin. She stopped at his side and called to Gran, "What's going on? Who is that?"

"Ain't sure yet. He's a stranger," the old man said.

"One of Redmor's hands?" she asked.

"Claims he ain't."

"Then fetch him on up like decent folk."

Gran gestured at Evan. "Get up."

"I need to use the stick," Evan said. "I can't walk without it."

"Use it then."

Evan got himself onto his feet. He leaned more heavily on the lance than he really had to, just in case anybody doubted he was lame. With a gesture of the revolver, Gran told him to go on ahead up the slope.

The woman came to meet him. She was middle-aged, stocky, familiar in a way Evan couldn't quite figure. Her eyes were a strange color, like storm clouds. So were the old man's. And the boy's. They were all kin, he thought. Likely she was the old man's daughter rather than his wife, and the boy her son. Likely they called the old man *Gran* for Grandpa.

Looking him up and down, she said, "You're a scruffy one. What's wrong with your leg?"

"Somebody shot me."

Narrow-eyed, Gran asked, "Why?"

The boy had come closer. He suggested, "Horse-thieving?"

"Trespassing, I reckon," Evan said. "I cut some wire. Me and my partner. They killed my partner, and damn near killed me."

The woman looked at Gran. "Redmor?"

"Likely," he answered. He turned back to Evan. "What'd you cut the wire for?"

"Hunting water."

The woman nodded. "Redmor."

"Who's this Redmor?" Evan asked.

"The only one in these parts as has water," she told him.

The boy worked up spit and let fly at the ground, as if he wished it were Redmor's face.

"I take it he ain't sharing none." Evan said.

"That's the trouble," Gran answered.

The woman said, "If you're shot in the leg, it ain't doing you no good standing there on it."

"No, ma'am," Evan agreed.

She turned to the old man, "Gran, fetch him on up to the house. We might as well set while we talk."

He nodded and gestured for Evan to follow the woman to the cabin.

Inside, it was cozy with a small fire on the hearth, and a large pot simmering over it. Gran motioned for Evan to sit down at the table, then sat down across from him. The boy followed them in. He stood near the door with the rifle lowered, but his finger still on the trigger.

Evan stretched out his injured leg. Indicating the bandanna tied around his thigh, the woman asked, "You hurting? Need doctoring?"

"It's healing," he said.

"I'll take a look." She hunkered to strip away the bandage.

Gruffly, the boy said, "He ain't told us yet what he's doing here."

"Boy's right," Gran eyed Evan. "What are you doing, sneaking up on us?"

"I wasn't sneaking up. I was just taking a look before I showed myself. I wanted to be sure you wasn't somebody else."

"Who?"

"The fellers who shot me."

Examining his wound, the woman said, "You're lucky the bullet went clear through. Didn't break anything. I can put on a poultice to speed up the healing."

"I'd be much obliged, ma'am." Evan replied. He turned back to Gran. "This Redmor, what's he look like?"

"Tall and skinny."

"He got a beard?"

Gran nodded.

The boy gave a laugh. "Nothing like Gran'pa's, though."

"Scruffy and dark-colored?"

"Yeah."

"He got a rider name of Hode?"

"That's him, alright," Gran said. "He's the one shot you?"

Evan recalled the words he'd overheard. "It was that feller, Hode, done it."

"He's Redmor's top hand," Gran told him.

"And Redmor's the devil's top hand," the boy added.

The woman had gone to a small chest and was rummaging through it. She looked over her shoulder at him. "Be thankful Redmor's a little-minded man. He could do a lot worse if he knowed what he was doing."

Gran nodded.

Evan asked, "This Redmor been giving you trouble, too?"

"He stole something from us. . . ." the boy started.

Gran gestured for him to be quiet, and told Evan, "He's giving trouble to every rancher around here. Drought's killing everybody, and he's dammed the only water left in the county."

The woman joined in. "There was plenty of water in these parts before Redmor dammed his springhead. Not long after that, the land begun drying up. As if he'd dammed every spring and tank and creek in the county."

"And the rain, too," the boy added. "Ain't been a cloud in the sky since he dammed that creek."

"If he's hurting you that much, why'n't you go after him?" Evan asked.

"We ain't the ones to do it," she said.

Gran said, "Folks tried talking to him. That didn't do any good so they threatened to bust down the dam. He said he'd kill any man set foot on his land. Now he's got men riding his fence, ready to shoot down anybody tries to get in."

Evan nodded, understanding now why he and Hank had been attacked. "But that don't give him the right to do it."

"In this country, a man takes what rights he's got the power to hold."

"We ain't got the power to take him," the boy said. "Not without mortal help . . ."

"Look out now," the woman interrupted. She'd finished preparing the poultice, and was ready to put it on Evan's leg. "This is gonna hurt at first."

"My granny used to say, *the stronger the cure the more it hurts.*" He tensed against the anticipated pain.

The touch of the poultice against the wound was like a spear of flame piercing into his flesh. Like getting shot all over again, he thought.

"Just sit still. It'll ease in a minute," she assured him. "You hungry?"

He had to draw a couple of breaths before he could find his voice. "Yes, ma'am."

"Vittles should be about ready." She knotted the bandage, then went to the fire to check the pot simmering over it. A whiff of it

seemed to satisfy her. She ladled up a plateful and set it in front of
Evan.

It was good, maybe the best stew Evan had ever eaten. Sure a
lot better than raw rattlesnake. It filled him with a drowsy warmth.
By the time he'd finished he could hardly keep his eyes open. He'd
half a mind that the woman had drugged him, half a mind that
there was something very strange about these people and this
place. Something unnatural. But before he could consider the
thought, he was asleep.

He dreamed he was in bright sunlight, astride the white mare.
There was no rein, but he didn't feel the need of one. The mare
knew where she was going. After a moment, he realized they were
in the arroyo near the rocks where he'd hid from Hode and
Redmor.

*She turned at the little drywash he'd squirmed down when he
was hunting cover, after his horse collapsed. At the top, the land
hardly looked familiar. It was carpeted with lush grass, dotted with
green brush. In the distance, he could see pronghorn grazing.*

*When he saw a fast-flowing creek ahead, he realized the mare
was carrying him along his own backtrack. That was where he and
Hank had been attacked. But there was no fence and no drought in
the dream.*

When he woke, he recalled nothing of the dream, but he did remember that when he flung himself onto his horse and ran from the
gunman who'd shot down Hank, he'd gone straight ahead.

He waited until they were all in the cabin together before he
brought up the idea he'd been pondering. He started by asking,
"You said Redmor has fence riders ready to shoot down anybody
who tries to cross his line?"

Gran nodded solemnly in reply.

"Suppose somebody had a way to get onto his land without
crossing his fence?"

"You know of a way?"

"Maybe. There's caves under this land like prairie dog burrows
and one of 'em opens out behind Redmor's fence. Do you know
the lay of his land?"

"Me and the boy both know it. All the land hereabout was open range before Redmor put that fence up."

"There's a dry creek back a ways," Evan hooked a thumb to indicate the direction. "You know how far the dam is from where his fence crosses that creek bed?"

"Half-mile at most. Just what you got in mind?"

"Suppose a man with a pack of blasting powder was to get in on foot near to that creek bed? You reckon he could get to the dam and blow it?"

The boy grinned, but Gran said, "Even if somebody could get past the fence riders, and bust the dam, he'd likely get caught before he could get out again."

"Suppose he went in at night and set a charge with a long fuse? Suppose he was well away from the dam before it blew?"

Gran gave Evan's words a long moment of consideration. With a slow nod, he admitted, "It might work. But I'm afraid it'd take a younger man than me."

Eagerly, the boy asked, "Just how could somebody get there without crossing the fence?"

The woman scowled at him. "You ain't thinking of doing it?"

"It'd take an *older* man than him," Evan said.

"You mean you?" she asked.

He nodded.

Gran eyed him. "Why would you do that for us?"

"Wouldn't be just for you," he said. "They killed my partner. I owe them for that."

"It'd be dangerous," the woman warned. "You could get yourself killed."

"Lot of ways a man can get himself killed," Evan answered. "Trailing cattle, riding the cars, even just drifting. But for a damned lot of luck, I'd be dead now in that arroyo back yonder."

"He's right about that," Gran said.

"I'd need blasting powder. And a gun. I lost mine back a ways."

"I know where to get hold of some of that dynamite stuff. You want a hand gun or a rifle?"

"Both, if you can get 'em."

"You'd need a guide, too," the boy said. "Somebody to show you where the dam is."

"Once I hit the creek bed, I can find it," Evan answered him.

Shaking his head, he repeated, "You'd need a guide."

Evan looked to the woman to protest, but she said, "Boy's right."

He argued that it would be a lot more dangerous for two than one. To his surprise, nobody backed him. Finally he agreed to let the boy accompany him as far as the arroyo and head him in the right direction.

It was a lot easier going back through the cavern than it had been coming. This time Evan carried a lantern, and no longer needed a stick to lean on. The moon was up, tipping the ridges with silver, when he and the boy emerged on the rocky wall of the arroyo.

By moonlight, he checked the weapons and dynamite the old man had got for him. There was plenty of fuse and a good stock of matches. Satisfied, he told the boy to get on home.

"I'll wait for you," the boy said.

"I might not come back this way," Evan replied.

"You better take this." The boy held out something.

Evan was surprised to see the Indian lance. He hadn't even noticed that the boy was bringing it along. He said, "I don't need a stick to walk now."

"You need this anyway."

Maybe the kid was right. Some men carried lucky coins, and the Indians had all kinds of charms. He'd had a run of luck since he'd found the lance. Maybe it was good medicine. Taking it, he headed out.

Beyond the rim of the arroyo, the land was cluttered with rocks and cut with gullies and ridges. A small wind skittered through the shadows, rolling bits of dry brush ahead of it. An owl crossed the face of the moon. Far away, a coyote sang to it.

Evan moved cautiously from shadow to shadow, watching for

any sign of riders. He froze as one passed in the distance. The man rode on, unaware of him.

He could smell the water before he reached it. The lake that had formed behind the dam lay in a broad hollow below a rocky ridge. He headed toward the peak of the ridge, figuring if Redmor had a guard watching over the dam, that was the likely place for him. Careful not to let himself be skylit, he sidled downwind, and crept toward the high point.

He caught no unnatural sounds or scents. At the peak, he looked out across the lake. In the moonlight, its breeze-ruffled surface glittered as if it were scattered with silver coins. He crouched motionless, scanning the land surrounding it.

The dam was a rough construction of earth and rock stretched across the hollow where the creek had once flowed. He moved toward it. On an outcrop where he could see the face of it, he stretched out to study it and decide how to plant the charges.

Suddenly there was a voice at his back. "I knew you'd be coming."

Snake-quick, he twisted onto one elbow, his other hand swinging up the rifle. But before he could turn far enough to see the speaker, a sharp blow sent the weapon flying out of his grip.

There'd been no warning sound. Not a footstep on gravel or rustle of clothing or whisper of breathing. Just the sudden voice.

The rifle gone, Evan lifted his empty hand and slowly finished turning his head. The figure he saw was silhouetted against the night sky, a tall skinny man with a fuzz of scruffy beard visible at his jaw line and a revolver in his hand. It was aimed at Evan.

"Redmor?" Evan said.

The tall man nodded. "You're the one my rider shot, ain't you?"

Evan didn't reply, but Redmor went on talking as if he had.

"I didn't know who you were then. I thought the ranchers had sent you. Wasn't till after I chased her and she got away that I figured out who she was. . . . that she was protecting you. . . . that's when I knew you'd be coming back to try again."

Puzzled, Evan asked, *"She?"*

"The White Mare," Redmor said it as if it were somebody's

name. "She ain't gonna get it, though. I'm no ordinary man. I got ancient blood. I got powers. I know the witch-stories and the secrets. I can make the potions and ride the winds and read the signs. I know what I got down there. I know she can't just take it away from me. And she can't kill me herself. Not while I have my powers. That's why she's sent you as her champion, ain't it?"

Evan shook his head. "I don't know what you're talking about."

"The White Mare." Redmor paused. As if surprised by the idea, and disappointed, he said, "You don't know, do you? You don't have any powers at all. You're just a common ordinary mortal, ain't you?"

"I reckon," Evan muttered. The man was crazy, he thought.

"I expected she'd send somebody with powers. A worthy opponent." Redmor gave a little shrug. "Well, maybe next time she will."

Evan caught the tone in his voice, and knew his finger was tightening on the trigger. Giving a sudden shove against the ground, he rolled. The bullet slammed into the ground where he'd been. But he was on his side, then up onto his knees. The Indian lance was under his hand. He heard the click as Redmor thumbed the hammer back for another shot. In the same instant, he flung the lance.

The glare and thunder of exploding gunpowder shattered the instant into flashes of image—the polished stone head of the lance slamming into Redmor—the revolver kicking itself from Redmor's grip as the lancehead hit his chest—behind Redmor's crumpling figure, a second moon rising over the ridge—only it wasn't the moon but the White Mare glowing as if she were made of light.

Evan blinked. Through the hazy afterimage of the gunshot, he looked toward the ridge. It lay dark and empty against the skyglow. He gave a bewildered shake of his head, and decided he'd only imagined the mare. Going as crazy as Redmor, he thought. Turning, he looked down at the fallen man.

Redmor lay on his side, his face to the moonlight. His mouth gaped, spilling liquid darkness. The lips twitched and a sound like the rattle of a snake came from his throat. The lips twisted it into a harsh mockery of a voice. A protest. "I can't die...."

"Hank died," Evan said. "At your orders."

"But I got powers."

A sudden voice. "What is sent returns threefold." Evan wheeled. It was the boy standing there behind him, looking down at Redmor's body.

"I told you not to come," Evan snapped at him.

The boy gazed at Redmor a moment longer, then looked up at Evan. "He's dead now."

"You get the hell back where it's safe," Evan said. "Those shots'll be bringing riders."

Paying no attention, the boy turned from him and started down the slope toward the lake.

"Hey!" Evan hurried after him.

At the water's edge the boy knelt, dipping his hands into the shimmering surface of the lake. And suddenly it wasn't the boy, but a woman with hair the color of moonlight.

Evan halted with a start. He stared at the figure before him—the woman from his dreams.

She gathered water into her hands and rose with it. The water seemed to pour upward in sheets and into the cup of her outheld hands, draining the lake, baring the crevice of the springhead at its bottom.

As the water withdrew, the dam began to crumble, rock tumbling from rock, scattering itself over the earth until nothing of it remained in place.

The woman's hands were filled with light that shimmered into the shape of a cup and, as Evan stared, became a golden goblet encrusted with the brilliant colors of precious gems. Water flowed from the cup, as if all the water of the lake she'd gathered were returning. It filled the springhead and flowed into the bed of the creek in a tumbling rush.

The cup within her hands became a cauldron ornamented with strange figures and stained with verdigris, and still the water poured from it. The cauldron became a clay bowl, painted with geometric patterns, and an intricately woven basket, and then a common cook pot. She tilted the pot, lowering it until the water that flowed from it was one with the waters in the spring, and once more it changed. As she lifted it again, it was something of a shape and color that his eyes could not define. She closed her cupped hands over it.

As it was hidden from his sight, Evan broke the trance that held him. Maybe it was a dream, or maybe he was crazy, or maybe the old Indian stories were right about animals that could talk and people who could change shape. Whatever it was, he wanted to make some sense of it all.

"What the hell is going on?" he demanded of the woman. "Who are you?"

She turned and looked at him, the moonlight in her face, the moon itself in her eyes.

She was the most beautiful thing he'd ever seen. For a moment he just stared. Then he remembered where he was. "We gotta get to cover. Those shots'll bring Redmor's men for sure."

"Not yet." She lifted her cupped hands, keeping the thing within them hidden from him. "While I hold this in this form, we are outside of time. They can't come until I am gone."

"What?"

"Believe me."

Thinking of his grandmother's tales, he asked, "What are you? Some kind of spirit?"

She didn't reply. Her smile became misty. As if she were fading.

He had a sudden feeling she was about to disappear. "Look here! I just killed a man. I thought I knew why, but I don't. I got a right to know."

She shimmered, and somehow she was three—the old man, the woman and the boy.

The woman said, "We are from a faraway place. Another realm. Another world. There, we are the keepers of a great treasure. It was stolen from us. We needed the help of a mortal to recover it. We took shapes familiar to you and posed the problem in mortal terms you could easily understand and accept."

As she spoke, they became the three women from his dreams. And then they were one again, the woman of moonlight.

He gestured toward her cupped hands. "That thing you took out of the water, that's your treasure?"

"Not our treasure. It belongs to all the world, and all beyond. We are its keepers—a *manifestation* of its keepers as it is a manifestation of the treasure."

"Manifestation?" he said in puzzlement.

"A lesser form of a greater thing. It is a symbol, a shadow, a reflection of the ever-full cauldron from which all eat, the cup of life from which all drink, the womb of life, the earth itself. The nexus of power."

He gave a shake of his head. "You lost me back yonder."

"Isn't it enough to know you've served a great purpose? It was stolen. It fell into the wrong hands and was wrongly used. You've ridden this land. You know the desolation that it caused."

"Are you saying that thing caused the drought?"

She nodded.

"How?" Afraid she wasn't going to reply, he added, "I got a right to know."

She considered for a moment, then said, "You have started a fire with a lens, have you not?"

He nodded, still bewildered.

"Sunlight alone will not start a fire. But it will, concentrated through the lens. Sunlight is not a thing you can catch in a bottle or hold in your hand but the glass can collect its power into a point that will set your tinder ablaze. You understand that?"

"Yeah."

"As best it can be explained in mortal concepts, our treasure is such a thing. It focuses power. As the lens collects the sunlight into a concentrated point, this has been used to collect the surrounding waters and concentrate them in one place. Redmor had the ability to do that much with it. But he was a small-minded man and could do only small damage. We had to recover it before it could fall into greater hands that could do greater harm. And now we must return it to its proper place." She was growing misty again. Fading as if she were dissolving in the moonlight.

Suddenly she steadied, a translucent figure before him. "When I'm gone, you will be in time again. Redmor's men will be coming. They'll find you."

"I'll be ready for them," he told her.

"They'll kill you."

"Maybe. But I'll kill some of them first."

She reached out toward him. "You may come with us if you wish."

"To your world?"

"Other mortals have done so in past times, and but few longed to return. The flow of time is slow and sweet in our realm. There, you may live in a springtime of joy for a thousand years."

"I'm obliged for the invite, ma'am," he answered. "But I got a job here I got to get done."

"A job?"

"Redmor's man, Hode, shot my partner in the back. I got to see justice done. Or go down trying."

"Justice," she said, "is a treasure worth dying for."

Then she was gone.

And Evan could hear the riders coming.

What You See . . .

---✠---

Alan Dean Foster

". . . bunions, lumbago, bad back, consumption, whooping cough, dysentery, yellow fever, heart problems, liver trouble, infertility! Afflictions of the eye, the ear, the nose and the throat! Broken bones, sprains, strains, disfigurations of the skin and suppuration of all kinds!"

Now the blacksmith, he had a disposition not dissimilar to that of the mules he frequently shod, but so suave and convincing was the stranger's pitch that the square-brick man with the arms like railroad ties stepped to the front of the milling crowd and squinted up at the platform.

"Thet leetle bottle, it can cure all thet?"

From the back of the garishly decorated wagon Doctor Mohet Ramses gazed down benevolently at the first (and hopefully not the last) of the warm afternoon's supplicants.

"Sir, I would not claim it were it not true." He held up the compact, winsome black bottle, letting the sunlight fall flush on the florid label. "All that and more can the Elixir of the Pharaohs cure."

"Then you best take some yourself," shouted someone from the back of the crowd. "Maybe it'll keep you from runnin' off at the mouth!"

Doctor Ramses was undaunted by the scattered laughter this rude sally brought forth. He drew himself up to his full height, which though just over six feet seemed greater because of his parsimonious construction, and glared haughtily at the cloddish loquator.

"For twenty years I have endured the slurs of disbelievers and yet fate finds me still plying my trade. Why is that, I ask you? It is because the Elixir of the Pharaohs works, my friends!"

The blacksmith scratched dubiously at his bewhiskered chin. "A dollar a bottle seems awful high, Doc."

Ramses leaned low, bringing his voice down with him. "Only when compared to what it can buy, my friend. How much is your health worth? How much another year of life, or two, or ten? For you see," he said, straightening and raising aloft the inimitable, the peerless black bottle, "this venerable Elixir not only cures, not only prevents, but actually *extends* the life of the user!

"Unlike the traveling charlatans you good people have doubtless encountered before, I do not claim that my wondrous tonic cures every ailment, every time. Only most ailments, most of the time. I have records of hundreds of exhaustively documented cases from across this great country and from the Continent itself in which the Elixir has proven itself time and time again. I speak only the truth when I say that it can add to your life, actually make you live longer."

"How much longer?" wondered a woman in the front row on whose cheeks the blush of youth had grown stale.

"A year per bottle, madam. One year of life, of good and vigorous and healthy exercise, for each bottle you ingest according to instructions. One dollar for three hundred and sixty-five days of continued subsistence on this good green Earth. Is that not worth a little sweat of thy brow?"

"A dollar a bottle's too high," said a farmer angrily. "At them rates we can't afford to try it."

Doctor Mohet Ramses smiled compassionately. "Ah, my good sir, all things are granted freely in Heaven but in this world, sad it is to say, nothing comes without cost. You should not think that you can't afford to purchase the Elixir of the Pharaohs, but rather that you can't *not* afford to buy it."

Near the front a middle-aged lady looked at her husband. She hadn't been feeling well lately; had if the truth be known been in fact doing poorly. A dollar was a lot of money, but . . . if it only did a tenth of what the Doctor claimed. . . .

She struggled with her purse and dug out a handful of coins, holding them up toward the wagon. "I'll buy a bottle, Doctor. What have I got to lose?"

"A dollar," her husband muttered under his breath.

She glared at him. "See if I give you any, William."

Doctor Ramses' smile widened as he exchanged brimming black bottles for coins. When one well-dressed citizen eagerly pressed a quarter eagle into the erstwhile physician's perfumed palm, he positively beamed.

Bit by bit the crowd thinned, clutching their precious bottles tightly to shirt or bodice. Eventually there was but a single old woman left. She was so small and insignificant Doctor Ramses hardly noticed her as he contentedly tallied his take for the day. Time it was to move on. Other towns waited just over the horizon, other needful communities beckoned. All needed his services, all doted on his presentation as eagerly as they did on his marvelous solution.

The Elixir really was a wondrous concoction, he knew. Versatile as well, depending as it did for the bulk of its constituency on whatever creek he happened to cut across whenever his stock was running low.

He very rarely had trouble because, unlike that of so many traveling snake-oil salesmen, his pitch was different. Contrary to the rest of his silver-tongued brethren he promised not merely cures, but hope. For when his purchasers passed on, it was invariably with the conviction that the Elixir of the Pharaohs had truly extended their lives. He smiled to himself. A difficult assertion to disprove, when the principal complainants against him were all dead.

Only then did he notice the woman. His initial reaction was to ignore her, but he hesitated. She had remained throughout his talk, and remained still after all others had departed. Her dress was simple patched homespun and the bonnet she wore to shield herself from the sun was fraying. No fine Irish lace decorated the hem of her dress, no clever tatting softened the edge of her cuffs. Still, he owed it to her to repeat the offer one last time. Mohet Ramses was nothing if not magnanimous.

He knelt on the platform. "Can I be of assistance, madame?"

The woman hesitated. On her face could be seen the after-effects of a long lonely life of hard work and toil. It was clear she was not used to speaking to anyone more educated than the town schoolmaster or the local parson. Her expression was a mournful mix of hope and despair. She managed a hesitant reply.

"It ain't fer me, Doctor, sir. It's Emmitt. My husband."

Doctor Ramses smiled tolerantly. "So I assumed, madame."

"He's in the wagon, Doctor." She pointed and Ramses noted a gutted buckboard and team tied to a rail outside the nearby general store. "Emmitt, he's gettin' on to still be herdin', but he just tells me to shut up . . . he don't mean nothin' by it . . . and gits on with his work."

"It happened yesterday. Got the last of our twenty head in the corral; time to market 'em, don't you know, and that cursed old nag of his spooked. Still don't know what done it, but Emmitt, he went a-flyin'. Panicked the cattle, one kicked him, and, well, I'd be beholden if you'd come an' see for yourself, Doctor."

Ramses hesitated. It really was time to pack up the store and get a move on. There was invariably some local who would ignore the finely printed instructions and chug an entire bottle of the noxious brew in hopes of quickly curing some bumptious black eye, or constipation, or some other mundane ill, only to have his hopes dashed. Whereupon, fiery of eye and palpitating of heart, he would set out in search of the good Doctor's whereabouts. As a purely prophylactic measure Ramses historically had found it prudent not to linger in the vicinity of prior sales.

As the streets were presently devoid of recent customers, however, this was an internal debate easily resolved.

"Tell me, madame; do you have a dollar?"

She nodded slowly. " 'bout all I do have right now, sir. See, when the cattle git sold, that's the only time all year Emmitt and me have any foldin' money. I was goin' to pay the regular doctor with it, but he don't come to town but once a week, and this bein' Friday I don't expect him for another four days." She sniffed and the leathery skin twitched. "My man's a tough one, but he took that kick right hard." She rubbed the back of one hand under her nose. "I ain't sure he can last another four days."

Doctor Ramses reached down to take the woman's hand comfortingly in his own. "Fear not, good woman. Your husband is about to receive a dose of the most efficacious medication known to nineteenth-century man. Lead the way, and I shall accompany you."

"God bless you, Doctor!"

"There now," he said as he hopped off the back of the floridly painted wagon, "control yourself, madame. It is only my Hippocritical duty I am doing."

He winced at the sight of the battered, lanky old man lying in the rear of the wagon. He lay on his back, atop a dirty, bloodied quilt, a feather pillow jammed beneath his head. His eyes were closed and his thin brown hair had long since passed retreating to the region above the temples. Several veins had ruptured in his nose, which reminded Ramses of a map he'd once sold which purported to depict in some detail the delta of the Mississippi.

A crude bandage had slipped from the left side of the old man's head. A glance revealed that the force of the blow he had received had caved in the bone. Dried blood had run and caked everywhere; on the pillow, on his weathered skull, on the floor of the buckboard. His mouth hung half open and his sallow chest heaved with pained reluctance. As they looked on, the aged unfortunate raised a trembling hand toward the woman. It fell back and Ramses had to fight to maintain the smile on his face. Turning away from the disagreeable scene he held out to the anxious woman a small black bottle.

"One dollar, madame. One dollar to extend your husband's life. A worthy trifle, I am sure you will agree."

She fumbled with her purse and Ramses, eager to be away from this provincial municipality, waited impatiently while she counted out the money in pennies and nickels. Only when the count had reached one hundred U.S. cents did he pass to her the precious container. She accepted it with trembling fingers.

"You're sure this'll work, Doctor?"

"My good woman, it has never been known to fail. Ten years." He thrust high a declamatory finger. "Ten years did I live among the multitudes of Heathen Aegypt, perusing the primordial scrolls, learning all there was to learn, acquiring great knowledge, until at last I understood the mystic formula of the great and wise Pharaohs. Trust in me, and all will be well."

In point of fact, Doctor Mohet Ramses had never been to Aegypt. But he had been to Cairo. Cairo, Illinois, where he had practiced a number of trades, none of which were remotely related to medicine, until the furious father of an outraged daughter had gone searching for him with gun in hand. At which point Doctor Mohet Ramses, alias Dickie Beals of Baltimore, Maryland, had sought and found expediency in a life on the road. A most profitable life.

The sun was going down, the town's two saloons were lighting up, and the venerable Doctor was anxious to be on his way.

"Good luck to you, good woman, and to your husband, who should begin soon to exhibit a salubrious response to the most noteworthy liquid. Give him a spoonful a day followed by a piece of bread and you will find yourself gazing in wonder upon the medical miracle of the Age. And now if you will excuse me, there are others who have need of my services, access to which I am sure you would not wish to deny them."

"No sir, no! And thank you, Doctor, thank you!" She clutched his hand and, much to his disgust, began to kiss it effusively. He drew it back with as much decorum as he could muster.

"A woman ought to consider carefully what she's kissin'."

The deep voice boomed out of the shadows and a man rode into view from behind Ramses' wagon. He was enormous, as was the preposterous mongrel of a steed he bestrode. For an instant Ramses panicked. Then he saw that the man was an utter stranger to him, and relaxed.

The rider wore thick buckskins and showed salty black hair that hung to his shoulders. An incipient conflagration in his beard would've died for lack of oxygen, so thick were the bristles. His eyes were the color of obsidian, and darker than a moonless night.

He dismounted from the ridiculous stallion and lumbered over. A huge hand reached toward the woman and she flinched instinctively.

"May I see that, ma'am?" His voice turned gentle as a cooing babe's.

"What . . . what for, sir?"

"I am by nature an inquisitive man, mother. I'd have a look to satisfy my curiosity." He squinted at Doctor Ramses. "Surely sir, as a man of learning, you've no objection?"

Ramses hesitated, then stiffened. "I, sir? Why should I have any objection? But you delay this poor soul's treatment." He indicated the wagon and its pitiful human cargo.

"Not for long, I reckon." He reached out and plucked the bottle from the woman's uncertain fingers.

Ramses had to repress a grin. If this stranger had been the aforementioned local physician, there might have been trouble, but there was nothing to fear from a gargantuan bumpkin like this. He watched amusedly as the giant opened the bottle and sniffed at the contents.

His smile vanished when the mountain man swallowed the oily contents in a single gulp.

The old woman let out a cry and, astonishingly, threw herself at the giant. She hardly came up to his waist, but that didn't stop her from flailing away at him with her tiny fists. She might as well have been trying to reduce Gibraltar to dust.

Gently the giant settled her. A thick finger wiped at her tears. "Easy, mother." He tossed the empty bottle to Ramses, who caught it reflexively. "There weren't nothin' in that bottle that could've helped your man."

"Now, sir," declared Ramses, a fount of mock outrage, "I really must protest! If you were a man of science I might accept. . . ."

The huge form turned to him. "Listen well, 'Doctor'. I am Mad

Amos Malone, and I am a man of many things. But what is in any
event called fer here ain't science." He jabbed a huge forefinger toward the buckboard. "That man there is dying, and he needs
somethin' rather stronger than what you're offerin' him. He wants
to live, and I aim to help him."

"You, sir?" It was growing dark rapidly. Night fell quickly on
the open plains. "How might you intend to do that?"

"By helpin' these folks to help themselves." He smiled reassur-
ingly at the old woman, yellowed teeth gleaming from within the
depths of the beard. "You just calm yourself, mother, and we'll see
what we can do."

Ramses thought to depart. There was nothing for him here but
a distraught old woman and a man crazy from too much time in the
wilderness. But Ramses was curious, and he already had the woman's dollar. Maybe the mountain man was some sort of competitor.
If he had something worthy to sell, they might, as any two men engaged in the same trade were occasionally wont to do, strike a bargain. The Doctor was ever ready and willing to improve his stock.

To his disappointment the mountain man returned from fum-
bling with his saddlebags with nothing but an old wooden cup. It
was scratched and chipped, and appeared to have been carved out
of a single piece of some light-colored hardwood. It had a thick
brim and was in appearance nothing remarkable.

He offered it to the old woman, whose tears were drying on her
cheeks. "Here, mother. Use this to give your man a drink of water."
He gestured toward the town pump, which sat in a small Spanish-
style square in the center of the street.

"Water?" She blinked in bewilderment. "What good will water
do my Emmitt? He needs doctorin'. He needs this man's medicine." She indicated Ramses, who smiled condescendingly.

Malone spoke solemnly. "Let him drink from that old cup,
mother, and if it don't help your husband, I'll buy you another bottle of this gentleman's brew myself." Whereupon he produced from
a pocket a shiny gold piece. Not U.S. issue, but a disk slick with
age and worn by time. Ramses's eyes widened as he recognized the
ornate cross and Spanish lettering on the visible side. In his whole

life he'd seen only a single piece of eight. It had belonged to a New Orleans gambler. What the mountain man flashed was worth rather more than a dollar. Ramses was glad he'd trusted his instincts and stayed.

"Sir, you are as noble as you are curious."

The giant's eyes seemed to disappear beneath overhanging thick black brows that drew down like a miniature portcullis. "Don't be too sure o' that, friend." It was not a threat, but neither did the big man's tone inspire Ramses to move nearer the speaker.

Unsteady and bewildered, the woman shuffled to the well. The men heard the pump handle creak, heard the attendant splash of water. She made her slow way back to them, and after eyeing the giant blankly, climbed with surprising agility into the back of the wagon. There she dubiously but lovingly tipped the wooden lip of the cup to her husband's parted lips.

"Here now, darlin'. You got to drink, even if it 'tis just water. You got to, so's this man'll buy us another bottle of the doctor's medicine."

The dying old man wheezed and tried but failed to lift his head. Some kind of unvoiced communication passed between them, as it can only between two people who have been married so long that the two have become one. She spilled the water into his mouth and he gagged, choking, the liquid running out over his parted, chapped lips and down his furrowed cheek. Ramses suppressed a smile. A pitiful exhibition, but one which given the circumstances he was quite willing to endure. In the giant's fingers, the piece of eight shimmered in the fading light.

The old rancher coughed again. A second time. Then he sat up. Not bolt upright, as if hit by lightning, or shakily, as if at any moment he might collapse again. Just steady and confident-like. His wife's eyes grew wide, while Ramses's arguably exceeded them in diameter.

With profound deliberation the old man turned to his wife and put his arms around her. The tears streaming down his face started to dissolve the coagulated blood. "Sorry, woman," he was mumbling. "Sorry to make you worry like thet."

"Oh, Emmitt, Emmitt!" She sat back from him, crying and smiling and half-laughing all at once. "You gonna listen to me now and git yourself a hand to do the heavy work?"

"Reckon I ain't got much choice." The rancher climbed effortlessly to his feet and extended a hand toward the beaming giant and the flabbergasted Ramses. "Mighty grateful to you, mister."

The mountain man nodded as he shook the proffered hand. "Glad to be o' service, sir. I could sense you were a good man, and I could see how serious you wanted to live."

"It weren't fer myself. Heck, I done had a decent life. But the woman, it would've gone hard on her. This way I got a little more time to make some better plans."

"It's good for a man to have plans, Emmitt," said the giant.

Leaping lithely from the buckboard, the rancher loosened the reins from the hitching rail, climbed back aboard, and lifted his startled wife into the seat alongside him. She almost forgot to hand the cup back to Malone, following which her husband chucked the reins. Jerking forward, the buckboard rattled up the dirt road that led out of town, kicking up dust as it passed the seeping pump.

Ramses had forgotten all about the piece of eight. His attention was now riveted on the old wooden cup. "Might I have a look at that vessel, sir?"

"Don't see why not." The giant handed it over.

Ramses scrutinized it as minutely as he'd ever inspected a suspect coin, turning it over and over in his fingers, feeling the scars in the old wood, lifting it to smell of the interior. It reeked of old rooms, and dampness, and something he couldn't quite place. Some fragrance of a faraway land, and perhaps also a distant time.

With utmost reluctance he passed it back. "What potion did you have in that, sir, that brought that man back from the dead? For the country of the dead was surely where he was headed. I saw his skull. It was well stove in and his brains were glistening in the sunlight."

" 'Tweren't no potion." The mountain man walked back to his lunatic steed and casually returned the cup to the unsecured saddlebag from whence it had come. "That man wanted to live. Out o' love for another. That right there's a mighty powerful medicine. Mighty powerful. Didn't need but a little nudge to help it along."

"Yes, of course." Then it was no potion, Ramses thought furiously, but the cup itself, the cup! "Might I ask where you acquired that vessel?"

"What, the grail? Won it off the Shemad Bey, Pasha of Tripoli, durin' a game o' chess we played anon my last sojourn along the Barbary Coast. After he'd turned it over, the old Pasha confessed to me that it had been stolen many times afore comin' his way. So I didn't see that harm in relievin' him of its possession. I reckon it's better off in my care than his, anyways." He pulled the straps of the saddlebag through both buckles and notched them tight.

"Your pardon sir," said Ramses, "but did you say 'grail'?"

"That's right. Belonged long time ago to a feller name of Emmanuel. Took his last swallow from it, I believe."

"You are jesting with me, sir."

"Nope." The giant walked down the street, his mount trailing alongside with a notable air of equine indifference. "When I jest, I laugh, and when I laugh, rivers bubble and mountains shake. You don't see no rivers bubblin' or mountains shakin' hereabouts now, do you?"

"Sir, we stand in the plains of the Missouri. There are no mountains hereabouts, and the nearest river is the Meramec some twenty miles to the south."

"Why 'tis right you are. I reckon you'll just have to take my word for it then."

"Sir, would you consider selling that gr . . . that drinking vessel? I will make you a fine offer for it, in gold."

" 'Tain't for sale, friend. Fer one thing, I got plenty o' gold. Fer t'other, it wouldn't work for you nohows."

"And why not?"

"The grail, see, it don't do nothin' by itself. It's just a cup, an ordinary drinkin' cup. It's what's in the heart and the soul of whomever's drinkin' from it that makes a difference. Most times it don't make no difference. Sometimes it do. I was glad it did tonight, but you cain't never be sure." He halted and Ramses saw they were standing outside the blacksmith shop and stable.

"Now if you'll excuse me, friend, I've been three days and nights on the back of this lamentable alibi of a horse and I've a might o' sleepin' to catch up on." With that he turned and entered the stable. Emerging a few minutes later, he strode off down the street toward the town's single hotel, from whose attached saloon could imprecisely be heard the brittle jollities of a banjo player in shifty voice.

Ramses was left standing solitaire in the starlight, thinking hard. The giant would be a bad man to cross, he ruminated. He'd seen the heavy Sharps rifle protruding from its scabbard on the side of the saddle. But the Promethean rustic had neglected even to lock the stable! And he'd taken careful notice of the fact that there were no locks on the saddlebags, not even a knot. Just a couple of straps on each one.

But Ramses was no simpleton. He returned to his wagon and mounted the seat, chucking the reins and making as much noise as possible on his ostentatious way out of town. The mountain man had refused to sell him the cup, and that was that, and like the honest soul that he was he was moving placidly on.

A mile out of town he set up a hasty camp by the bank of a running stream, tethering one of his horses to a convenient cottonwood while hoping there were no acquisitive Indians or white men about. He made and drank some strong coffee, considered the night sounds and the stars, and round about three a.m. saddled up his other animal and rode quietly back into town.

The wooden buildings were shadowy now, the two saloons as silent as the distant church which dominated the far end of the main street. Dismounting outside the stable, he kept a wary eye on the distant hotel. The door hardly creaked as he edged it aside just enough to slip through. His excitement rose as through the dim light he saw that the mountain man's animal stood where he'd left it in the farthest stall.

Ramses could move fast when he needed to, whether running from irate fathers or official representatives of the law. He moved fast now, the straw hissing under his feet as he hurried to the far end of the building. The dozing horses and one mule ignored him.

Lifting the stall door as he opened it so the hinges wouldn't creak he stepped inside. Facing him, the improbably large quadruped filled the smelly enclosure from wall to wall. At the back of the stall the saddlebags lay draped across a pile composed of saddle and tack.

Turning sideways, he attempted to slip between the animal's mass and the unyielding stall panels.

"C'mon there, boy. Give us a little room. Move on over just a bit, won't you?"

Swinging its mottled face to cast a skewed eye at him, the ludicrous creature emitted a soft snort and promptly lowered its head to begin cropping at the straw underhoof.

"Come on, damn you!" Ramses put both hands on the animal's flank and shoved, bracing himself against the wall and putting all his weight into the effort. He might as well have been trying to convert a reluctant Jesuit.

Breathing hard, Ramses deposed on the four-legged barricade-to-his-intent a few choice non-medical terms. He bent and passed through the slats of the stall wall into the vacant stall next to it, then carefully slipped in again near the rear, taking care to keep an eye on the horse's oversized rear hooves. It continued to ignore him, wholly intent on the available fodder.

The saddlebag's straps yielded easily to his deft fingers. He'd filch the cup and be clean out of the county before morning.

Lifting the nap, he dug around inside until his hand closed over the unyielding wooden cylinder. Extracting his prize, he held it up to the available light. In the moonlight it was outstanding in its ordinariness, and for an instant he wondered if there were more than one of the vessels. That was absurd, he knew. There was only one of what he sought. Only one in all the world, and now it was his, his!

He turned it in his fingers, letting the moonlight play across the bowl and rim. So plain, he mused. So utterly unremarkable. It was slightly bigger than he remembered it, but then his first and only

previous view had been clouded by astonishment and the realiza-
tion of inherent possibilities.

His gaze narrowed. There was a hint of movement within the
vessel. Lingering water, or possibly some more viscous liquid.

Something crept out of the bowl to wrap itself around his left
wrist.

Startled, he inhaled sharply. At the sound of his soft gasp the
horse looked back wearily. Then it delivered itself of a decidedly
disinterested whinny and returned to its browsing.

A panicked Ramses tried to shake loose of the cup. He flung
his hand about wildly and banged the vessel against the back of the
stall. But the old wood was tough and the sinuous band around his
wrist was like a steel cable. It was gray in hue and ichorous and
glacier-wet. As he fought to extricate himself it began to snake further up his arm. With his free hand he fumbled frantically for the
derringer he kept always in his right shirt pocket. As he did so
he made rapid breathing sounds, like a dog after a long run, as he
struggled to scream but failed.

Before his wide, disbelieving eyes a second serpentine coil
emerged from the interior of the cup to wrap itself around his head,
blocking one of his eyes. It was cold and slick, cold as ice. The tip
forced itself past his clamped lips and down his throat. He started
to gag.

Tilted towards him, the depths of the cup revealed a pair of
eyes. They were about the size and shape of a sparrow's eggs,
bright red with little black pupils centered on fiery crimson. Of any
face they might front there was no sign. As he goggled madly two
more emerged below the first pair.

Then he saw that all four were all part of the same countenance, which he finally got a good look at. He did scream then, but
the sound was muffled by the tentacle swelling inside his throat,
and no one heard.

In the stalls across the way two dray animals, a mare and a
gelding, looked on motionlessly. Well, they were not quite motionless. Both were trembling violently and sweat was pouring down
their withers.

The mountain man's steed munched straw while ignoring the flailing, thrashing man who occasionally bounced off his hindquarters and legs.

More tentacles erupted from the abyssal depths of the cup, far more than it should have been able to hold. They lashed and bound the softly screaming, utterly desperate Mohet Ramses before they began to retract, dragging the unfortunate Doctor with them. As he didn't fit inside the bowl of the vessel nearly as efficiently, there ensued a great many cracking and rending noises as he was pulled in, until only his spasmodically kicking legs were visible protruding beyond the smooth rim. Finally they too vanished, and lastly his fine handmade shoes, and then he was all gone.

It was quiet again in the stable. Across from the silent stall the dray pair gradually ceased their shivering.

As the other guests looked on in fascination, Amos Malone rose early and ate breakfast enough for any three men. Then he made his way outside. A few other pedestrians were about. They glanced occasionally in his direction, but not always. Unusual men frequented the frontier, and Malone was larger but not necessarily more unusual than some the townsfolk had seen previously.

At the smithy he chatted awhile with the owner, then paid him his fee and entered the stable next door.

"Well, Worthless," he informed his steed as he set blanket and saddle on the broad back, "I promise you some oats first decent-sized town we hit. You look like you had an uneventful night." The stallion snorted at Malone as he cinched the saddle tight, shaking its head and mane.

The mountain man hefted the bulky saddlebags and prepared to secure them behind the heavy saddle. As he did so he noticed the cup, lying on its side in the dirt. Plonking the awkward load astride Worthless's butt he bent to pick up the stray vessel, considering it thoughtfully in the morning light. The old jet-black wood drew in the sunshine like a vampire sucking blood. With a sigh he moved to place it back in its container.

"Told him," he muttered. "That ain't the way it works. A smart man doesn't go foolin' around in another feller's kit." Reaching inside the near saddlebag, he pulled out a second cup and held it up to the light. The morning rays turned the burnished cedar the color of Solomon's gold, pure and radiant.

"Course, it didn't help him that he got ahold o' the wrong grail."

Storyville, Tennessee

— ✠ —

Richard Gilliam

Almost no one at Drake's Crossing remembers Billy Ray Colton. How one cold January morning in 1917 his mama dressed him warm and handed him a locket with her picture in it. How she cried as the family waved goodbye to the train, and how proud she felt that the town had mostly turned out to see her son go off to war. The Great War. The War to End Wars. The best of all possible wars. The war from which Billy Ray Colton never returned, indeed the war which he never reached, Billy Ray having been killed in a New Orleans whorehouse while waiting on a transport order to France to join General Pershing and the American Expeditionary Forces.

Please excuse that I have begun this tale by speaking of someone who is of no difference to the things that were to happen later. Such is as life often is. Things that seem important make very little difference at all, while the world continues to create directions of no apparent choosing whatsoever. At the time, all of Drake's Crossing mourned, and it was said that Billy Ray had died defending the honor of a lady, though, of course, this was merely something that was said, and not something that was true at all.

My tale would be much easier if the story that brought The Dandy to Drake's Crossing had been told to him by Billy Ray Colton, or even better still if the zombie I'll get to later had been Billy Ray himself. Alas, that is not what happened. The Dandy heard of the treasure cave from a drummer, and the zombie was

149

just an ordinary nigra who had had the misfortune to run afoul of Marie Laveau and her Crescent City domain.

You might think Billy Ray's death was important in making the Navy decide to close down Storyville, but it just is not so. The whorehouse where Billy Ray died was uptown, not in Storyville, one of the few brothels that operated outside the permitted area. No, the Navy closed down the Storyville District in the fall of 1917, and that is where this tale begins, Billy Ray having been cold dead four months at this happening. I will speak not again of Billy Ray Colton, and ask that you forget about him altogether. It is God's duty to remember such persons, His burden to grieve, His joy to forgive. God gives different tasks to each of us, and my charge is to tell the story that follows to those who would hear.

The Dandy was from one of the best families of Louisiana, New Orleans being a major provider of dandies in these days, Charleston long past having gone the way of decline. His daddy was in shipping, and his mama had been a beauty of some repute. She had died in childbirth, when The Dandy was five, and perhaps my tale would have no fool if she had lived to teach more to her son. It was about the time of his sister's presenting to cotillion that The Dandy began to frequent the environs of Storyville, and quickly became a favorite of the crib girls there, to say nothing of the madams who welcomed anyone with an easy purse and genteel manners.

While many travelers will tell you that Lulu White's Mahogany Hall was the most posh of all bordellos, The Dandy most often graced the house at 341 Basin Street, said house being under the careful management of Willie O. Barrera and staff. Neither elegant nor mannered, the house of Willie O. Barrera was known for its special trade, and The Dandy counted himself lucky to have known women of most races there, including an Oriental girl from distant China, having won at auction the right to be her deflowerer.

On one side of this house was a fire station. I mention it merely to let you know that Storyville in no way suffered from a lack of civic amenities. The entire purpose of Storyville was to set apart the cribs and the brothels from the decent parts of New Orleans, and such facilities as the firehouse evidenced the keeping of the pact between the city and the Storyville District.

Across the Conti Street side of the house, for 341 Basin Street had a favourable corner location, was the St. Louis Cemetery No. 1. Perhaps you have heard of this landmark, for it is the resting place of many persons who were famous in their time. Paul Morphy, the father of modern chess, lies there, as does Alexander Milne, the miser-philanthropist, after whom the Milneburg resort was named. Most folks will tell you that Marie Laveau has her tomb there, too, though this profaning of consecrated ground is denied by the more Christian persons of the area. The Dandy had been some few years too young to have met "The Queen of the Voodoos," but he felt great admiration for her, and smiled whenever he was present at the mentioning of her name.

Much makings had occurred concerning the possible closure of the Storyville District, but The Dandy, like most patrons of the houses, paid little mind to the threats. To close Storyville would be to open prostitution to the entire city, to allow harlots to ply their trade at large throughout the town. No city had yet discovered a way to eliminate its sporting life, and few thought the U.S. Navy would be so foolish as to abolish the sensible limits of Storyville. But such was the case, for on November 12, 1917, the U.S. government, once and forever, laid Storyville to rest.

The Dandy had been away to Galveston for some months when this ill-chosen act occurred, performing an errand his father had requested, performing it without enthusiasm, a simple messenger hand-delivering contracts to the port authority there. That he was meant for more than such menial tasks, The Dandy knew. He was meant for greatness, meant for importance, for such is the birthright of an only son born to wealthy parents. After a period of entertainment, The Dandy grew tired of the Mexican women who were the only even nominally exotic fare offered by the houses of the Texas coast, and thus he returned by direct freighter to New Orleans and to the house at 341 Basin Street.

A colder night New Orleans had not seen for many a November. The lack of persons on the street, thus, did not concern The

Dandy as he approached the door of the two-story house. His custom was to knock, for a gentleman always requested entrance when calling upon a lady, no matter how scarlet her profession. Rumor had it that Willie Barrera had purchased two Arab girls, sisters from a Turkish harem, such talent made all the more difficult to obtain these days, given Turkey's belligerent status in world affairs. The Dandy had had Arab girls on occasion, and preferred them above all others. Some unscrupulous madams would try to pass Jewish girls off as Arabs, but The Dandy could tell the difference—the Jewish girls lay there without passion, while the raven-haired Arab women welcomed you deeply into their firm embrace. I say this not to speak against Jewish girls, for I have heard they make good and loving wives, but such was the opinion of The Dandy that Jews made very poor courtesans, and he was far from alone in this opinion, such view being widely held in cosmopolitan cities such as New Orleans.

A thick, low bank of clouds dampened the light of the city. The Dandy heard the eye-slat of the wooden door open and close, followed by the welcoming creak of hinges inviting his entrance.

The parlor was dark, very dark, and it was here that The Dandy sensed much was amiss. Yet but a small hurricane lamp lit the parlor, its light much too inadequate for the large room.

"I knew'd you'd come," said the voice, and The Dandy instantly recognized his welcomer.

"Miss Lauren, how good to see you again," The Dandy replied, and though he smiled the smile of a gentleman, he much doubted the goodness of his greeting.

"They closed us down, the Navy did. The fools finally did it," said the woman.

"My goodness no," said The Dandy, with somewhat mock concern, confident that closed simply meant relocated. "And Willie? What of Willie? And the rest of the girls?"

"Don't know for sure. Not here. Just me here. I gots to stay. Some talk of moving uptown. Heard a few houses done that already. Not me though. I gots to stay here."

"Oh, Miss Lauren. You can move, too. Any madam would want you. Doesn't matter where the house is," said The Dandy.

"Yes it does," she replied. "Yes it does. . . ."

"The furniture—it's gone—Willie had it moved somewhere. Find out. Go there," said The Dandy, eager himself to know the new location.

"You don't understand. I gots to stay here. I gots to stay close to Marie."

"Laveau?" asked The Dandy, his customary smile absent from his face.

"She wants to meet you. You gots a task to do. For her, and for me."

"Marie is dead," said The Dandy.

"Marie ain't never been really dead," came the reply. "Can't be really dead since she give herself to the voodoos so many years ago. She don't move much no more, but I knows she ain't dead neither."

"Marie is dead," said The Dandy, this time more wishing it true than stating a fact.

"She wants to meet you, she does. I'll take you to her. Not too far, just under the street and into old St. Louis No. 1."

"Under the street?"

"Why, yes—a tunnel," Lauren replied. "Into Marie's parlor. Just a few steps, not far. Come, let's go."

"Wait," said The Dandy.

"Don't stall Marie, now. You knows she can put the big come hither on you if she needs to. Why do you think you came back from Galveston just now, came here first and on this day? You heard Marie call. Now don't make her expend herself to bring you to audience. She needs her strength, just like us all do. Now come."

The woman lifted the lantern, and for the first time The Dandy sensed the desolate barrenness of the house. Always before there had been piano music, and the soft cooing of the crib girls entreating the favour of the guests. The sounds of good times, the reassuring sounds of companions in sin, mutual venturers into the worlds of pleasure. The darkness glowered from all sides, and neither the ceiling nor the walls were at all distinct. He followed the light, and the silhouette of the woman, extending his hands to his side, so that he might touch some doorway or window, and perhaps reorient his sense of location in this house he had visited so often, but now which seemed alien and cold.

"Down here," said Lauren, motioning toward an unlit fireplace. "There's a small door in the rear."

The Dandy first thought of his clothes, and the soot in the fire-place, but as the door opened, his concerns focused at what lay at the tunnel's end.

"Marie . . . is there?" he asked, seeing that Lauren had entered the passageway.

"She's waiting for you," came the muffled reply. "Best to hurry now."

The Dandy's hands shook as he bent, grabbing the open door. A loud clang startled him, and he realized his foot had knocked over the grating at the edge of the fireplace.

"You want to wake the dead?" Lauren shouted. She was well into the tunnel now.

The woman's chuckle brought a shameful scorn to the visage of The Dandy. He would not be mocked by any woman, and he certainly would not allow himself to be ridiculed by a whore. Disregarding his fear, he stepped strongly into the tunnel, only to feel his feet slide from under him as he did.

The woman did not notice, or at least did not acknowledge his fall. Righting himself, The Dandy was surprised to find he could stand in the passage. The walls were of fine masonry, and both sides of the floor were lined with sandbags, absorbing what little moisture seeped through.

"Marie's magic keeps it dry," said Lauren, standing some few feet away. "Marie's magic and the best masons in New Orleans. Marie always did say you shouldn't rely only on magic. Nothing wrong with bricks and mortar."

The Dandy saw the woman smile, and relaxed as she did. Indeed, he thought, the magic of the dry tunnel was mostly in the quality of its construction. The water table was high in New Orleans, but even so, some shallow underground construction was possible, though drainage for spring floods was always needed.

"We're almost there. Step up." Lauren said, holding her lantern so as to shine onto a slight stairway.

No door blocked the tunnel's end, and The Dandy could see Lauren's light casting toward an open room.

"Marie's chambers," said Lauren. "I'll light us some candles."

There is a dread of which men do not speak, and of which most hope not to feel, or, at least, not to allow others to know that they feel. The Dandy now felt such a dread, and if I say that his heart was barely up to the challenge, please do not think that I mean to name him a coward, for I have said to you already that he was a fool, and there is many a dead fool who wishes he had instead been born a coward.

No, the death that comes to us all was not to yet come to The Dandy, indeed, if it had, this tale would be much the shorter, and you would have to find some other way to hear of the cave The Dandy was soon to visit, and of the wonderful treasure he would find there.

The Dandy knew none of this, not even the drummer's tale he would hear later this same night. For him, each candle brought forth a new terror. A feather at the first, a cross at the second, a book at the third, a portrait at the fourth, a cabinet of vials at the fifth, and then, and then . . .

As Lauren lighted the sixth candle, the corpse of a large negro male, standing erect, came into view.

"My brother," she said. "He's why I gots to stay. So you can help him."

"Your brother?" The Dandy asked. "You're so much . . ."

"Lighter skinned?" Lauren completed the question. "Yes. I am lighter skinned. We had different fathers. Luke's father was black, a slave. My father once owned our mother. . . ."

"You're so young—that war was fifty years ago. . . ."

"So it was," Lauren replied. "Like I said, I gots to stay."

"Your brother," The Dandy said. This time the words were not a question.

Lauren cast her head downward. "Luke. He don't belong here. Even Marie say so. Luke, he just trying to do good and ended up finding bad. I *knew* I was doing bad. Luke was just trying for my sake."

She paused. "Marie's candle is the biggest."

As the light from the seventh candle filled the room, The Dandy gasped—Marie, her face dried and twisted, dressed in her purple finest and sitting upon a great chair, elevated from the floor by a sturdy platform of finished wood.

"Luke, he guards Marie," said Lauren. "Except now he'll be guarding you."

The Dandy's body shuddered, though his sight stayed fixed upon the two corpses.

"I've promised Marie I'd tend to her. Drains Marie a lot, keeping an undead at her call. She wants you to take my brother. Let him be your manservant. Let him watch over you," Lauren added.

"Guard . . . me?" said The Dandy. Words came not easy to his mouth.

"Marie says you'll know what to do. Says you always figured you gots a special greatness ahead of you. Luke here is a gift. It's what I made Marie promise. Luke's freedom, if I takes care of her. Always."

"How can Luke be free if he's mine?" asked The Dandy, regaining a measure of composure.

"Luke's a gift to me, not you," snapped Lauren. "I just asked him to help you. Marie says it's best for everyone if he does."

"Helps me do what?"

"I guess Marie knows. At least for now just take him as your servant. Most white folks would like a servant what don't talk back." She grinned.

"And you?"

"Like I said. I tends Marie. Harder by the year to keep this place safe. Marie used to protect all of Storyville, but she's grown weak lately, weak since they been trying to put a stop to us all. . . ."

"The Navy?"

"The Navy don't believe in Marie. If they did, she might hold some power over them. The Navy just believe in its own self. Too much for Marie to stop them when they decided to close Storyville." Lauren sighed.

"How long?"

"Who knows?" Lauren replied. "Now that you come, I'll close the house. Marie can keep her chambers here without too much trouble. People still come and leave offerings—upstairs at her marker. She gets new powers when they does. Or at least stronger old ones. Marie will last. Don't you worry 'bout Marie and me."

The Dandy nodded. "Your brother—anything I need to know? Keep him out of the sun, maybe?"

"He can go in the sun, though like anyone else, his skin'll burn if you keep him there too long," answered Lauren. "No need to feed him, and since he's not bound to you, Marie's enchantment should last long enough."

"Enchantment?" The Dandy coughed as he spoke.

"What Marie done. How he be this way."

"How did he get to be this way?"

"Trying to save me," Lauren sighed. "Big fool came off the farm and thought he could save his sister from being a whore. Marie didn't take too kindly to losing her students. Always promised, though, that she'd let him go free someday."

Lauren stopped, and looked toward the portrait. "I made the promise more attractive. Marie needs me to tend to her, and I need Marie just to stay alive."

The Dandy looked at Marie, then to Lauren's brother, and then at the woman. "Why should I take him?"

"Because Marie asked you to, and because you know you've always admired Marie."

"And what am I to do?"

"Marie says you'll find out." Lauren grinned. "Marie's not wrong about such things."

A smile came across the face of The Dandy. "Yes. The truthfulness of Marie's powers are well known."

"I needs to tell you. There more forces at work than you

knows. I made Marie promise me my brother would be free. Not just free from this place, but free from the enchantment, too. Don't know what that means to you, but Marie tells me you may find something valuable, sort of as payment for your troubles."

The smile grew bigger. "Something valuable." He grinned wide. "Just like I thought. A fortune of my own. No more having to ask my father every time I need money."

"Could be," the woman replied. "Marie don't really say. Just that something you may find may be valuable."

The Dandy looked again at the nigra, and then at his sister.

"He's already wearing livery," she said. "He'll do whatever you ask, but, remember, he's free to go his own way. Ask his help and you'll get more than if you order him around."

"I'll treat him well."

"Marie knows that. That's why she picked you—that and how you was always smiling when her name was mentioned. Marie likes you, too."

The Dandy smiled. "Shall we go?"

"You and Luke go. I gots to stay. Luke, he sees in the dark real good. Just follow him and he'll gets you out safe."

"And then?"

"And then you be choosing what to do for yourself. Marie can't follow you. She needs to keep her powers for this place. Would weaken her too much to see something what's far from here. That come hither she put to Galveston wore her down. Maybe the last big spell she could cast."

"And how do I know what to choose?"

"Fool question," snarled Lauren. "Fool question from a fool. Now go. Luke will lead you. Leave Marie and me alone."

For the remainder of the night, The Dandy and his newfound manservant wandered aimlessly, first through the French Quarter, then by the docks, until finally, just before dawn, The Dandy found himself outside one of the few taverns in the Crescent City of which he had not previously been a patron.

"Caleb's Beacon," he muttered, reading the hand-lettered wooden sign. "Clarence Jefferson, proprietor."

The Dandy looked to his companion, and wondered what to do with him. The huge negro turned away, walked a few steps, and sat by the curb. Satisfied with this solution, The Dandy entered the establishment through the partially opened door.

As I said, it was near dawn, and The Dandy was much attracted by the smell of bacon and eggs, which wafted from the building. For a person whose nature was much that of a rake, The Dandy was not possessed by the demon alcohol, though he had more than sufficient vices to compensate.

A gruff-looking man stood to the rear of the room, near doors that The Dandy took to be those of the kitchen. The man glanced indifferently toward The Dandy, gestured toward a corner table, and waited.

"Bacon and eggs," said The Dandy, as he walked across the room to his seat. The host nodded, then turned and entered the kitchen.

The Dandy looked at the other tables. Only three were occupied. Two well-dressed men sat together in the far corner, and The Dandy took them to be merchants. Two more sat at a table near the door. They wore the garb of longshoremen. A gray-haired portly man sat at a small table near the center of the room. His dress coat was much too tight, and his tie matched poorly his food-stained shirt.

"Good morning, sir." The portly man spoke, then took a sip of coffee.

"Good morning," said The Dandy, trying to sound uninterested.

"Up early we are today. Like I say, got to be up early to get ahead in the world." The man smiled.

The Dandy nodded.

"May I join you?" he asked, not waiting for a reply. "My name's Wally. Wally, King of the Child Book Salesmen. Oh, don't worry, I'm not trying to sell the Child Book to you. Doubt you have any children. Am I right?"

The Dandy winced. "I am not married."

"Well, Wally is rarely wrong about who's a Child Book customer and who isn't. Fine thing, the Child Book. If you have children someday, you can look me up then. Let's share a breakfast now."

The Dandy started to object, but as he began, the kitchen doors opened. The gruff man, looking even more gruff than before, placed two plates of breakfast on The Dandy's table.

"Best bacon and eggs in New Orleans," Wally said, taking his fork in hand. "Can't fix gumbo worth crap, but I sure do come here for breakfast when I'm in town."

"Where are you from?" asked The Dandy.

"All over, truly. Well, all over the Southeast, anyway. Come from Virginia to start with, but I've been from California to Florida in my time."

"I mean, where is home now?"

"Don't have a home," sighed Wally. "Atlanta, I guess. That's where the Child Book home office is. I only go there for sales conferences, though. Don't sell too many Child Books sitting in sales meetings."

"I can understand," said The Dandy, finding small talk a strain.

"See a lot when you travels, you do. Seen it all, from the Rough Riders down in Tampa to the big quake in Frisco in '06. Yep, ole Wally been around a bit."

"President Roosevelt and the Rough Riders?"

"Yep. Sold a Child Book to old Teddy himself, except he wasn't president yet, of course. Luckiest thing that ever happened to me, maybe. Got a picture of Teddy reading the Child Book. Sure did sell a lot of Child Books for me over the years."

"That was a lucky sale," said The Dandy.

"Sure was. About the only other lucky break I got was finding my way out of the mountains one winter when I got lost up in Tennessee."

"You got lost in the Smokies?"

"Sure did. Was trying to get from Chattanooga back to Virginia, and was fool enough to try to drive my own wagon. Got lost something fierce, just as a big winter storm headed in. Thought I was dead for sure, snowbound in the mountains."

"What happened? How did you get out?"

"Strangest thing. I found this cave. My horses had run off, so I left the wagon and started traveling in the snow. Headed east, toward the sunrise, figuring that was as good a plan as any. Headed up this mountain. Knew there weren't nothing I could reach on the side of it I was on, so I was hoping to get up high where maybe I could see a town if the storm cleared."

"Smart thinking," said The Dandy, growing more interested.

"Thanks." Wally smiled. "Didn't work like I thought, though. The sun stayed in one place, instead of passing overhead like it ought to. Weren't no sun at all, but a fire set in the mouth of a cave. Some hunter's fire, I guess. Never knew for sure. Got myself warm, first thing, then slept though the night, and the storm was gone by morning."

"You were lucky."

"Yes. I was, but the strange part was still to come. I was still lost, remember. And there wasn't a road or a town in sight."

"So, what happened?"

"Well, the fire was burning low, and I had no food anyway. Water certainly wasn't a problem, since I could easily melt a little snow. Seemed to me like I had no choice. I could be warm, and starve to death, or take my chances in the snow."

"Obviously, you made it to safety."

"Yes, I did. But not like you think. I set out in the snow, and quickly was just as lost as I had been before. Doubled back on my own tracks a couple of times, so I knew I wasn't getting nowhere. It was near night, and I was lucky the wind hadn't covered up where I'd walked, but it hadn't, so I made it back to the cave."

"Was there still a fire?"

"Barely. Just warm embers, really. And no dry wood handy. Not a broken limb in sight."

"What about your wagon? Wasn't it made of wood?"

"The wagon was too far, and I probably couldn't have found it, anyway."

"Bet you were pretty hungry," said The Dandy, looking at the two plates with their uneaten food.

"Hungry is too mild a word. I was starving, literally. Fortunately, I was also tired. The wind was hard, so I went a good bit deeper into the cave, where the cold wasn't so bad. Fell asleep real easily."

"What next, Wally?" The Dandy asked.

"Funniest thing. I thought I'd died the next morning. Woke up smelling coffee. Food, too. I guess the hunters had come back in the night and rebuilt the fire. The sun was full up when I woke. Mountain types aren't known to wait at a place much after dawn. They were gone, but they'd left a pot of coffee and a pan of grits."

"Did you follow their tracks?"

"Weren't no tracks. The snow had come again, and I was pretty much back where I was two days before, except I was warm and had eaten a little."

"So you waited? They came back?"

"Waiting made sense. The fire was warm and the storm was bad. The next night I slept by the fire, so they'd see me if they returned, but they didn't."

Wally sipped his coffee, then continued. "It was right before dawn, when a dog started licking my face. Attracted by the warmth of the fire, I suppose. Don't know, really. Right friendly hound, the big sort of dog that a hunter might use. I petted him, and he wagged his tail real good, so I knew he liked me. Didn't have nothing better to do, so I followed the dog out of the cave, hoping he'd lead me to the hunters. He took me to the town, instead, a little place called Drake's Crossing. Stayed there a couple of days until the storm broke, then went on my way."

"Sounds like quite an adventure. What happened to the hound?" asked The Dandy.

"Don't rightly know. Didn't much think about him at the time, once I saw the town. Got myself to the first house and collapsed. Fortunately, it was the pastor's home, and he had a guest room. Slept nearly a day, I did, before I got up."

The Dandy nodded. "You were lucky."

"Maybe not," said Wally. "I missed finding the treasure there. Seems there's a legend about the cave. It gives treasure to people according to their worth. My worth was to be left alive. . . ."

"The world needs Child Book salesmen, Wally. Maybe the cave knew that," said The Dandy, only mocking his companion slightly. There was no doubt in The Dandy's mind that he would soon be visiting Tennessee.

"Well, you may be right," said Wally. "I'd like to think there are better families in the world now, because I sell them the Child Book. Wish I'd taken the time to have a family."

"Anything more about the cave? It's pretty easy to find once you get to Drake's Crossing?"

"The locals seemed to think so, at least. Most of them go there once. Some find old coins, or a doll, or an Indian bow. There's supposed to be the ruins of a settler house nearby, though I never seen it."

"Any really big finds?"

"They say the best find what they're looking for deep in the caves. Hard to say, since I didn't go there on a treasure hunt. You know how legends go. Probably someone found a silver dollar up there one day and the story got bigger every time it was told. That sort of thing."

"Most likely so, Wally." The Dandy had heard enough. He thought of Marie and of the cave, and he smiled. "That's a real fine story you told, but we got eggs getting cold here. Think it's time for us to eat."

The Dandy was surprised to find that the train connected into Drake's Crossing. A spur line, really, used mostly for logging, but with passenger service out of Chattanooga. Luke was little trouble. He purchased two private passages, one for himself, and one in the colored's car, much to the amazement of the ticket clerk, who knew that only the really great gentlemen of the day purchased private passage for their servants.

Luke never questioned or complained, but The Dandy was well

aware that Luke *could* choose a separate path, so he was most careful to treat the negro well. While a servant is a convenience to a gentleman when he travels, a servant that can see in the dark is a more than considerable asset when exploring a cave, and The Dandy took special care to thank Luke each time he toted their bags, or performed some other task.

When they arrived at the station at Drake's Crossing, The Dandy was concerned to see the expression on Luke's face had changed. Not for the worse, really, since Luke now occasionally smiled, but The Dandy had become accustomed to his companion's stoic manners, and seeing Luke react favorably to his surroundings made The Dandy uncomfortable.

Drake's Crossing had a hotel of sorts, a series of small cabins, used by tourists come to visit the Appalachians. When The Dandy inquired about separate accommodations for coloreds, he was told the town had neither coloreds, nor housing for them, and that his servant was welcome to stay in the same cabin as The Dandy.

Few things surprise a gentleman who comes from a town so wicked as New Orleans, let alone one who only short days ago stood himself in front of the queen of the voodoos. The innkeeper quickly noticed the look of astonishment on the face of The Dandy, and the increasing smile on the face of his otherwise gaunt companion. Slavery was rare in the mountains, explained the innkeeper, and few negroes had moved into the area after the war. The reason was partially economic—slaves were useful on plantations, of which the area had none—but also the reason was partially the personality of the area. Mountain people valued the independence their isolation gave them, and the attempts to use slaves as loggers had failed badly the few times it had been tried.

The Dandy bore not so greatly the bigotries of his kind. The prejudice he felt in his heart was one of arrogance toward the poor. He thought far less of white trash than of colored, since the colored had the burden of their skin to keep them from the better-paying jobs. Perhaps the racial ambivalence of the bordellos had had some ameliorating effect. The Dandy had known many women of color, and had shared a game of cards or dice often with their men.

He spent no time at all in the cabin, having brought with him from New Orleans hiking clothes, torches, and digging implements. He had no rope. Were he to need rope he could surely buy some.

Although The Dandy wished to avoid suspicion, he nonetheless felt he could trust the innkeeper enough to ask nonchalantly if there were walking trails or caves in these mountains. The answer was yes to both, and conveniently, there was a marked trail which ran near the latter. And thus, though night was approaching, The Dandy and his companion set off to find the cave.

Need I tell you that come the dark The Dandy lost the trail, and that he insisted to Luke that they go north, when Luke could see the pathway went east? To ask directions is not enough in life. One must not ignore that which is true, nor ignore those who see more clearly. Alas, such is the way of the fool, to deny that which has been shown—though, in truth, I know there to be some fool in us all.

The night was cold, very cold, and the coat The Dandy wore was only a little successful in keeping him warm. Fearful of the many rocks and sharp cliff-faces, The Dandy found a wind-protected niche, and slept a sleep of sorts, as best he could.

Luke stood nearby, unconcerned with the cold. He faced the east, as though he was confident of what would come, and it was only by chance that The Dandy was awake when first dawn came.

The early glow of the morning cast an amber brightness onto the mountain, and was soon replaced by the bright yellow of the sun. As the sun came to view, Luke began to walk, with the air of confidence which comes all too seldom to those of low birth.

The Dandy followed. What else was he to do? Maybe an hour passed, as the negro led the way up the mountain.

Luke reached the cave first, The Dandy having steadily fallen more behind. Luke waited, and then waited some more when The Dandy asked if he could rest before they entered.

Whatever was in the cave would still be there a few minutes later, The Dandy reckoned, drinking the last of the water in his canteen. Luke nodded, and pointed into the cave.

The Dandy rose, noticing the natural light stopped maybe seventy feet into the mouth. He lit a torch, and Luke winced when the flame leaped near his face. The Dandy stepped forward, and soon was well into the passageway.

Luke lumbered along, much more slowly than he had walked when finding this place. The cavern had turned twice, and they were well past any glimpse of the sun.

The Dandy charged ahead until the passageway split. Intuitively, he waited on Luke, who selected the pathway to the right without hesitation. About ten paces forward, Luke stopped and bent to the ground.

The Dandy's heart beat with excitement as he saw Luke's hand take hold of something from the floor. Luke turned, holding the item for The Dandy to see. It was a bird, a dove of some sort, and The Dandy was sorely disappointed that the find had been so slight.

Luke placed the object in the knapsack, and began walking again. Another passage split occurred, this time with three choices. Luke entered the middle one, and again stopped after ten steps or so. He bent, picked up a small metal cross, and held it near the face of his companion.

Though the item held no particular value, The Dandy sensed that they were coming closer to finding better treasure. Luke moved onward, weaving between several narrow boulders, and finally climbed up a hole in the roof.

The Dandy remarked to himself at how dry the caves were, then thought this made sense, given that water most often flowed down a mountain, rather than accumulated near the top. He followed Luke up into the hole, struggling with his torch as he did.

Luke had already found the next object, and The Dandy laughed aloud when he saw it was a copy of the Child Book. The Dandy thumbed through it, found one of Wally's business cards, then handed the book back to Luke.

Luke smiled, then added the book to the other objects he was carrying. They walked a ways, took another passage, and stopped.

The fourth object was more deeply buried, and The Dandy

wondered how well Luke could dig into the hardened floor. Luke's hands were strong, and it took but a few moments to unearth the tiny object.

The Dandy's heart stopped, then started again. He knew the locket before Luke opened it, knew that it was the locket he had carelessly lost just after his twelfth birthday, knew before Luke opened it that the locket would contain a picture of his long-dead mother.

The Dandy cried, and felt very, very alone.

Luke paused, and sat on a large outcropping, several feet above the floor. He moved not to comfort his distressed companion, but neither did he abandon him, and so they stayed there for hours, though how many I cannot say.

After a time, The Dandy's sobs lessened, as if he had no tears left in his body. He did not sleep, but neither did he rise, lying stressfully upon the cave's floor.

What he thought in those hours, I am not to say, for there are burdens so powerful that to know them can destroy a person. I may tell you, however, that after a great time had passed The Dandy did a remarkable thing. He reached deep within himself, found his strength, regained his composure, and stood.

Luke arose also, and once again began his walk. The Dandy stepped more surely now, more confident of his purpose. Another ceiling hole loomed ahead, and The Dandy scarcely gave Luke time to clear his feet before grabbing the rim.

The fifth object lay covered in damp silt. It was a fairly good-sized trunk, and when he opened it, The Dandy found a great many interesting objects inside. There were chains and locks, and keys to open the locks, and some locks which were open and could not be closed. There were toys from his childhood, and trophies from his school days. There were model ships of all sorts—racing ships and ocean liners, cargo vessels, and a very pretty sailing boat that bore the name *Lauren* on the side. The Dandy marveled at this great find, felt some of the warmth return to him he had lost while lying on the cavern's floor.

He found a small cup, which bore his name, and which he remembered using as a toddler. He smiled as he turned to show the find to Luke, but the negro was gone.

Hurriedly, The Dandy arose, dashing into the dark. His torch burned dim, and he fell hard as he tripped over an unseen hole.

The Dandy righted himself, seeing that the torch had fallen downward into the next level. He started to climb after it, but hesitated. The drop to the next floor was long, and he could see well enough to tell that once he descended, he would be unable to reenter the upper chamber.

Luke had not gone that way, of this The Dandy was certain, for he had heard no sound which surely a jump of this sort would cause. He could go to the chest, and wait on Luke's possible return, or he could proceed forward, and hope to catch up. Attempting to recover the torch was out of the question if he were to rejoin his companion.

The light from the bottom of the pit provided a mark point, by which The Dandy judged his progress moving along the cave's floor. On his knees he crawled, and more than once he jammed his fingers onto sharp rocks.

The pit was long behind him now, and he could feel a choice of passages ahead of him. The Dandy took none of them, instead standing and raising his hands toward the ceiling. He found a grip, and raised himself upward.

The chamber was large, and a radiant light came from the distant end. There, in front of a glowing mirror, stood Luke. The Dandy ran, his feet sure along the path.

Luke glanced at The Dandy's approach, and turned again toward the mirror. The reflection was that of a younger Luke, full of vitality and charm. In one part of the mirror The Dandy saw Luke as a infant, nursing at his mother's breast. In another was Luke in the Bayou, fishing for supper, and in yet another was Luke helping to birth a foal. At the center of the mirror was Lauren, and she smiled warmly at her brother. Luke smiled back, gazing into her eyes, watching sadly as a dark mist swept her away.

The mirror went blank, though the glow remained. Luke motioned for The Dandy to take his place.

Though you and I know clearly this is what The Dandy should have done, we must temper our judgment of him by wondering if we would want to face ourselves so fully. I have said to you that The Dandy was a fool, and perhaps his failure is mitigated somewhat if I tell you that this was to be the last foolish act he would ever commit. We have all missed opportunities we should have taken, and it was The Dandy's regret to pass this one by.

Luke sighed, and placed his arms around his companion. Tears came to the big man's eyes, as he held The Dandy next to his chest. He looked at his friend and smiled, pointing to the center of three doors.

As the pair stepped through the entrance, a most marvelous sight appeared. A woman, in flowing robes and wearing a tiara, beckoned them toward her. In her hand she held a bowl, and The Dandy knew he had never seen a more wonderful sight. Light filled the room, and the smell of roses drifted through the air.

She handed the bowl to Luke, and The Dandy could see the transformation from within. Those impurities which remained within Luke turned to smoke, and were drawn down to the floor, absorbed into the rock. A glow, not unlike that of the woman, came from within Luke, and The Dandy cried at the beauty of the sight.

Luke looked to The Dandy, and then to the woman, but she gave no sign. Turning, he handed the cup to The Dandy.

A light came over The Dandy, as it had over Luke. Alas, the light could reach no farther into The Dandy than he himself had seen, so the transformation was only partially completed. Much smoke swirled, and made its way from him, so much so, that Luke had to step back, lest he cough. The Dandy thought he might feel a great burden lifted, but instead, he became aware of the greatness of the burden which remained within him.

The woman stepped forward and took the cup from the hands of The Dandy. "Not now," she said, understandingly. "Not yet."

The Dandy nodded, though he could no longer see the woman or see Luke. A light filled his eyes, obscuring all else.

"Not yet," he heard once more, as the smell of roses drifted away.

* * *

Almost no one at Drake's Crossing remembers The Dandy.
How one cold November morning in 1917 he wandered out of the
mountains, blind and starving, lost in the sun, saved by the caring
of those who found him, and by the story he gave to them in return. . . .

Somewhere in Her Dying Heart

✛

Lisa Lepovetsky

Somewhere in her dying heart she tastes
the hearths laid waste by the seven who soar
on leathery wings, spawning darkness and death
like mutated seed from their blackened thighs.
She's known forever what she must do, and plucks
her tongue from her head, then her eyes.

She wails from the lindens and ash as virgin snow
laces through the wood to cover her naked toes,
and she dances in the dark to keep her soul
from freezing to stone. She parts her lips
as an owl rips the beating heart from a hare

and she imagines her husband, her king, as he
wastes, protected, in his magnificent granite tomb
on the cliffs behind her, sunset bleeding
across the skies like the ragged gash a lance
tore through the pale muscled thighs she loves.

She shudders, and a cold red tear struggles
to her chin. But colder anger keeps the promise
burning in her womb. She waits. The seven come
at last, icy shards blasting her like glass,
but she is ready and the deadly questions spatter

from her ruined lips like shot, pelting them with
truths that sear and bubble through their veins
until their faces split like overripe pods.
She tastes the ichor of their blood, and drinks
their life from the bony chalices they leave behind.

Hell-Bent for Leather

─────────── ✠ ───────────

Jeremiah E. Phipps

Walter sat in the leather bar, nursing his beer.

All around him people strutted their tough stuff. The music was loud and the air was heavy with cigarette smoke. Leather-clad people were laughing, dancing, flirting.

Normally, it was his kind of place, his favorite bar in Tampa, as a matter of fact. Not tonight. He was distracted. He pressed the cold bottle of beer against his forehead and closed his eyes.

It hadn't been his fault. He wasn't even moving. The truck backed into him. Simple.

Not simple. It was his second crunched cab this month. They didn't even apologize when they fired him. At least they could have made up some story about insurance rates to soften the blow. But, no. It was goodbye, Walter, and out the door. Sure, he had some money saved up, but he was dead in Tampa as a cabby. He opened his eyes.

Someone had sat down on the stool next to him. She was sitting backwards, leaning against the bar, legs crossed, one foot swinging in time with the music as she watched the crowd. She was a killer.

Short leather skirt, bare midriff. Her gently heaving embonpoint was barely concealed by a leather bra that was mostly straps and open places. Red hair and green eyes.

She turned to Walter and smiled, instantly breaking his heart and almost, but not quite, driving the image of his crushed cab from his troubled mind.

"Nice jacket," she said.

Walter suddenly realized that he was still wearing his cabby outfit. The scarred-up leather jacket, while comfortable, was not nearly as fashionable as his usual leather-bar attire. And his faded jeans and scuffed boots were not exactly high-class. He blushed, and stammered something that came out more like a croak than words. She didn't seem to mind, and her friendly green eyes locked onto him with interest.

"I've seen you in here before," she said. "What's your name?"

"Walter Johns," he said, extending a suddenly sweaty hand that she took in a soft, but firm handshake. "Do I know you?"

"I doubt it," she said. "Every time I've been in here before I've been with my ex-boyfriend. He's 6'10' and 320 pounds. Most people don't look much past that, if you know what I mean. But Mr. Bubba King is history now. I don't need that kind of grief in my life. Oh, I forgot, my name is Moon."

Walter tried to hide the involuntary laugh, but it escaped anyway. The twinkle in her eyes, if anything, increased.

"I'm sorry," Walter said. "But what kind of a name is Moon?"

"My parents were flower children in the 60's, and they named me Moonlet. Everybody calls me Moon, and I'm used to it by now. Hey, it could have been worse. They could have named me after a body part."

Walter choked back another laugh and started coughing. Moon reached over and thumped him on the back.

"Let's get out of here," she said.

"What?"

"I don't feel like drinking or dancing. This place reminds me of Bubba. You got a car? Let's go to the beach."

Walter left his unfinished beer on the bar along with a dollar tip.

"This is a car?" asked Moon as she climbed into the passenger side.

"Nash Metropolitan," Walter said. "You don't see many of these babies anymore."

"We're not going to see this one long, either," she said. "Every fender you got here is busted all to pieces and it looks like someone with heavy boots has been dancing on the roof."

"Not my fault," Walter said. "Things just seem to happen to me. Be sure and slam the door. It's a little bent, and won't close unless you slam it hard."

They drove down Curlew Road, across Causeway Boulevard to the far end of Honeymoon Island, past the scattered houses to the deserted beach. The moon was low on the horizon, and the water lapped gently on the sand.

They took their shoes off and walked slowly up and down the beach, turning shells over with their toes as they spilled the dark secrets of their souls and bared their hearts to one another. Ospreys drifted silently overhead. Walter was amazed that Moon was so easy to talk with, and so open, too. After she had shucked her clothes and taken a quick skinny-dip, Walter felt bold enough to hold her hand. She did not pull her soft, warm hand away from his.

It turned out that they were both unemployed and facing a bleak and uncertain future. They shared this dismal fate together, without benefit of unemployment compensation.

For Moon had been a secretary and research assistant for her ex-boyfriend Bubba, who, in spite of his mammoth size, had an unexpected literary bent, editing a soft-core pornographic wrestling magazine. Moon's job had ended the moment she refused to let him demonstrate the Hungarian Choke Hold on her in their bedroom. She was penniless, destitute, and out on the streets.

They sat on the beach to watch the sun go down. Walter risked putting his arm around her. She turned to him, her green eyes serious.

"So how long you been into leather?" she whispered in a deep, lusty voice.

Walter was drifting with the nearness of her. Her sweet smell was mixed with the soft scent of leather and the tang of the salt water. He closed his eyes, and thought back to his childhood.

"Sandy Amoros," he said dreamily.

"What?"

"Last game of the 1955 World Series. Yogi Berra hit a long drive to the left field fence. Sandy ran for it and made an unbelievable catch. Stole a three-run homer and turned it into an easy double play. Saved the game and the Series. The ball hit his Wilson A2000 glove with a solid thunk you could hear around the world. They called it *The Catch* from that day on. It was the only World Series the Brooklyn Dodgers ever won. I've been into leather ever since the ball hit his glove."

"Hey! Just how old *are* you?" she asked, pulling away just a little bit. "Were you there?"

"No," he said, his eyes still closed. "I've never been to New York. But I've seen the play a thousand times on ESPN. You don't have to be present at a miracle to know when one happens. Maybe someday I'll meet him."

"Excuse me," said Moon. "I'm not much of a baseball fan, but I do believe Mr. Amoros is dead. He had that sugar disease like my friend Wanda. I always read stories about the sugar disease."

"That's what he'd like you to believe," said Walter. "A lot of celebrities fake their deaths when the glare of the spotlight gets too bright. Elvis and Mama Cass come to mind right away."

"I always wondered what really happened to Cass Elliot," Moon said in a faraway voice, snuggling closer. "Such a beautiful voice."

Baseball. Walter could taste the popcorn and peanuts. Feel the soft leather glove. They held each other in a chaste embrace. They kissed, lightly and gently. She tasted of salt with the hint of spearmint chewing gum.

"Look," he said, lost in his dream.

The sun was setting on the Gulf. As the last part of it slid into the water a green flash split the sky like a laser going off. At that instant two Navy jets flew down the beach about ten feet above their heads.

"Wow!" Moon said.

"Did you hear it?" Walter asked, his ears ringing from the thunder of the jets.

"What?" she said, slapping her ear. "I can't hear a thing."

"It was a message," he said.

"What?" she shouted.

"A message," he yelled.

"From who?" she bellowed. "Or is it whom?"

"Sandy Amoros," he roared, grabbing her hand. "He needs his glove. We've got to go."

She stumbled to her feet. "Where are you taking me?" she shouted.

"New York," he thundered. "The Big Apple."

Their hearing came back to normal about the time they hit the I-95 cutoff at Daytona Beach and headed north.

"This is crazy," Moon said. "We're chasing a dead man."

"No," said Walter. "Editing pornographic wrestling magazines is crazy. Getting your jollies with the Hungarian Choke Hold is crazy. What we are doing is noble and decent."

"What's so noble about finding the glove Sandy Amoros used in the 1955 World Series?"

"I told you what he said to me."

"And I still think it was nothing but your ears ringing from the jets."

"No, it was a vision, a true vision. *I have lost it, and you will find it.* Sandy spoke to me, as clearly as you are now."

"I must be mumbling," she said.

"What?"

"I must be hungry," she said.

With a screech, Walter swung the Nash Metropolitan off an exit, shedding both side mirrors in the process. He pulled into the drive-in window of the nearest fast-food joint.

"Can't we go in?" Moon asked.

"No time," said Walter. "Every second counts."

"Welcome to Rancho Deluxe," said the plastic cowboy hat through its rusted speaker grill. "May I take your order?"

"I'll take two Big Daddy Burgers and a side order of ribs. Five cups of black coffee. Lots of extra napkins." He turned to Moon. "What do you want?"

"They got salads?" she asked.

"Eat some real food," Walter said. "We got a long drive ahead of us."

"I'm a vegetarian," she said softly.

"What?"

"I don't eat meat. It's a matter of principle."

"You wear leather, but you don't eat meat?"

She nodded, and blushed. He grinned. He knew at that moment he was in love for sure.

"Throw some rabbit food in there too," he yelled to the plastic cowboy hat. "One of every salad you got."

As they drove north, they tossed the empty bags and drink cups into what passed for a backseat in the tiny car. Somewhere around the turnoff to Flagler Beach the back bumper fell off the Nash. As it did, Walter winked at Moon and floored his mighty steed, which topped out at 62 miles per hour, thanks to the lost weight, a generous tail wind, and a tank of high-test.

"I've never been north of Jacksonville," Moon said, chewing on a carrot as they sputtered through the darkness. "Can we stop at Savannah? I read something about that town once in a book."

"No time," said Walter, pulling the plastic lid off another cup of black coffee. "We got to make tracks."

"How about Pedro's South of the Border? Please? I've heard ever so much about it. My friend Wanda went there on her honeymoon. Just south of the North Carolina border. It's supposed to be a real beautiful place."

"I think we can handle Pedro's, if we make it snappy," said Walter. "It's on the way and I'll probably need more gas by then."

"You ever been to Pedro's?"

"No," said Walter, swerving around an armadillo. "I've never been north of Jacksonville, either."

"What? How are you going to get us to New York?"

"I looked at a map once," he said. "I've got cabby in my blood. Trust me."

She did, and slept all the way through Georgia and most of South Carolina, waking only when Walter pulled into Pedro's South of the Border.

He filled the tank and got another half-dozen cups of coffee to go while Moon wandered. He found her at the check-out counter, buying a pack of tiny firecrackers, a postcard, and a stamp.

"Let's go," he said. "No time to spare."

"We got to wait one minute while I write my postcard." She said it with such conviction that Walter dared not press the point.

She leaned on the lottery counter and licked the end of a pencil she'd pulled from the rack. With great care she wrote a short message and an address, then put the stamp on. "Who you writing?" Walter asked.

"My mother," she said.

"You never mentioned your mother."

"She died ten years ago," said Moon. "I always write her a postcard whenever I go someplace. I have to make up an address of course, but that doesn't much matter. I figure she knows. I sent her a card from Disney World once."

Walter gave Moon a hug. They dropped the card in the mailbox and headed north.

The trip was a blur of empty coffee cups and heavy traffic. The tailpipe fell off the Nash in Richmond, and they lost a quarter panel just outside of Baltimore. Moon dozed as the miles rolled by.

"Whoa! What is this?" she asked as she woke with a start.

"Lincoln Tunnel," said Walter, tossing another empty coffee cup in back. "We're almost there."

"I never been in a tunnel before," she said.

"Sure you have," he said. "You slept through one in Baltimore."

"What's above us?" she asked.

"Water," Walter said. "The Hudson River."

"I don't think I like this very much," Moon said.

"It won't last long," said Walter. "Nothing does."

They came out of the tunnel and were funneled into downtown New York City.

"I never seen so many people in my entire life," said Moon. "So many cars. And look at these buildings; they must be twenty stories tall! How we gonna find Sandy's glove in all this mess?"

"Trust me," said Walter.

She did, and they rode around for over an hour with Walter sticking his head out the window every block or two and sniffing the air like a bloodhound.

"There," he said.

"Sam's Sport Shoppe? The one with all those going out of business signs?"

"That's the place," said Walter, cutting a hard right in front of a bus and bouncing up on the sidewalk. "Let's go."

"Those signs are covered with dust," said Moon. "They look like they've been hanging there for a hundred years. Walter, I think we're making a big mistake."

"Sandy had a lifetime batting average of .255, which is okay, but not real great," said Walter. "He was, at best, a mediocre fielder. But that day, and *that* glove lifted him above most mortal men. It was a golden moment. Trust me."

Moon shook her head with doubt, but followed him into the store. "Look," he said.

And sure enough there was a whole wall full of Sandy Amoros signature model gloves, maybe 500 of them, with a sign saying that prices had been cut to the bone. Moon watched him stand in front of the display for about two whole minutes before he lurched forward and grabbed one.

"This is it," he said, riding a caffeine high that wouldn't quit. "This is his original glove. I just know it is."

"It looks like all the rest," said Moon, her heart breaking. To have come so far . . .

"No, look," he said excitedly. "See this crack? And this fold? It's got to be the real one." He pulled out two twenty-dollar bills and slapped them on the counter, grabbing her and pulling her out the door without waiting for his change.

"What next?" Moon asked, as Walter intimidated a poor meter maid with an inspired impression of a raving lunatic.

"Now we find Sandy," said Walter, tossing parking tickets in the air as he dove behind the wheel. "Don't forget to slam the door. And trust me."

She did, but after two aimless hours of wandering through downtown New York City traffic, she began to have some doubts.

"Are you sure that's the right glove?"

"Yes."

"Are you sure Sandy lives in New York?"

"Pretty sure."

"Well, he wasn't in the phone book."

"An important man like him wouldn't have a listed number, honey," Walter said, giving Moon's hand a squeeze. "They're not like the rest of us."

"I'm afraid we've made a big—"

"Hey! Hang on!" Walter cut across four lanes of solid traffic, bouncing off two cabs and a Winnebago, screeching through a highly illegal U-turn with the skill of a Juan Fangio on LSD and the daring of a Hunter Thompson with a mouthful of reds. When they slammed against the curb in front of the condo, the driver's door fell off and Walter jumped out.

"You can't—" That was all the doorman got out before Walter pushed him to the sidewalk and went to the man standing under the awning.

"Here's your glove, Mr. Amoros," he said, handing him the Wilson A2000. "I'm Walter, and this here's my friend Moon."

"Pleased to meet you, sir," said Moon, who only had a couple of bruises from Walter's Mario Andretti imitation.

"Glove?" said Amoros.

"The 1955 World Series," huffed Walter. "Last game."

Sandy Amoros gave a rueful grin. "I'm sorry, son, but the original glove is in a museum."

"No," said Moon. "I don't believe it. We came all this way . . ." Her heart broke to see the expression on Walter's face.

"Sorry, Mr. Amoros," said the doorman, coming up all hot and bothered. "They should never—"

"Where's my car, James?" he asked.

"I called for it an hour ago, Mr. Amoros," said the doorman. "The limousine service said—"

"This is the third time this week," said Sandy Amoros. "I'll never make it now."

"Where do you have to go?" asked Walter.

"Children's Hospital," said Amoros. "I'm visiting their cancer ward to sign baseballs for the kids. I'll be incognito, of course. I'll have on my dark glasses, and nobody could ever read my handwriting anyway, especially on a baseball. But I'll never make it now. Even a helicopter couldn't get me there on time."

"I can," said Walter.

"In that?" asked Amoros, pointing to the Nash, which was spewing steam from its radiator and had one headlight hanging down by its wires.

"Trust me," said Walter.

Sandy Amoros looked most doubtful.

"Trust him," said Moon, grabbing him by the hand. "He knows what he's doing." She dragged the retired baseball player to the car and climbed into the trash-filled backseat as Sandy Amoros got in the passenger side. Walter floored it, cutting off two BMWs and a Mercedes as he pulled into traffic.

"Do you know where you're going, son?" asked Amoros.

"Sure," said Walter. "I read a map once. Got it right here in my head."

"God help us," said Amoros, holding the dashboard as they ricocheted off a Chevy and into a Ford.

"Darn!" cried Walter as a cop running hot with full lights and siren cut him off. "Only five blocks to go."

Moon rose up in the back with a Big Daddy Burger sack stuck to her head. She lit the pack of firecrackers and tossed it out the window.

"Hit it, baby!" she yelled as Walter grabbed first gear and drove around the cops ducking for cover. "We're going to make it. We *have* to make it!"

And they did make it. With two minutes to spare. A shaken Sandy Amoros got out of the car.

"Thanks, friends," he said. "This will mean a lot to these kids."

"You're welcome, Mr. Amoros," said Walter. "I'm sorry we bothered you."

"No bother," he said, and looked thoughtful for a second. "Say, you want a job?"

"Say what?"

"You want a job? I need a reliable driver."

"I'm your man," said Walter.

"And you back there. What kind of a name is Moon?"

"It's the name my mama gave me."

"I need a secretary and research assistant. People are always writing me, even though most of them think I'm dead. You interested?"

"Sure."

"Wait for me here," said Amoros. "I think we've got a great future together. And, by the way, that *is* the right glove, I'd know it anywhere. Thanks for getting it back to me. Makes a difference with the kids. At least with the ones who believe." He turned away and went into the hospital.

"Marry me, Moon," said Walter as they watched him walk away.

"What?"

"I want to marry you. We got prospects now, and a future, too. But take that bag off your head, it looks silly."

She took the bag off, wadded it up and bounced it off the back of his head.

"We got to find a souvenir store," she said.

"Why?" he asked.

"I need to buy a postcard. A woman doesn't get married without telling her mama first. It's a rule. Trust me."

He did.

They were married a week later in a dark and cozy leather bar in Brooklyn. The bride was dressed in a stunning brown leather outfit, and looked terrific. The groom wore his finest black leathers. Sandy Amoros was in attendance, wearing his dark glasses and a big floppy leather hat for a disguise. He gave the bride away, and bought drinks for the house. Afterwards, they all went to a ball game.

The home team won. They were all very happy.

Atlantis

——✠——

Orson Scott Card

Kemal Akyazi grew up within a few miles of the ruins of Troy; from his boyhood home above Kumkale he could see the waters of the Dardanelles, the narrow strait that connects the waters of the Black Sea with the Aegean. Many a war had been fought on both sides of that strait, one of which had produced the great epic of Homer's *Iliad.*

This pressure of history had a strange influence on Kemal as a child. He learned all the tales of the place, of course, but he also knew that the tales were Greek, and the place was of the Greek Aegean world. Kemal was a Turk; his own ancestors had not come to the Dardanelles until the fifteenth century. He felt that it was a powerful place, but it did not belong to him. So the *Iliad* was not the story that spoke to Kemal's soul. Rather it was the story of Heinrich Schliemann, the German explorer who, in an era when Troy had been regarded as a mere legend, a myth, a fiction, had been sure not only that Troy was real but also where it was. Despite all scoffers, he mounted an expedition and found it and unburied it. The old stories turned out to be true.

In his teens Kemal thought it was the greatest tragedy of his life that Pastwatch had to use machines to look through the millennia of human history. There would be no more Schliemanns, studying and pondering and guessing until they found some artifact, some ruin of a long-lost city, some remnant of a legend made true again. Thus Kemal had no interest in joining Pastwatch. It was not

185

history that he hungered for—it was exploration and discovery that he wanted, and what was the glory in finding the truth through a machine?

So, after an abortive try at physics, he studied to become a meteorologist. At the age of eighteen, heavily immersed in the study of climate and weather, he touched again on the findings of Pastwatch. No longer did meteorologists have to depend on only a few centuries of weather measurements and fragmentary fossil evidence to determine long-range patterns. Now they had accurate accounts of storm patterns for millions of years. Indeed, in the earliest years of Pastwatch, the machinery had been so coarse that individual humans could not be seen. It was like time-lapse photography in which people don't remain in place long enough to be on more than a single frame of the film, making them invisible. So in those days Pastwatch recorded the weather of the past, erosion patterns, volcanic eruptions, ice ages, climatic shifts.

All that data was the bedrock on which modern weather prediction and control rested. Meteorologists could see developing patterns and, without disrupting the overall pattern, could make tiny changes that prevented any one area from going completely rainless during a time of drought, or sunless during a wet growing season. They had taken the sharp edge off the relentless scythe of climate, and now the great project was to determine how they might make a more serious change, to bring a steady pattern of light rain to the desert regions of the world, to restore the prairies and savannahs that they once had been. That was the work that Kemal wanted to be a part of.

Yet he could not bring himself out from the shadow of Troy, the memory of Schliemann. Even as he studied the climatic shifts involved with the waxing and waning of the ice ages, his mind contained fleeting images of lost civilizations, legendary places that waited for a Schliemann to uncover them.

His project for his degree in meteorology was part of the effort to determine how the Red Sea might be exploited to develop dependable rains for either the Sudan or central Arabia; Kemal's immediate target was to study the difference between weather patterns during the last ice age, when the Red Sea had all but disappeared, and the present, with the Red Sea at its fullest. Back and forth he went through the coarse old Pastwatch recordings, gathering data on sea level and on precipitation at selected points inland. The old TruSite I had been imprecise at best, but good enough for counting rainstorms.

Time after time Kemal would cycle through the up-and-down fluctuations of the Red Sea, watching as the average sea level gradually rose toward the end of the ice age. He always stopped, of course, at the abrupt jump in sea level that marked the rejoining of the Red Sea and the Indian Ocean. After that, the Red Sea was useless for his purposes, since its sea level was tied to that of the great world ocean.

But the echo of Schliemann inside Kemal's mind made him think: What a flood that must have been.

What a flood. The ice age had locked up so much water in glaciers and ice sheets that the sea level of the whole world fell. It eventually reached a low enough point that land bridges arose out of the sea. In the north Pacific, the Bering land bridge allowed the ancestors of the Indies to cross on foot into their great empty homeland. Britain and Flanders were joined. The Dardanelles were closed and the Black Sea became a salty lake. The Persian Gulf disappeared and became a great plain cut by the Euphrates. And the Bab al Mandab, the strait at the mouth of the Red Sea, became a land bridge.

But a land bridge is also a dam. As the world climate warmed and the glaciers began to release their pent-up water, the rains fell heavily everywhere; rivers swelled and the seas rose. The great south-flowing rivers of Europe, which had been mostly dry during the peak of glaciation, now were massive torrents. The Rhone, the Po, the Strimon, the Danube poured so much water into the Mediterranean and the Black Sea that their water level rose at about the same rate as that of the great world ocean.

The Red Sea had no great rivers, however. It was a new sea,

formed by rifting between the new Arabian plate and the African, which meant it had uplift ridges on both coasts. Many rivers and streams flowed from those ridges down into the Red Sea, but none of them carried much water compared to the rivers that drained vast basins and carried the melt-off of the glaciers of the north. So, while the Red Sea gradually rose during this time, it lagged far, far behind the great world ocean. Its water level responded to the immediate local weather patterns rather than to worldwide weather.

Then one day the Indian Ocean rose so high that tides began to spill over the Bab al Mandab. The water cut new channels in the grassland there. Over a period of several years, the leakage grew, creating a series of large new tidal lakes on the Hanish Plain. And then one day, some fourteen thousand years ago, the flow cut a channel so deep that it didn't dry up at low tide, and the water kept flowing, cutting the channel deeper and deeper, until those tidal lakes were full, and brimmed over. With the weight of the Indian Ocean behind it the water gushed into the basin of the Red Sea in a vast flood that in a few days brought the Red Sea up to the level of the world ocean.

This isn't just the boundary marker between useful and useless water level data, thought Kemal. This is a cataclysm, one of the rare times when a single event changes vast reaches of land in a period of time short enough that human beings could notice it. And, for once, this cataclysm happened in an era when human beings were there. It was not only possible but likely that someone saw this flood—indeed, that it killed many, for the southern end of the Red Sea basin was rich savannah and marshes up to the moment when the ocean broke through, and surely the humans of fourteen thousand years ago would have hunted there. Would have gathered seeds and fruits and berries there. Some hunting party must have seen, from the peaks of the Dehalak mountains, the great walls of water that roared up the plain, breaking and parting around the slopes of the Dehalaks, making islands of them.

Such a hunting party would have known that their families had been killed by this water. What would they have thought? Surely that some god was angry with them. That the world had been done away, buried under the sea. And if they survived, if they found a way to the Eritrean shore after the great turbulent waves settled down to the more placid waters of the new, deeper sea, they would tell the tale to anyone who would listen. And for a few years they could take their hearers to the water's edge, show them the treetops barely rising above the surface of the sea, and tell them tales of all that had been buried under the waves.

Noah, thought Kemal. Gilgamesh. Atlantis. The stories were believed. The stories were remembered. Of course they forgot where it happened—the civilizations that learned to write their stories naturally transposed the events to locations that they knew. But they remembered the things that mattered. What did the flood story of Noah say? Not just rain, no, it wasn't a flood caused by rain alone. The "fountains of the great deep" broke open. No local flood on the Mesopotamian plain would cause that image to be part of the story. But the great wall of water from the Indian Ocean, coming on the heels of years of steadily increasing rain—*that* would bring those words to the storytellers' lips, generation after generation, for ten thousand years until they could be written down.

As for Atlantis, everyone was so sure they had found it years ago. Santorini—Thios—the Aegean island that blew up. But the oldest stories of Atlantis said nothing of blowing up in a volcano. They spoke only of the great civilization sinking into the sea. The supposition was that later visitors came to Santorini and, seeing water where an island city used to be, assumed that it had sunk, knowing nothing of the volcanic eruption. To Kemal, however, this now seemed far-fetched indeed, compared to the way it would have looked to the people of Atlantis themselves, somewhere on the Mits'iwa Plain, where the Red Sea seemed to leap up in its bed, engulfing the city. *That* would be sinking into the sea! No explosion, just water. And if the city were in the marshes of what was now the Mits'iwa Channel, the water would have come, not just from the southeast, but from the northeast and the north as well, flowing among and around the Dehalak mountains, making islands of them and swallowing up the marshes and the city with them.

Atlantis. Not beyond the pillars of Hercules, but Plato was right to associate the city with a strait. He, or whoever told the tale to him, simply replaced the Bab al Mandab with the greatest strait that he had heard of. The story might well have reached him by way of Phoenicia, where Mediterranean sailors would have made the story fit the sea they knew. They learned it from Egyptians, perhaps, or nomad wanderers from the hinterlands of Arabia, and "within the straits of Mandab" would quickly have become "within the pillars of Hercules," and then, because the Mediterranean itself was not strange and exotic enough, the locale was moved outside the pillars of Hercules.

All these suppositions came to Kemal with absolute certainty that they were true, or nearly true. He rejoiced at the thought of it: There was still an ancient civilization left to discover.

Everyone knew that Naog of the Derku people was going to be a tall man when he grew up, because his father and mother were both tall and he was an unusually large baby. He was born in floodwater season, when all the Engu clan lived on reed boats. Their food supply, including the precious seed for next year's planting, was kept dry in the seedboats, which were like floating huts of plaited reeds. The people themselves, though, rode out the flood on the open dragonboats, bundles of reeds which they straddled as if they were riding a crocodile—which, according to legend, was how the dragonboats began, when the first Derku woman, Gweia, saved herself and her baby from the flood by climbing onto the back of a huge crocodile. The crocodile—the first Great Derku, or dragon—endured their weight until they reached a tree they could climb, whereupon the dragon swam away. So when the Derku people plaited reeds into long thick bundles and climbed aboard, they believed that the secret of the dragonboats had been given to them by the Great Derku, and in a sense they were riding on his back.

During the raiding season, other nearby tribes had soon learned to fear the coming of the dragonboats, for they always carried off captives who, in those early days, were never seen again. In other tribes when someone was said to have been carried off by the crocodiles, it was the Derku people they meant, for it was well known that all the clans of the Derku worshipped the crocodile as their savior and god, and fed their captives to a dragon that lived in the center of their city.

At Naog's birthtime, the Engu clan were nestled among their tether trees as the flooding Selud River flowed mudbrown underneath them. If Naog had pushed his way out of the womb a few weeks later, as the waters were receding, his mother would have given birth in one of the seedboats. But Naog came early, before highwater, and so the seedboats were still full of grain. During floodwater, they could neither grind the grain into flour nor build cooking fires, and thus had to eat the seeds in raw handfuls. Thus it was forbidden to spill blood on the grain, even birthblood; no one would touch grain that had human blood on it, for that was the juice of the forbidden fruit.

This was why Naog's mother, Lewik, could not hide alone in an enclosed seedboat for the birthing. Instead she had to give birth out in the open, on one of the dragonboats. She clung to a branch of a tether tree as two women on their own dragonboats held hers steady. From a near distance Naog's father, Twerk, could not hide his mortification that his new young wife was giving birth in full view, not only of the women, but of the men and boys of the tribe. Not that any but the youngest and stupidest of the men was overtly looking. Partly because of respect for the event of birth itself, and partly because of a keen awareness that Twerk could cripple any man of the Engu that he wanted to, the men paddled their boats toward the farthest tether trees, herding the boys along with them. There they busied themselves with the work of floodwater season—twining ropes and weaving baskets.

Twerk himself, however, could not keep from looking. He finally left his dragonboat and climbed his tree and watched. The women had brought their dragonboats in a large circle around the woman in travail. Those with children clinging to them or bound to them kept their boats on the fringes—they would be little help, with their hands full already. It was the older women and the young girls who were in close, the older women to help, the younger ones to learn.

But Twerk had no eyes for the other women today. It was his wide-eyed, sweating wife that he watched. It frightened him to see her in such pain, for Lewik was usually the healer, giving herbs and ground-up roots to others to take away pain or cure a sickness. It also bothered him to see that as she squatted on her dragonboat, clinging with both hands to the branch above her head, neither she nor any of the other women was in position to catch the baby when it dropped out. It would fall into the water, he knew, and it would die, and then he and everyone else would know that it had been wrong of him to marry this woman who should have been a servant of the crocodile god, the Great Derku.

When he could not contain himself a moment longer, Twerk shouted to the women: "Who will catch the baby?"

Oh, how they laughed at him, when at last they understood what he was saying. "Derku will catch him!" they retorted, jeering, and the men around him also laughed, for that could mean several things. It could mean that the god would provide for the child's safety, or it could mean that the flood would catch the child, for the flood was also called derkuwed, or dragonwater, partly because it was aswarm with crocodiles swept away from their usual lairs, and partly because the floodwater slithered down from the mountains like a crocodile sliding down into the water, quick and powerful and strong, ready to sweep away and swallow up the unwary. Derku will catch him indeed!

The men began predicting what the child would be named. "He will be Rogogu, because we all laughed," said one. Another said, "It will be a girl and she will be named Mehug, because she will be spilled into the water as she plops out!" They guessed that the child would be named for the fact that Twerk watched the birth; for the branch that Lewik clung to or the tree that Twerk climbed; or for the dragonwater itself, into which they imagined the child spill-

ing and then being drawn out with the embrace of the god still
dripping from him. Indeed, because of this notion Derkuwed became a childhood nickname for Lewik's and Twerk's baby, and
later it was one of the names by which his story was told over and
over again in faraway lands that had never heard of dragonwater or
seen a crocodile, but it was not his real name, not what his father
gave him to be his man-name when he came of age.

After much pushing, Lewik's baby finally emerged. First came
the head, dangling between her ankles like the fruit of a tree—that
was why the word for *head* was the same as the word for *fruit* in
the language of the Derku people. Then as the newborn's head
touched the bound reeds of the dragonboat, Lewik rolled her eyes
in pain and waddled slowly backward, so that the baby flopped out
of her body stretched along the length of the boat. He did not fall
into the water, because his mother had made sure of it.

"Little man!" cried all the women as soon as they saw the sex
of the child.

Lewik grunted out her firstborn's baby-name. "Glogmeriss,"
she said. *Glog* meant "thorn" and *meriss* meant "trouble"; together
they made the term that the Derku used for annoyances that turned
out all right in the end, but which were quite painful at the time.
There were some who thought that she wasn't naming the baby at
all, but simply commenting on the situation, but it was the first
thing she said and so it would be his name until he left the company of women and joined the men.

As soon as the afterbirth dropped onto the dragonboat, all the
other women paddled nearer—like a swarm of gnats, thought
Twerk, still watching. Some helped Lewik pry her hands loose
from the tree branch and lie down on her dragonboat. Others took
the baby and passed it from hand to hand, each one washing a bit
of the blood from the baby. The afterbirth got passed with the baby
at first, often dropping into the floodwater, until at last it reached
the cutting woman, who severed the umbilical cord with a flint
blade. Twerk, seeing this for the first time, realized that this might
be how he got his name, which meant "cutting" or "breaking." Had
his father seen this remarkable thing, too, the women cutting a

baby off from this strange belly-tail? No wonder he named him for it.

But the thing that Twerk could not get out of his mind was the fact that his Lewik had taken off her apron in full view of the clan, and all the men had seen her nakedness, despite their efforts to pretend that they had not. Twerk knew that this would become a joke among the men, a story talked about whenever he was not with them, and this would weaken him and mean that he would never be the clan leader, for one can never give such respect to a man that one laughs about behind his back.

Twerk could think of only one way to keep this from having the power to hurt him, and that was to confront it openly so that no one would laugh behind his back. "His name is Naog!" cried Twerk decisively, almost as soon as the baby was fully washed in river water and the placenta set loose to float away on the flood.

"You are such a stupid man!" cried Lewik from her dragon-boat. Everyone laughed, but in this case it was all right. Everyone knew Lewik was a bold woman who said whatever she liked to any man. That was why it was such a mark of honor that Twerk had chosen to take her as wife and she had taken him for husband—it took a strong man to laugh when his wife said disrespectful things to him. "Of course he's naog," she said. "All babies are born naked."

"I call him Naog because *you* were naked in front of all the clan," answered Twerk. "Yes, I know you all looked when you thought I couldn't see," he chided the men. "I don't mind a bit. You all saw my Lewik naked when the baby came out of her—but what matters is that only *I* saw her naked when I put the baby in!"

That made them all laugh, even Lewik, and the story was often repeated. Even before he became a man and gave up the baby-name Glogmeriss, Naog had often heard the tale of why he would have such a silly name—so often, in fact, that he determined that one day he would do such great deeds that when the people heard the word *naog* they would think first of him and his accomplishments, before they remembered that the name was also the word for the tabu condition of taking the napron off one's secret parts in public.

As he grew up, he knew that the water of derkuwed on him as a baby had touched him with greatness. It seemed he was always taller than the other boys, and he reached puberty first, his young body powerfully muscled by the labor of dredging the canals right among the slaves of the dragon during mudwater season. He wasn't much more than twelve floodwaters old when the grown men began clamoring for him to be given his manhood journey early so that he could join them in slave raids—his sheer size would dishearten many an enemy, making him despair and throw down his club or his spear. But Twerk was adamant. He would not tempt Great Derku to devour his son by letting the boy get ahead of himself. Naog might be large of body, but that didn't mean that he could get away with taking a man's role before he had learned all the skills and lore that a man had to acquire in order to survive.

This was all fine with Naog. He knew that he would have his place in the clan in due time. He worked hard to learn all the skills of manhood—how to fight with any weapon; how to paddle his dragonboat straight on course, yet silently; how to recognize the signs of the seasons and the directions of the stars at different hours of the nights and times of the year; which wild herbs were good to eat, and which deadly; how to kill an animal and dress it so it would keep long enough to bring home for a wife to eat. Twerk often said that his son was as quick to learn things requiring wit and memory as to learn skills that depended only on size and strength and quickness.

What Twerk did not know, what no one even guessed, was that these tasks barely occupied Naog's mind. What he dreamed of, what he thought of constantly, was how to become a great man so that his name could be spoken with solemn honor instead of a smile or laughter.

One of Naog's strongest memories was a visit to the Great Derku in the holy pond at the very center of the great circular canals that linked all the Derku people together. Every year during the mud season, the first dredging was the holy pond, and no slaves were used for *that*. No, the Derku men and women, the great and the obscure, dredged the mud out of the holy pond, carried it away in baskets, and heaped it up in piles that formed a round lumpen wall around the pond. As the dry season came, crocodiles a-wandering in search of water would smell the pond and come through the gaps in the wall to drink it and bathe in it. The crocodiles knew nothing of danger from coming within walls. Why would they have learned to fear the works of humans? What other people in all the world had ever built such a thing? So the crocodiles came and wallowed in the water, heedless of the men watching from trees. At the first full moon of the dry season, as the crocodiles lay stupidly in the water during the cool of night, the men dropped from the trees and quietly filled the gaps in the walls with earth. At dawn, the largest crocodile in the pond was hailed as Great Derku for the year. The rest were killed with spears in the bloodiest most wonderful festival of the year.

The year that Naog turned six, the Great Derku was the largest crocodile that anyone could remember ever seeing. It was a dragon indeed, and after the men of raiding age came home from the blood moon festival full of stories about this extraordinary Great Derku, all the families in all the clans began bringing their children to see it.

"They say it's a crocodile who was Great Derku many years ago," said Naog's mother. "He has returned to our pond in hopes of the offerings of manfruit that we used to give to the dragon. But some say he's the very one who was Great Derku the year of the forbidding, when he refused to eat any of the captives we offered him."

"And how would they know?" said Twerk, ridiculing the idea. "Is there anyone alive now who was alive then, to recognize him? And how could a crocodile live so long?"

"The Great Derku lives forever," said Lewik.

"Yes, but the true dragon is the derkuwed, the water in flood," said Twerk, "and the crocodiles are only its children."

To the child, Naog, these words had another meaning, for he had heard the word *derkuwed* far more often in reference to himself, as his nickname, than in reference to the great annual flood. So to him it sounded as though his father was saying that *he* was the true dragon, and the crocodiles were his children. Almost at once he realized what was actually meant, but the impression lingered in the back of his mind.

"And couldn't the derkuwed preserve one of its children to come back to us to be our god a second time?" said Lewik. "Or are you suddenly a holy man who knows what the dragon is saying?"

"All this talk about this Great Derku being one of the ancient ones brought back to us is dangerous," said Twerk. "Do you want us to return to the terrible days when we fed manfruit to the Great Derku? When our captives were all torn to pieces by the god, while *we,* men and women alike, had to dig out all the canals without slaves?"

"There weren't so many canals then," said Lewik. "Father said."

"Then it must be true," said Twerk, "if your old father said it. So think about it. Why are there so many canals now, and why are they so long and deep? Because we put our captives to work dredging our canals and making our boats. What if the Great Derku had never refused to eat manfruit? We would not have such a great city here, and other tribes would not bring us gifts and even their own children as slaves. They can come and visit our captives, and even buy them back from us. That's why we're not hated and feared, but rather *loved* and feared in all the lands from the Nile to the Salty Sea."

Naog knew that his father's manhood journey had been from the Salty Sea all the way up the mountains and across endless grasslands to the great river of the west. It was a legendary journey, fitting for such a large man. So Naog knew that he would have to undertake an even greater journey. But of that he said nothing.

"But these people talking stupidly about this being that same Great Derku returned to us again—don't you realize that they will want to put it to the test again, and offer it manfruit? And what if the Great Derku *eats* it this time? What do we do then, go back to doing all the dredging ourselves? Or let the canals fill in so we

can't float the seedboats from village to village during the dry season, and so we have no defense from our enemies and no way to
ride our dragonboats all year?"

Others in the clan were listening to this argument, since there
was little enough privacy under normal circumstances, and none at
all when you spoke with a raised voice. So it was no surprise when
they chimed in. One offered the opinion that the reason no manfruit
should be offered to this Great Derku was because the eating of
manfruit would give the Great Derku knowledge of all the thoughts
of the people they ate. Another was afraid that the sight of a powerful creature eating the flesh of men would lead some of the
young people to want to commit the unpardonable sin of eating
that forbidden fruit themselves, and in that case all the Derku people would be destroyed.

What no one pointed out was that in the old days, when they
fed manfruit to the Great Derku, it wasn't *just* captives that were
offered. During years of little rain or too much rain, the leader of
each clan always offered his own eldest son as the first fruit, or, if
he could not bear to see his son devoured, he would offer himself
in his son's place—though some said that in the earliest times it
was always the leader himself who was eaten, and they only started
offering their sons as a cowardly substitute. By now everyone expected Twerk to be the next clan leader, and everyone knew that he
doted on his Glogmeriss, his Naog-to-be, his Derkuwed, and that
he would never throw his son to the crocodile god. Nor did any of
them wish him to do so. A few people in the other clans might
urge the test of offering manfruit to the Great Derku, but most of
the people in all of the tribes, and all of the people in Engu clan,
would oppose it, and so it would not happen.

So it was with an assurance of personal safety that Twerk
brought his firstborn son with him to see the Great Derku in the
holy pond. But six-year-old Glogmeriss, oblivious to the personal
danger that would come from the return of human sacrifice, was
terrified at the sight of the holy pond itself. It was surrounded by
a low wall of dried mud, for once the crocodile had found its way
to the water inside, the gaps in the wall were closed. But what kept

the Great Derku inside was not just the mud wall. It was the row on row of sharpened horizontal stakes pointing straight inward, set into the mud and lashed to sharp vertical stakes about a hand's-breadth back from the point. The captive dragon could neither push the stakes out of the way nor break them off. Only when the flood-water came and the river spilled over the top of the mud wall and swept it away, stakes and all, would that year's Great Derku be set free. Only rarely did the Great Derku get caught on the stakes and die, and when it happened it was regarded as a very bad omen.

This year, though, the wall of stakes was not widely regarded as enough assurance that the dragon could not force his way out, he was so huge and clever and strong. So men stood guard constantly, spears in hand, ready to prod the Great Derku and herd it back into place, should it come dangerously close to escaping.

The sight of spikes and spears was alarming enough, for it looked like war to young Glogmeriss. But he soon forgot those puny sticks when he caught sight of the Great Derku himself, as he shambled up on the muddy, grassy shore of the pond. Of course Glogmeriss had seen crocodiles all his life; one of the first skills any child, male or female, had to learn was how to use a spear to poke a crocodile so it would leave one's dragonboat—and therefore one's arms and legs—in peace. This crocodile, though, this dragon, this god, was so huge that Glogmeriss could easily imagine it swallowing him whole without having to bite him in half or even chew. Glogmeriss gasped and clung to his father's hand.

"A giant indeed," said his father. "Look at those legs, that powerful tail. But remember that the Great Derku is but a weak child compared to the power of the flood."

Perhaps because human sacrifice was still on his mind, Twerk then told his son how it had been in the old days. "When it was a captive we offered as manfruit, there was always a chance that the god would let him live. Of course, if he clung to the stakes and refused to go into the pond, we would never let him out alive—we poked him with our spears. But if he went boldly into the water so far that it covered his head completely, and then came back out alive and made it back to the stakes without the Great Derku taking him and eating him, well, then, we brought him out in great honor. We said that his old life ended in that water, that the man we had captured had been buried in the holy pond, and now he was born again out of the flood. He was a full member of the tribe then, of the same clan as the man who had captured him. But of course the Great Derku almost never let anyone out alive, because we always kept him hungry."

"*You* poked him with your spear?" asked Glogmeriss.

"Well, not me personally. When I said that *we* did it, I meant of course the men of the Derku. But it was long before I was born. It was in my grandfather's time, when he was a young man, that there came a Great Derku who wouldn't eat any of the captives who were offered to him. No one knew what it meant, of course, but all the captives were coming out and expecting to be adopted into the tribe. But if *that* had happened, the captives would have been the largest clan of all, and where would we have found wives for them all? So the holy men and the clan leaders realized that the old way was over, that the god no longer wanted manfruit, and therefore those who survived after being buried in the water of the holy pond were *not* adopted into the Derku people. But we did keep them alive and set them to work on the canals. That year, with the captives working alongside us, we dredged the canals deeper than ever, and we were able to draw twice the water from the canals into the fields of grain during the dry season, and when we had a bigger harvest than ever before, we had hands enough to weave more seedboats to contain it. Then we realized what the god had meant by refusing to eat the manfruit. Instead of swallowing our captives into the belly of the water where the god lives, the god was giving them all back to us, to make us rich and strong. So from that day on we have fed no captives to the Great Derku. Instead we hunt for meat and bring it back, while the women and old men make the captives do the labor of the city. In those days we had one large canal. Now we have three great canals encircling each other, and several other canals cutting across them, so that even in the driest season a Derku man can glide on his dragonboat like a crocodile from any part of our land to any other, and never have to drag it across dry earth. This is the greatest gift of the dragon to us, that we can have the labor of our captives instead of the Great Derku devouring them himself."

"It's not a bad gift to the captives, either," said Glogmeriss. "Not to die."

Twerk laughed and rubbed his son's hair. "Not a bad gift at that," he said.

"Of course, if the Great Derku really loved the captives he would let them go home to their families."

Twerk laughed even louder. "They have no families, foolish boy," he said. "When a man is captured, he is dead as far as his family is concerned. His woman marries someone else, his children forget him and call another man father. He has no more home to return to."

"Don't some of the ugly-noise people buy captives back?"

"The weak and foolish ones do. The gold ring on my arm was the price of a captive. The father-of-all priest wears a cape of bright feathers that was the ransom of a boy not much older than you, not long after you were born. But most captives know better than to hope for ransom. What does *their* tribe have that we want?"

"I would hate to be a captive, then," said Glogmeriss. "Or would *you* be weak and foolish enough to ransom me?"

"You?" Twerk laughed out loud. "You're a Derku man, or will be. We take captives wherever we want, but where is the tribe so bold that it dares to take one of *us*? No, we are never captives. And the captives we take are lucky to be brought out of their poor, miserable tribes of wandering hunters or berry-pickers and allowed to live here among wall-building men, among canal-digging people, where they don't have to wander in search of food every day, where they get plenty to eat all year long, twice as much as they ever ate before."

"I would still hate to be one of them," said Glogmeriss. "Because how could you ever do great things that everyone will talk about and tell stories about and remember, if you're a captive?"

All this time that they stood on the wall and talked, Glogmeriss never took his eyes off the Great Derku. It was a terrible creature, and when it yawned it seemed its mouth was large enough to swallow a tree. Ten grown men could ride on its back like a dragonboat. Worst of all were the eyes, which seemed to stare into a man's heart. It was probably the eyes of the dragon that gave it its name, for *derku* could easily have originated as a shortened form of *derk-unt*, which meant "one who sees." When the ancient ancestors of the Derku people first came to this floodplain, the crocodiles floating like logs on the water must have fooled them. They must have learned to look for eyes on the logs. "Look!" the watcher would cry. "There's one with eyes! Derk-unt!" They said that if you looked in the dragon's eyes, he would draw you toward him, within reach of his huge jaws, within reach of his curling tail, and you would never even notice your danger, because his eyes held you. Even when the jaws opened to show the pink mouth, the teeth like rows of bright flame ready to burn you, you would look at that steady, all-knowing, wise, amused, and coolly angry eye.

That was the fear that filled Glogmeriss the whole time he stood on the wall beside his father. For a moment, though, just after he spoke of doing great things, a curious change came over him. For a moment Glogmeriss stopped fearing the Great Derku, and instead imagined that he *was* the giant crocodile. Didn't a man paddle his dragonboat by lying on his belly straddling the bundled reeds, paddling with his hands and kicking with his feet just as a crocodile did under the water? So all men became dragons, in a way. And Glogmeriss would grow up to be a large man, everyone said so. Among men he would be as extraordinary as the Great Derku was among crocodiles. Like the god, he would seem dangerous and strike fear into the hearts of smaller people. And, again like the god, he would actually be kind, and not destroy them, but instead help them and do good for them.

Like the river in flood. A frightening thing, to have the water rise so high, sweeping away the mud hills on which they had built the seedboats, smearing the outsides of them with sun-heated tar so they would be watertight when the flood came. Like the Great Derku, the flood seemed to be a destroyer. And yet when the water

receded, the land was wet and rich, ready to receive the seed and
give back huge harvests. The land farther up the slopes of the
mountains was salty and stony and all that could grow on it was
grass. It was here in the flatlands where the flood tore through like
a mad dragon that the soil was rich and trees could grow.

I will *be* the Derkuwed. Not as a destroyer, but as a lifebringer.
The real Derku, the true dragon, could never be trapped in a cage
as this poor crocodile has been. The true dragon comes like the
flood and tears away the walls and sets the Great Derku crocodile
free and makes the soil wet and black and rich. Like the river, I
will be another tool of the god, another manifestation of the power
of the god in the world. If that was not what the dragon of the deep
heaven of the sea intended, why would he have made Glogmeriss
so tall and strong?

This was still the belief in his heart when Glogmeriss set out on
his manhood journey at the age of fourteen. He was already the
tallest man in his clan and one of the tallest among all the Derku
people. He was a giant, and yet well-liked because he never used
his strength and size to frighten other people into doing what he
wanted; on the contrary, he seemed always to protect the weaker
boys. Many people felt that it was a shame that when he returned
from his manhood journey, the name he would be given was a silly
one like Naog. But when they said as much in Glogmeriss's hearing, he only laughed at them and said, "The name will only be silly
if it is borne by a silly man. I hope not to be a silly man."

Glogmeriss's father had made his fame by taking his manhood
journey from the Salty Sea to the Nile. Glogmeriss's journey therefore had to be even more challenging and more glorious. He would
go south and east, along the crest of the plateau until he reached
the legendary place called the Heaving Sea, where the gods that
dwelt in its deep heaven were so restless that the water splashed
onto the shore in great waves all the time, even when there was no
wind. If there was such a sea, Glogmeriss would find it. When he
came back as a man with such a tale, they would call him Naog
and none of them would laugh.

* * *

Kemal Akyazi knew that Atlantis had to be there under the waters of the Red Sea; but why hadn't Pastwatch found it? The answer was simple enough. The past was huge, and while the TruSite I had been used to collect climatalogical information, the new machines that were precise enough that they could track individual human beings would never have been used to look at oceans where nobody lived. Yes, the Tempoview had explored the Bering Strait and the English Channel, but that was to track long-known-of migrations. There was no such migration in the Red Sea. Pastwatch had simply never looked through their precise new machines to see what was under the water of the Red Sea in the waning centuries of the last ice age. And they never *would* look, either, unless someone gave them a compelling reason.

Kemal understood bureaucracy enough to know that he, a student meteorologist, would hardly be taken seriously if he brought an Atlantis theory to Pastwatch—particularly a theory that put Atlantis in the Red Sea of all places, and fourteen thousand years ago, no less, long before civilizations arose in Sumeria or Egypt, let alone China or the Indus Valley or among the swamps of Tehuantapec.

Yet Kemal also knew that the setting would have been right for a civilization to grow in the marshy land of the Mits'iwa Channel. Though there weren't enough rivers flowing into the Red Sea to fill it at the same rate as the world ocean, there were still rivers. For instance, the Zula, which still had enough water to flow even today, watered the whole length of the Mits'iwa Plain and flowed down into the rump of the Red Sea near Mersa Mubarek. And, because of the different rainfall patterns of that time, there was a large and dependable river flowing out of the Assahara basin. Assahara was now a dry valley below sea level, but then would have been a freshwater lake fed by many rivers and spilling over the lowest point into the Mits'iwa Channel. The river meandered along the nearly level Mits'iwa Plain, with some branches of it joining the Zula River, and some wandering east and north to form several mouths in the Red Sea.

Thus dependable sources of fresh water fed the area, and in

rainy season the Zula, at least, would have brought new silt to freshen the soil, and in all seasons the wandering flatwater rivers would have provided a means of transportation through the marshes. The climate was also dependably warm, with plenty of sunlight and a long growing season. There was no early civilization that did not grow up in such a setting. There was no reason such a civilization might not have grown up then.

Yes, it was six or seven thousand years too early. But couldn't it be that it was the very destruction of Atlantis that convinced the survivors that the gods did not want human beings to gather together in cities? Weren't there hints of that anti-civilization bias lingering in many of the ancient religions of the Middle East? What was the story of Cain and Abel, if not a metaphorical expression of the evil of the city-dweller, the farmer, the brother-killer who is judged unworthy by the gods because he does not wander with his sheep? Couldn't such stories have circulated widely in those ancient times? That would explain why the survivors of Atlantis hadn't immediately begun to rebuild their civilization at another site: They knew that the gods forbade it, that if they built again their city would be destroyed again. So they remembered the stories of their glorious past, and at the same time condemned their ancestors and warned everyone they met against people gathering together to build a city, making people yearn for such a place and fear it, both at once.

Not until a Nimrod came, a tower-builder, a Babel-maker who defied the old religion, would the ancient proscription be overcome at last and another city rise up, in another river valley far in time and space from Atlantis, but remembering the old ways that had been memorialized in the stories of warning and, as far as possible, replicating them. We will build a tower so high that it *can't* be immersed. Didn't Genesis link the flood with Babel in just that way, complete with the nomad's stern disapproval of the city? This was the story that survived in Mesopotamia—the tale of the beginning of city life there, but with clear memories of a more ancient civilization that had been destroyed in a flood.

A more ancient civilization. The golden age. The giants who

once walked the earth. Why couldn't all these stories be remembering the first human civilization, the place where the city was invented? Atlantis, the city of the Mits'iwa Plain.

But how could he prove it without using the Tempoview? And how could he get access to one of those machines without first convincing Pastwatch that Atlantis was really in the Red Sea? It was circular, with no way out.

Until he thought: Why do large cities form in the first place? Because there are public works to do that require more than a few people to accomplish them. Kemal wasn't sure what form the public works might take, but surely they would have been something that would change the face of the land obviously enough that the old TruSite I recordings would show it, though it wouldn't be noticeable unless someone was looking for it.

So, putting his degree at risk, Kemal set aside the work he was assigned to do and began poring over the old TruSite I recordings. He concentrated on the last few centuries before the Red Sea flood—there was no reason to suppose that the civilization had lasted very long before it was destroyed. And within a few months he had collected data that was irrefutable. There were no dikes and dams to prevent flooding—that kind of structure would have been large enough that no one would have missed it. Instead there were seemingly random heaps of mud and earth that grew between rainy seasons, especially in the drier years when the rivers were lower than usual. To people looking only for weather patterns, these unstructured, random piles would mean nothing. But to Kemal they were obvious: In the shallowing water, the Atlanteans were dredging channels so that their boats could continue to traffic from place to place. The piles of earth were simply the dumping-places for the muck they dredged from the water. None of the boats showed up on the TruSite I, but now that Kemal knew where to look, he began to catch fleeting glimpses of houses. Every year when the floods came, the houses disappeared, so they were only visible for a moment or two in the TruSite I: flimsy mud-and-reed structures that must have been swept away in every flood season and rebuilt again when the waters receded. But they were there, close by the hillocks that marked the channels. Plato was right again—Atlantis grew up around its canals. But Atlantis was the people and their boats; the buildings were washed away and built again every year.

When Kemal presented his findings to Pastwatch he was not yet twenty years old, but his evidence was impressive enough that Pastwatch immediately turned, not one of the Tempoviews, but the still-newer TruSite II machine to look under the waters of the Red Sea in the Massawa Channel during the hundred years before the Red Sea flood. They found that Kemal was gloriously, spectacularly right. In an era when other humans were still following game animals and gathering berries, the Atlanteans were planting amaranth and ryegrass, melons and beans in the rich wet silt of the receding rivers, and carrying food in baskets and on reed boats from place to place. The only thing that Kemal had missed was that the reed buildings weren't houses at all. They were silos for the storage of grain, built watertight so that they would float during the flood season. The Atlanteans slept under the open air during the dry season, and in the flood season they slept on their tiny reed boats.

Kemal was brought into Pastwatch and made head of the vast new Atlantis project. This was the seminal culture of all cultures in the old world, and a hundred researchers examined every stage of its development. This methodical work, however, was not for Kemal. As always, it was the grand legend that drew him. He spent every moment he could spare away from the management of the project and devoted it to the search for Noah, for Gilgamesh, for the great man who rode out the flood and whose story lived in memory for thousands of years. There had to be a real original, and Kemal would find him.

The flood season was almost due when Glogmeriss took his journey that would make him into a man named Naog. It was a little early for him, since he was born during the peak of the flood, but everyone in the clan agreed with Twerk that it was better for a manling so well-favored to be early than late, and if he wasn't already up and out of the flood plain before the rains came, then he'd have to wait months before he could safely go. And besides, as

Twerk pointed out, why have a big eater like Glogmeriss waiting out the flood season, eating huge handfuls of grain. People listened happily to Twerk's argument, because he was known to be a generous, wise, good-humored man, and everyone expected him to be named clan leader when sweet old ailing Dheub finally died.

Getting above the flood meant walking up the series of slight inclines leading to the last sandy shoulder, where the land began to rise more steeply. Glogmeriss had no intention of climbing any higher than that. His father's journey had taken him over those ridges and on to the great river Nile, but there was no reason for Glogmeriss to clamber through rocks when he could follow the edge of the smooth, grassy savannah. He was high enough to see the vast plain of the Derku lands stretching out before him, and the land was open enough that no cat or pack of dogs could creep up on him unnoticed, let alone some hunter of another tribe.

How far to the Heaving Sea? Far enough that no one of the Derku tribe had ever seen it. But they knew it existed, because when they brought home captives from tribes to the south, they heard tales of such a place, and the farther south the captives came from, the more vivid and convincing the tales became. Still, none of them had ever seen it with their own eyes. So it would be a long journey, Glogmeriss knew that. And all the longer because it would be on foot, and not on his dragonboat. Not that Derku men were any weaker or slower afoot than men who lived above the flood—on the contrary, they had to be fleet indeed, as well as stealthy, to bring home either captives or meat. So the boy's games included footracing, and while Glogmeriss was not the fastest sprinter, no one could match his long-legged stride for sheer endurance, for covering ground quickly, on and on, hour after hour.

What set the bodies of the Derku people apart from other tribes, what made them recognizable in an instant, was the massive development of their upper bodies from paddling dragonboats hour after hour along the canals or through the floods. It wasn't just paddling, either. It was the heavy armwork of cutting reeds and binding them into great sheaves to be floated home for making boats and ropes and baskets. And in older times, they would also have

developed strong arms and backs from dredging the canals that surrounded and connected all the villages of the great Derku city.
Slaves did most of that now, but the Derku took great pride in
never letting their slaves be stronger than they were. Their shoulders and chests and arms and backs were almost monstrous compared to those of the men and women of other tribes. And since the
Derku ate better all year round than people of other tribes, they
tended to be taller, too. Many tribes called them giants, and others
called them the sons and daughters of the gods, they looked so
healthy and strong. And of all the young Derku men, there was
none so tall and strong and healthy as Glogmeriss, the boy they
called Derkuwed, the man who would be Naog.

So as Glogmeriss loped along the grassy rim of the great plain,
he knew he was in little danger from human enemies. Anyone who
saw him would think: There is one of the giants, one of the sons
of the crocodile god. Hide, for he might be with a party of raiders.
Don't let him see you, or he'll take a report back to his people.
Perhaps one man in a pack of hunters might say, "He's alone, we
can kill him," but the other hunters would jeer at the one who
spoke so rashly. "Look, fool, he has a javelin in his hands and
three tied to his back. Look at his arms, his shoulders—do you
think he can't put his javelin through your heart before you got
close enough to throw a rock at him? Let him be. Pray for a great
cat to find him in the night."

That was Glogmeriss's only real danger. He was too high into
the dry lands for crocodiles, and he could run fast enough to climb
a tree before any pack of dogs or wolves could bring him down.
But there was no tree that would give a moment's pause to one of
the big cats. No, if one of *them* took after him, it would be a fight.
But Glogmeriss had fought cats before, on guard duty. Not the
giants that could knock a man's head off with one blow of its paw,
or take his whole belly with one bite of its jaws, but still, they were
big enough, prowling around the outside of the clan lands, and
Glogmeriss had fought them with a hand javelin and brought them
down alone. He knew something of the way they moved and

thought, and he had no doubt that in a contest with one of the big cats, he would at least cause it grave injury before it killed him.

Better not to meet one of them, though. Which meant staying well clear of any of the herds of bison or oxen, antelope or horses that the big cats stalked. Those cats would never have got so big waiting around for lone humans—it was herds they needed, and so it was herds that Glogmeriss did *not* need.

To his annoyance, though, one came to *him.* He had climbed a tree to sleep the night, tying himself to the trunk so he wouldn't fall out in his sleep. He awoke to the sound of nervous lowing and a few higher-pitched, anxious moos. Below him, milling around in the first grey light of the coming dawn, he could make out the shadowy shapes of oxen. He knew at once what had happened. They caught scent of a cat and began to move away in the darkness, shambling in fear and confusion in the near darkness. They had not run because the cat wasn't close enough to cause a panic in the herd. With luck it would be one of the smaller cats, and when it saw that they knew it was there, it would give up and go away.

But the cat had not given up and gone away, or they wouldn't still be so frightened. Soon the herd would have enough light to see the cat that must be stalking them, and then they *would* run, leaving Glogmeriss behind in a tree. Maybe the cat would go in full pursuit of the running oxen, or maybe it would notice the lone man trapped in a tree and decide to go for the easier, smaller meal.

I wish I were part of this herd, thought Glogmeriss. Then there'd be a chance. I would be one of many, and even if the cat brought one of us down, it might not be me. As a man alone, it's me or the cat. Kill or die. I will fight bravely, but in this light I might not get a clear sight of the cat, might not be able to see in the rippling of its muscles where it will move next. And what if it isn't alone? What if the reason these oxen are so frightened yet unwilling to move is that they know there's more than one cat and they have no idea in which direction safety can be found?

Again he thought, I wish I were part of this herd. And then he thought, Why should I think such a foolish thought twice, unless the god is telling me what to do? Isn't that what this journey is for, to find out if there is a god who will lead me, who will protect me, who will make me great? There's no greatness in having a cat eviscerate you in one bite. Only if you live do you become a man of stories. Like Gweia—if she had mounted the crocodile and it had thrown her off and devoured her, who would ever have heard her name?

There was no time to form a plan, except the plan that formed so quickly that it might have been the god putting it there. He would ride one of these oxen as Gweia rode the crocodile. It would be easy enough to drop out of the tree onto an ox's back—hadn't he played with the other boys, year after year, jumping from higher and higher branches to land on a dragonboat that was drifting under the tree? An ox was scarcely less predictable than the dragonboat on a current. The only difference was that when he landed on the ox's back, it would not bear him as willingly as a dragonboat. Glogmeriss had to hope that, like Gweia's crocodile frightened of the flood, the ox he landed on would be more frightened of the cat than of the sudden burden on his back.

He tried to pick well among the oxen within reach of the branches of the tree. He didn't want a cow with a calf running alongside—that would be like begging the cats to come after him, since such cows were already the most tempting targets. But he didn't want a bull, either, for he doubted it would have the patience to bear him.

And there was his target, a full-sized cow but with no calf leaning against it, under a fairly sturdy branch. Slowly, methodically, Glogmeriss untied himself from the tree, cinched the bindings of his javelins and his flintsack and his grainsack, and drew his loin-cloth up to hold his genitals tight against his body, and then crept out along the branch until he was as nearly over the back of the cow he had chosen as possible. The cow was stamping and snort-ing now—they all were, and in a moment they would bolt, he knew it—but it held still as well as a bobbing dragonboat, and so Glogmeriss took aim and jumped, spreading his legs to embrace the animal's back, but not *so* wide that he would slam his crotch against the bony ridge of its spine.

He landed with a grunt and immediately lunged forward to get his arms around the ox's neck, just like gripping the stem of the dragonboat. The beast snorted and bucked, but its bobbing was no worse than the dragonboat ducking under the water at the impact of a boy on its back. Of course, the dragonboat stopped bobbing after a moment, while this ox would no doubt keep trying to be rid of him until he was gone, bucking and turning, bashing its sides into other oxen.

But the other animals were already so nervous that the sudden panic of Glogmeriss's mount was the trigger that set off the stampede. Almost at once the herd mentality took over, and the oxen set out in a headlong rush all in the same direction. Glogmeriss's cow didn't forget the burden on her back, but now she responded to her fear by staying with the herd. It came as a great relief to Glogmeriss when she leapt out and ran among the other oxen, in part because it meant that she was no longer trying to get him off her back, and in part because she was a good runner and he knew that unless she swerved to the edge of the herd where a cat could pick her off, both she and he would be safe.

Until the panic stopped, of course, and then Glogmeriss would have to figure out a way to get *off* the cow and move away without being gored or trampled to death. Well, one danger at a time. And as they ran, he couldn't help but feel the sensations of the moment: The prickly hair of the ox's back against his belly and legs, the way her muscles rippled between his legs and within the embrace of his arms, and above all the sheer exhilaration of moving through the air at such a speed. Has any man ever moved as fast over the ground as I am moving now? he wondered. No dragonboat has ever found a current so swift.

It seemed that they ran for hours and hours, though when they finally came to a stop the sun was still only a palm's height above the mountains far across the plain to the east. As the running slowed to a jolting jog, and then to a walk, Glogmeriss kept waiting for his mount to remember that he was on her back and to start trying to get him off. But if she remembered, she must have decided she didn't mind, because when she finally came to a stop, still in the midst of the herd, she simply dropped her head and began to graze, making no effort to get Glogmeriss off her back.

She was so calm—or perhaps like the others was simply so exhausted—that Glogmeriss decided that as long as he moved slowly and calmly he might be able to walk on out of the herd, or at least climb a tree and wait for them to move on. He knew from the roaring and screaming sounds he had heard near the beginning of the stampede that the cats—more than one—had found their meal, so the survivors were safe enough for now.

Glogmeriss carefully let one leg slide down until he touched the ground. Then, smoothly as possible, he slipped off the cow's back until he was crouched beside her. She turned her head slightly, chewing a mouthful of grass. Her great brown eye regarded him calmly.

"Thank you for carrying me," said Glogmeriss softly.

She moved her head away, as if to deny that she had done anything special for him.

"You carried me like a dragonboat through the flood," he said, and he realized that this was exactly right, for hadn't the stampede of oxen been as dangerous and powerful as any flood of water? And she had borne him up, smooth and safe, carrying him safely to the far shore. "The best of dragonboats."

She lowed softly, and for a moment Glogmeriss began to think of her as being somehow the embodiment of the god—though it could not be the crocodile god that took this form, could it? But all thoughts of the animal's godhood were shattered when it started to urinate. The thick stream of ropey piss splashed into the grass not a span away from Glogmeriss's shoulder, and as the urine spattered him he could not help but jump away. Other nearby oxen mooed complainingly about his sudden movement, but his own cow seemed not to notice. The urine stank hotly, and Glogmeriss was annoyed that the stink would stay with him for days, probably.

Then he realized that no *cow* could put a stream of urine between her forelegs. This animal was a bull after all. Yet it was scarcely larger than the normal cow, not bull-like at all. Squatting down, he looked closely, and realized that the animal had lost its testicles somehow. Was it a freak, born without them? No, there was a scar, a ragged sign of old injury. While still a calf, this animal had had its bullhood torn away. Then it grew to adulthood, neither cow nor bull. What purpose was there in life for such a creature as that? And yet if it had not lived, it could not have carried him through the stampede. A cow would have had a calf to slow it down; a bull would have flung him off easily. The god had prepared this creature to save him. It was not itself a god, of course, for such an imperfect animal could hardly be divine. But it was a god's tool.

"Thank you," said Glogmeriss, to whatever god it was. "I hope to know you and serve you," he said. Whoever the god was must have known him for a long time, must have planned this moment for years. There was a plan, a destiny for him. Glogmeriss felt himself thrill inside with the certainty of this.

I could turn back now, he thought, and I would have had the greatest manhood journey of anyone in the tribe for generations. They would regard me as a holy man, when they learned that a god had prepared such a beast as this to be my dragonboat on dry land. No one would say I was unworthy to be Naog, and no more Glogmeriss.

But even as he thought this, Glogmeriss knew that it would be wrong to go back. The god had prepared this animal, not to make his manhood journey easy and short, but to make his long journey possible. Hadn't the ox carried him southeast, the direction he was already heading? Hadn't it brought him right along the very shelf of smooth grassland that he had already been running on? No, the god meant to speed him on his way, not to end his journey. When he came back, the story of the unmanned ox that carried him like a boat would be merely the first part of his story. They would laugh when he told them about the beast peeing on him. They would nod and murmur in awe as he told them that he realized that the god was helping him to go on, that the god had chosen him years before in order to prepare the calf that would be his mount.

Yet this would all be the opening, leading to the main point of the story, the climax. And what that climax would be, what he would accomplish that would let him take on his manly name, Glogmeriss could hardly bear to wait to find out.

Unless, of course, the god was preparing him to be a sacrifice. But the god could have killed him at any time. It could have killed him when he was born, dropping him into the water as everyone said his father had feared might happen. It could have let him die there at the tree, taken by a cat or trampled under the feet of the oxen. No, the god was keeping him alive for a purpose, for a great task. His triumph lay ahead, and whatever it was, it would be greater than his ride on the back of an ox.

The rains came the next day, but Glogmeriss pressed on. The rain made it hard to see far ahead, but most of the animals stopped moving in the rain and so there wasn't as much danger to look out for. Sometimes the rain came down so thick and hard that Glogmeriss could hardly see a dozen steps ahead. But he ran on, unhindered. The shelf of land that he ran along was perfectly flat, neither uphill nor downhill, as level as water, and so he could lope along without wearying. Even when the thunder roared in the sky and lightning seemed to flash all around him, Glogmeriss did not stop, for he knew that the god that watched over him was powerful indeed. He had nothing to fear. And since he passed two burning trees, he knew that lightning could have struck him at any time, and yet did not, and so it was a second sign that a great god was with him.

During the rains he crossed many swollen streams, just by walking. Only once did he have to cross a river that was far too wide and deep and swift in flood for him to cross. But he plunged right in, for the god was with him. Almost at once he was swept off his feet, but he swam strongly across the current. Yet even a strong Derku man cannot swim forever, and it began to seem to Glogmeriss that he would never reach the other side, but rather would be swept down to the salt sea, where one day his body would wash to shore near a party of Derku raiders who would recognize from the size of his body that it was him. So, this is what happened to Twerk's son Glogmeriss. The flood took him after all.

Then he bumped against a log that was also floating on the current, and took hold of it, and rolled up onto the top of it like a dragonboat. Now he could use all his strength for paddling, and soon he was across the current. He drew the log from the water and embraced it like a brother, lying beside it, holding it in the wet grass until the rising water began to lick at his feet again. Then he dragged the log with him to higher ground and placed it up in the notch of a tree where no flood would dislodge it. One does not abandon a brother to the flood.

Three times the god has saved me, he thought as he climbed back up to the level shelf that was his path. From the tooth of the cat, from the fire of heaven, from the water of the flood. Each time a tree was part of it: The tree around which the herd of oxen gathered and from which I dropped onto the ox's back; the trees that died in flames from taking to themselves the bolts of lightning meant for me; and finally this log of a fallen tree that died in its home far up in the mountains in order to be my brother in the water of the flood. Is it a god of trees, then, that leads me on? But how can a god of trees be more powerful than the god of lightning or the god of the floods or even the god of sharp-toothed cats? No, trees are simply tools the god has used. The god flings trees about as easily as I fling a javelin.

Gradually, over many days, the rains eased a bit, falling in steady showers instead of sheets. Off to his left, he could see that the plain was rising up closer and closer to the smooth shelf along which he ran. On the first clear morning he saw that there was no more distant shining on the still waters of the Salty Sea—the plain was now higher than the level of that water; he had left behind the only sea that the Derku people had ever seen. The Heaving Sea lay yet ahead, and so he ran on.

The plain was quite high, but he was still far enough above it that he could see the shining when it came again on a clear morning. He had left one sea behind, and now, with the ground much higher, there was another sea. Could this be it, the Heaving Sea?

He left the shelf and headed across the savannah toward the water. He did not reach it that day, but on the next afternoon he stood on the shore and knew that this was not the place he had been looking for. The water was far smaller than the Salty Sea, smaller even than the Sweetwater Sea up in the mountains from which the Selud River flowed. And yet when he dipped his finger into the water and tasted it, it *was* a little salty. Almost sweet, but salty nonetheless. Not good for drinking. That was obvious from the lack of animal tracks around the water. It must usually be saltier than this, thought Glogmeriss. It must have been freshened somewhat by the rains.

Instead of returning to his path along the shelf by the route he had followed to get to this small sea, Glogmeriss struck out due south. He could see the shelf in the distance, and could see that by running south he would rejoin the level path a good way farther along.

As he crossed a small stream, he saw animal prints again, and among them the prints of human feet. Many feet, and they were fresher than any of the animal prints. So fresh, in fact, that for all Glogmeriss knew they could be watching him right now. If he stumbled on them suddenly, they might panic, seeing a man as large as he was. And in this place what would they know of the Derku people? No raiders had ever come this far in search of captives, he was sure. That meant that they wouldn't necessarily hate him—but they wouldn't fear retribution from his tribe, either. No, the best course was for him to turn back and avoid them.

But a god was protecting him, and besides, he had been without the sound of a human voice for so many days. If he did not carry any of his javelins, but left them all slung on his back, they would know he meant no harm and they would not fear him. So there at the stream, he bent over, slipped off the rope holding his javelins, and untied them to bind them all together.

As he was working, he heard a sound and knew without looking that he had been found. Perhaps they *had* been watching him all along. His first thought was to pick up his javelins and prepare for battle. But he did not know how many they were, or whether they were all around him, and in the dense brush near the river he might be surrounded by so many that they could overwhelm him easily, even if he killed one or two. For a moment he thought, The god protects me, I could kill them all. But then he rejected that idea. He had killed nothing on this journey, not even for meat, eating only the grain he carried with him and such berries and fruits and roots and greens and mushrooms as he found along the way. Should he begin now, killing when he knew nothing about these people? Perhaps meeting them was what the god had brought him here to do.

So he slowly, carefully finished binding the javelins and then slung them up onto his shoulder, being careful never to hold the javelins in a way that might make his watcher or watchers think that he was making them ready for battle. Then, his hands empty and his weapons bound to his back, he splashed through the stream and followed the many footprints on the far side.

He could hear feet padding along behind him—more than one person, too, from the sound. They might be coming up behind him to kill him, but it didn't sound as if they were trying to overtake him, or to be stealthy, either. They must know that he could hear them. But perhaps they thought he was very stupid. He had to show them that he did not turn to fight them because he did not want to fight, and not because he was stupid or afraid.

To show them he was not afraid, he began to sing the song of the dog who danced with a man, which was funny and had a jaunty tune. And to show them he knew they were there, he bent over as he walked, scooped up a handful of damp soil, and flung it lightly over his shoulder.

The sound of sputtering outrage told him that the god had guided his lump of mud right to its target. He stopped and turned to find four men following him, one of whom was brushing dirt out of his face, cursing loudly. The others looked uncertain whether to be angry at Glogmeriss for flinging dirt at them or afraid of him because he was so large and strange and unafraid.

Glogmeriss didn't want them to be either afraid or angry. So he let a slow smile come to his face, not a smile of derision, but rather a friendly smile that said, I mean no harm. To reinforce this idea, he held his hands out wide, palms facing the strangers.

They understood him, and perhaps because of his smile began to see the humor in the situation. They smiled, too, and then, because the one who was hit with dirt was still complaining and trying to get it out of his eyes, they began to laugh at him. Glogmeriss laughed with them, but then walked slowly toward his victim and, carefully letting them all see what he was doing, took his waterbag from his waist and untied it a little, showing them that water dropped from it. They uttered something in an ugly-sounding language and the one with dirt in his eyes stopped, leaned his head back, and stoically allowed Glogmeriss to bathe his eyes with water.

When at last, dripping and chagrined, the man could see again, Glogmeriss flung an arm across his shoulder like a comrade, and then reached out for the man who seemed to be the leader. After a moment's hesitation, the man allowed Glogmeriss the easy embrace, and together they walked toward the main body of the tribe, the other two walking as closely as possible, behind and ahead, talking to Glogmeriss even though he made it plain that he did not understand.

When they reached the others they were busy building a cookfire. All who could, left their tasks and came to gawk at the giant stranger. While the men who had found him recounted the tale, others came and touched Glogmeriss, especially his strong arms and chest, and his loincloth as well, since none of the men wore any kind of clothing. Glogmeriss viewed this with disgust. It was one thing for little boys to run around naked, but he knew that men should keep their privates covered so they wouldn't get dirty. What woman would let her husband couple with her, if he let any kind of filth get on his javelin?

Of course, these men were all so ugly that no woman would want them anyway, and the women were so ugly that the only men who would want them would be these. Perhaps ugly people don't care about keeping themselves clean, thought Glogmeriss. But the women wore aprons made of woven grass, which looked softer than the beaten reeds that the Derku wove. So it wasn't that these people didn't know how to make cloth, or that the idea of wearing clothing had never occurred to them. The men were simply filthy and stupid, Glogmeriss decided. And the women, while not as filthy, must be just as stupid or they wouldn't let the men come near them.

Glogmeriss tried to explain to them that he was looking for the Heaving Sea, and ask them where it was. But they couldn't understand any of the gestures and handsigns he tried, and his best efforts merely left them laughing to the point of helplessness. He gave up and made as if to leave, which immediately brought protests and an obvious invitation to dinner.

It was a welcome thought, and their chief seemed quite anxious for him to stay. A meal would only make him stronger for the rest of his journey.

He stayed for the meal, which was strange but good. And then, wooed by more pleas from the chief and many others, he agreed to sleep the night with them, though he halfway feared that in his sleep they planned to kill him or at least rob him. In the event, it turned out that they *did* have plans for him, but it had nothing to do with killing. By morning the chief's prettiest daughter was Glogmeriss's bride, and even though she was as ugly as any of the others, she had done a good enough job of initiating him into the pleasures of men and women that he could overlook her thin lips and beakish nose.

This was not supposed to happen on a manhood journey. He was expected to come home and marry one of the pretty girls from one of the other clans of the Derku people. Many a father had already been negotiating with Twerk or old Dheub with an eye toward getting Glogmeriss as a son-in-law. But what harm would it do if Glogmeriss had a bride for a few days with these people, and then slipped away and went home? No one among the Derku would ever meet any of these ugly people, and even if they did, who would care? You could do what you wanted with strangers. It wasn't as if they were people, like the Derku.

But the days came and went, and Glogmeriss could not bring

himself to leave. He was still enjoying his nights with Zawada—as near as he could come to pronouncing her name, which had a strange click in the middle of it. And as he began to learn to understand something of their language, he harbored a hope that they could tell him about the Heaving Sea and, in the long run, save him time.

Days became weeks, and weeks became months, and Zawada's blood-days didn't come and so they knew she was pregnant, and then Glogmeriss didn't want to leave, because he had to see the child he had put into her. So he stayed, and learned to help with the work of this tribe. They found his size and prodigious strength very helpful, and Zawada was comically boastful about her husband's prowess—marrying him had brought her great prestige, even more than being the chief's daughter. And it gradually came to Glogmeriss's mind that if he stayed he would probably be chief of these people himself someday. At times when he thought of that, he felt a strange sadness, for what did it mean to be chief of these miserable ugly people, compared to the honor of being the most ordinary of the Derku people? How could being chief of these grub-eaters and gatherers compare to eating the common bread of the Derku and riding on a dragonboat through the flood or on raids? He enjoyed Zawada, he enjoyed the people of this tribe, but they were not his people, and he knew that he would leave. Eventually.

Zawada's belly was beginning to swell when the tribe suddenly gathered their tools and baskets and formed up to begin another trek. They didn't move back north, however, the direction they had come from when Glogmeriss found them. Rather their migration was due south, and soon, to his surprise, he found that they were hiking along the very shelf of land that had been his path in coming to this place.

It occurred to him that perhaps the god had spoken to the chief in the night, warning him to get Glogmeriss back on his abandoned journey. But no, the chief denied any dream. Rather he pointed to the sky and said it was time to go get—something. A word Glogmeriss had never heard before. But it was clearly some kind of food, because the adults nearby began laughing with anticipatory delight and pantomiming eating copious amounts of—something.

Off to the northeast, they passed along the shores of another small sea. Glogmeriss asked if the water was sweet and if it had fish in it, but Zawada told him, sadly, that the sea was spoiled. "It used to be good," she said. "The people drank from it and swam in it and trapped fish in it, but it got poisoned."

"How?" asked Glogmeriss.

"The god vomited into it."

"What god did that?"

"The great god," she said, looking mysterious and amused.

"How do you know he did?" asked Glogmeriss.

"We saw," she said. "There was a terrible storm, with winds so strong they tore babies from their mothers' arms and carried them away and they were never seen again. My own mother and father held me between them and I wasn't carried off—I was scarcely more than a baby then, and I remember how scared I was, to have my parents crushing me between them while the wind screamed through the trees."

"But a rainstorm would sweeten the water," said Glogmeriss. "Not make it salty."

"I told you," said Zawada. "The god vomited into it."

"But if you don't mean the rain, then what do you mean?"

To which her only answer was a mysterious smile and a giggle. "You'll see," she said.

And in the end, he did. Two days after leaving this second small sea behind, they rounded a bend and some of the men began to shinny up trees, looking off to the east as if they knew exactly what they'd see. "There it is!" they cried. "We can see it!"

Glogmeriss lost no time in climbing up after them, but it took a while for him to know what it was they had seen. It wasn't till he climbed another tree the next morning, when they were closer and when the sun was shining in the east, that he realized that the vast plain opening out before them to the east wasn't a plain at all. It was water, shimmering strangely in the sunlight of morning. More water than Glogmeriss had ever imagined. And the reason the light shimmered that way was because the water was moving. It was the Heaving Sea.

He came down from the tree in awe, only to find the whole tribe watching him. When they saw his face, they burst into hysterical laughter, including even Zawada. Only now did it occur to him that they had understood him perfectly well on his first day with them, when he described the Heaving Sea. They had known where he was headed, but they hadn't told him.

"There's the joke back on you!" cried the man in whose face Glogmeriss had thrown dirt on that first day. And now it seemed like perfect justice to Glogmeriss. He had played a joke, and they had played one back, an elaborate jest that required even his wife to keep the secret of the Heaving Sea from him.

Zawada's father, the chief, now explained that it was more than a joke. "Waiting to show you the Heaving Sea meant that you would stay and marry Zawada and give her giant babies. A dozen giants like you!"

Zawada grinned cheerfully. "If they don't kill me coming out, it'll be fine to have sons like yours will be!"

Next day's journey took them far enough that they didn't have to climb trees to see the Heaving Sea, and it was larger than Glogmeriss had ever imagined. He couldn't see the end of it. And it moved all the time. There were more surprises when they got to the shore that night, however. For the sea was noisy, a great roaring, and it kept throwing itself at the shore and then retreating, heaving up and down. Yet the children were fearless—they ran right into the water and let the waves chase them to shore. The men and women soon joined them, for a little while, and Glogmeriss himself finally worked up the courage to let the water touch him, let the waves chase him. He tasted the water, and while it was saltier than the small seas to the northwest, it was nowhere near as salty as the Salt Sea.

"This is the god that poisoned the little seas," Zawada explained to him. "This is the god that vomited into them."

But Glogmeriss looked at how far the waves came onto the shore and laughed at her. "How could these heavings of the sea reach all the way to those small seas? It took days to get here from there."

She grimaced at him. "What do you know, giant man? These waves are not the reason why this is called the Heaving Sea by those who call it that. These are like little butterfly flutters compared to the true heaving of the sea."

Glogmeriss didn't understand until later in the day, as he realized that the waves weren't reaching as high as they had earlier. The beach sand was wet much higher up the shore than the waves could get to now. Zawada was delighted to explain the tides to him, how the sea heaved upward and downward, twice a day or so. "The sea is calling to the moon," she said, but could not explain what that meant, except that the tides were linked to the passages of the moon rather than the passages of the sun.

As the tide ebbed, the tribe stopped playing and ran out onto the sand. With digging stones they began scooping madly at the sand. Now and then one of them would shout in triumph and hold up some ugly, stony, dripping object for admiration before dropping it into a basket. Glogmeriss examined them and knew at once that these things could not be stones—they were too regular, too symmetrical. It wasn't till one of the men showed him the knack of prying them open by hammering on a sharp wedgestone that he really understood, for inside the hard stony surface there was a soft, pliable animal that could draw its shell closed around it.

"That's how it lives under the water," explained the man. "It's watertight as a mud-covered basket, only all the way around. Tight all the way around. So it keeps the water out!"

Like the perfect seedboat, thought Glogmeriss. Only no boat of reeds could ever be made *that* watertight, not so it could be plunged underwater and stay dry inside.

That night they built a fire and roasted the clams and mussels and oysters on the ends of sticks. They were tough and rubbery and they tasted salty—but Glogmeriss soon discovered that the very saltiness was the reason this was such a treat, that and the juices they released when you first chewed on them. Zawada laughed at him for chewing his first bite so long. "Cut it off in smaller bits," she said, "and then chew it till it stops tasting good and then swallow it whole." The first time he tried, it took a bit of doing to swallow it without gagging, but he soon got used to it and it *was* delicious.

"Don't drink so much of your water," said Zawada.

"I'm thirsty," said Glogmeriss.

"Of course you are," she said. "But when we run out of fresh water, we have to leave. There's nothing to drink in this place. So drink only a little at a time, so we can stay another day."

The next morning he helped with the clam-digging, and his powerful shoulders and arms allowed him to excel at this task, just as with so many others. But he didn't have the appetite for roasting them, and wandered off alone while the others feasted on the shore. They did their digging in a narrow inlet of the sea, where a long thin finger of water surged inward at high tide and then retreated almost completely at low tide. The finger of the sea seemed to point straight toward the land of the Derku, and it made Glogmeriss think of home.

Why did I come here? Why did the god go to so much trouble to bring me? Why was I saved from the cats and the lightning and the flood? Was it just to see this great water and taste the salty meat of the clams? These are marvels, it's true, but no greater than the marvel of the castrated bull-ox that I rode, or the lightning fires, or the log that was my brother in the flood. Why would it please the god to bring me here?

He heard footsteps and knew at once that it was Zawada. He did not look up. Soon he felt her arms come around him from behind, her swelling breasts pressed against his back.

"Why do you look toward your home?" she asked softly. "Haven't I made you happy?"

"You've made me happy," he said.

"But you look sad."

He nodded.

"The gods trouble you," she said. "I know that look on your face. You never speak of it, but I know at such times you are thinking of the god who brought you here and wondering if she loved you or hated you."

He laughed aloud. "Do you see inside my skin, Zawada?"

"Not your skin," she said. "But I could see inside your loincloth when you first arrived, which is why I told my father to let me be the one to marry you. I had to beat up my sister before she would let me be the one to share your sleeping mat that night. She has never forgiven me. But I wanted your babies."

Glogmeriss grunted. He had known about the sister's jealousy, but since she was ugly and he had never slept with her, her jealousy was never important to him.

"Maybe the god brought you here to see where she vomited."

That again.

"It was in a terrible storm."

"You told me about the storm," said Glogmeriss, not wanting to hear it all again.

"When the storms are strong, the sea rises higher than usual. It heaved its way far up this channel. Much farther than this tongue of the sea reaches now. It flowed so far that it reached the first of the small seas and made it flow over and then it reached the second one and that, too, flowed over. But then the storm ceased and the water flowed back to where it was before, only so much saltwater had gone into the small seas that they were poisoned."

"So long ago, and yet the salt remains?"

"Oh, I think the sea has vomited into them a couple more times since then. Never as strongly as that first time, though. You can see this channel—so much of the seawater flowed through here that it cut a channel in the sand. This finger of the sea is all that's left of it, but you can see the banks of it—like a dried-up river, you see? That was cut then, the ground used to be at the level of the rest of the valley there. The sea still reaches into that new channel, as if it remembered. Before, the shore used to be clear out there, where the waves are high. It's much better for clam-digging now, though, because this whole channel gets filled with clams and we can get them easily."

Glogmeriss felt something stirring inside him. Something in

what she had just said was very, very important, but he didn't know what it was.

He cast his gaze off to the left, to the shelf of land that he had walked along all the way on his manhood journey, that this tribe had followed in coming here. The absolutely level path.

Absolutely level. And yet the path was not more than three or four man-heights above the level of the Heaving Sea, while back in the lands of the Derku, the shelf was so far above the level of the Salt Sea that it felt as though you were looking down from a mountain. The whole plain was enormously wide, and yet it went so deep before reaching the water of the Salt Sea that you could see for miles and miles, all the way across. It was deep, that plain, a valley, really. A deep gouge cut into the earth. And if this shelf of land was truly level, the Heaving Sea was far, far higher.

He thought of the floods. Thought of the powerful current of the flooding river that had snagged him and swept him downward. And then he thought of a storm that lifted the water of the Heaving Sea and sent it crashing along this valley floor, cutting a new channel until it reached those smaller seas, filling them with saltwater, causing *them* to flood and spill over. Spill over where? Where did their water flow? He already knew—they emptied down into the Salt Sea. Down and down and down.

It will happen again, thought Glogmeriss. There will be another storm, and this time the channel will be cut deeper, and when the storm subsides the water will still flow, because now the channel will be below the level of the Heaving Sea at high tide. And at each high tide, more water will flow and the channel will get deeper and deeper, till it's deep enough that even at low tide the water will still flow through it, cutting the channel more and more, and the water will come faster and faster, and then the Heaving Sea will spill over into the great valley, faster and faster and faster.

All this water then will spill out of the Heaving Sea and go down into the plain until the two seas are the same level. And once that happens, it will never go back.

The lands of the Derku are far below the level of the new sea, even if it's only half as high as the waters of the Heaving Sea are now. Our city will be covered. The whole land. And it won't be a trickle. It will be a great bursting of water, a huge wave of water, like the first gush of the floodwater down the Selud River from the Sweetwater Sea. Just like that, only the Heaving Sea is far larger than the Sweetwater Sea, and its water is angry and poisonous.

"Yes," said Glogmeriss. "I see what you brought me here to show me."

"Don't be silly," said Zawada. "I brought you here to have you eat clams!"

"I wasn't talking to you," said Glogmeriss. He stood up and left her, walking down the finger of the sea, where the tide was rising again, bringing the water lunging back up the channel, pointing like a javelin toward the heart of the Derku people. Zawada followed behind him. He didn't mind.

Glogmeriss reached the waves of the rising tide and plunged in. He knelt down in the water and let a wave crash over him. The force of the water toppled him, twisted him until he couldn't tell which way was up and he thought he would drown under the water. But then the wave retreated again, leaving him in the shallow water on the shore. He crawled back out and stayed there, the taste of salt on his lips, gasping for air, and then cried out, "Why are you doing this! Why are you doing this to my people!"

Zawada stood watching him, and others of the tribe came to join her, to find out what the strange giant man was doing in the sea.

Angry, thought Glogmeriss. The god is angry with my people. And I have been brought here to see just what terrible punishment the god has prepared for them. "Why?" he cried again. "Why not just break through this channel and send the flood and bury the Derku people in poisonous water? Why must I be shown this first? So I can save myself by staying high out of the flood's way? Why should I be saved alive, and all my family, all my friends be destroyed? What is their crime that I am not also guilty of? If you brought me here to save me, then you failed, God, because I refuse to stay, I will go back to my people and warn them all, I'll tell them what you're planning. You can't save me alone. When the flood comes I'll be right there with the rest of them. So to save me, you must save them all. If you don't like *that,* then you should have drowned me just now when you had the chance!"

Glogmeriss rose dripping from the beach and began to walk, past the people, up toward the shelf of land that made the level highway back home to the Derku people. The tribe understood at once that he was leaving, and they began calling out to him, begging him to stay.

"I can't," he said. "Don't try to stop me. Even the god can't stop me."

They didn't try to stop him, not by force. But the chief ran after him, walked beside him—ran beside him, really, for that was the only way he could keep up with Glogmeriss's long-legged stride. "Friend, Son," said the chief. "Don't you know that you will be king of these people after me?"

"A people should have a king who is one of their own."

"But you *are* one of us now," said the chief. "The mightiest of us. You will make us a great people! The god has chosen you, do you think we can't see that? This is why the god brought you here, to lead us and make us great!"

"No," said Glogmeriss. "I'm a man of the Derku people."

"Where are they? Far from here. And there is my daughter with your first child in her womb. What do they have in Derku lands that can compare to that?"

"They have the womb where *I* was formed," said Glogmeriss. "They have the man who put me there. They have the others who came from that woman and that man. They are my people."

"Then go back, but not today! Wait till you see your child born. Decide then!"

Glogmeriss stopped so abruptly that the chief almost fell over, trying to stop running and stay with him. "Listen to me, father of my wife. If you were up in the mountain hunting, and you looked down and saw a dozen huge cats heading toward the place where your people were living, would you say to yourself, Oh, I suppose the god brought me here to save me? Or would you run down the mountain and warn them, and do all you could to fight off the cats and save your people?"

"What is this story?" asked the chief. "There are no cats. You've seen no cats."

"I've seen the god heaving in his anger," said Glogmeriss. "I've seen how he looms over my people, ready to destroy them all. A flood that will tear their flimsy reed boats to pieces. A flood that will come in a single great wave and then will never go away. Do you think I shouldn't warn my mother and father, my brothers and sisters, the friends of my childhood?"

"I think you have new brothers and sisters, a new father and mother. The god isn't angry with *us*. The god isn't angry with you. We should stay together. Don't you *want* to stay with us and live and rule over us? You can be our king now, today. You can be king over me, I give you my place!"

"Keep your place," said Glogmeriss. "Yes, a part of me wants to stay. A part of me is afraid. But that is the part of me that is Glogmeriss, and still a boy. If I don't go home and warn my people and show them how to save themselves from the god, then I will always be a boy, nothing but a boy, call me a king if you want, but I will be a boy-king, a coward, a child until the day I die. So I tell you now, it is the child who dies in this place, not the man. It was the child Glogmeriss who married Zawada. Tell her that a strange man named Naog killed her husband. Let her marry someone else, someone of her own tribe, and never think of Glogmeriss again." Glogermiss kissed his father-in-law and embraced him. Then he turned away, and with his first step along the path leading back to the Derku people, he knew that he was truly Naog now, the man who would save the Derku people from the fury of the god.

Kemal watched the lone man of the Engu clan as he walked away from the beach, as he conversed with his father-in-law, as he turned his face again away from the Gulf of Aden, toward the land of the doomed crocodile-worshippers whose god was no match for the forces about to be unleashed on them. This was the one, Kemal knew, for he had seen the wooden boat—more of a watertight cabin on a raft, actually, with none of this nonsense about taking animals two by two. This was the man of legends, but seeing his face, hearing his voice, Kemal was no closer to understanding him than he had been before. What can we see, using the TruSite II? Only what is visible. We may be able to range through time, to see the most intimate, the most terrible, the most horrifying, the most inspiring moments of human history, but we only see them, we only hear them, we are witnesses but we know nothing of the thing that matters most: motive.

Why didn't you stay with your new tribe, Naog? They heeded your warning, and camped always on higher ground during the monsoon season. They lived through the flood, all of them. And when you went home and no one listened to your warnings, why did you stay? What was it that made you remain among them, enduring their ridicule as you built your watertight seedboat? You could have left at any time—there were others who cut themselves loose from their birth tribe and wandered through the world until they found a new home. The Nile was waiting for you. The grasslands of Arabia. They were already there, calling to you, even as your own homeland became poisonous to you. Yet you remained among the Engu, and by doing so, you not only gave the world an unforgettable story, you also changed the course of history. What kind of being is it who can change the course of history, just because he follows his own unbending will?

It was on his third morning that Naog realized that he was not alone on his return journey. He awoke in his tree because he heard shuffling footsteps through the grass nearby. Or perhaps it was something else that woke him—some unhearable yearning that he nevertheless heard. He looked, and saw in the faint light of the thinnest crescent moon that a lone baboon was shambling along, lazy, staggering. No doubt an old male, thought Naog, who will soon be meat for some predator.

Then his eyes adjusted and he realized that this lone baboon was not as close as he had thought, that in fact it was much bigger, much *taller* than he had thought. It was not male, either, but female, and far from being a baboon, it was a human, a pregnant woman, and he knew her now and shuddered at his own thought of her becoming the meal for some cat, some crocodile, some pack of dogs.

Silently he unfastened himself from his sleeping tree and dropped to the ground. In moments he was beside her.

"Zawada," he said.

She didn't turn to look at him.

"Zawada, what are you doing?"

Now she stopped. "Walking," she said.

"You're asleep," he said. "You're in a dream."

"No, *you're* asleep," she said, giggling madly in her weariness.

"Why have you come? I left you."

"I know," she said.

"I'm returning to my own people. You have to stay with yours." But he knew even as he said it that she could not go back there, not unless he went with her. Physically she was unable to go on by herself—clearly she had eaten nothing and slept little in three days. Why she had not died already, taken by some beast, he could not guess. But if she was to return to her people, he would have to take her, and he did not want to go back there. It made him very angry, and so his voice burned when he spoke to her.

"I wanted to," she said. "I wanted to weep for a year and then make an image of you out of sticks and burn it."

"You should have," he said.

"Your son wouldn't let me." As she spoke, she touched her belly.

"Son? Has some god told you who he is?"

"He came to me himself in a dream, and he said, 'Don't let my father go without me.' So I brought him to you."

"I don't want him, son *or* daughter." But he knew even as he said it that it wasn't true.

She didn't know it, though. Her eyes welled with tears and she sank down into the grass. "Good, then," she said. "Go on with your journey. I'm sorry the god led me near you, so you had to be bothered." She sank back in the grass. Seeing the faint gleam of light reflected from her skin awoke feelings that Naog was now ashamed of, memories of how she had taught him the easing of a man's passion.

"I can't walk off and leave you."

"You already did," she said. "So do it again. I need to sleep now."

"You'll be torn by animals and eaten."

"Let them," she said. "You never chose me, Derku man, I chose *you*. I invited this baby into my body. Now if we die here in the grass, what is that to you? All you care about is not having to watch. So don't watch. Go. The sky is getting light. Run on ahead. If we die, we die. We're nothing to you anyway."

Her words made him ashamed. "I left you knowing you and the baby would be safe, at home. Now you're here and you aren't safe, and I can't walk away from you."

"So run," she said. "I was your wife, and this was your son, but in your heart we're already dead anyway."

"I didn't bring you because you'd have to learn the Derku language. It's much harder than your language."

"I would have had to learn it anyway, you fool," she said. "The baby inside me is a Derku man like you. How would I get him to understand me, if I didn't learn Derku talk?"

Naog wanted to laugh aloud at her hopeless ignorance. But then, how would she know? Naog had seen the children of captives and knew that in Derku lands they grew up speaking the Derku language, even when both parents were from another tribe that had not one word of Derku language in it. But Zawada had never seen the babies of strangers; her tribe captured no one, went on no raids, but rather lived at peace, moving from place to place, gathering whatever the earth or the sea had to offer them. How could she match even a small part of the great knowledge of the Derku, who brought the whole world within their city?

He wanted to laugh, but he did not laugh. Instead he watched over her as she slept, as the day waxed and waned. As the sun rose he carried her to the tree to sleep in the shade. Keeping his eye open for animals prowling near her, he gathered such leaves and seeds and roots as the ground offered the traveler at this time of year. Twice he came back and found her breath rasping and noisy; then he made her wake enough to drink a little of his water, but she was soon asleep, water glistening on her chin.

At last in the late afternoon, when the air was hot and still, he squatted down in the grass beside her and woke her for good, showing her the food. She ate ravenously, and when she was done, she embraced him and called him the best of the gods because he didn't leave her to die after all.

"I'm not a god," he said, baffled.

"All my people know you are a god, from a land of gods. So large, so powerful, so good. You came to us so you could have a human baby. But this baby is only half human. How will he ever be happy, living among *us,* never knowing the gods?"

"You've seen the Heaving Sea, and you call *me* a god?"

"Take me with you to the land of the Derku. Let me give birth to your baby there. I will leave it with your mother and your sisters, and I will go home. I know I don't belong among the gods, but my baby does."

In his heart, Naog wanted to say yes, you'll stay only till the baby is born, and then you'll go home. But he remembered her patience as he learned the language of her people. He remembered the sweet language of her people. He remembered the sweet language of the night, and the way he had to laugh at how she tried to act like a grown woman when she was only a child, and yet she couldn't act like a child because she was, after all, now a woman. Because of me she is a woman, thought Naog, and because of her and her people I will come home a man. Do I tell her she must go away, even though I know that the others will think she's ugly as I thought she was ugly?

And she is ugly, thought Naog. Our son, if he *is* a son, will be ugly like her people, too. I will be ashamed of him. I will be ashamed of her.

Is a man ashamed of his firstborn son?

"Come home with me to the land of the Derku," said Naog. "We will tell them together about the Heaving Sea, and how one day soon it will leap over the low walls of sand and pour into this great plain in a flood that will cover the Derku lands forever. There will be a great migration. We will move, all of us, to the land my father found. The crocodiles live there also, along the banks of the Nile."

"Then you will truly be the greatest among the gods," she said, and the worship in her eyes made him proud and ill-at-ease, both at once. Yet how could he deny that the Derku were gods? Compared to her poor tribe, they would seem so. Thousands of people living in the midst of their own canals; the great fields of planted grain stretching far in every direction; the great wall of earth surrounding the Great Derku; the seedboats scattered like strange soft boulders; the children riding their dragonboats through the canals; a land of miracles to her. Where else in all the world had so many people learned to live together, making great wealth where once there had been only savannah and floodplain?

We live like gods, compared to other people. We come like gods out of nowhere, to carry off captives the way death carries people off. Perhaps that is what the life after death is like—the *real* gods using us to dredge their canals. Perhaps that is what all of human life is for, to create slaves for the gods. And what if the gods themselves are also raided by some greater beings yet, carrying *them* off to raise grain in some unimaginable garden? Is there no end to the capturing?

There are many strange and ugly captives in Derku, thought Naog. Who will doubt me if I say that this woman is my captive? She doesn't speak the language, and soon enough she would be used to the life. I would be kind to her, and would treat her son well—I would hardly be the first man to father a child on a captive woman.

The thought made him blush with shame.

"Zawada, when you come to the Derku lands, you will come as my wife," he said. "And you will not have to leave. Our son will know his mother as well as his father."

Her eyes glowed. "You are the greatest and kindest of the gods."

"No," he said, angry now, because he knew very well just exactly how far from "great" and "kind" he really was, having just imagined bringing this sweet, stubborn, brave girl into captivity. "You must never call me a god again. Ever. There is only one god, do you understand me? And it is that god that lives inside the Heaving Sea, the one that brought me to see him and sent me back here to warn my people. Call no one else a god, or you can't stay with me."

Her eyes went wide. "Is there room in the world for only one god?"

"When did a crocodile ever bury a whole land under water forever?" Naog laughed scornfully. "All my life I have thought of the Great Derku as a terrible god, worthy of the worship of brave and terrible men. But the Great Derku is just a crocodile. It can be killed with a spear. Imagine stabbing the Heaving Sea. We can't even touch it. And yet the god can lift up the whole sea and pour it over the wall into this plain. *That* isn't just a god. That is *God*."

She looked at him in awe; he wondered whether she understood. And then realized that she could not possibly have understood, because half of what he said was in the Derku language, since he didn't even know enough words in *her* language to think of these thoughts, let alone say them.

Her body was young and strong, even with a baby inside it, and the next morning she was ready to travel. He did not run now, but even so they covered ground quickly, for she was a sturdy walker. He began teaching her the Derku language as they walked, and she learned well, though she made the words sound funny, as so many captives did, never able to let go of the sounds of their native tongue, never able to pronounce the new ones.

Finally he saw the mountains that separated the Derku lands from the Salty Sea, rising from the plain. "Those will be islands," said Naog, realizing it for the first time. "The highest ones. See? They're higher than the shelf of land we're walking on."

Zawada nodded wisely, but he knew that she didn't really understand what he was talking about.

"Those are the Derku lands," said Naog. "See the canals and the fields?"

She looked, but seemed to see nothing unusual at all. "Forgive me," she said, "but all I see are streams and grassland."

"But that's what I meant," said Naog. "Except that the grasses grow where we plant them, and all we plant is the grass whose seed we grind into meal. And the streams you see—they go where we want them to go. Vast circles surrounding the heart of the Derku lands. And there in the middle, do you see that hill?"

"I think so," she said.

"We build that hill every year, after the floodwater."

She laughed. "You tell me that you aren't gods, and yet you make hills and streams and meadows wherever you want them!"

Naog set his face toward the Engu portion of the great city. "Come home with me," he said.

Since Zawada's people were so small, Naog had not realized that he had grown ever taller during his manhood journey, but now as he led his ugly wife through the outskirts of the city, he realized that he was taller than everyone. It took him by surprise, and at first he was disturbed because it seemed to him that everyone had grown smaller. He even said as much to Zawada—"They're all so small"—but she laughed as if it were a joke. Nothing about the place or the people seemed small to *her*.

At the edge of the Engu lands, Naog hailed the boys who were on watch. "Hai!"

"Hai!" they called back.

"I've come back from my journey!" he called.

It took a moment for them to answer. "What journey was this, tall man?"

"My manhood journey. Don't you know me? Can't you see that I'm Naog?"

The boys hooted at that. "How can you be naked when you have your napron on?"

"Naog is my manhood name," said Naog, quite annoyed now, for he had not expected to be treated with such disrespect on his return. "You probably know of me by my baby name. They called me Glogmeriss."

They hooted again. "You used to be trouble, and now you're naked!" cried the bold one. "And your wife is ugly, too!"

But now Naog was close enough that the boys could see how very tall he was. Their faces grew solemn.

"My father is Twerk," said Naog. "I return from my manhood journey with the greatest tale ever told. But more important than that, I have a message from the god who lives in the Heaving Sea. When I have given my message, people will include you in my story. They will say, 'Who were the five fools who joked about Naog's name, when he came to save us from the angry god?' "

"Twerk is dead," said one of the boys.

"The Dragon took him," said another.

"He was head of the clan, and then the Great Derku began eating human flesh again, and your father gave himself to the Dragon for the clan's sake."

"Are you truly his son?"

Naog felt a gnawing pain that he did not recognize. He would soon learn to call it grief, but it was not too different from rage. "Is this another jest of yours? I'll break your heads if it is."

"By the blood of your father in the mouth of the beast, I swear that it's true!" said the boy who had earlier been the boldest in his teasing. "If you're his son, then you're the son of a great man!"

The emotion welled up inside him. "What does this mean?" cried Naog. "The Great Derku does not eat the flesh of men! Someone has murdered my father! He would never allow such a thing!" Whether he meant his father or the Great Derku who would never allow it even Naog did not know.

The boys ran off then, before he could strike out at them for being the tellers of such an unbearable tale. Zawada was the only one left, to pat at him, embrace him, try to soothe him with her voice. She abandoned the language of the Derku and spoke to him soothingly in her own language. But all Naog could hear was the news that his father had been fed to the Great Derku as a sacrifice for the clan. The old days were back again, and they had killed his father. His father, and not even a captive!

Others of the Engu, hearing what the boys were shouting about, brought him to his mother. Then he began to calm down, hearing her voice, the gentle reassurance of the old sound. She, at least, was unchanged. Except that she looked older, yes, and tired. "It was your father's own choice," she explained to him. "After floodwater this year the Great Derku came into the pen with a human baby in its jaws. It was a two-year-old boy of the Ko clan, and it happened he was the firstborn of his parents."

"This means only that the Ko clan wasn't watchful enough," said Naog.

"Perhaps," said his mother. "But the holy men saw it as a sign from the god. Just as we stopped giving human flesh to the Great Derku when he refused it, so now when he claimed a human victim, what else were we to think?"

"Captives, then. Why not captives?"

"It was your own father who said that if the Great Derku had taken a child from the families of the captives, then we would sacrifice captives. But he took a child from one of our clans. What kind of sacrifice is it, to offer strangers when the Great Derku demanded the meat of the Derku people?"

"Don't you see, Mother? Father was trying to keep them from sacrificing anybody at all, by making them choose something so painful that no one would do it."

She shook her head. "How do you know what my Twerk was trying to do? He was trying to save *you*."

"Me?"

"Your father was clan leader by then. The holy men said, 'Let each clan give the firstborn son of the clan leader.' "

"But I was gone."

"Your father insisted on the ancient privilege, that a father may go in place of his son."

"So he died in my place, because I was gone."

"If you had been here, Glogmeriss, he would have done the same."

He thought about this for a few moments, and then answered only, "My name is Naog now."

"We thought you were dead, Naked One, Stirrer of Troubles," said Mother.

"I found a wife."

"I saw her. Ugly."

"Brave and strong and smart," said Naog.

"Born to be a captive. I chose a different wife for you."

"Zawada is my wife."

Even though Naog had returned from his journey as a man and not a boy, he soon learned that even a man can be bent by the pressure of others. So far he had *not* bent: Zawada remained his wife. But he also took the wife his mother had chosen for him, a beautiful girl named Kormo. Naog was not sure what was worse about the new arrangement—that everyone else treated Kormo as Naog's real wife and Zawada as barely a wife at all, or that when Naog was hungry with passion, it was always Kormo he thought of. But he remembered Zawada at such times, how she bore him his first child, the boy Moiro; how she followed him with such fierce courage; how good she was to him when he was a stranger. And when he remembered, he followed his duty to her rather than his natural desire. This happened so often that Kormo complained about it. This made Naog feel somehow righteous, for the truth was that his first inclination had been right. Zawada should have stayed with her own tribe. She was unhappy most of the time, and kept to herself and her baby, and as the years passed, her babies. She was never accepted by the other women of the Derku. Only the captive women became friends with her, which caused even more talk and criticism.

Years passed, yes, and where was Naog's great message, the one the god had gone to such great trouble to give him? He tried to tell it. First to the leaders of the Engu clan, the whole story of his journey, and how the Heaving Sea was far higher than the Salty Sea and would soon break through and cover all the land with water. They listened to him gravely, and then one by one they counseled with him that when the gods wish to speak to the Derku people, they will do as they did when the Great Derku ate a human baby. "Why would a god who wished to send a message to the Derku people choose a mere *boy* as messenger?"

"Because I was the one who was taking the journey," he said.

"What will you have us do? Abandon our lands? Leave our canals behind, and our boats?"

"The Nile has fresh water and a flood season, my father saw it."

"But the Nile also has strong tribes living up and down its shores. Here we are masters of the world. No, we're not leaving on the word of a boy."

They insisted that he tell no one else, but he didn't obey them. In fact he told anyone who would listen, but the result was the same. For his father's memory or for his mother's sake, or perhaps just because he was so tall and strong, people listened politely— but Naog knew at the end of each telling of his tale that nothing had changed. No one believed him. And when he wasn't there, they repeated his stories as if they were jokes, laughing about riding a castrated bull ox, about calling a tree branch his brother, and most of all about the idea of a great flood that would never go away. Poor Naog, they said. He clearly lost his mind on his manhood journey, coming home with impossible stories that he obviously believes and an ugly woman that he dotes on.

Zawada urged him to leave. "You know that the flood is coming," she said. "Why not take your family up and out of here? Go to the Nile ourselves, or return to my father's tribe."

But he wouldn't hear of it. "I would go if I could bring my people with me. But what kind of man am I, to leave behind my mother and my brothers and sisters, my clan and all my kin?"

"You would have left me behind," she said once. He didn't answer her. He also didn't go.

In the third year after his return, when he had three sons to take riding on his dragonboat, he began the strangest project anyone had ever seen. No one was surprised, though, that crazy Naog would do something like this. He began to take several captives with him upriver to a place where tall, heavy trees grew. There they would wear out stone axes cutting down trees, then shape them into logs and ride them down the river. Some people complained that the captives belonged to everybody and it was wrong for Naog to have their exclusive use for so many days, but Naog was such a large and strange man that no one wanted to push the matter.

One or two at a time, they came to see what Naog was doing with the logs. They found that he had taught his captives to notch them and lash them together into a huge square platform, a dozen strides on a side. Then they made a second platform crossways to the first and on top of it, lashing every log to every other log, or so it seemed. Between the two layers he smeared pitch, and then on the top of the raft he built a dozen reed structures like the tops of seedboats. Before floodwater he urged his neighbors to bring him their grain, and he would keep it all dry. A few of them did, and when the rivers rose during floodwater, everyone saw that his huge seedboat floated, and no water seeped up from below into the seedhouses. More to the point, Naog's wives and children also lived on the raft, dry all the time, sleeping easily through the night instead of having to remain constantly wakeful, watching to make sure the children didn't fall into the water.

The next year, Engu clan built several more platforms following Naog's pattern. They didn't always lash them as well as he had, and during the next flood several of their rafts came apart—but gradually, so they had time to move the seeds. Engu clan had far more seed make it through to planting season than any of the other tribes, and soon the men had to range farther and farther upriver, because all the nearer trees of suitable size had been harvested.

Naog himself, though, wasn't satisfied. It was Zawada who pointed out that when the great flood came, the water wouldn't rise gradually as it did in the river floods. "It'll be like the waves against the shore, crashing with such force . . . and these reed shelters will never hold against such a wave."

For several years Naog experimented with logs until at last he had the largest movable structure ever built by human hands. The raft was as long as ever, but somewhat narrower. Rising from notches between logs in the upper platform were sturdy vertical posts, and these were bridged and roofed with wood. But instead of using logs for the planking and the roofing, Naog and the captives who served him split the logs carefully into planks, and these were smeared inside and out with pitch, and then another wall and ceiling were built inside, sandwiching the tar between them. People were amused to see Naog's captives hoisting dripping baskets of water to the roof of this giant seedboat and pouring them out onto it. "What, does he think that if he waters these trees, they'll grow like grass?" Naog heard them, but he cared not at all, for when they spoke he was inside his boat, seeing that not a drop of water made it inside.

The doorway was the hardest part, because it, too, had to be able to be sealed against the flood. Many nights Naog lay awake worrying about it before building this last and largest and tightest seedboat. The answer came to him in a dream. It was a memory of the little crabs that lived in the sand on the shore of the Heaving Sea. They dug holes in the sand and then when the water washed over them, their holes filled in above their heads, keeping out the water. Naog awoke knowing that he must put the door in the roof of his seedboat, and arrange a way to lash it from the inside.

"How will you see to lash it?" said Zawada. "There's no light inside."

So Naog and his three captives learned to lash the door in place in utter darkness.

When they tested it, water leaked through the edges of the door. The solution was to smear more pitch, fresh pitch, around the edges of the opening and lay the door into it so that when they lashed it the seal was tight. It was very hard to open the door again after that, but they got it open from the inside—and when they could see again they found that not a drop of water had got inside. "No more trials," said Naog.

Their work then was to gather seeds—and more than seeds this time. Water, too. The seeds went into baskets with lids that were lashed down, and the water went into many, many flasks. Naog and his captives and their wives worked hard during every moment of daylight to make the waterbags and seedbaskets and fill them. The Engu didn't mind at all storing more and more of their grain in

Naog's boat—after all, it was ludicrously watertight, so that it was sure to make it through the flood season in fine form. They didn't have to believe in his nonsense about a god in the Heaving Sea that was angry with the Derku people in order to recognize a good seedboat when they saw it.

His boat was nearly full when word spread that a group of new captives from the southeast were telling tales of a new river of salt-water that had flowed into the Salty Sea from the direction of the Heaving Sea. When Naog heard the news, he immediately climbed a tree so he could look toward the southeast. "Don't be silly," they said to him. "You can't see the Salty Shore from here, even if you climb the tallest tree."

"I was looking for the flood," said Naog. "Don't you see that the Heaving Sea must have broken through again, when a storm whipped the water into madness. Then the storm subsided, and the sea stopped flowing over the top. But the channel must be wider and longer and deeper now. Next time it won't end when the storm ends. Next time it will be the great flood."

"How do you know these things, Naog? You're a man like the rest of us. Just because you're taller doesn't mean you can see the future."

"The god is angry," said Naog. "The true god, not this silly crocodile god that you feed on human flesh." And now, in the urgency of knowing the imminence of the flood, he said what he had said to no one but Zawada. "Why do you think the true god is so angry with us? Because of the crocodile! Because we feed human flesh to the Dragon! The true god doesn't want offerings of human flesh. It's an abomination. It's as forbidden as the forbidden fruit. The crocodile god is not a god at all, it's just a wild animal, one that crawls on its belly, and yet we bow down to it. We bow down to the enemy of the true god!"

Hearing him say this made the people angry. Some were so furious they wanted to feed him to the Great Derku at once, but Naog only laughed at them. "If the Great Derku is such a wonderful god, let *him* come and get me, instead of you taking me! But no, you don't believe for a moment that he *can* do it. Yet the *true* god had the power to send me a castrated bull to ride, and a log to save me from a flood, and trees to catch the lightning so it wouldn't strike me. When has the Dragon ever had the power to do *that*?"

His ridicule of the Great Derku infuriated them, and violence might have resulted, had Naog not had such physical presence, and had his father not been a noble sacrifice to the Dragon. Over the next weeks, though, it became clear that Naog was now regarded by all as something between an enemy and a stranger. No one came to speak to him, or to Zawada, either. Only Kormo continued to have contact with the rest of the Derku people.

"They want me to leave you," she told him. "They want me to come back to my family, because you are the enemy of the god."

"And will you go?" he said.

She fixed her sternest gaze on him. "You are my family now," she said. "Even when you prefer this ugly woman to me, you are still my husband."

Naog's mother came to him once, to warn him. "They have decided to kill you. They're simply biding their time, waiting for the right moment."

"Waiting for the courage to fight me, you mean," said Naog.

"Tell them that a madness came upon you, but it's over," she said. "Tell them that it was the influence of this ugly foreign wife of yours, and then they'll kill her and not you."

Naog didn't bother to answer her.

His mother burst into tears. "Was this what I bore you for? I named you very well, Glogmeriss, my son of trouble and anguish!"

"Listen to me, Mother. The flood is coming. We may have very little warning when it actually comes, very little time to get into my seedboat. Stay near, and when you hear us calling—"

"I'm glad your father is dead rather than to see his firstborn son so gone in madness."

"Tell all the others, too, Mother. I'll take as many in my seedboat as will fit. But once the door in the roof is closed, I can't open it again. Anyone who isn't inside when we close it will never get inside, and they will die."

She burst into tears and left.

Not far from the seedboat was a high hill. As the rainy season neared, Naog took to sending one of his servants to the top of the hill several times a day, to watch toward the southeast. "What should we look for?" they asked. "I don't know," he answered. "A new river. A wall of water. A dark streak in the distance. It will be something that you've never seen before."

The sky filled with clouds, dark and threatening. The heart of the storm was to the south and east. Naog made sure that his wives and children and the wives and children of his servants didn't stray far from the seedboat. They freshened the water in the waterbags, to stay busy. A few raindrops fell, and then the rain stopped, and then a few more raindrops. But far to the south and east it was raining heavily. And the wind—the wind kept rising higher and higher, and it was out of the east. Naog could imagine it whipping the waves higher and farther into the deep channel that the last storm had opened. He imagined the water spilling over into the salty river-bed. He imagined it tearing deeper and deeper into the sand, more and more of it tearing away under the force of the torrent. Until finally it was no longer the force of the storm driving the water through the channel, but the weight of the whole sea, because at last it had been cut down below the level of low tide. And then the sea tearing deeper and deeper.

"Naog." It was the head of the Engu clan, and a dozen men with him. "The god is ready for you."

Naog looked at them as if they were foolish children. "This is the storm," he said. "Go home and bring your families to my seedboat, so they can come through the flood alive."

"This is no storm," said the head of the clan. "Hardly any rain has fallen."

The servant who was on watch came running, out of breath, his arms bleeding where he had skidded on the ground as he fell more than once in his haste. "Naog, master!" he cried. "It's plain to see—the Salty Shore is nearer. The Salty Sea is rising, and fast."

What a torrent of water it would take, to make the Salty Sea rise in its bed. Naog covered his face with his hands. "You're right," said Naog. "The god is ready for me. The true god. It was for this hour that I was born. As for *your* god—the true god will drown him as surely as he will drown anyone who doesn't come to my seedboat."

"Come with us now," said the head of the clan. But his voice was not so certain now.

To his servant and his wives, Naog said, "Inside the seedboat. When all are in, smear on the pitch, leaving only one side where I can slide down."

"You come too, husband," said Zawada.

"I can't," he said. "I have to give warning one last time."

"Too late!" cried the servant with the bleeding arms. "Come now."

"You go now," said Naog. "I'll be back soon. But if I'm not back, seal the door and open it for no man, not even me."

"When will I know to do that?" he asked in anguish.

"Zawada will tell you," said Naog. "She'll know." Then he turned to the head of the clan. "Come with me," he said. "Let's give the warning." Then Naog strode off toward the bank of the canal where his mother and brothers and sisters kept their dragonboats. The men who had come to capture him followed him, unsure who had captured whom.

It was raining again, a steady rainfall whipped by an ever-stronger wind. Naog stood on the bank of the canal and shouted against the wind, crying out for his family to join him. "There's not much time!" he cried. "Hurry, come to my seedboat!"

"Don't listen to the enemy of the god!" cried the head of the clan.

Naog looked down into the water of the canal. "Look, you fools! Can't you see that the canal is rising?"

"The canal always rises in a storm."

Naog knelt down and dipped his hand into the canal and tasted the water. "Salt," he said. "Salt!" he shouted. "This isn't rising because of rain in the mountains! The water is rising because the Salty Sea is filling with the water of the Heaving Sea. It's rising to cover us! Come with me now, or not at all! When the door of my seedboat closes, we'll open it for no one." Then he turned and loped off toward the seedboat.

By the time he got there, the water was spilling over the banks of the canals, and he had to splash through several shallow streams where there had been no streams before. Zawada was standing on top of the roof, and screamed at him to hurry as he clambered onto the top of it. He looked in the direction she had been watching, and saw what she had seen. In the distance, but not so very far away, a dark wall rushing toward them. A plug of earth must have broken loose, and a fist of the sea hundreds of feet high was slamming through the gap. It spread at once, of course, and as it spread the wave dropped until it was only fifteen or twenty feet high. But that was high enough. It would do.

"You fool!" cried Zawada. "Do you want to watch it or be saved from it?"

Naog followed Zawada down into the boat. Two of the servants smeared on a thick swatch of tar on the fourth side of the doorway. Then Naog, who was the only one tall enough to reach outside the hole, drew the door into place, snuggling it down tight. At once it became perfectly dark inside the seedboat, and silent, too, except for the breathing. "This time for real," said Naog softly. He could hear the other men working at the lashings. They could feel the floor moving under them—the canals had spilled over so far now that the raft was rising and floating.

Suddenly they heard a noise. Someone was pounding on the wall of the seedboat. And there was shouting. They couldn't hear the words, the walls were too thick. But they knew what was being said all the same. Save us. Let us in. Save us.

Kormo's voice was filled with anguish. "Naog, can't we—"

"If we open it now we'll never close it again in time. We'd all die. They had every chance and every warning. My lashing is done."

"Mine too," answered one of the servants.

The silence of the others said they were still working hard.

"Everyone hold on to the side posts," said Naog. "There's so much room here. We could have taken on so many more."

The pounding outside was in earnest now. They were using axes to hack at the wood. Or at the lashings. And someone was on top of the seedboat now, many someones, trying to pry at the door.

"Now, O God, if you mean to save us at all, send the water now."

"Done," said another of the servants. So three of the four corners were fully lashed.

Suddenly the boat lurched and rocked upward, then spun crazily in every direction at once. Everyone screamed, and few were able to keep their handhold, such was the force of the flood. They plunged to one side of the seedboat, a jumble of humans and spilling baskets and water bottles. Then they struck something—a tree? The side of a mountain?—and lurched in another direction entirely, and in the darkness it was impossible to tell anymore whether they were on the floor or the roof or one of the walls.

Did it go on for days, or merely hours? Finally the awful turbulence gave way to a spinning all in one plane. The flood was still rising; they were still caught in the twisting currents; but they were no longer caught in that wall of water, in the great wave that the god had sent. They were on top of the flood.

Gradually they sorted themselves out. Mothers found their children, husbands found their wives. Many were crying, but as the fear subsided they were able to find the ones who were genuinely in pain. But what could they do in the darkness to deal with bleeding injuries, or possible broken bones? They could only plead with the god to be merciful and let them know when it was safe to open the door.

After a while, though, it became plain that it wasn't safe *not* to open it. The air was musty and hot and they were beginning to pant. "I can't breathe," said Zawada. "Open the door," said Kormo.

Naog spoke aloud to the god. "We have no air in here," he said. "I have to open the door. Make it safe. Let no other wave wash over us with the door open."

But when he went to open the door, he couldn't find it in the darkness. For a sickening moment he thought: What if we turned completely upside down, and the door is now under us? I never thought of that. We'll die in here.

Then he found it, and began fussing with the lashings. But it was hard in the darkness. They had tied so hurriedly, and he wasn't thinking all that well. But soon he heard the servants also at work, muttering softly, and one by one they got their lashings loose and Naog shoved upward on the door.

It took forever before the door budged, or so it seemed, but when at last it rocked upward, a bit of faint light and a rush of air came into the boat and everyone cried out at once in relief and gratitude. Naog pushed the door upward and then maneuvered it to lie across the opening at an angle, so that the heavy rain outside wouldn't inundate them. He stood there holding the door in place, even though the wind wanted to pick it up and blow it away—a slab of wood as heavy as that one was! While in twos and threes they came to the opening and breathed, or lifted children to catch a breath of air. There was enough light to bind up some bleeding injuries, and to realize that no bones were broken at all.

The rain went on forever, or so it seemed, the rain and the wind. And then it stopped, and they were able to come out onto the roof of the seedboat and look at the sunlight and stare at the distant horizon. There was no land at all, just water. "The whole earth is gone," said Kormo. "Just as you said."

"The Heaving Sea has taken over this place," said Naog. "But we'll come to dry land. The current will take us there."

There was much debris floating on the water—torn-up trees and bushes, for the flood had scraped the whole face of the land. A few rotting bodies of animals. If anyone saw a human body floating by, they said nothing about it.

After days, a week, perhaps longer of floating without sight of land, they finally began skirting a shoreline. Once they saw the smoke of someone's fire—people who lived high above the great valley of the Salty Sea had been untouched by the flood. But there was no way to steer the boat toward shore. Like a true seedboat, it drifted unless something drew it another way. Naog cursed himself for his foolishness in not including dragonboats in the cargo of the boat. He and the other men and women might have tied lines to the seedboat and to themselves and paddled the boat to shore. As it was, they would last only as long as their water lasted.

It was long enough. The boat fetched up against a grassy shore. Naog sent several of the servants ashore and they used a rope to tie the boat to a tree. But it was useless—the current was still too strong, and the boat tore free. They almost lost the servants, stranding them on the shore, forever separated from their families, but they had the presence of mind to swim for the end of the rope.

The next day they did better—more lines, all the men on shore, drawing the boat further into a cove that protected it from the current. They lost no time in unloading the precious cargo of seeds, and searching for a source of fresh water. Then they began the unaccustomed task of hauling all the baskets of grain by hand. There were no canals to ease the labor.

"Perhaps we can find a place to dig canals again," said Kormo.

"No!" said Zawada vehemently. "We will never build such a place again. Do you want the god to send another flood?"

"There will be no other flood," said Naog. "The Heaving Sea has had its victory. But we will also build no canals. We will keep no crocodile, or any other animal as our god. We will never sacrifice forbidden fruit to any god, because the true god hates those who do that. And we will tell our story to anyone who will listen to it, so that others will learn how to avoid the wrath of the true god, the god of power."

Kemal watched as Naog and his people came to shore not far from Gibeil and set up farming in the El Qa' Valley in the shadows of the mountains of Sinai. The fact of the flood was well known, and many travelers came to see this vast new sea where once there had been dry land. More and more of them also came to the new village that Naog and his people built, and word of his story also spread.

Kemal's work was done. He had found Atlantis. He had found

Noah, and Gilgamesh. Many of the stories that had collected around those names came from other cultures and other times, but the core was true, and Kemal had found them and brought them back to the knowledge of humankind.

But what did it mean? Naog gave warning, but no one listened. His story remained in people's minds, but what difference did it make?

As far as Kemal was concerned, all old-world civilizations after Atlantis were dependent on that first civilization. The *idea* of the city was already with the Egyptians and the Sumerians and the people of the Indus and even the Chinese, because the story of the Derku people, under one name or another, had spread far and wide—the Golden Age. People remembered well that once there was a great land that was blessed by the gods until the sea rose up and swallowed their land. People who lived in different landscapes tried to make sense of the story. To the island-hopping Greeks Atlantis became an island that sank into the sea. To the plains-dwelling Sumerians the flood was caused by rain, not by the sea leaping out of its bed to swallow the earth. Someone wondered how, if all the land was covered, the animals survived, and thus the account of animals two by two was added to the story of Naog. At some point, when people still remembered that the name meant "naked," a story was added about his sons covering his nakedness as he lay in a drunken stupor. All of this was decoration, however. People remembered both the Derku people and the one man who led his family through the flood.

But they would have remembered Atlantis with or without Naog, Kemal knew that. What difference did his saga make, to anyone but himself and his household? As others studied the culture of the Derku, Kemal remained focused on Naog himself. If anything, Naog's life was proof that one person makes no difference at all in history. He saw the flood coming, he warned his people about it when there was plenty of time, he showed them how to save themselves, and yet nothing changed outside his own immediate family group. That was the way history worked. Great forces sweep people along, and now and then somebody floats to the surface and becomes famous but it means nothing, it amounts to nothing.

Yet Kemal could not believe it. Naog may not have accomplished what he *thought* his goal was—to save his people—but he did accomplish something. He never lived to see the result of it, but because of his survival the Atlantis stories were tinged with something else. It was not just a golden age, not just a time of greatness and wealth and leisure and city life, a land of giants and gods. Naog's version of the story also penetrated the public consciousness and remained. The people were destroyed because the greatest of gods was offended by their sins. The list of sins shifted and changed over time, but certain ideas remained: That it was wrong to live in a city, where people get lifted up in the pride of their hearts and think that they are too powerful for the gods to destroy. That the one who seems to be crazy may in fact be the only one who sees the truth. That the greatest of gods is the one you can't see, the one who has power over the earth and the sea and the sky, all at once. And, above all, this: That it was wrong to sacrifice human beings to the gods.

It took thousands of years, and there were places where Naog's passionate doctrine did not penetrate until modern times, but the root of it was there in the day he came home and found that his father had been fed to the Dragon. Those who thought that it was right to offer human beings to the Dragon were all dead, and the one who had long proclaimed that it was wrong was still alive. The god had preserved him and killed all of them. Wherever the idea of Atlantis spread, some version of this story came with it, and in the end all the great civilizations that were descended from Atlantis learned not to offer the forbidden fruit to the gods.

In the Americas, though, no society grew up that owed a debt to Atlantis, for the same rising of the world ocean that closed the land bridge between Yemen and Djibouti also broke the land bridge between America and the old world. The story of Naog did not touch there, and it seemed to Kemal absolutely clear what the cost of that was. Because they had no memory of Atlantis, it took the people of the Americas thousands of years longer to develop civilization—the city. Egypt was already ancient when the Olmecs first built amid the swampy land of the bay of Campeche. And because they had no story of Naog, warning that the most powerful of gods rejected killing human beings, the old ethos of human sacrifice remained in full force, virtually unquestioned. The carnage of the Mexica—the Aztecs—took it to the extreme, but it was there already, throughout the Caribbean basin, a tradition of human blood being shed to feed the hunger of the gods.

Kemal could hardly say that the bloody warfare of the old world was much of an improvement over this. But it was different, and in his mind, at least, it was different specifically because of Naog. If he had not ridden out of the flood to tell his story of the true God who forbade sacrifice, the old world would not have been the same. New civilizations might have risen more quickly, with no stories warning of the danger of city life. And those new civilizations might all have worshiped the same Dragon, or some other, as hungry for human flesh as the gods of the new world were hungry for human blood.

On the day that Kemal became sure that his Noah had actually changed the world, he was satisfied. He said little and wrote nothing about his conclusion. This surprised even him, for in all the months and years that he had searched hungrily for Atlantis, and then for Noah, and then for the meaning of Noah's saga, Kemal had assumed that, like Schliemann, he would publish everything, he would tell the world the great truth that he had found. But to his surprise he discovered that he must not have searched so far for the sake of science, or for fame, or for any other motive than simply to know, for himself, that one person's life amounted to something. Naog changed the world, but then so did Zawada, and so did Kormo, and so did the servant who skinned his elbows running down the hill, and so did Naog's father and mother, and . . . and in the end, so did they all. The great forces of history were real, after a fashion. But when you examined them closely, those great forces always came down to the dreams and hungers and judgments of individuals. The choices they made were real. They mattered.

Apparently that was all that Kemal had needed to know. The next day he could think of no reason to go to work. He resigned from his position at the head of the Atlantis project. Let others do the detail work. Kemal was well over thirty now, and he had found the answer to his great question, and it was time to get down to the business of living.

Invisible Bars

------- ✠ -------

Dean Wesley Smith

The Saturday afternoon the genie popped in, Jay would have much rather been out playing golf.

No mere mortal could have invented such a perfect golf afternoon; temperature in the low sixties, trees just getting their first spring growth, the smell of freshly cut grass in the air, and a soft wind out of the West. Jay watched the trees sway gently over his neighbor's barbecue. A perfect wind to make that final hole almost reachable. A perfect day for golf for everyone except Jay. His quest was doomed. Today he was to fight the piles of junk in the garage and do battle with a genie.

Somewhere, in the long-distant, snow-filled past, before the weatherman had said, "Clear and sunny through the weekend," Jay had promised Eva he would clean out the garage. A stupid promise even during the worst of weather. But he had given it with his most sincere smile to make up for an indiscretion he desperately wanted forgotten. Now no amount of shouting, pleading, or repromising could get him to that first tee.

Trapped. Jailed in a prison of his own making. Doomed to clog his nose with dust, cover his fingers with grease, and fill his hair with cobwebs. He was to suffer the torture of years of accumulated junk while his polished golf clubs sat against the trunk of his car.

The garage was into him for an hour of lost golf, one nasty cut on his right calf, and every cuss word he could think of, when he found the genie's lamp. It was in a box of garbage Eva had bought at a fall auction just to get a salt shaker which matched Aunt Edna's. Jay remembered that the entire box had cost him five bucks. He'd tossed it in the garage figuring he'd look at it later.

This fine spring golf day wasn't exactly the later he'd had in mind. The genie's lamp was buried clear to the bottom under an old ice skate, a dozen pink shelf brackets, and two burnt toasters. It was the standard Arab oil lamp Jay had seen in at least a dozen movies.

Jay looked longingly out at the sun-covered driveway and his golf clubs and then back at the lamp. Too bad genies didn't exist. He held the lamp up. "It ought to be worth at least a buck at the garage sale," he said to himself. Then he did the natural thing. He rubbed the lamp on his shirt sleeve.

A low rumble shook the garage, knocking the backyard hose off its tail. A bright flash blinded Jay, sending pinwheels of colored dots spinning against the inside of his eyelids. Slowly, the pinwheel cleared and Jay opened his eyes. The genie stood with his arms crossed and legs spread, right smack in the middle of the oil spot.

Jay dropped the lamp on the floor and stared open-mouthed for a moment before breaking down into complete laughter. He just couldn't help it. The big guy looked like a clown from the circus in his baggy knickers, sleeveless vest, and turban.

But the big guy didn't even crack a smile, so Jay slowly contained his laughter enough to go to the open garage door. "All right, you guys," he called out. "Good gag, but enough of this." He tried to spot the hiding place of his golfing buddies. This prank had to be their doing. They'd be close enough to see it. They must have planted the lamp in the box right before he started the clean-up. Jay looked at the big guy. "Ralph sent you, didn't he?"

The big guy didn't answer. He just stood there in the oil spot, arms folded, staring straight ahead. A Ralph trick. A little more elaborate, maybe, but a typical Ralph stunt. "All right," Jay said, making his voice sound as tough as he could without laughing. "What's going on?"

"You have three wishes, O master," the genie said, his deep, loud voice echoing in the garage. "But first you must prove your-self worthy."

That did it. Jay dropped down on an orange crate howling with choking laughter. And every time he tried to hold himself under control, he'd look up at the guy with the baggy knickers and start howling all over again. He was amazed he couldn't hear Ralph and the guys laughing from their hiding places.

"What's so funny?" Eva stopped in the kitchen door and stared at the big man. The genie never took his gaze off the wall. "Oh, I'm sorry," Eva said. "I didn't know you had a visitor." Eva kept staring at the guy and slowly her eyes glazed over.

Jay knew that look. He'd seen it for the first time back when they were dating. They'd gone to a triple-X movie and her eyes glazed over after only ten minutes. He'd seen it again two years ago when she'd had the affair. She didn't think he knew, but for al-most a month he'd come home and her eyes would have that look. He just wished she'd look at him like that again sometime.

Jay glanced quickly out the garage door. No sign of Ralph or anyone. They were going to make him play this gag out. He stood, moved up in front of the big guy, stuck out his hand and said, "My name's Jay Fenimore. This is my garage. Who are you?"

"I am the Genie of the Lamp." This time the volume of the guy's voice damn near deafened Jay.

Jay covered his ears and shouted back at the guy. "Who sent you?" He had no idea why he was shouting. It just seemed he needed to.

"You called me!" The garage trembled with that answer. Jay shook his head and hoped that someday his ears would quit ring-ing. He made a quick inspection of the area around the genie-fellow, looking for any type of sound system or wires. Not one sign of speakers, but that didn't mean there weren't any. He'd heard about those fancy new CIA gadgets. He couldn't imagine how Ralph had gotten hold of one. Anything was possible.

Jay went back to a position between the genie and the wall. "Quietly now," Jay shouted up at the genie. "Tell me what you're doing here."

"I've come to grant you three wishes if you are worthy." The guy's voice was even louder and deeper. At this rate, they'd be listening downtown in another sentence. Eva had her hands over her ears and the dazed look seemed to be fading.

Jay looked quickly from Eva to the genie. He'd have to play along until Ralph and the guys pulled their *gotcha*. They'd laugh all the way to the golf course.

"What do I have to do?" Jay asked and quickly covered his ears.

"My test is simple. Make a wish that I cannot grant. Then I will give you three that I can."

"Any three?"

"Yes!" the genie said. One of the dirty panes of glass in the back garage window shattered. The big guy didn't seem to notice.

"You've got to quiet him down!" Eva shouted. She looked scared.

Jay agreed. "Would you please move outside?" Jay pointed at the open garage door and started to lead the way. Three of his neighbors stood in the middle of the street staring.

"NO!" the genie said. "I cannot move until you answer my test." This time nothing broke, but it seemed as if the house took a few seconds to stop shaking. Jay waved to the neighbors and pulled the garage door closed. Then he moved quickly over beside Eva.

"For heaven's sake, don't ask him another question until I figure out who's behind all this."

"But who is he?" Eva asked. "Where's he from?"

"I am the Genie of the Lamp. I came because I was summoned."

Another pane of glass exploded out of the garage window and Jay heard a shattering in the kitchen.

"May I have ten minutes to consider my answer?"

"Yes," the genie said. It sounded slightly softer. Jay wasn't sure if it really was or if he was just going deaf. He pushed Eva back into the kitchen and closed the door.

"Should we call the police?" Eva asked.

Jay shook his head. Calling the police was always Eva's first thought. "No. I'm going to play along and give him a damn answer. Just as soon as I think of one."

"But if he *is* a real genie," Eva asked, "how can there be a wish he can't grant? What happens if you ask and he can grant it?"

"Then he will get only what he thinks I cannot grant," the genie said from out in the garage. "But the person he is now will not like it."

More glass shattered in the cabinets. Jay pushed Eva toward them. "See what's broken, and don't ask another question. He can hear us through the walls."

Eva nodded and started opening cupboard doors. Jay sat down at the kitchen table and tried to think. All he'd wanted to do was play golf. That damn simple. But no, now he was stuck with some prankster. Or worse yet, a real genie.

And if this guy was a real genie, what wish couldn't he grant? What kind of stupid test was this? In all the genie movies he'd seen, the person with the lamp just got three wishes. Not once did they have to pass any test. They sometimes got shot for owning the lamp, but never was there a test. Someone had made up new rules in the genie business.

Eva set a can of beer in front of Jay, and dropped down into the seat beside him. Jay knew when she brought him a beer, she was really worried. She actually believed that was a real genie out there. He was starting to believe it, too.

Jay looked around the small kitchen and sighed. Many nights over the past few years he'd thought of this room as prison. Not that he hadn't started out like everyone else, wanting a home and a family. He had. But now they just felt like weights. He'd started out loving his job. Now, he could barely drag himself to work. His entire life had become one prison linked to another. All he really wanted to do was play golf. If that guy was a genie, maybe Jay could get some golf time out of this mess. But first Jay had to think of a wish the genie could not grant. Stupid test. Wasn't finding the lamp enough?

Jay took a long drink of the beer and tried to think. What wish couldn't a real genie grant? Maybe there was somewhere the genie couldn't go, like the moon. Probably any good, self-respecting genie could go there. And if Jay asked for that, he'd be stuck on the moon.

Maybe there was something the genie couldn't bring to him, like a building or a bridge. He had a sudden flash of the Empire State Building sticking up out of the middle of his subdivision.

"Your time is up," the genie said. Jay held on to the kitchen table and studied the new cracks in the ceiling paint. This poor house wasn't going to take much more.

"I'm coming!" Jay shouted at the garage door. This house may have become his prison over the last few years, but it still made him angry when someone threatened it.

Suddenly, Jay knew the way out. Knew without a doubt what he would ask for. It was so easy. He knew the one thing the genie couldn't grant him. One simple wish. That's all it would take. Then he could play golf for the rest of his life.

Jay smiled at Eva, motioned for her to be quiet, then led her out the back door. The genie was still standing in the middle of the oil spot, legs apart, arms folded across his chest.

"I'm ready," Jay said, winking at Eva.

"Good," the genie said. "Make a wish that I cannot grant and I will give you three that I can."

Jay stepped over in front of the genie and took a deep breath. "My wish is simple. I wish to remain the same flesh-and-blood man I am now, living here like I do now, while being free from every conceivable prison that makes up my life."

There was a very long and very loud silence. Jay could feel his heart pounding against his chest. There was no way the genie could grant that wish. No way.

Slowly, the genie looked down at Jay. Jay shivered under the genie's stare. He felt naked, as if everything he'd ever done or ever thought lay open.

After only a moment, the genie closed his eyes and started laughing softly. It was a quiet laugh in comparison and Jay doubted anyone outside the garage could hear it.

"You are very resourceful," the genie said in a normal voice. "And your wish has come the closest to succeeding than all the thousands of your kind I have met over the centuries."

"You mean you can grant that wish?" Jay asked. He didn't know whether to be happy or afraid.

Eva took hold of Jay's arm. "You can't take him. He did nothing to deserve this."

The genie again laughed softly. "I have no plans of taking him. I only plan to grant his wish."

"But you said I wouldn't like what I would get," Jay said. "I would love the freedom from all of life's prisons."

"I don't think so," the genie said sadly. "Many before you sought out the Holy Grail in hopes of finding eternal life and escape from the prisons of their own bodies and they were never successful. They looked for a drinking cup to solve their problems. They never looked inside. I have seen that you are a proud, intelligent man trapped by what you were taught and the rules around you. Those are the prisons you refer to. Your body, your home, your work. You see that you stand within them and you see the bars that hold you. But inside of working around and with those bars that define your life, you have done nothing. You have only waited, hoping to find that *Grail* to free you."

"Please," Jay said. "I really . . ."

"I am sorry," the genie said, "but you see, I too am bound by rules. You wished to remain the same flesh-and-blood man, yet be totally free from the prisons that make up your life. So be it."

The genie waved his hand in the air above Jay as he said, "The only man totally free from the prisons of life is one who cannot see that he is in them."

There was a bright flash that sent dots spinning in front of Jay's eyes, followed quickly by a rumbling thunder. The last pane of glass in the garage window dropped out and broke on the concrete.

"They really should ban those jets and their sonic booms," Jay said as he finished sweeping up the broken glass and handed the broom to Eva. Then he reached down and picked up the old rusted cup out of a box of junk. He stared at it a moment, trying to figure out why it looked familiar. "Eva, you want this?"

Eva looked over her shoulder at the cup as she started to sweep up the dust around the oil spot. "I don't think so. Give it to the rummage people."

Jay studied the cup for a moment wondering just what anyone would use it for, then tossed it on the growing pile heading for re-sale. It landed between an old lamp and his polished golf clubs.

That Way Lies Camelot

-✝-

Janny Wurts

The May sunlight that fell through the windows was serene enough
to trigger a violence of resentment and hurt. Lynn Allen hurled a
sodden, crumb-gritty sponge in the sink and ran her fingers through
hair that fell thick to her shoulders, in neglected need of a cut.
Childless, still single at thirty-three, she held little enough in common with a younger sister whose pretty, homey kitchen reflected
family cheer at every turn. And what could anybody say to comfort
a sibling who was divorced, a mother of three, with her eldest just
barely twelve and lying in a coma, not expected to last out the day?

Words failed. Despair raged in like flood tide.

Wretched with the helplessness that overran them all over
Sandy's terminal illness, Lynn blinked and roused and wiped damp
palms on her jeans. She tried to regroup, to recover a grip on the
immediate, while at the end of the gravel drive outside, a school
bus slowed to a grind of gears; stopped to a squeal of brakes.

The front door banged.

"Damn it!" Raw with exasperation, Lynn repeated the same
check she'd completed five minutes earlier. There'd been no forgotten books or sweaters in the breakfast nook then; she hadn't
overlooked a misplaced brown bag lunch. No dab hand with kids,
she'd thought she'd done miracles to get her nephews out the door
on time for school without their incessant bickering firing her temper.

In typically eight-year-old smugness, Tony hollered bad news from the hallway. "Dog pen's empty, Aunt Lynn! Grail's run off again."

And the front door, left open, wafted air strongly scented with bursting pre-summer greenery. The patter of the boy's running sneakers diminished down the porch stair as he raced headlong toward the waiting bus.

"Damned *stupid* flea-bag of a mutt!" Lynn clenched her fists, feeling sloppy and out of synch in clothes more suited for weekend picnics. The dog's timing couldn't be worse; and worse, couldn't be helped. He would have to be rounded up before he finished dining from the neighbor's upset trash cans, and nosed out more original mischief that would incite some busybody's complaint to the county dog catchers. Ragged already from grief and exhaustion, Ann was shortly going to be coping with the funeral of a son. Given hassles with the insurance company over hospital expenses worth more than her house, the last thing she needed would be another fine for an unleashed pet.

The dog was Sandy's, after all. Obligation to a child, who could not be spared by all the torments of modern medicine, would invoke motherly sentiment by the bucket. The scrofulous yellow hound, with its torn ear and its ridiculous shambling gait, would be redeemed. An ounce of common sense suggested the creature should be better off abandoned to be humanely destroyed.

Through the window, washed in early, blinding brightness, Lynn saw Tony's neon jacket disappear inside the doorway of the bus. Brian, just ten, had boarded already. One problem less, with the boys off her hands; which left the damnfool dog. Lynn moved mechanically to the closet and snatched the first jacket to hand, an anorak that was baggy and grease-stained enough to have belonged to Annie's ex. She grimaced and pulled the thing on. It felt worse than her face, which any other day would have been tastefully made up for her work as design manager for a New York advertising firm.

But her job, as well as the tacked-together appointments she called a social life, had been wrenched to a halt by Sandy's relapse.

The event had impelled her to acts of insanity: to cash in her un-
used vacation time and leave the office in a hair-pulling rush.

Her boss's shouting troubled her. "There might not be any job
here for you, whenever the hell you get back!"

And her reply, as filled with female bitchiness as any chauvin-
ist could wish, to find fault for firing her later: "My nephew is ill,
and I'm driving to New Hampshire to help my sister. If you've got
a problem with that, then take my resignation in writing, sideways,
down the first orifice you can reach."

She'd slammed the office door upon a thunderstruck, stupefied
silence; and although she'd stayed absent for a month and sent no
word, nobody from the firm so much as phoned.

Presently on her knees in the silvery pile of Annie's living
room carpet, Lynn smothered a halfway hysterical laugh. Just now
the convolutions of high-pressure employment seemed a picnic, beside the daily management of young boys, and keeping tabs on one
alley-bred mutt. She scrounged under the coffee table, careful not
to upset the empty pizza box with its cache of stale crumbs, and
stretched to rescue her sneakers. These had somehow been kicked
so far underneath the sofa they were wedged against the back strut.
Grunting other inexpressible frustrations in epithets over the dog,
she sauntered across waxed floors and expensive orientals to the
doorway, still open and decorated with a wreath that had Easter
eggs wired in withered sprigs of hemlock.

The decoration had stayed up, forgotten, in the crush of concerns that followed Sandy's sudden onset of infections and the
ugly, inescapable diagnosis that every agonizing scientific remedy
had bought little more time, and no cure.

Lynn crossed the white and green painted New England porch,
squinted through light that hurt, and dissected the muddle of shade
cast by a privet hedge whose wild growth reflected the absence of
a husband. Though the fence wasn't torn, and the wire gate on its
sagging hinges was still wrapped shut with chain, the dog's pen
stood deserted. The infamous Grail had departed on another of his
happy gallivants.

She sighed. Grail. What a stupid name for an ungainly mutt

that loped like a roll of discarded shag carpet, propped askew on four legs. A creature nobody would have wanted, in right mind or not; but as a shambling stray towed home on a length of twine that showed signs of its salvage from the gutter, he had not been easily refused. Not when his plight had been championed by Sandy, who had sneaked outside unseen, still shaky and pale from the effects of his chemotherapy treatments. The huge eyes and gaunt face of leukemia in remission had overturned practicality, which would have been fine if the idiot dog had been content to enjoy his good fortune.

But the mongrel was friendly and brainless, and possessed by a penchant for wandering. He chewed through ropes, dug under wire fences, then progressed to other escape methods as unfathomable in their art as Houdini's. It had been Grandfather Thomas who had called the creature Grail; the name stuck because of his young owner's obsession for Arthurian legend, and for the hours the whole family spent in godforsaken searches that seemed as regular and futile as crusades.

"Do us all a service and charge in front of a delivery truck," Lynn grumbled to the creature's absent spirit. She kicked a stone and hiked after its savage ricochet down the drive. Over the grit and sparkle of gravel left mounded by the melt of last season's snowdrifts, she rounded the hedge toward the neighbor's yard.

Charlie Mitchell still wore his bathrobe, sash and hem flapping as he ill-temperedly chased down a bread wrapper caught by the wind. The trash can stood righted amid a chewed litter of The Colonel's colored packaging. Obviously Grail had feasted and departed. Poised to beat a quick retreat, Lynn moved too late.

White hair askew and pajama cuffs grayed from the dew, Charlie pounced on the plastic. He gave a crow of triumph, swiveled around, and realized in embarrassment that his antics had been observed. Flustered by his unaccustomed burst of exercise, he called in carping irritation, "Damned dog lit off for the woods an hour ago! Get wise and buy him a chain, can't you? It's illegal to shoot dogs out of hand in this state. Or by God, I'd have loaded my shotgun and blown the mutt to the devil."

Lynn choked back excuses that a chain had failed already. Grail's brainless skull was narrow like a snake's, and collars slid off him like so many layers of shed skin. The chain, hacked off a foot from its swivel clip, now fastened an equally useless gate. She produced a polite apology for her sister's sake, and returned in resignation toward the house.

Inside, cut off from the gusty freshness of bursting azaleas and tulips, the rooms were sun-washed and silent. The waxed antiques and stylish hardwoods seemed too warm with life, their expensive comforts disjointed by a wider setting of tragedy. Lynn gritted her teeth unconsciously as she passed by Sandy's room, with its counterpane bedspread and clutterless floors, all too painfully neat. Unlike Tony, who slept like a hot dog in a bun, Sandy tended to rip his bedclothes off wholesale and leave them tousled in heaps. Photos of medieval castles lined the walls, as well as an old poster, lovingly framed, from a stage production of *Camelot*. The books and toy knights were not scattered across the rugs, nor arrayed for a charge against Saxons. They sat ranked in rows on the shelf, helms and ribboned trappings dulled by a layer of soft dust. As if Sandy's boisterous presence had been subdued, reduced already to a shadow that diminished the vibrance of his memory. Lynn pressed a hand to her mouth and hurried the length of the hallway, her track automatically bending to avoid the clutter of the younger boys' toys.

But the desk in the corner of the master bedroom offered no haven at all.

Lynn sat, elbows crackling in stacks of envelopes that showed not a curlicue of Annie's idle doodles. The mail lay as it had come, unopened, or else torn apart in fierce bursts, contents rifled for information. North sky through the casement blued the oblong, windowed cellophane; the return addresses of medical labs and oncologists, printed starkly in thermographed typefaces only preferred anymore by doctors, lawyers, and funeral homes.

Off to one side, bent-cornered and half buried, lay the unsent application for the charity that granted the wishes of terminally ill children. Only the blanks that related to Sandy's condition were filled out; the doctors' signatures meticulously collected in heavy-handed, near illegible scrawls. The last sentences, in defiant schoolboy printing, requested a visit to the Round Table of King Arthur. After that, unfilled lines stretched in rows. The memory still cut, of the aftermath, with Ann driven to the edge. "My God, Lynn. Sandy's old enough to know that a trip to the past is impossible!"

At this desk, in this chair, Ann had sat white-faced over the pens and the papers gathered up from the kitchen table. She wept in despairing exasperation that the one wish her boy chose to long for was beyond human resource to fulfill.

Later, around the rubber-soled tread of busy nurses and the unending interruptions of hospital routine, they tried to coax Sandy to reconsider. Donated funds could send kids to Disney World, let them play with circus clowns, allow them to meet famous rock stars, or tour the set of a movie. But sending a boy back to King Arthur's court was just not a practical aspiration.

Too thin, too pale, his scrawny hand clenched on the wrist that had bruised red and purple from too close acquaintance with needles, Sandy stayed adamant. He would see Camelot, or go nowhere at all.

Lynn swore and blinked back tears. It wasn't as if they couldn't have sent the kid to a Renaissance fair, or a summertime recreation staged by the Society for Creative Anachronism. Yet Sandy scorned the idea of a staged joust. He wanted real chivalry, and swords that drew blood, as if the savage bright danger of a legendary past could negate the horrors he endured through his illness.

"You know," he confided to his mother, "men got hurt in Arthur's time, and suffered wounds, and it was for a *cause*. Knights died for other people, Mom. I hurt, and I'll die too, but nobody will be better or get saved."

A boy's view: more than just desire, that leaped reason's restraint and became dreaming obsession. The tissue of tears and salvation for him; agony to the family he'd leave behind. Ann had pulled a tissue from her purse, blown her nose, and put the subject behind as best she could. She gave Sandy a hug and insisted it probably didn't matter anyway, as grants to bring joy to terminally ill children usually were awarded to cystic fibrosis cases. Leukemia, these days, was considered the less devastating disease.

Not Sandy's aggressive form, this was true.

Battered by platitudes that even the child could sense were meaningless, Sandy never complained. Colorless as the pillows he lay on, his features made over into an eerie, premature old age by the hair loss caused by his treatments, he had comforted his mother by pretending most diligently to forget.

Now, stung to useless fury by this fortitude, Lynn plowed aside the paper clutter that mapped a child's last month of life. She grabbed the phone and jabbed numbers fiercely.

The line rang once. Ann answered. She sounded beat to her socks.

Lynn made a failed attempt to sound cheerful. "Still there?"

A wrung-out sigh came back. "Still there. At least he still shows breathing and a heartbeat." A pause, as Annie roused enough to take worried notice of the time. "Did Brian miss the bus?"

Lynn blinked faster, and felt tears trace hot lines down her cheeks. She could not, so easily, brush away the vision in her mind, of Sandy lying lost in a sea of adult-sized sheets, his wasted form diminished by the monitors and the tubes, overhanging his bed like modern-time carrion vultures awaiting his moment of death. "Brian and Tony are at school, and fine. I called because Grail's got out."

An interval of shared exasperation. "That dog. He's probably picking the chicken bones out of Charlie Mitchell's trash. You'd think the old coot would spend a few bucks and buy cans with lids that fit. The ones he hangs onto are a lunch invitation to coons and every other passing animal."

"Grail ate the trash already. Now he's run off to the woods." The unspoken question dangled—should Lynn abandon the mutt and drive to the hospital, or embark on a cross-country bushwhack?

"You'd better find him, I suppose." In the background, over the faintly heard tones of a nurse and a doctor conversing, Ann said,

"Just a minute." A muffled roar as her hand smothered the receiver. She came back, tiredly resigned. "There's little enough to do here, anyway."

"Hang on," said Lynn. "I'll join you soon as I can." She dropped the receiver in its cradle, swearing like a sailor, because at that moment she hated life. She ached from sad certainty that Ann wanted her off to find the dog because even now she held out for a miracle. Outraged motherhood would not accept that Sandy's final hour must happen soon. He would not wake up, recover, and come home; but as long as life still lingered, it was unthinkable to Ann not to have a dog waiting, to bark and lick Sandy's hands in greeting.

"Damn, damn, damn," said Lynn, her eyes now dry to her fury, and her insides clenched in misery. "There ought to be a law against mothers outliving their children."

But there was no law, beyond the one outside the window, in cycles eternally unaffected. Nature wove all of spring's fabric of rebirth, in the flight of nesting barn swallows, and in the sunlight falling immutably gold over maples crowned with unfolded leaves.

Lynn shoved up from the desk, returned to the kitchen, and dug through the clutter of children's drawings and coupons for the spare ring of keys. She locked up a house made cozy for living, but that echoed empty as a tomb. She slammed the door, set the dead bolt, and crossed the back yard to the woods in a blaze of targetless anger.

For Ann, and for Sandy's memory, she'd find the blasted dog.

Grail was the sort who tore up great grouts of earth with his hind feet just after he defecated. Assuredly no tracker, Lynn nonetheless could not miss the divots chopped out of the grass and raked in showers across the patio as evidence of Grail's blithe passage. A smeared print or two remained in the mud by the swingset; these pointed unerringly into the shade, and should have been companioned by the sneaker treads of a young boy, were it Saturday, and Sandy not mortally ill.

Lynn crossed the dried weeds that edged the sandbox. Dandelions pushed yellow heads through the stalks of last year's burdock.

The woods lay beyond, and through them, well trodden by young boys, was the path that led to the fort they had built out of sticks. The birches threw out new leaves, pale lit in sunlight as doubloons. The path was strewn with the drying wings of fallen maple seeds, and snarled mats of rotted twigs. If a dog had passed, nose to ground on the scent of a possum or hot after the tails of running squirrels, no sign remained. The path dipped toward the stream, the soft, moss-grown banks speared by unfurling shoots of skunk cabbage, and ranked on drier soil, the half-spread umbrellas of May apples. Across the narrow current lay the fort. Lynn paused. Naturally the water was high at this season, last summer's stepping stones washed out or submerged.

A fallen log offered the only crossing and an exercise in balance not attempted since childhood. Hesitation over a patch of wet bark cost her a slip. Lynn splashed knee-deep in a sink-hole. One leg of her jeans, one sock, and one expensive designer sneaker became as icily sodden as her mood.

Hating Grail with fresh energy, she sat, and skinned the rest of the way across on her fanny. The far bank was reached without mishap beyond a torn pocket and sadly tattered dignity.

Longingly she mused upon clothing that was pastel and fluffy. The smell of the oil-stained anorak made her feel off, and if the staff in the office were to see her, their worship of her unflappable grooming would suffer a shock beyond salvage. Well, they could all perish of missed deadlines, Lynn thought venomously, and she smiled as she arose and dusted off particles of bark.

Winter had not been kind to the lean-to that comprised the boys' fort. Snow load had caved in the roof. One wall sagged inward, and the wooden shield on which Sandy had sketched his make-believe coat of arms rested on the ground, weathered bare of poster paint. The unicorn lay dulled to shabby gray. A rusty can contained water, black leaves, and assorted bent nails. Beyond a snarl of moldered string and a burst cushion, a trash bin still held whittled sticks, imaginatively fleshed out as lances. Sad pennons decked the ends, cut from old pillow slips that dampness had freckled with mildew.

Nowhere, anywhere, was there sign or sound of Grail.

Lynn sighed and sat down on a boulder. She listened to the chuckle of the stream, wiggled toes that squelched in the wet sneaker, and finally undid the laces. Her hands got chilled as she wrung out her cuff and her sock. The gravel and mud ingrained in the knit she could do little about; too depressed for annoyance, she hoped the stores still carried laces to co-ordinate with last year's fashion colors. She shoved her wet calf to warm in a patch of sunlight, and cupped her chin in her palms.

A catbird in its plain gray squalled outrage from a maple. Lynn watched its discontent, abstracted.

How foolish to feel sloppy in jeans and no make-up on a weekday. Now adorned in mud, bits of bark, and dead leaves, her own problems seemed dwindled to insignificance. The man she'd hoped would become serious, who'd never phoned through to Ann's to inquire; the silly stresses abandoned at the office; her boss's tantrum at her leaving; all these seemed reduced, re-framed in the triteness of a sitcom.

By contrast, Ann's efforts at handling the pending loss of her boy seemed unapproachable; as pitiless and futile as a modern-day search to define the true Chalice of Christ. Everywhere one turned lay Sandy's memory; and where recollection had not trodden, new things cut the heart no less fiercely. The awareness never ceased, that this sight, or that fresh experience, could have stirred the boy to delight.

For two years, he'd had so little, between the doctors and the treatments, and the jail-like isolation necessary to shelter him from infection.

Lynn slapped her wet pants leg. Days like this, under spring sunshine with the hope ripped out from under all of them, she felt like suing Almighty God, that He would allow a little boy to be born, solely to suffer anguish and die. New age philosophies and spiritual metaphors simply ceased to have meaning, when Sandy had sat straight with pencil clenched in hand, demanding impossible wishes.

His own way of asking, perhaps, for something the healthy oth-

erwise took for granted. A fit of rebellion, that life, for him, was
as unreachable a dream as a quest in historical legend.

That moment, the rusty, deep-throated bay that was Grail's split
the woodland stillness. Jolted to recovery of her purpose, Lynn
jammed on her shoe and stood up. The sound came again, from upstream. She jogged, her wet sneaker squishing, and hoped the mutt
hadn't flushed a deer. Grail might run dead crooked, his hind legs
flailing crabwise a foot offset from his forepaws, but he could go
on tireless for miles. As the damp sock wadded up on her heel and
began instantly to chafe a new blister, Lynn determined she was
not going to chase that dog one step further than her breath lasted.

That promise she broke in sixty seconds.

In the ten minutes it took to track Grail down, she raked one
arm on a briar, and ruined her other sneaker in a slithering step
across a pit of black mud between swamp hummocks.

The sight of Grail gave no cheer.

He was wet, had been rolling in something nameless and noisome, and his coat was screwed into wiry ringlets like an Aire-
dale's. His butt was raised, burr-coated tail waving like a whip, and
his snout was jammed to the eyeballs in the cleft of a half-rotted
stump.

Lynn flagged back to a walk. "Grail!"

The dog yiped, inhaled mold, and loosed a forceful sneeze into
the stump. The beat of his tail increased tempo; beyond that, her
summons was ignored.

Lynn walked up beside him. "Grail," she snapped. "Unwedge
your face and come here."

Moist   .own eyes rolled in her direction. Grail gave another
muffled bark.

"I damned well don't want to share in your hunt for snails!"
Lynn reached out, twined two fists in the dank ruff, and pulled.

Grail's hide rolled like bread dough, gave and peeled back until
his bones seemed suspended in a bladder. She dragged him stiff-
legged out of the cleft, and wondered belatedly whether he had a
skunk or a muskrat held cornered and angry inside.

That possibility shortened her temper. Manhandling the dog like an alligator wrestler, Lynn hauled back from the stump.

"Bless my buttons and whiskers!" piped a voice over Grail's frustrated whining. From the inside of the stump, somebody waspishly continued, "It's long enough you took then, silly dog, to heed the plain voice of reason."

Grail yapped. Lynn started, and all but lost her grip on his hair as the animal scrabbled frantically forward. Jerked off balance, her uncut bangs caught in her eyelashes, Lynn glimpsed the absolute impossible: a little brown man about three inches high stepped smartly out of the tree stump.

He had red cheeks, and chestnut whiskers that unfurled like frost-burned moss over a green waistcoat buttoned with brass. He wore leather boots, tan leggings, and a rakish cap topped with a jay's feather. At sight of Lynn, he shrieked in high-pitched anger.

She had no chance to stay startled. Grail tore out of her hands in a snarling bound, and as the man skipped backward in agile panic, rammed his muzzle back into the cleft with staccato, hair-raising yaps.

Knocked to her knees by the fracas, Lynn sat heavily on her rump. "Jesus Christmas!" She wasn't in the habit of having hallucinations; particularly ones of muskrats looking like little brown men who wore green waistcoats and talked. Where paired-off folk made decisions by compromise and committee, she had learned, living alone, to call her shots as they came.

She scrambled up out of the leaves and hit Grail in a shoulder tackle. He bucked, he heaved, he whined in piteous protest. After a lot of scratching and flying sticks, she managed to drag him aside. She then placed her face where the dog's had been, and, ignoring Grail's muddy nose as it poked at her neck and ear, looked into the dim cranny with its rings of old fungus and spider webs.

She almost caught a stick in the eye, one with a brass-shod tip, brandished by the furious little man. She yelled at the scrape on her cheek. He stumbled back with raised eyebrows, cursing in a language she'd never heard.

Certainly he was real enough to draw blood. Lynn dabbed at

her face, while the man stepped back. Apologetic, he tucked his stick under one jacketed arm and spoke. "Ah, miss, so it's you." His skin was seamed like a walnut shell, and his eyes upon her might have been merry had he not been bristling with indignation. "It's a wish you'll be wanting, I presume. Though far likely it is I'd rather treat for my freedom with the dog."

"That can be arranged." Sourly, Lynn licked a bloody fingertip, and swore.

Pressed and heaving at her shoulder, Grail sensed her shift in attitude. He rammed in for another go at the stump, while the little man hopped and shrieked.

"Wait! Wait! Lady, I misspoke myself, I did truly. Pull off that dog, do please. For your own Christian conscience, let me go."

Damp, dirty, and possessed by a sense of unreality that yielded an irritation equal to her captive's, Lynn said, "Why should I?"

The little man folded his arms. He puffed out his cheeks, looking at once diffident and crafty. He shuffled his boots, whacked his stick against the walls of his wooden prison, and finally faced her. "Well," he conceded. "There is the wee matter of a wish. You do have me caught, not so fairly, mind! But it's trapped I would be, I suppose, if you slipped your hold on that hound."

"And so I get a wish?" Lynn suppressed a rise of hysterical laughter. The strain, the surprise, the total weirdness of what was taking place smashed her off-balance in a rush. "I need no wishes granted," she said tartly, and finished, defiantly flippant, with the thought uppermost in her mind. "It's Sandy's wish needs the attention."

"Ah!" The brown man sighed. He sidled, leaned a shoulder against the stump wall and frowned with a bushy furrow of brows. "A sick boy, it is, who begs a visit to Arthur's Round Table?" He gave a cranky shrug in reply to Lynn's astounded stare, and his anger swiftly melted to sad compassion. "You do know, miss, that yon one is soon to die."

The grief hit hard and too fast, that even a supernatural figment in the form of a finger-sized man could know and be helpless before incurable disease. Lynn choked back sudden tears.

The man strove quickly to console her. "Ah, miss, it's not so very hopeless as all that. Just hard. You ken how it is in this creation. Every living creature must choose its time and its place. Such is the maker's grand way. Your boy, now, Sandy. If he's to have what he desires, somebody's going to have to convince him to change his mind." The stick moved and slapped boot leather in reproof. "Somebody being me, no doubt. That's hard work, just for a wish. Hard work." He pinned her again with dark, restless eyes, his annoyance grown piquant as she opened her mouth, perhaps to ridicule; surely, foolishly to question. Humans did that, would in fact spit on good fortune when, like Grail, it bounded its way through their front door.

"Be still now," snapped the man. "Let me think! Its *my* freedom I'm wanting, and yon's a muckle hard course you've set me if I'm going to fix a way to win it!"

With that, the little fellow deflated, plumped himself down, and set his elbows on his knees and his chin in cupped palms, to ponder the gravity of his dilemma.

The boisterous Grail had against all his nature grown still, and Lynn seized the moment to take stock. She unlocked her hand from the dog's neck, reawakened to discomforts both mental and physical. One pant leg was icily soaked. She had sticks and leaves in her hair, an astonishing departure. But these upsets paled to insignificance before the fact that she could exchange conversation and bargain with a creature that by rights belonged in the province of fairy tales.

After the briefest cogitation, she concluded that her nerves were too worn from the strain of dealing with Sandy's illness. That was enough to wrestle without battling further with a situation that confounded logic. Either the creature in the stump was a pixie or a leprechaun, or something else of that ilk; or else she was irrevocably crazy.

The truth in the verdict was unlikely to help Sandy, either way.

The next instant the matter resolved itself. With no warning, and a blinding quick movement, the little man shot to his feet and bolted for the opening in the stump.

Illusions didn't bid for escape. Lynn ducked to block off the cleft, and collided shoulder to shoulder with Grail's snarling lunge to achieve the same end.

The combined effect startled the little man back with his hands palm out in supplication. "Mercy! It's crushed by your blundering about, you'll have me. And unfairly, too, I might add, since I've figured a chance for the boy to have what he's wishing."

Grail whined doubtfully and rolled his eyes.

Unwilling to credit the mutt with intelligence, but touched by the self-same distrust, Lynn glared down at the little man. In vindication for bruised dignity and a growing sense of the ridiculous, she was determined to extract satisfaction, even if the next moment she woke up, rumpled in her bedclothes, to discover the whole event a silly dream. "You tried to get away," she accused.

The brown man sulked. "What if I did?" He crammed chubby hands in the pockets of his waistcoat and started with agitation to pace. "I'm caught still, and trying desperate hard to remedy that unfortunate mistake!"

Grail snarled, as if the creature might be lying. In a blend of acerbity and sarcasm that was her way of fending off what could not in conscience be taken seriously, Lynn sighed. "You don't look to me like a man keeping his half of a bargain."

The little fellow winced, then looked affronted. His roving carried him over a blackened acorn cap and across the musty confines of the stump. Removed from Grail's muzzle enough to feel secure, he stopped and folded his arms, booted foot tapping. "Is it so? And what are you thinking? That meddling with a boy's dying, not to mention playing hob with a time frame that passes through legend, is easy? Wishes, which you human sorts almost *never* bother asking, are *grueling business*!"

Sore from stooping, Lynn eased her knees by leaning a companionable arm across Grail's rawboned shoulder blade. Noisome wet fur was no substitute for upholstery, but the touch of an ordinary animal had become a necessary comfort. She looked a great deal less disgruntled now than her captive, which brought the shrewdness of her management background to the immediate fore.

If she was going to play the fool and talk extortion with a fey being inside a rotted stump, Sandy may as well have a crack at the benefits. "Then, to go free, you'll have to show me some results."

The tiny man sidled; a sly grin tipped up one corner of his mouth, and he stroked at his wiry fall of whiskers. "It is hard work I'll be going off to then, lady. To fix your boy's wish, truth to tell. For that you'll be having to let me out." He stepped in brash confidence toward the daylight that shone through the cleft.

Lynn's outraged "What?" tangled with Grail's sudden snarl. The pelted muscle under her shoulder surged as the dog rammed headfirst and growling into the opening in the stump. A scuffle ensued. For a moment, the animal's bulk obscured sight of what transpired within.

Then Grail's tail whipped straight. His buttocks heaved and he backed up. Clenched in between rows of bared teeth, the little man swung from his waistcoat, his arms waving, his terrified shouts thin as a bird's cries over the growls of the dog. The stick whipped the air to and fro, shining like a little brass pin, and about as uselessly effective.

Lynn spared a moment for sympathy, mostly for the fact that the little fellow was probably perishing of dog breath. Discounting his clothes, the rest of him was unmarked, however much his shrieks suggested otherwise.

"Put me down!" he screeched. "Oh, lady, for pity, I can't be fixing wishes as a dog's snack. Surely it's wise enough you are, and merciful also, to be seeing that!"

Lynn set her jaw and said nothing.

Grail sat, lips peeled back and trembling above his victim. The little man kicked in agitation. "You need me to make arrangements, don't you? Well, true it is I can't *do that* sick with beast stink and prisoned inside a stump!"

"How do I know your word is good?" Touched to acerbity, Lynn sat down to set her head level with Grail's. She fingered the damp cuff of her jeans. "Really, if you're going to be trusted, I should go along as observer, to be certain the terms of Sandy's wish are fully met."

The man's arms fell to his sides with a faint slap. His whiskers drooped. He hung like a mouse from Grail's jaws, a forlorn morsel with a fat belly that strained at his rows of brass buttons. "I'm not lying. Spit on my luck if I am."

Grail's brown eyes held level with Lynn's, imploring canine prudence, and oddly, knowingly, infused with a wisdom no dog she'd ever known had possessed. A queer chill shot through her. In a dark, unbreached corner of her mind, conviction grew, that the dog's purpose was and always had been *to find such a tiny man, and take him captive.*

But of course in cold logic, that was ridiculous.

Pressed unbearably against the realities of a child's terminal disease, and faced by unspeakable suffering and now the bitter ending of Sandy's life, Lynn found reason a poor arbiter. Hope and superstition this moment seemed infinitely more kindly. Grave, supremely detached from the ongoing cruelties at the hospital, she sighed. To the tiny man she said, "That's not good enough."

"Bother and fiddlesticks!" cried the man. Jostled by movement of the jaws that prisoned him, he rolled widened eyes in trepidation.

Grail looked befuddled, as if his nasal passages had sprouted an itch from too heady a scent of the supernatural. The little man observed this, growing alarmed. He evidently understood that in canines, heavy sneezes often ended with an unkindly whap of muzzle and teeth against the ground. "I'll show you the results in a dream!" he hollered in sharpened anxiety. "It's not so simple, you'll appreciate, with a wish involving more than one party, and one of them with scarcely an hour left to live. You're wasting time!"

"I think not." Punched inside by reminder of Sandy's condition, and sorry for Ann, waiting alone and unsupported for an ending her heart could not encompass, Lynn held hard to the last fragment of detachment still left to her. "That's not good enough. Dreams can be manipulated, I must assume, or the dog who holds your coattails would be satisfied. Grail hasn't seen fit to let you go."

"You'd have me set the Sight on you!" howled the man. Dangling, he managed to look irked as he folded his arms across his chest. "Well that's another wish!"

Lynn glowered levelly back. "That's no wish, but proper surety."

"Ah, it's hard, hard in the heart, that humans can be, you female sorts most of all." The man waved a miniature fist. "An unchancy business it is, always, dealing with modern-day mortals." He unlimbered a wrist to wag a finger, cuff buttons flashing like pin heads. "You folk muddle about wide awake, most times, with your dreams the most living part of you. Did you know as much, you'd fare better." When this diatribe left Lynn without comment, the brown man fixed her with a glare that made her tingle. "Well, it's not my part to adjust your mortal ills and your muckle mistaken thinking! Very well, miss. As you wish. If you're the blundering sort who sets no stock by dreams, it's the Sight you'll get to witness my part in the bargain. But sorrow you'll find, and weeping too, when you long to be quit of the gift afterwards!"

This was delivered in vindication, not warning, for the little man raised his hand and flicked his fingers, as if to splat water in Lynn's face.

She saw no physical projectile. But something struck her forehead just below the hairline. A golden bloom rinsed her eyesight, a painless dazzle that flared and faded, and left her senses momentarily encapsulated. As if a bubble had been spun around her consciousness, she felt as if physically suspended.

She raised her head, gasped; the wood she knew was altogether gone. No skunk cabbage grew; no May apples. The ground was a living carpet of shining myrtle. She breathed a chillier, more fragrant air; the trees all about were old oaks, huge towering crowns shafted with midday sunlight. The ground fell away, toward a clearing floored in ivy and moss, and sheltered by water-channeled outcrops.

Little men that lurked in stumps were one thing. *This,* a forest setting more appropriate to a page of medieval romantic illustration, was too much.

Lynn opened her mouth to cry out.

"Be quiet, fool woman!" The little man rapped her fingers with his stick, which caused her a violent start. "Wake him up, and you'll spoil Sandy's wish!"

Muddled, unable to re-orient herself, Lynn whispered, "Wake who up?"

Apparently the little man and the mongrel dog had made their peace, for in course of a wild search, she located him, seated in his spit-dampened waistcoat, astride Grail's thick ruff. The brass-tipped stick now pointed toward something a ways off in the undergrowth.

Lynn peered through twining runners of ivy, and saw what looked like bits of basket woven out of sticks. Closer scrutiny revealed a young man, black-haired and high browed, and barely past his boyhood. He appeared to be asleep. A cheek as innocent and clear-complexioned as a peach rested on uncallused knuckles. His limbs were well made, though delicately muscled, and over his simple tunic he wore what looked to be shoulder pads and breast plate all woven out of willow fronds and twigs.

"My God," breathed Lynn.

The little man bristled. "Not God!" He went on to snap in an undertone, "Just the magic you've demanded of me, and no more."

Lynn could not quite stifle awe. "Who is he?"

"Your Sandy will know." The little man clapped his palms together in a silent explosion of fey power.

Lynn's hair bristled. A jolt hammered through her that rocked her awareness to its root. She blinked, shaken by its passage, and then stopped, slammed cold still, by the sight of Sandy standing barefoot in his hospital gown. He stepped forward and paused, eye to eye with the creature on Grail's back.

The tubes, the needles, the paraphernalia of medical science that inadequately sought to prolong his life had all gone. Bruises remained, under his eyes and on his arms and in the hollow of his shoulder; the stitchery left by weeks upon weeks of IV needles. He still looked sick and thin, all knobby white limbs and a neck that rose frail as a stem. His eyes shone sunken and huge, haunted yet by the shadows of his suffering.

"Sandy!" gasped Lynn.

But he did not look at her. The little brown man addressed him and his ears seemed sealed to other words.

"You'll be knowing who that is, lying there?" The stick twitched toward the sleeper, and a hand miraculously tiny twined in a fall of chestnut whiskers.

Languid as if sleepwalking, Sandy turned his head. He regarded the young man in his bed of ivy and moss, and a yearning transformed his face with life. Incandescent in delight, he almost laughed. "Perceval!"

"You'll be knowing the legend, then," prompted the fey man who had brought both together, the sleeping young man and a dying boy's spirit, to a woodland Lynn could not place in any ecosystem known to modern earth.

"Of course I know." Sandy's excitement broke through his weakness, made his thin voice ring with derisive joy. "Perceval was son to a rebel king, thrown down by King Arthur's justice. He was raised in isolation by his mother in a far off tower. She hoped he would become a priest, and escape the fate of his father, to die in battle. But when from a distance Perceval saw some knights riding, he was struck by the sun on their armor. He asked what sort of creatures they were, for their beauty left him in awe. His mother, afraid he would leave her to take up fighting and bloodshed, told him he had seen angels."

"And so lost him," the little man picked up, as Sandy's enraptured recitation trailed off. "For young Perceval replied that there was no more worthy quest than to follow God's angels to heaven." The little man cracked a smile filled with crafty sharp teeth and inclined his head toward the sleeper. "Well, so you're seeing," he confided to Sandy. "Yon lies Perceval, who set off wearing armor he wove out of sticks, that he could be as like unto the saintly hosts as possible until his reunion with them should be fulfilled."

Sandy knotted bony hands together. He gazed in admiration at the young man, whom he knew would go on from this clearing, to win his place at Arthur's Round Table and be one of the chosen few who would glimpse the Holy Grail. Drinking in details for sheer delight, Sandy stared: at the fine, shiny dark hair, unblemished in health; at the unstained innocence of the face. He looked at the hands, palms soft and unmarked; at muscles too delicate to have done much more than hold books.

The hero worship in his look became marred by dawning doubt. "He's a wimp."

The little man said nothing.

Sandy's study encompassed the wrists that lay lax in the moss, unmarred by even a briar scrape. Troubled sorely, he swung around and glared in accusation at the little man. "You lied. That can't be Perceval. He doesn't at all look like the sort who would go for hard rides and bloody fighting."

And Lynn, understanding a thing, held her breath, while the little brown man answered him reasonably.

"You're part right, my boy. But I never lie. That's Perceval, there, and you've spoken the heart of the problem, his and yours. For within the next hour, your two fates must resolve. You will be greeting God's angels, and he will wake up to discover his 'angels' are earthly clay in the form of tough-mannered, battle-trained knights."

"Oh!" Sandy stepped back, his soul laid bare by longing. "If *only* we could change places!"

"Said is done!" cried the little man, and he clapped his hands with a crack that shattered the stillness.

Sandy vanished.

Birds started up from the trees, and the young man in his armor of sticks sat up, a look of raw startlement on his face. He raised his arms, stared at his palms as if flesh, bone and nerve were appendages that belonged to a stranger. Then he looked wildly about until his gaze found and locked on the little man. "You've done it!" And he smiled as though all the world had been reborn between his two hands.

"So I have." The little man laughed and pointed westward through the forest. "That way lies Camelot, young Perceval. Fare you well, on all your quests, until the last, until the day you sight the Grail."

Lynn came back to herself, with Grail's tongue dragging and dragging across her cheek. She sat in soggy leaf mould, one shoulder braced against a stump whose cleft was now empty.

She shivered once, violently; in distaste she pushed off the dog. For once, Grail gave over his affections with deference to the person being mauled. He backed off, sat, and looked at her. His tail whacked up a storm of forest detritus. His expression looked inordinately pleased.

Lynn shivered again. Chilled by uncanny experience, and also by her soaked shoe and pants cuff, she looked about, as if expecting the woods to be somehow momentously different.

They were not.

May sunlight slashed the trunks of the birch trees like knife cuts limned in gold; the catbird's mate sang at her nesting, and two squirrels ran scolding in a territorial squabble through the bursting leafy crowns overhead.

It did not seem a day for miniature men and bright wishes. Neither did it seem any more appropriate a time for a twelve-year-old boy to lie dying.

Lynn cursed. Whatever had befallen her, be it illness, hallucination, or stark raving madness, she had an obligation, now that Grail was found. She must hurry on to the hospital to lend her support to Ann.

That moment, ridiculously, she recalled she'd neglected to bring a leash. Grail seemed to need none, creature of obscure contradictions that he was. For the first time in his miserable life, he came when called. Apparently content for once to follow, he frisked at Lynn's heels all the way back to the house. More surprising, he stepped meekly into his pen at her bidding; and once there, lay down, nose to tail, to fall asleep. He looked like an old string mop, stiff-curled as if dried in ocher paint.

Lynn left him. Inside the house, her intent bent exclusively on the logistics entailed in joining Ann quickly at the hospital. Shoes,

one muddy, one damp; dirty jeans, oil-stained anorak; all flew off
her into a heap. She wanted a shower, but settled with splashing
cold water on her face. Too pressed to fuss over details, she
snatched khaki slacks, a silk blouse, and a tailored jacket from the
closet. She had dress for success down to reflex, and her thoughts
she held firmly to practicality, until the first cog slipped in her reg-
imen.

She realized she'd left the shoes that went best with the jacket
in the city. Her desperate self-control fled.

Frowning, frantic not to think, and still barefoot, she dug her
make-up case out of the bathroom and parked in front of the mirror. Trivia refused its role; would not keep her preoccupied. She
froze through a moment of silent struggle; to focus on anything
and everything onerously ordinary, that she not be overset to dis-
turbance over what had or had not occurred out in the woods.

Tiny men, and brown thoughts; she was as much in denial of
Sandy's straits as webbed about in the peculiar insanity Grail had
lured her to tread. Dangerous ground. Better to debate her choice
of lipstick.

She rummaged through her cosmetics and selected a shade of
cover-up to conceal the nick on her cheek. Then she glanced up at
the mirror. And stopped dead.

Where her own features should have looked out at her, she saw
instead a different view. Ann, seated in her untidy cardigan with
her back bowed and her face in her hands, beside a bed in a hospital room.

"No!" Lynn shoved her knuckles against her mouth in denial,
even as memory of the little man's protest mocked her. *If you're
the blundering sort who set no stock by dreams, it's the Sight you'll
get, to witness my part in the bargain. But sorrow you'll find, and
weeping too, when you long to be quit of the gift afterwards!*

The ache in her died to a whisper. "No." But the deathbed view
of her nephew bound her senses, as vitally real as if she were present at her sister's shoulder.

No recrimination, no fear, no sense of disorientation or disbe-
lief could tear her attention from the body, supine under white

sheets. The pastel hospital gown betrayed by its lack of wrinkles how far removed from life and movement lay the consciousness that delineated Sandy.

Lynn choked a breath through her tightened throat, then stopped, even breathing suspended.

For the motionless boy on the bed sighed slightly and opened his eyes.

They shone, blue and enormous in the subdued, artificial lighting of the hospital. Dark as marks in charcoal, his brows sketched a puzzled frown. Too weak and emaciated to do more, he regarded the sterile white walls, the plastic pitchers, the raised side rails, and the IV line dangling at his shoulder as if he had never in his life known such sights.

He looked as if witness to marvels.

Lynn caught her breath in a gasp. She knew like a blow, *that this was not Sandy, looking out through the eyes of his face.* She stood, frozen and trapped before the vision of a perfect stranger residing in Sandy's failing flesh.

The boy noticed Ann at that moment. Perhaps he heard her stifled weeping, or was drawn by her forlorn posture as she convulsed in silenced grief. He raised the hand not burdened with needles, dragged limp fingers across the sheet, and gave her a brushing touch.

Ann started up as if shot. "Sandy?"

He blinked as she caught his wrist. "My God, my God," she cried in wonder and jagged-edged joy.

He looked at her. The familiarity of the gesture tore at Lynn's heart for the fact that he had no cowlicks left to tumble brown hair across his eyes.

Because of that, she and Ann both saw: the boy's hollowed features were lit from within by a burning, unearthly rapture. "Lady," he whispered in an accent that sounded gallant and antique. "You must not weep for me. It is promised. I go on to God's glory, to meet His most beautiful angels."

The fingers in Ann's chilled hand tightened one last time, and the spirit, lightly held, left the flesh.

* * *

Lynn came back to herself, gripping the sink too tightly. Wild-eyed, her own face stared back from the mirror. The pin-prick cut showed livid against her pallor, and her chest ached as, in tears, she recovered herself with a cry.

A strange, exalted exhilaration possessed her, snapped at once by sharp grief at the jangling intrusion of the telephone.

She stumbled out to reach the hallway extension.

"Lynn?" said Ann's voice as she answered. "It's over. He's gone, just this minute." She paused for a wondering breath. "You wouldn't think it, but it happened beautifully. He woke up to tell me . . ."

Words failed her, and Lynn couldn't bear it. "He's gone to meet the angels."

Startled, still drifty with shock, Ann came back in surprise. "Lynnie, how could you know?"

Lynn crouched, weak-kneed, and steadied herself on an elbow that ground with real pain against the baseboard. "Never mind," she answered. "It doesn't matter."

But it did; the uncanny proofs remained with her. Into old age, the fey man's gift of Sight never left her; and Grail never wandered again.

Hitchhiking Across an Ancient Sea

✛

Kristine Kathryn Rusch

The prairie grass, rich and tall and fine, tickles my chest as I walk. A child could get lost here. I'm six-eight, and I feel dwarfed by the endless vista of grasses, undulating in the breeze. The air smells fresh, like a sea breeze, and I wonder what Karen will think as she stands at the edge of the prairie, land stretching far as the eye can see.

The rain slanted sideways the day Nikki arrived, hard, pelting rain without chill, the kind of storm unique to the Pacific coast. I had just pulled my boat in—the day's catch not quite what I expected—when she stopped in front of McIver's Store.

She was driving a brand-new Volvo, dark blue, obviously a tourist car because the paint-job wouldn't have survived in the salt-laden air more than a month. Her legs were long, her hair dark and red, her eyes covered with sunglasses despite the darkness of the day. But it wasn't so much her body I was looking at. It was the air of silence she carried around her, like a piece of fragile glass separating her from the world. Sylvia Plath called that glass a bell jar, and I hadn't seen one since my mother's shattered twenty-five years before.

I left the boat and the catch to Bill, my assistant, and I hurried up the sand-covered path, not caring that I still wore my rain gear and smelled of fish. I pushed open the screen door, and let it slam back with a bang. McIver's smelled of coffee, day-old donuts, and woodsmoke. She stood in front of the cash register, sunglasses still on, hands shaking as she counted out fifteen dollars for her groceries.

Long tapered nails, painted red. Two nails on the right hand broken below the skin line. Polish chipped on the other three. A bruise growing purple between her thumb and her forefinger. I couldn't turn away, not even then.

"Help you, Denny?" Old Man McIver asked, caution in his voice. He had seen the glasses, seen the bruise, put it all together. And he knew me. Remembered when I arrived, just as bruised, just as silent.

I grabbed the coffee pot, and poured the old brew into the remaining styrofoam cup. "Cold one," I said. "Damn rain kept up all day."

"Surprised you go out in it," McIver said. "Most of the other boys spend their days in Ike's, drinking and waiting for the clouds to clear."

"Most of the other boys make a half-assed living off the sea." The cup warmed my hands.

She didn't look up as she took the packages from McIver. "There's a sign in your window about cottages."

He glanced at her, then at me, both looks measuring and tough. "Yup. You interested by the week or the month?"

"Month," she said.

He stared at me, pale blue eyes going watery in the store's dim light. I grabbed my cup and went outside, the message clear. He wasn't going to say a thing until I left. He saw my interest, knew that common wounds bind deep. He wanted me to leave her alone.

I leaned against a post for a minute, watching the rain slant in front of me like someone sketched it in the air. Then I wandered back down to the boat.

She and I would have time enough for talking later.

Took three nights driving to get here. Karen woke up once in Montana, looked at a daybreak sky full of clouds from the fires in Yellowstone, and said, "It's pretty, Dad."

"Yes," I said. "It is." And thought briefly about stopping. Who came to Montana, after all? It was long and rugged and cold. There was fishing in clear mountain streams. Not a living, maybe, but a way of life.

Then I looked over at her little four-year-old face pressed into the pillow, almost blocking the view from the passenger window, the Volvo's plastic cracked from too much wear, and knew Montana was too harsh for us. We belong in Kansas, in prairie grasses that extend forever, willows that bow over a patch of land like islands rising out of the sea. The land is old, and has seen more bloodshed than the rest of the West combined.

So much death that a little more only enriches the soil, enriches the land.

Bloody Kansas.

We've come home.

When I first arrived in Emmett's Cove, I wore a three-piece suit and shoes that shined so clearly I could see my own reflection. My only experience out of doors had been a two-day camping trip in Yosemite, where I'd spent most of my time staring at Sequoias and wondering if trees that tall were filled with wisdom. Height and wisdom once had a correlation for me: I had gotten into Northwestern on a basketball scholarship—basketball being the only escape from Chicago's South Side, at least for boys like me. I blew out my knee second term and pulled a week's worth of all-nighters in the hospital, studying so that I could stay even if I never walked again. I walked, but not on the court, and by the time I graduated, I had a straight-A average, and enough recommendations to get me into Harvard Law.

I graduated summa cum laude, turned down jobs with prestige firms in New York and L.A., and returned to the South Side, thinking that even though I was in private practice, I could be the Clarence Darrow of my generation. Five Cook County detectives mistaking me for a five-nine robber in a ski mask ("why else you in the neighborhood, boy?"—a nightstick across the mouth preventing me from saying my office was half a block away), and a six-week stay in Sacred Heart Hospital changed my mind on that. Somehow I had thought that the law degree would protect me from the ignorance and violence I had grown up with. But nothing could protect me—I couldn't even protect myself against five armed men. Perhaps it was that knowledge, more than the beating, that made me leave.

So ten years later, I knew how Nikki felt when she arrived in that Volvo: wanting space and silence in a place where no one knew her name; wishing she could hide her face, and the story it told; hoping no one would see, and wanting someone to ask, one small question, a tiny show of concern.

Places like Emmett's Cove, though, the concern came in glances, in questions not asked, in answers not given, and in one hundred dollars rent for a furnished cabin that would command over five hundred dollars in the height of the season. There was also warmth, if you knew how to find it, and loneliness, everywhere you looked.

The motel room smells musty. Thin chenille bedspreads cover rubbery old blankets. Karen balks at sleeping in daylight, but I can see the exhaustion in the shadows that hollow out her eyes.

I stand at the window until her breathing evens, staring at a grouping of cottonwood trees that breaks my view of the prairie. The motel is old, used as little as the highway now that the interstate sweeps cars by this forgotten expanse of land. People here are as taciturn as people on the coast, but they're different, rooted. It's as if the land has reached up and wrapped itself around their ankles, drawing them inward like a slow quicksand no one wants to fight.

My daughter sighs in her sleep. She is the best of both of us: skin a fine milk chocolate, hair a deep brown with red highlights—not quite auburn, not quite black. Wrapped in the chenille, she looks small and desperate, her tiny hands clutching a stuffed dog that somehow survived the fiery house.

We need roots, Karen and I. Not a past to chase us like an angry demon across a burning landscape, but roots to hold us, so we can turn and face that past with the strength of generations.

I hope we'll find that strength here, in the prairie, on land that once stood beneath the waters of an ancient sea.

I found the cottage easily enough. Nikki made no attempt to hide the Volvo, which spoke of two possibilities: she had been planning her escape for a long time and the Volvo was new; or no one remained to look for her. Her lack of caution suggested no one remained.

Every evening, she walked on the beach, arms wrapped around her despite the oversized cable-sweater she wore. I began bringing my boat back early, sometimes abandoning a sweet run, much to Bill's chagrin. He worked with me because I *worked,* one of the few in this town who refused to let the sea beat me. I learned fishing from Old Man McIver during two tough years when I was always cold, always aching. I figured that if the sea beat me, I would have nothing left, having let the urban jungle close its door behind me.

A week into my changed routine, Bill abandoned a line to see me standing at the prow. His gaze followed mine, rooted on Nikki standing near Cutter's Rock, looking thin and forlorn. He stared with me for a moment, then grunted. "That explains it," he said, and went back to his work.

But it didn't, not really. I had lived in Emmett's Cove for a decade. Lived alone, had few friends, and never dated. My house had become my refuge, filled with hundreds of books, recordings, and videos. Sometimes I drove inland, sold my fish to a handful of stores beyond my regulars, or attended a class in Portland or Salem, but rarely did I spend time with anyone else.

And I was not the only one with this solitary routine. Emmett's Cove stood at the mouth of an isolated stretch of beach. Highway 101 went through, but most drivers never made it that far. They turned on one of the highways leading to civilization. Emmett's Cove would have died decades before if it weren't for the great fishing just off the inlet. Tourists drove through in the summer, but most drove on, searching for towns with artsy-crafty shops and twenty-four-hour grocery stores. Part-time fishermen took the summer cabins, and everyone else belonged.

Or was a refugee like me, running from an unsettled score, a violent past. Living in a kind of stasis, waiting for the world to catch up.

That night I got off the boat, removed my gear, and washed up in the small shed at the edge of the dock. Bill took care of the line and the catch, shaking his head all the while. I walked down the beach to Cutter's Rock, keeping my pace friendly, splashing at the wave's edges to make my presence known.

Still, Nikki jumped when I said hello.

She wasn't wearing her sunglasses. Her right eye was purplish yellow and swollen almost shut. Four fading bruises ran like fingerprints down one cheek, with a matching thumb near her jaw. She didn't smile at me. In fact, she took half a step back.

I held out my hands to show I meant no harm. My height, my very presence on an Oregon beach was enough to unnerve most people. "I come in peace," I said, only half humorously.

She nodded once, gaze skittering away from me like a stone atop of waves. I stood beside her. From the land, the ocean looked like a picture postcard, dressed up with salt and sea tang, an unreal vista. On the boat, I felt like a beetle on the back of a lion. One false move and I would fall to my death.

"It's like standing on the edge of the world," she said.

Maybe that was what it was. We had run so far, we couldn't run any farther. The coastal mountains rose behind us like giants guarding a fairy land.

"Sometimes I pretend that the rest of the world has gone away," I said. "There's only us, here. Now."

I got the smile then. It lit her entire face, made the bruises fade, gave her a beauty I only suspected she possessed. "I wish," she said, the words plaintive and full of such longing that I felt to continue the conversation would diminish us both.

We stood, side by side, until the ocean swallowed the sun, and night surrounded us.

* * *

At daybreak, Karen and I walk down the dusty back highway that will lead us to the creek. I have filled my backpack with two vacuum bottles filled with water, prepackaged sandwiches from the grocery store, and a bunch of bananas. Karen carries her stuffed dog, not quite understanding this pilgrimage, but willing to go along with it.

As the road plunges into the prairie, she stops and holds up her hands, a wordless request that I carry her. I pick her up and we stare at the grass. Waves ripple through it as the breeze touches it. Karen watches with a solemnity she once had for the ocean. The stuffed dog lies between us, a soft barrier. Dust whirls around us. The day will be hot.

At the base of the hollow stand three oak trees. A half-dry creek runs between them, and on one side is a half-collapsed barn. A few yards away, a fireplace stands like a lone sentry.

A hundred and thirty-five years ago, my great-grandmother hid under the hay in this barn, listening as white men circled outside, their dogs baying. She had seen her father attacked by dogs— barely enough of him left to lynch, she once said—and she knew if she got found the dogs wouldn't get her first. For three hours, she didn't move, scarcely breathed, felt hay tickle her nose, her chin, her very being.

Finally they left. At dawn, her contact, a big, eastern white man named Sam came, wrapped her in a blanket and stuck her in the back of his cart like a slab of sausage. He went through three picket points, telling guards in a joking tone that he had runaway slaves in the back of his cart. The guards all laughed, never checked, and she made it to Chicago, where she lived long enough to tell a little boy that if she had it to do over again, she would have gone back to Kansas, because that was where freedom began.

"Is this it?" Karen asks, clearly disappointed.

"This is it," I say, wishing that it felt more like home.

Somehow I expected the earth to reach up here and grab me, small vines that would circle my ankles and pull me inward. But my daughter and I sit in the shade, feeling the humidity grow as the sun shortens the shadows. I feel the history, seeping out of the land. If I close my eyes, I can almost see my great-grandmother's childish face, drawn tight with terror. And before her, the generation of nomadic peoples who fished the prairie as if the sea waters never retreated. The land was old, and I was only a heartbeat in its history.

"Ready to go?" I ask.

Karen nods.

I take her hand, and we make our way back up the dusty trail, the heat fierce against our backs. We have nowhere left to go. Our search for home is like the Christian search for the grail. It rises like a beacon before us, but we can never touch it. We will remain, forever, hitchhikers crossing an ancient sea.

The first time was as natural as breathing. One moment we were in Nikki's living room, the next between the sheets, my dark hand covering her white. She tasted of rainwater and summer sunshine. And I was gentle, especially after I saw the scars tracing her skin like war wounds.

She never told me. I never asked. But over the years I pieced it together.

He had been a colleague, a bit older, more confident. The attraction was rich and fine, fraught with danger that blossomed under stress or after too many drinks. And she, somehow, grew to believe she deserved it, grew to think his fists were part of his love. Until the night in the grocery store parking lot, where a fight erupted into a beating, the beating into a brawl. She lost the baby; he lost his life; and at the hospital, the detective told her they would file no charges, since it was clearly self-defense.

To the detective perhaps. To Nikki the incident spoke of the possibilities of love. She wore the bell jar as protection, guarding a side I would never touch, no matter how gentle my fingers, how soft my tone. After Karen, the bell jar became more fragile— perhaps a baby's cries were more threatening than my masculine needs—and when it shattered, the shards fell over all of us.

* * *

Another man resides in the hotel. Fortyish, he fancies himself a midwestern Christo. He is working on a masterpiece in the prairie. He will unveil it in two days.

We sit on rusted metal lawn furniture and drink beer in late summer twilight, just after I put Karen to bed. His hands are gnarled, his face sea-weathered. I wonder if he has lived on the coast.

I tell him about my search. He laughs, voice booming across the expanse of land.

"People like you," he says, "do not know how to live. You encounter tragedy and flee as if it were the enemy, instead of embracing it and all of its possibilities. And because you run, you do not feel, and because you do not feel, you do not live."

I stand then, unwilling to let a man I hardly know make pronouncements about my life.

"See?" he says. "You run, even now."

I go inside. The day's heat is trapped in here. Karen's legs poke out of the sheets, her hair sprawled across the pillow. I close the windows, turn on the ancient air conditioner, figuring its rattle is preferable to the heat. Karen sighs once and turns. I cover her, then sit in the darkness and watch her sleep.

I knew even before the sirens began. Out on the boat, just beyond the inlet, I made Bill turn back. "Squall?" he asked.

"Not exactly," I said.

Perhaps I saw unconscious cues. Perhaps I saw the smoke. Or perhaps I had a premonition. It didn't matter. What mattered was that, as soon as the boat scraped the dock, I was off and running toward the house.

Smoke billowed around the point, black and ugly. The sirens started when I was two blocks away. I arrived to find Karen on the front lawn, arms wrapped around her stuffed dog, rocking back and forth. The house was engulfed—not even the volunteer fire-fighters would go inside.

There had been small signs, sure. An unexplained fire on top of the stove. A space heater catching a towel. Somehow I always found a reason that had nothing to do with Nikki. Karen didn't understand that towels on heaters caused fires. Karen splattered grease on the stove. Never noticing, of course, that each time, Karen had been outside, safe and protected, her stuffed dog for company.

Hard to believe that a woman I loved was unstable. Harder still to believe that all the things we never talked about, all the hints, the imagined stories, may not have linked us after all.

I didn't want to think that I had not been enough, that the shattered place inside Nikki finally engulfed her like fire engulfed the wooden house.

All Karen and I had left was the Volvo. The insurance man tracked us down, didn't meet my gaze when he apologized for the death of my wife, as if it were his fault, as if his insurance didn't provide the proper magic. His check bought us clothes and the ability to travel. I rented the boat to Bill, and we left.

Running again from the scene of a crime.

The day of the unveiling is cool and spring-like, odd for Kansas in July. We wander down a gravel road, a group of pilgrims united only in our quest to see what an artist has created in the prairie heat.

Karen walks beside me, stuffed dog tucked under her arm. He has not left her side since the fire, her own magic against all future tragedies. She holds me too, as if her grip ensures that I will never leave her.

We haven't talked about the fire, have said little to each other since we left the coast. The shadows under her eyes have grown deeper, and I wonder if perhaps I was wrong. Perhaps we should have stayed and faced the burned-out ruin, discussed the scars that tragedy left.

I pick Karen up and squeeze her. She squawks in protest, I put her down, and we walk together, part of a Kansas crowd going to see a Kansas event.

The artist is there, sitting on top of his pickup truck, as immobile as a statue. He doesn't acknowledge me, even when I wave. He watches the people pass by, listens as the gasps rise.

I am taller, so I can see it from the rise. Three sails rising out of prairie grass, looking forever like a ship sailing the inland sea. The grass undulates around it, waves battering its sides. An emptiness flows through me, a longing deeper than any I had ever felt before.

Karen tugs my arm. "Daddy," she says, and I realize she cannot see. I pick her up, feeling her four-year-old weight. Someday she will be too big to hold. Someday, she will be all grown up, with passions of her own.

I point and her gaze follows, then she gasps and squirms again. I cannot hold her. She slips through my arms and into the grass, only the ripples showing her passage.

"Karen!" I follow, half embarrassed by her outburst, but unable to prevent her passage. The artist stands on his truck, watching. The crowd is silent. I trace the ripples as I would the wake of a boat, and reach the sails a moment after Karen.

They are three tall masts pounded into the earth, the grass hollowed out around them to simulate a ship. She walks around and around, looking lost. Then she kicks a sail. The shiver runs along the mast, makes the fabric flap in a nonexistent breeze.

"It's not real," she says.

I grab her, pull her into my arms. She fights against me for a moment, then collapses against my shoulder, deep racking sobs flowing from her chest. The passion missing from me and my wife has found a home in our child. The roots I'm searching for Karen already has. They're on a coast half a continent away, near a burned-out house overlooking the sea.

"I'm sorry," I say, and the words have more power than I ever thought they could. I stand and carry my sobbing daughter out of the waving grass.

She is right. The sea is not here. It receded eons ago to a world filled with sharp edges, with cliffs and rocks and slanting rain. Odd to have found a beacon and be blinded by its light. I never knew what I had because I never let myself see.

I emerge covered with dirt and straw. Like my great-grandmother, a hundred and thirty-five years before, I feel free. She was right. Freedom begins in Kansas, but she was wrong too. It is something we can take home with us. And I learned it, not from an old woman near death, but from a young girl near birth.

The artist smiles at us as we walk past. Karen shifts in my arms, body calm after her bout of tears. I nod once, glad to be embracing life.

Visions

—✠—

Lawrence Watt-Evans

So I'm at my ex-wife's place, I've just dropped the kid off after another weekend of asking what she's doing with her life and being told, "Nothing much." I'm sitting in my car in the driveway, I didn't go inside because I don't need to hear Cheryl asking, "Where'd we go wrong?" for the two thousand and sixth time, I'm dreading the drive home and I'm feeling depressed as hell, and sort of empty—I get that way when I drop Annie-Beth off, sometimes, and the drive back doesn't help any, you can get really morbid alone in your car. It is not an emotional high point. I've got the key in the ignition but the car's turned off, Annie-Beth hates getting out when the motor's running, she's always afraid the car's going to start up by itself and run over her foot or drag her away by the seat belt or something. She's gone inside, the door was unlocked, I didn't see Cheryl, and I'm just sitting there wondering why I don't start the car and get on with it, when this golden light pours in, the color of honey, like I'm parked under the golden arches, or one of those weird yellow streetlights they use some places, only it's richer than that, it's the color of the yellow in the stained-glass windows I saw as a kid—I never see that color anymore, they don't look the same anymore.

For a minute I just stare at my hands, there in my lap, and everything looks rich and strange, and then I realize the light's coming from somewhere in front of me, and I think oh my God, Cheryl's garage is on fire, so I look up, and . . .

I can't describe it. It's not a fire. It's a cup, hanging in the air right above the hood ornament, but it's not just a cup, and it's not exactly there, it's like it's everywhere at once, like I can see right through it into all of the world at the same time, and this golden glow is pouring off it in waves, in surging tides of light, and then it's gone and there's just Cheryl's garage with the old bracket where the basketball backboard fell off years ago and the knothole in the fascia with the bird's nest sticking out.

And I just sit there, staring, with my mouth open. I don't jump out to look for it, which would have been the sensible thing, I just sit there. I don't know why. It's only after I've been staring for a couple of minutes that I realize my God, that thing was *beautiful,* it was the most beautiful thing I've ever seen, it was *fabulous.*

And I'm still sitting there, gaping at the air, when the door of the house opens and Cheryl comes out, and she stands there on the top step with her arms folded across her chest, and calls to me, "What's the matter, won't the car start?"

I shake my head, more to clear it than to say no, and I wave to her and say, "No, I was just thinking." Then I finally start the car and I back it out onto the street before she can ask what I was thinking about.

And I drive down the street and turn the three corners to get out of the subdivision, and I cruise down the highway, and all the time I'm not really thinking, I'm on autopilot, I've driven this route a hundred times so it doesn't need any thought, and my brain is still in a daze, because it was so *beautiful,* shining there, and it was so *strange.*

And then when I'm pulling onto the interstate it finally hits me, it registers at long last, that what I saw was impossible, it just couldn't have happened, golden whatchamacallits don't appear out of nowhere and hang in the air and then vanish, not in real life. I start thinking up all these cockamamie explanations, how it could be a hologram, or a trick of the light, or something wrong with my eyes, or all this stuff, but really, I know all along it isn't any of those things.

And I know what it *was,* too, I'm not stupid and I had a half-decent education, but I can't buy that, not yet, I'd have to think I was crazy, or that the whole world was crazy.

Real people don't see visions of the Holy Grail in their ex-wives' driveways.

But my God, what else could it be?

(My God. That's good. That's just exactly right.)

So I'm cruising down I-70 at sixty or so, and the sun's going down behind me and my lights are on, the sky's all rose-colored fire to either side and going dark straight ahead, and it's one of those days when you think you can really see the earth is curved, that if you aren't careful you'll just fly off into space, gravity seems weak and temporary, the kind of evening when I get feeling weird anyway, I'm not depressed anymore but I'm feeling very weird indeed, and after a while, somewhere around Exit 76, I stop trying to rationalize it, and I say, "Okay, Rob, old boy, you saw the Holy Grail. You had an honest-to-God vision."

Actually, I start to say it a little more profanely than that, I start to call it "a fucking vision," but that's wrong, I can't get the word out, so I switch to "goddamned vision" and that's worse.

An honest-to-God vision. That's what it was. That's what I say.

And when I say that, when I let myself say that, let the words come out, I see a golden light ahead of me, and at first I think it's headlights coming the other way, then I think it's a fire, maybe Baltimore's burning down, then maybe it's just the city lights, but then I see it and I know what it is.

It's the Grail, going on before me.

It's the *vision* of the Grail, anyway.

You know, I wish I could tell you what it was like, but I can't. There aren't the words. You can't think about it in words when you're seeing it. You can't really think about it at all. It just is, and you have to accept it, you have to look at it and accept it. It's a little like that feeling you get from TM, when it goes just exactly right, and it's a little like sex, when that's really good, but it isn't really like anything.

The peace of God, I suppose it is.

It scares the hell out of me, and it feels wonderful, all at the same time. So I slam on the brakes and pull over to the shoulder.

It hangs there, in the sky in front of me, beckoning me, and I close my eyes, and I have to fight to keep them closed, so I can think. I can feel that golden light through my eyelids, like sunlight all over me. I try to ignore it, because I want to *think*.

And what I think is, "Why me?"

In the old stories, the way I remember them, it was the pure young knights who were granted visions of the Holy Grail— Perceval and Galahad and that crowd. Role models of male chastity who go barging around the countryside killing people in fair fights.

This is frankly not how I picture myself. As far as I know I have yet to kill anything bigger than the beagle I backed my dad's car over once when I was a kid, which was not a fair fight, nor were my mortal combats with house mice and cockroaches and the like exactly formal duels. And while I have sometimes been sexually inactive for a few months at a stretch, it was never, after the age of seventeen, entirely intentional. If you want to get away from the hard-core chastity angle and look for a model of undying faithfulness and true romantic love, Cheryl will tell you that while I could certainly be worse, I am not exactly the perfect example there, either. And finally, while I am convinced that my work as an insurance adjuster is respectable and necessary and that I deserve my salary, while I have sometimes helped out folks in distress, always assuming their premiums were up to date and the claims looked legit, I will be the first to admit that this does not make me the moral equivalent of a Knight of the Round Table.

So I am forced to conclude that either God really does move in mysterious ways and we've all misunderstood the whole schmear these last thousand years or so and I am somehow worthy of this honor, or that I'm going completely crazy and none of this is happening, or that it happens to a whole lot of people who just don't talk about it and it's worked its way down the scale to me, or that the whole thing is completely random.

None of these is what you might call a comforting view of the universe, but with that golden light on my eyelids it's sort of hard to think that the universe might be a nasty place after all. I am not depressed at all when that light's shining on me, the empty feeling I usually have after I drop Annie-Beth off is not there at all, I feel full right to the top, if you see what I mean. It's an effort to not just sit back and enjoy it, and I force myself to think, about anything.

I try to imagine what I will say about this at the office. "So, Rob, how was the weekend? Have a good time with Annie-Beth?"

"Oh, sure, had a fine time. Saw the Holy Grail on the way home."

This does not strike me as something that will go over well. I try to imagine the answers.

"Oh, yeah, I've seen that. Pretty, isn't it?"

"Get in your way while you were driving? I hate it when that happens."

"You just wait right here, Rob, I have a call to make to a doctor I know."

This does not appeal to me, even though I'm giggling like an idiot, which seems like a pretty undignified reaction to the Holy Grail itself, but I can't help it.

And under the giggling and the euphoria I am beginning to feel seriously put upon. I mean, I didn't ask for this. I'm no King Arthur looking to keep a bunch of bored homicidal maniacs in armor busy. I'm no Galahad out looking for new worlds to conquer. I'm not even Indiana Jones. And wasn't the Grail supposed to have been taken into Heaven?

And what am I supposed to do about it? Visions *mean* something, don't they? The traditional thing is to go questing after the bloody thing, right? But I don't want to go questing.

So I open my eyes and I call out loud, "Why me?"

No one answers, of course; I'm sitting alone in my car beside the interstate, there isn't anyone else there to answer me. God doesn't appear. No angels descend from Heaven.

"What do you want me to do?" I shout.

Nobody answers. The thing just hangs there, shining God's

glory down on me. I sit there and stare at it for a moment, and then I say, "The hell with it," and I throw the transmission into drive and I pull back on the highway and I go home.

And when I get to the Beltway, I go south, and the Grail goes north.

This is a shock; I'd been figuring it would go on ahead of me and hang over the city somewhere, maybe over the Inner Harbor, or maybe it would go on out over the Atlantic. I hadn't figured it would be following the roads, you know? In fact, I'm so surprised that I pull over on the shoulder again, and I turn around in my seat and I watch, and the whole thing, cup and halo and glow, vanishes behind the sign pointing to I-95 north to New York, and it's gone, it doesn't reappear.

And isn't *that* a kick in the head. If I decide I *do* want to go questing, it occurs to me that New York might be the place to start.

Which figures. After all, if you want *anything* in this great country of ours, don't you go to either New York or L.A.? I've always heard you can get anything at all in the Big Apple, but it hadn't occurred to me before that very moment, there on the Baltimore Beltway, that that included the Holy Grail.

And with the glow gone, I suddenly find myself thinking about a whole bunch of stuff that I hadn't before, stuff that I am not happy about. Isn't there something in the stories about no man gets more than one shot at the Grail? Have I just ruined my entire life by not making a U-turn across the median and heading north? Am I going to spend the rest of my life regretting the loss of that nifty warm feeling I got?

Jeez, I don't like that idea. Makes God sound like some kind of drug pusher, luring in the suckers with a taste of the Grail's light, getting them hooked. And giving someone one chance at something without telling him what the hell is going on, or that he's got the one and only chance, or what it is it's a chance at . . . what kind of God would do that?

I'm giving God more thought sitting there on the Beltway than I had in years, you understand. I was never very devout, either—yet another way I'm no Galahad. But when there's a thing like that . . .

I don't feel like I'm going to suffer because the thing's gone, but you can't always tell right away about things like that, maybe it's just afterglow, maybe I could still turn around and go after it, maybe I could turn at the next exit and head for New York.

And I reach a decision. I put the car in gear and I get back on the highway, and I drive south to my exit, and I don't turn around. I go home.

Because I am not interested in spending years questing after that golden glow. I am not interested in proving myself to anyone, not even God.

All my life I've been looking for things, and being disappointed with them when I find them—if I find them. I've been looking for things without knowing what I was looking for, looking for love and money and sex and all the things people look for. The Holy Grail would be one more. I might know what it looks like, but I don't know what it *is,* or what I'd do with it if I found it. And if I found it, and *it* was a disappointment—think of that for a minute. Think how empty I felt after my marriage broke up. Think how I feel when my kid is bored with me. Think how I feel when my job turns dull and the clients hate me because I won't pay enough and the company's pissed that I'm paying anything.

And think how much worse it would be to touch the Grail and then lose it.

Besides, I realize that I don't need any new quests. I haven't finished the old ones.

And when I get in the house I go straight to the phone and I call Cheryl, and I apologize for bothering her. I ask if she really wants to talk about where we went wrong, because if she does, maybe I'm ready to listen.

I'm not sure, you understand, but maybe.

And I'm planning ahead. I'm thinking about getting back together, or if we're too far apart, of at least tying up the loose ends. I'm thinking about getting to know my kid. I'm thinking about doing my job right.

We talk, and we make a date.

And when the vision of the Grail turns up again a few days later, I just smile and enjoy the glow.

It's been coming every week or two ever since, and I don't know why any more than I did that first time. No one else ever sees it. It doesn't get any closer or any further away. It always heads off to the northeast. Maybe it's not a visitation from God at all, maybe it's just a UFO or something; maybe I'm about to be kidnapped by aliens. I don't know. I don't let it bother me.

I tell Cheryl about it, she just laughs and says that if there was ever anyone less likely than me to go haring off after a Holy Grail, she can't imagine who. She doesn't see it, doesn't feel the glow, but she laughs.

It's good to hear her laugh. And I'm not going on any quest for the Grail.

I have plenty of old quests to finish up.

And maybe, when they're all done, maybe someday when I've finished the ones I started, maybe then I'll take a trip up to New York, or wherever it leads. Maybe I'll see what I find there. Maybe I'll take Cheryl and Annie-Beth.

And if it's not the Holy Grail we find there, well, what the hell. I'm pretty sure that these last few weeks I've found *something*.

The Awful Truth in Arthur's Barrow

———— ✠ ————

Lionel Fenn

Kent Montana stepped wearily into the Heathrow Airport reception area, slightly groggy from his overnight flight from the United States. His eyes felt lined with gravel, his arms were lined with lead, and the carry-on luggage could have used a forklift to hurry it along. He yawned, dropped his bag to the floor, and stretched.

That's when he noticed the man with the grenade.

It was also when he noticed the reception area was unusually empty, as was the jetway behind him. He did manage to glimpse a spot of Harris Tweed cowering behind a ticket counter, but the fact that the man with the grenade was closer attracted most of his attention. Besides, the tweed wanted pressing.

"Are you he?" the armed man demanded hoarsely.

Kent also noticed, and getting pretty tired of it he was, that the pin was not where it was supposed to be; i.e., in the grenade.

"Dammit, man, answer me!"

Weary as he was, and sick unto death of the British Air pilot's seven-hour guide lecture across a pitch-black Atlantic Ocean, and fed up with a portly seat mate who had insisted on reading every magazine on the aircraft aloud and in varying awful dialects, he suspected that responding with a perfectly acceptable, under the circumstances, "Bugger off," might not, in this case, be the wisest choice.

"Who," he said instead, "are you looking for?"

The man, who was of average height and deep enough into

middle age to be damn near old, a little hefty, and dressed in a suit that had seen better days during the Great War, scowled. "He's rather tall without being silly about it, has quiet ginger hair, a fairly squared jaw, walks as if he were a bleedin' baron, and has a Scottish accent on account of he's a Scot. He's also a baron."

"Ah," said Kent. "Him."

The man squinted, pointed with the grenade again and shouted, "By God, you're him!"

Kent yawned.

"A cool one, you are," the man said with grudging admiration.

Kent didn't disabuse him. Instead, he picked up his bag, walked straight over, and said in a low voice, "My mother hired you, didn't she."

The man stared. "I beg your pardon?"

"My mother. You're one of her paid assassins, aren't you."

"The hell I am," the man responded indignantly.

"Then what the hell are you doing with that grenade?"

The man reared back. "Here, here, your lordship, no need to shout." Suddenly, before Kent could scream, run, or otherwise express his growing distress, the man took his arm and hustled him down the passageway toward Immigration. "It's all quite simple, really," the man explained as they hurried on. "My name is Basil. Basil Forthwaite, and I need your help desperately."

Rustlings in the corners, in the rooms they passed, behind and ahead of them, convinced Kent that someone, probably the SAS, was preparing to launch an attack to free him.

"Oh, don't worry about them." Forthwaite said, squinting over his shoulder. "You're royalty. They won't shoot."

They swept around a corner, and the Immigration area opened before them. A clerk at one of the stations gaped, ducked, and threw Kent the stamp, which he used to log himself in as he walked. A few moments later they were zipping down the escalator to the baggage retrieval area. Which was deserted. And quiet.

"Listen, Mr. Forthwaite," he said.

"No need, no need," the man replied. "Your bags?"

Kent nodded toward the end of his left arm.

"Ah. Splendid." He guided them then to the terminal's main area.

The clank of a rifle's bolt being thrown echoed through the huge room.

"Look," Kent said, "I think you've made a mistake."

Forthwaite smiled, shook his head, and aimed for the glass doors to the outside. "No, no, no, I've planned it all very carefully."

Kent glanced around. He saw no one. Nothing. But he sensed more than one barrel of some weapon or other homing in on Forthwaite's skull. "You don't get it."

"Of course not. I have the grenade. They wouldn't dare."

"Mr. Forthwaite," he said, keeping his voice low, "we are in England, correct? Of course we are. I am a Scot, am I not? Of course I am. I am a baron with privileges not available to the masses, correct? Times are lousy here these days, true? Consider, if you will, the implications."

Forthwaite frowned, stopped, looked around, and said, "My God, they'll shoot."

"Probably."

"They won't care if they hit you while they're trying to get me."

"Probably."

"Jesus."

Immediately, the man began an intricate, convoluted, dizzying series of encircling motions around Kent as he brandished the grenade and led him somewhat fitfully through the exit. No one fired. No one popped out to stop them. No one, in fact did anything, not even when Forthwaite pointed to a boxy black vehicle illegally parked at the curb and ordered him inside.

"It's a cab," Kent said, scanning the area.

"Not just a cab, your lordship," the man corrected, opened the door, shoved Kent in, darted around the other side, leapt in behind the wheel, and sped off.

Kent unsprawled himself from the back seat and checked all the windows.

Nothing.

Not even a porter.

So this is what it's come to, he thought glumly; kidnapped by a nutter with a grenade, and no one comes to the rescue.

That's when he realized that the man was driving with both hands; that's when he realized the grenade was quivering on the seat beside him.

"Jesus!" he shouted, and lunged for the door and would have jumped out, speed or no speed, if the door had a handle, or a window that rolled down, or glass in the window that wasn't embedded with wire mesh. "Jesus!"

He stared at the grenade.

Forthwaite glanced into the rear view mirror and chuckled.

"It's a lighter," he said.

Kent glared. "A lighter."

"A lighter."

"You tricked me as well as kidnapped me."

Forthwaite chuckled good-naturedly.

"You could have gotten us both killed, you idiot."

Forthwaite shrugged. "It was worth it. I need you. The country needs you. It's entirely possible that the entire world may need you."

Kent picked up the grenade, tossed it up, dropped it, cringed ever so sightly, and braced himself against the ceiling as the cab veered onto the motorway and sped westward at such velocity that he soon found himself intrigued at the modifications so obviously made in the vehicle's engine. Not that it did his abruptly queasy stomach any good, but considering the handleless doors, the reinforced windows, and the unnervingly high rate of speed, escape for the moment seemed impossible. He therefore suggested to himself that he might as well lean back, enjoy the scenery, and in some manner discover exactly what it was that the clearly insane gent wanted, at which time he would then move on to planning the method of obtaining his freedom.

"What do you want?" he asked sternly.

Barons were well-known for getting to the point.

Forthwaite blasted the horn at a rather large coach, passed it in every illegal way possible, and said, "You've heard of the Holy Grail, no doubt."

Kent allowed as how he had read the stories when he was but a child and his nanny hadn't yet tried to kill him.

"I know where it is."

His mother wanted him dead so she could ditch the title, sell the family estate, and move to Majorca with her coterie of undiscriminating studs; his nanny had wanted him dead because she was being paid to want him dead. And the man obviously wanted him dead just for the hell of it.

Forthwaite glanced in the rear view mirror. "I am not joking, your lordship. I have intimate knowledge of the Grail's whereabouts, but I need you to help me."

Kent hated questions like the one he was about to ask, but he'd been in the habit of asking them for so long that he hardly ever cursed himself afterward: "Why me?"

"You'll see."

I'll see, thought Kent, sniffed, crossed his legs, and stared out at the blur that passed for English countryside.

"Professor Forthwaite," he began.

The man glared. "How did you know I was a professor?"

"Because," said Kent, "it's always a professor who's found the Holy Grail, isn't it, and usually in some antique shop in the Midlands, or a London cellar hitherto undiscovered because of the Blitz, or an abandoned church once used by migrant druids, or in a barrow excavated only in hopes of finding some bones and a couple of quids' worth of tin cups. It's been your life's work, hasn't it. Studying the legends, the ancient maps, the esoteric works of monks who hadn't anything better to do, and the diaries of Norman lords who could barely spell their own names. There was a map found in the binding of some book or other, and after decades of intense geological and geographical research, you've deciphered the scribblings and are determined to bring the Grail into the light of day, with no thought for your own betterment, but only so Mankind can save itself from certain destruction."

Beat that, you little shit, he thought, crossing his arms baronially over his chest.

Forthwaite passed a line of seventeen army lorries before he responded: "Interesting."

Kent raised an eyebrow. Not only did he hate asking questions, he also hated it when the other guy said, "Interesting." Such a pronouncement was usually the harbinger of unpleasant revelations. Unpleasant revelations usually meant he was probably going to be killed, usually unpleasantly. In this case, most likely in a high-speed modified-taxi crash.

"Well?" Forthwaite said several miles later. "Aren't you going to ask why it's interesting?"

"No," said Kent.

The police car sirened up beside them. The driver motioned them to pull over, and slow down while they were at it. Forthwaite immediately rolled down his window, jerked a thumb over the shoulder to his passenger, and mouthed, *Baron. Late. Royalty stuff.* And shrugged.

The constable glared at Kent, rolled his eyes, and the patrol car eased away.

Amazing, Kent thought; why the hell didn't I ever think of that?

They passed silently, except for the roaring taxi, through several towns, several more villages, and more sheep pastures than he could count. His stomach grumbled. He complained that he was hungry, and the professor told him it wouldn't be very long now before they reached their destination.

"Which is?"

"Crenywddydde," was the answer.

Kent sat up. "But that's in Wales!"

The professor nodded.

"God, how fast have you been going?"

"You don't want to know," was the somber, ominous answer.

Got that right, Kent thought glumly as the taxi began to slow and the scenery unblurred. What he also didn't know was why the professor thought that he, Kent, believed this fanciful tale of locating the Holy Grail. At least once a decade somebody found the legendary relic only to find it was Aunt Dora's company teapot or something. Why was this different? Why was the professor so anxious to have him, Kent, by his side that he was forced to result in a public kidnapping? Was this man as innocent and nuts as he appeared? Was he perhaps not the only person involved in this picaresque plot? My God, could there actually be minions?

The taxi pulled off the motorway onto a narrow, just barely two-lane country road flanked by high hedgerows. As the road alternately dipped and climbed, Kent tried to enjoy the lush greens, the soft browns, the vibrant wildflower colors; unfortunately he couldn't help wondering what would happen if a large tractor came around that far bend up there. Actually, he knew what would happen; he just wondered how long he'd lie in the wreckage before anyone came to help.

The tractor appeared when the taxi was not forty yards from the bend.

Forthwaite yelped and wrenched the wheel.

Kent yelped and froze.

The tractor didn't swerve, didn't duck, didn't make a single maneuver to avoid the collision. Only the professor's quick hand on the wheel swept them around the monstrous charging vehicle with only loud and terrifying wrenching of metal to prove that the farm implement had actually struck them.

At the bend itself Forthwaite stopped and twisted around to stare through the rear window. "He ... tried to kill us!" he declared.

Kent was also staring after the tractor, which was moving at a speed quite unnatural to the size of the thing. "Yes," he said thoughtfully. "I believe he did."

"My lord," the professor gasped. "I knew they were angry, but I never suspected ..." He turned immediately back to the wheel and refired the engine.

"Who is angry?" Kent asked.

There was no answer.

Of course, Kent thought; of course.

Ten minutes later, when the hedgerows vanished, they pulled into a small village of not more than half a dozen buildings the most prominent of which was a Tudor inn called The Green Gawain, on the right. Forthwaite pulled into the paved front yard and parked next to a small red sports car.

"Do I have your word you won't escape?"

Kent looked around. "To where?"

"Good enough."

He opened his door, slipped out, eyed Kent warily through the back window, then opened Kent's door and leapt back. Kent got out, stretched, took a deep breath of fresh Welsh country air, glanced at the scratches and huge long dent the murderous tractor had put in the taxi's left side, shuddered at the possibilities, and finally nodded a question at the inn's entrance. The professor nodded back, and together they stepped inside.

"Well, well, well, what have we here?" Kent said.

"A foyer," answered the professor helpfully.

And indeed it was a foyer, or, more accurately, a long hall that ended at an upward flight of stairs. On the right was a half-glass door that led into a dining room; on the left was a frosted glass door that led into the bar. On the walls were wood pegs for hats and coats and sweaters; none of the pegs were in use. The dining room was empty, although all the tables had been set. The staircase sat in shadow.

Forthwaite pushed the bar door open and motioned Kent to follow, leading him to a booth on the far wall.

The bar was empty.

Kent checked his watch—just about noon, and the bar was empty. Damn, he thought as he dropped onto the worn wooden seat and folded his hands on the chipped and worn table. Damn.

"As you can see," the professor said, gesturing to the room, "there's no one here."

Kent nodded.

"It's because of the Grail, you see."

"Out searching for it, are they?"

"Dead they are. Most of them."

Kent blinked. Slowly. Once.

Forthwaite closed his eyes and leaned back with a sigh. "You know a lot, your lordship," he said, "but you don't know it all. Not by half."

Then an attractive dark-haired woman pushed through the door and cried, "Dad!"

"Daughter," Forthwaite replied without much enthusiasm.

The woman, in her early thirties, jeans, a white sweater, and hiking boots, raced to the booth and embraced the professor, who did not return the favor. She leaned away. "You've been driving again."

He nodded.

"Did you find him?"

He nodded.

"Will he help us?"

He shrugged.

"Why that bleedin' toff bastard! Who the bleedin' hell does he think he is?"

"Kent Montana," said Kent Montana. "And you're the daughter who, as it turns out, is the only one who believed in your father's quest when the others scorned and vilified him. And now that it may be too late, you're the only one who'll stand up and fight with him against whatever it is you're fighting against." He smiled at the astonished look on the professor's face. "Get a job in the movies," he explained, "and you learn a lot."

He reached across the table and shook the woman's hand; the woman smiled cautiously.

"Gwynneth," she said. "Sorry your lordship, but it's been such a trial."

"I can imagine."

She smiled openly for the first time. "Yes. Yes, I believe you can at that." With that, she slid from the booth and hurried to the bar where she helped herself to three pints of bitter. Once returned and the drinks parceled out, she gazed into the dark liquid and sighed as her father told her of the attempted murder. Kent thought the least she could have done was gasp a little, or cry a "How dreadful for you!" but all she did was sigh.

He did not much care for the implication of resignation in that sigh; it smacked altogether too much of something the Forthwaites had gotten used to.

She smiled sourly when she saw his expression. "They think he's crazy, you see. They think he's read it wrong or robbed them of a chance to make their fortunes. They don't understand that he's trying to save their lives."

"I thought they were mostly dead."

"Well, they are, some. But not all. As you've already found out."

"Ah." He had a thought; he didn't like it, but he had it anyway. "And you need me as a hostage to prevent the ones still alive from preventing you from completing your excavations."

She sniffed, sipped her drink, smiled. "Not exactly."

"What, not exactly."

"Actually, we were rather hoping you'd talk them out of it."

He stared.

"Being an actor and such," she explained. "You're good with words. Father isn't, obviously. You explain that Father needs time to complete his work and save them all, including the world, and . . ." Her smile became strained. "Awful, isn't it."

He agreed.

"Especially," she added, "with the mood they're in."

"Afraid?" he asked.

"Pissed is more like it." She turned to her father. "And they're out there now, Father."

Forthwaite paled impossibly.

"Where?" Kent asked against his better judgment.

"Arthur's Barrow."

"Where . . . the . . . Grail . . . is."

Gwynneth shook her head. "Not quite, your lordship, not quite."

Kent didn't like the sound of that. He didn't like the sound of the taxi being crunched by the murderous tractor either, but they had survived that bit; this one he wasn't so sure about, especially when the professor reached into his jacket pocket and pulled out a large, lethal, loaded gun and suggested that they make haste before the village lost the last of its viable inhabitants. When Kent suggested that three people weren't going to do much good against a mob, the professor acknowledged the possibility but also allowed as how he could not, in good conscience, permit them to race blindly to their collective Welsh dooms. Kent, although he had a conscience as decent as most and better than half a dozen he could name off the top of his head, suggested that getting oneself dead on behalf of a mob that didn't know any better wasn't exactly going to help the mob save itself from whatever danger it was in by storming a barrow. The professor gave him the point, but pointed out that one could hardly storm a bump in the ground, and what the villagers were doing, actually, was attempting to dig for the Holy Grail.

"Which," he added as they hurried outside and into the taxi, "doesn't exist."

Let me get his straight, Kent thought as the taxi exploded out of the village and onto a cow path that led across a series of picturesque, low rolling hills; I've been kidnapped at the point of a cigarette lighter, hauled into Wales in record time, been nearly squashed by murderous farm equipment, had two sips of pretty fair bitter, and am now cruising suicidally across a bucolic field in order to stop some people from digging for something that doesn't exist, which will kill them when they find it.

Furthermore, it's the Holy Grail that doesn't exist, even though the professor has claimed that he knows where it is.

Furthermore, this Grail that doesn't exist can be found in something called Arthur's Barrow, which is an omen if I ever heard one.

Lastly, the sonofabitch is going to hit that tree if he doesn't—

The taxi stopped.

Gwynneth and the professor leapt out.

Kent, being a more sedate sort of person in the face of danger and ugly death, took his bloody time.

Then the three of them walked away from the tree that had almost been demoted to splinters and climbed a gentle green slope, at the top of which was a short flat space that led to a slope heading in the other direction; which is to say, down. The land beyond was a magnificently large fallow field that stretched to a dim line of mist-enshrouded mountains. Protruding from the bottom of the slope was a green mound some eight to nine feet high and covered with mown grass. It was also covered with a score of firm-faced men armed with shovels and picks, while an equal number of women stood on the ground and waved handkerchiefs and shawls of encouragement. They were laughing, every one of them.

"Arthur's Barrow," guessed Kent.

The professor nodded. "And we're too late." He puffed his ruddy cheeks and blew out a long sorrowful breath. "Since the very beginning, men have tried to find the Grail, you know. They don't always call it a grail, but it doesn't matter. When they begin their journey, they find themselves, every one of them, embarking on an impossible quest. But it doesn't stop them, does it; it doesn't stop them at all." He smiled at Kent ruefully. "I suppose we all have a Grail in our lives though, wouldn't you say, your lordship? A search for Truth, Meaning, a need to find explanation in a world beyond explanation?" He pointed down the slope. "Those people's Grail is the road out of abject poverty and people making fun of their language and their ways. And they think they've found it in the barrow."

Gwynneth nodded sadly, then took the gun from her father's hand, aimed it, and fired.

Kent jumped, but not as high as the man who used to hold a shovel in his hand and now held nothing but a long stick of thick wood, which he dropped instantly when Gwynneth cocked the hammer and took aim again. The others had already rid themselves of their tools and had climbed swiftly down the barrow's sides.

The professor glared at them.

They glared back.

Gwynneth wanted to know if she should pop one of them, just as an example.

Kent wanted to know, though not aloud, if anyone would miss

him if he snuck off, stole the taxi, and got his noble ass back to London.

When the gun sort of quavered meaningfully in his direction, he smiled baronially and, at the woman's suggestion, made his way down the slope. Before he was halfway to the bottom, and it wasn't far in the first place, one of the women recognized him. Under ordinary circumstances, he wouldn't have minded; under the present circumstances, however, being recognized didn't help his anonymity one bit.

As several of the villagers scrambled in their pockets for something they could use for autograph inscription, a burly, curly-headed young man stepped out of the crowd and clamped his hands on his hips.

"You can't stop us, Professor," he said to the professor, who had walked down the slope behind Kent but ahead of the gun. "You know we're right."

The crowd muttered.

Forthwaite shook his head. "Thomas Burton, you're a fool. I've told you a hundred times you're wasting your time. There's no Grail in there."

The crowd murmured.

An old woman in voluminous skirts, a yellowing shawl wrapped around her yellowing hair, and boots high enough to wade across the Tiber, pushed her way to Burton's side. "If there ain't nothing special in there," she said cannily, "what you'd bring *him* here for?"

The crowd mumbled.

The professor raised his hands for silence. "As you know," he said, "barrows have been used for countless centuries for burial mounds."

The crowd stopped mumbling.

Kent had a feeling.

"These mounds often contain nothing more than dirt, dust, and bones. Yet once in a great while they yield fascinating glimpses of culture long since vanished into the mists of time." He pulled a pen from his jacket pocket and pointed at the air as if addressing a blackboard. "Now in most barrows, the preliminary chamber . . ."

Kent sighed. He hated these explanatory bits, when the professor, or the scientist, went on endlessly about what everybody already knew except for a couple of people in the back row. He glanced at Gwynneth, then slopped his hands into his pockets and continued on down the slope. He passed through the crowd, and not one of them paid him any mind despite the earlier stir. A shrug without moving his shoulders, and he wandered over to the barrow. Its back end indeed merged with the hill, and he moved to the other side where, to his probable regret, he found the other end already breached by an entrance shored up with fresh timber.

He stared at the dark hole.

He sniffed.

He barely moved when Thomas Burton came to his side and nodded toward the barrow. "Spooky, isn't it." The handsome young man said. "We was going through the top because nobody wanted to go through there."

"Wise," Kent said.

"You going in?"

"With luck, not in my lifetime."

They could hear the professor answer a question from his audience, followed by a smattering of applause.

"You think the Grail is really in there?" Thomas asked somewhat fearfully.

"Do you?" Kent said pointedly.

The young man took off his cap, scratched his head thoughtfully, and toed at the ground with one boot. "Hope so. We've lost it all, otherwise." He gestured at the field behind them. "Lovely and all, but it's too far from the main roads for tourists, the mines are played out, and me mam's radio program lost its last sponsor yesterday." He looked directly at Kent. "We're desperate, you might say."

Kent realized that he had arrived at a crossroad. As much as he hated the explanatory bits, he hated the crossroads worse because he never seemed to be able to pick the right direction. He decided to play it safe.

"Your mother has a radio program?"

Thomas nodded. "Maggie's Midnight Madness, she calls it. It's on . . ."

"Oh my God," Kent gasped. "Your mother is *the* Maggie Burton, the Midnight Mother of Mayhem and Ballroom Music?"

The young man nodded proudly.

Kent nodded resignedly. Wouldn't you know it, he thought; come to a crossroads, don't pick a direction just to be safe, and you end up going somewhere anyway. Who would have thought that right here, in the middle of Wales, in the middle of a field, in the middle of nowhere, he would come across the one woman, the one program, the one blessed thing that had kept him going during his middle youth years when all seemed ranged against him, especially his mother's hired Highland assassins.

And now all would be lost unless Crenywddydde was saved.

The crowd applauded, but began mumbling again, politely and ominously. If form followed mumble, they would soon storm the hill, disarm the daughter, beat Forthwaite all to hell, storm the barrow, and probably find that whatever was in there wasn't what they thought.

"The professor," Kent said, "mentioned something about a lot of villagers dying."

Thomas pointed. "They went in, they didn't come out. Lots of screaming, though, and odd lights and things. Sounded like mam's Midsummer Marvel Show. You know, the one with the sacrifices and—"

Kent cut him off with a wave of his hand. Then he dug deep within himself, couldn't get lost, found his way back out, and said with more gusto than he felt, which wasn't any at all, "You have a torch?" Thomas pulled a long electric torch from his hip pocket.

"You have a weapon?"

"I do," Gwynneth said from his other side, and showed him the gun.

The mumbling became a rumbling.

"Why aren't you helping your father?" Kent asked.

"Because you're going in, you'll need help, and I'm the one with a gun." she answered simply, albeit with a touch of smugness.

Kent sighed.

Gwynneth noted that he did that a lot; Kent noted that sighing a lot was an indication of the Fate and Destiny he hadn't been able to avoid once, not once, dammit, since he'd been born; Thomas noted that Fate and Destiny were sometimes redundant, like now; Kent acknowledged the play on words with a sigh he hastily explained had nothing to do with Fate or Destiny but with the fact that he had finally realized he could not let a part of his childhood fade into history without a struggle and that, perhaps, he had actually been on a Quest of his own without realizing it all along. A Quest for the perfect role, the perfection of his acting craft, the reach for the stars, the grab for the brass ring, the creation of a foundation of a life devoted to making people understand themselves through the Art of the Theater and a couple of movies.

All this was his Quest.

All this was his Dream.

All this was his Life.

"Winter's coming," Gwynneth said. "If you're going to keep on like that, I'm going to need a coat or something."

Kent grabbed the torch from Burton's hand.

The rumbling became an angry shouting.

"At my side," he ordered as only a baron can. He took Gwynneth's shoulders. "Go help your father, the poor fool, he needs you now."

And then, with a straightening of his shoulders, he switched on the torch and stepped into Arthur's Barrow.

A moment later he stepped back out again and said, "Thomas, I know you're secretly in love with the professor's daughter and you want to fight by her side to protect her equally secret love for you, but I'm the damn baron here and I'm waiting."

Thomas blinked. "Oh."

And together they stepped back into Arthur's Barrow.

The first thing Kent thought was: It's damn cold in here.

The second thing was: There's a door here, old and banded in iron, with curious symbols upon it that loosely translated into *keep out or die,* something not usually associated with the likes of the Holy Grail.

The third thing was: The door's already open and if I go in there I'm going to die, just like it says.

Damn; if it isn't one thing, it's another.

He went through the door.

There was a chamber. A large chamber. Dirt walls, dead weeds and stuff hanging from the ceiling, dirt floor, crawling black things scuttling away from the light that flashed across the dirt walls and dead weeds and dirt floor. Set into the walls were ancient and serviceable torches which young Burton instantly set about lighting so that their golden flickering glow chased the shadows into the deepest corners.

In the middle of the floor, resting on rust-stained stone blocks, was a long ornate box, its silver and gold trim tarnished by time, the gems embedded in the lid sparkling as if Time meant nothing to them when it came to sparkling and looking good, the chains that lay on the dirt floor around the box looking like chains that had laid around for a hell of a long time.

"That must be it," Thomas whispered reverently. "That must be where the Grail is."

Kent was astounded. Not because of young Burton's observation, but because he had always believed that the Grail was a small thing, like a goblet or a chalice; but the size of the box before them indicated either a lot of packing material to prevent denting, or that the Grail was large enough to climb into.

Something, he decided, isn't right.

"I'll open it," Thomas said eagerly.

"No. Hang on. Something's not right."

"What's wrong?"

Kent pointed the now-useless electric torch toward a previously unseen niche in the far wall. There, in a neat row, were a number of skeletons. Human skeletons. Fresh human skeletons. Gleaming white fresh human skeletons. Then he directed the young man's attention to the chains, noting how they'd been hacked into several rusty pieces by the axes that lay beneath them. Next he directed the young man's attention to the box, which clearly displayed marks indicating that, until very recently, those same chains had been wrapped securely around it. Lastly, with a grunt that was more of a groan, he noted that the lid of the box was not square with its base.

Then he watched as young Burton added the skeletons, the axes, the chains, and the lid, and took a long step backward.

That, Kent thought wearily, is what I was afraid of.

Damn.

"So," the professor said from the doorway, "you would not listen to me, would you, you meddling fools." He had a demonic gleam in his eyes. He had a gun. He also had his daughter, who was thrust into the chamber and into young Burton's astonished-but-ready arms. "You thought I was crazy. Insane. Out of my mind for claiming I had discovered that for which Mankind had been searching for hundreds of years." He cackled. "And now you want to open that box and see for yourself if I've discovered nothing more than dust, or . . . the Holy Grail!"

"Father, please!" Gwynneth begged.

The mad gleam became a glow.

The hand with the gun rose menacingly.

"They laughed at me, you know," Forthwaite whispered as he stepped into the chamber and closed the door behind him. "They thought I was mad when I told them they were wrong."

Kent, without making too much of a fuss about it, searched the chamber for something he could use as a weapon that would get to the professor before the professor's bullet got to him.

Forthwaite cackled. "All the manuscripts, all the stories, all those horrid, horrid movies."

"Hey," Kent said.

The professor lifted his head and looked down his cheeks at them. "Monks, you know. It was the monks."

Thomas held Gwynneth a little closer; Gwynneth held Thomas

a little closer; Kent backed away slowly along the length of the box, running his left hand along the ancient, rotting sides.

"They were supposed to be the only educated ones, did you know that? Back then, they were the only ones who knew how to write." Forthwaite laughed, and it was a decidedly nasty laugh that perfectly matched the gun he waved through the air. "But the simpletons couldn't spell!"

"Father, what are you saying?" Gwynneth demanded anxiously and, considering the hold her no longer secret lover had on her, a little breathlessly.

Kent stumbled over the chains and grabbed the edge of the Grail's container to steady himself. He froze. He stared at the lid. He told himself that he did not feel the vibrations emanating from the box because boxes that tended to be a thousand years old did not, under any circumstances, vibrate.

"Professor," said young Burton, "you're not making any sense. Put down the gun. We won't hurt you. We'll . . . we'll go away and never speak of this to anyone."

"They're in there, boys!" a man's voice shouted from outside. "Break the door in!"

Forthwaite snickered, and drooled a little. "You don't understand, do you? You have no idea what I'm talking about."

Young Burton hesitated before nodding.

The professor laughed insanely.

Kent examined the gems, the jewels, the patterns, the faded but still visible inscriptions in the lid.

A massive weight thundered against the ancient door, which trembled but held.

Forthwaite fired into the air.

The thundering stopped.

Gwynneth screamed shortly, and Thomas gasped manfully.

Kent shook his head and decided not to think what he was thinking, because if he thought about it long enough, he'd realize that he knew exactly what the mad professor was talking about, and he didn't want to know what the mad professor was talking about, because if he knew, then he'd have to do something; and if he did something, he'd probably get himself pretty shot.

Forthwaite backed the couple off with an angry gesture, reached down, and picked up a length of rusty chain. "Tie yourselves up and be quick about it," he commanded as he tossed the chain to Thomas.

Young Burton scowled his refusal, and winced when the chain struck his chest.

The professor cocked the hammer.

Gwynneth begged her father to see reason, that he'd never get out of here alive, that no one wanted to steal his secrets, and no one need be harmed if only he'd put down the gun and talk to her as one adult to another.

Thomas, however, seeing the wisdom of demurring as well as deferring to a greater ballistic power, wrapped the chain around one wrist, wrapped more around Gwynneth's two wrists, then neatly flipped his hand so that the chain wrapped itself around his other wrist.

"Now your ankles," the professor commanded.

A pounding began on the door, and muffled cries of alarm were heard above them through the roof of the barrow.

Young Burton looked pointedly at his shackled hands.

The professor glared, and ordered Kent to shackle their ankles, then tie himself up and toss himself into a corner. Preferably the one with all the bones.

"Which bones?" Kent asked innocently, stalling.

"Them bones," the professor snarled ungrammatically.

"Them bones?" Kent leaned over the box to peer into the niche. "Which ones? It's getting damp in here, I chill easily."

"Them dry bones," the professor declared impatiently. "Do it!" He aimed at Kent's heart.

"Wait," said Kent hastily. "I'd like to say something."

"Father, please, hear the word of the lord."

"Baron," Kent said automatically.

Forthwaite fired.

Young Burton yelped as the bullet winged his left arm, and

dropped to his knees, pulling Gwynneth down with him, who yelped when her head struck the edge of the Grail's container, and she swooned into a daze which young Burton couldn't help her with, since, when he instinctively lifted his hands to catch her, he clocked himself in the forehead with the chains and swooned himself into a daze.

Kent, meanwhile, took advantage of the diversion to leap to stand at the head of the box, while, at the same time, the professor fired at the door to stop all that damn pounding and shouting, and leapt to stand at the foot of the box.

"By my count," Kent said, "you have one bullet left, Basil. If you miss, I'll be very pleased to have your head."

The professor smiled so evilly some of the dirt fell from the ceiling, and more than half the cobwebs Kent hadn't noticed before began to sway. "No matter, your lordship. It is not my only weapon."

Kent followed his gaze to the box, then looked up without raising his head and gestured toward the poor souls who had been stripped of life and flesh and muscle and sinew and organs and a couple of warts.

"They were all men, weren't they," he said.

Forthwaite gasped in astonishment.

"And they were slaughtered by whatever's in this box."

Forthwaite's jaw slackened.

The pounding returned, albeit tentatively.

Kent grabbed the lid on either side and made to slide it off.

"No, you fool!" Forthwaite shouted.

Kent smiled.

The professor wiped a nervous sleeve over his mouth, sopping up most of the drool which had turned into foam. "You have . . . you have no idea."

"But I do," said Kent.

"You don't."

"I do so."

"You can't."

"I can."

Forthwaite's eyes narrowed suspiciously. "Prove it."

The pounding gathered some moral courage and grew louder; Gwynneth groaned; young Burton moaned.

A cold wind began to circle through the chamber, causing the torches to dance and the dust to rise and the bones to clatter.

"Her name," said Kent, "was Gayiewynoleiy. A woman of such unnatural beauty that men slayed each other merely for a glimpse of her, and women tried to slay her so that they would not have this unearthly beauty as competition they could not hope to meet, much less beat. Sadly for the men, she was a nun. But the adoration shown her, not to mention the fact that the other nuns kept trying to murder her, filled her with temptation. For the pleasures of the flesh. For freedom. For money. But most of all, for power." He shook his head at the folly. "She destroyed the convent and all who lived therein, and some say she made a pact with the Devil, for after that day, no man could come near her without . . ." And he nodded toward what was left of the village men who had so boldly and greedily stormed the barrow, opened the previously unsealed door, and hacked off the chains. "And so they entombed her by trickery and deceit, bound her with blessed chains, wrote her story as a warning to all men everywhere against the allure of power in all its heinous forms, and left no record of the place where they placed her body."

He took a breath.

"This place."

He thumped the box.

"This body."

He stepped aside when the box thumped back.

"But how, man?" Forthwaite demanded. "How in God's name did you know all that?"

"I read the box."

"You what?"

Kent pointed to the inscriptions. "I read the box." His eyes widened. "Didn't you read the box?"

"I read the manuscripts."

"Ah. Well, see, I read the box."

The professor leaned heavily against the box and shook his head. "All these years," he muttered. "Every penny I had, every penny I could borrow, steal, beg, implore, urge, or pilfer, so that I could study the stories and their origins in their original form." He groaned angrily. "And you read the goddamn box."

Kent almost felt sympathy for the man except that the gun was still aimed at his heart even in the throes of woe and self-pity. "I suspect you were going to bring this to a conference, weren't you. All those dons and scientists and university colleagues who had been laughing at you all this time. You were going to show them what is in here, weren't you. Of course, you weren't going to be in the room at the time, but you were going to have your revenge, Basil, weren't you. You were going to have your revenge."

"Still am."

Kent frowned.

"Have to start with you, though."

Kent wondered where he'd gone wrong. He'd read the damn box, knew the real story, knew who was in here, knew what the professor had planned, and now the professor was supposed to see the error of his ways and not sink to the level of the scoundrels who had persecuted him all his life.

The pounding, fortified not only with moral courage but also no one shooting at it anymore, intensified.

Gwynneth and Thomas used the wall to brace themselves to their feet, a little dazed but nonetheless unhurt except for the welts on their heads that bled ever so slightly.

"Father," Gwynneth said, "is all that true?"

The professor, torn between grief and madness but not very, nodded.

"Yes," said Kent. "There is no Holy Grail. Do you think those Round Table knights would have tramped all over grimy, disgusting, medieval creation just for a goblet, no matter how holy? Do you really believe a bunch of robust, healthy young men actually destroyed a kingdom for some pounded metal no one had ever seen? Do you honestly believe Galahad was so pure and prissy that he didn't get horny once in a while?"

He thumped the lid for emphasis.

The lid thumped back.

Damn, he thought; I hate it when it does that.

"No. There is no Holy Grail. But there is the ..."

He paused.

There was neither dramatic music nor hysterical wailing nor shrieking violins to mark the tense moment.

He sighed.

"... *Holy Gail.*"

The professor screamed, and fired.

Gwynneth screamed and dropped to the floor, yanking a screaming Thomas with her.

Kent, although not screaming, wasn't entirely inaudible when Forthwaite's madness overtook him and he thrust aside the lid.

The barrow trembled violently.

The pounding stopped.

Clots and clumps and big chunks of dirt fell from the ceiling and the walls and rose from the floor, while the wind howled now and tore the bones asunder and put all the torches out but one.

Kent staggered until he struck a wall, and told himself that if he was really seeing what he was seeing, then he needed glasses because he couldn't be seeing what he was seeing because it was impossible, except for the thumping which should have warned him.

A fierce violet glow exploded from the coffin, for such it was now that everybody knew the true story, and the professor threw up his hands in terror as an ethereal figure in an equally glowing white gown rose supernaturally from the coffin's bed. Though Kent was behind it, there was no mistaking the fact that the figure belonged to a woman. And if her back was any indication, her front was amazing.

Young Burton stammered in shock and burgeoning lust until Gwynneth threw herself as best she could over his body.

Kent realized the world was doomed unless somebody did something pretty damn soon.

Gail did.

She tossed her luxurious ebony hair over her soft rounded shoulders, raised her slender arms, pointed all her enticing fingers at the professor, and laughed in such a way that even though the chamber roared with wind and groans and falling wall parts, the laughter echoed as if streaming up a long tunnel from the very depths of Hell.

Forthwaite threw himself at the door in a futile attempt to escape.

Gail laughed again.

And suddenly, amazingly, the professor's clothes fell away in heaps of ash though there had been no flame; then his flesh bubbled and fell away in heaps of ash, though there had been no fire; then all the rest of him except his bones fell away in the usual manner, until nothing but his skeleton, fresh, white, and gleaming, remained.

At the moment Kent lunged for the floor, lunged back to his feet, and before the hideously gorgeous woman who had condemned all mankind to perdition through lust and vice could turn and fix him with her magic, he swung the ax he had snatched from the floor in his lunge.

Blade met neck.

Steel parted flesh.

Bone shattered.

The head wobbled, wavered, and finally toppled into the coffin.

Kent wasted no time in tossing the ax aside, apologizing to young Burton for nearly taking off his good parts, throwing the lid back on, and grabbing the chains in order to rebind the Holy Gail back in her eternally damned resting place. Seconds later young Burton unbound himself from Gwynneth and assisted him, as did Gwynneth. Seconds after that the wind died, the dust settled, and the ceiling began to fall in rather forcibly.

They flung open the door and fled through the villagers who were waiting outside; the villagers, seeing the flight, fled in sympathetic panic; the barrow, once emptied, gushed with a horrid violet light that spilled into the sky while, coincidentally, the field began to roll and rumble as if in the hands of the Welsh earthquake god.

There was more screaming, some yelling, some falling down and running about before it all ended.

And when it all ended, Kent stood in the middle of the field. Alone. Watching the villagers straggle thankfully off to their humble homes. Watching Gwynneth and young Burton up on the hill embrace, kiss, and walk off into the sunset. Watching steam and smoke curl from the place where the barrow had once been.

"Hey!" he called after anyone who would listen.

Something wasn't right.

"Hey!"

After all, he was the hero, for crying out loud. He had saved the world, saved the woman, saved the temporary sidekick, and saved his own baronial buns in the bargain, not to mention the radio program that had so shaped his youth.

So for this he got to stand in the middle of a field all by himself, his clothes a mess, dirt all over his face, with no one to kiss passionately or even offer him a congratulatory drink?

"Hey!"

He flapped his hands against his legs in frustration.

Then he heard the taxi start up and realized that he'd have to walk all the way back to the inn. For this I uncovered the awful truth about the Holy Gail in Arthur's Barrow and proved, once and for all, that Galahad wasn't a complete idiot?

It clouded over.

He looked up.

"Don't," he said.

It rained.

He sighed.

Reunion

—✠—

Brian M. Thomsen

I lost all feeling from the waist down, weeks, maybe months, ago.

"*. . . and this is the old-timer of the ward. How are you doing today, Percy?*"

Giles is one of the good ones. He doesn't really know that I'm still here, that I haven't already slipped off to the la-la-land of the great beyond. He still treats me like a human being, and not just some withered old husk.

I wish we had met before this place. Before . . .

"*This is Max. He'll be filling in while I'm away at my time-share.*"

I remember Fire Island in July.

"*Can he hear us? He doesn't even blink.*"

"*Does it matter? I'd like to think that his suffering is over, but if he can still hear us, I'd like to think that he still deserves some respect and courteous conversation. Now roll him over onto his side. Careful, those bedsores look mean. Sorry, Percy.*"

"*Should we change the sheets as well?*"

"*No, the doctor wants to examine him first. A new doctor is going to look you over, Percy. Doctor Arnold is summering in Spain, and won't be back 'til September, the lucky old troll. Don't you just hate him?*"

I remember Spain, and I remember France, and Italy, and England. So many places, so many years. I remember Camelot and Arthur and Bors and the quest.

The Grail.

I remember it all, I think.

It's a bit of a jumble and things seem slightly out of order and I don't know how long it's been. There are gaps. The doctor said the lesions could cause amnesia, aphasia, and dementia, and he was partially right on all accounts. Too much to remember. Too much life.

I can't even remember how long I've been lying in this bed.

So many lives.

Too many goodbyes.

I think I still remember the first one, the last time I saw Bors. . . .

"But Perceval, we must return to Arthur. We must," said Bors, pleading for me to accompany him.

"You can if you want to. There's more to the world than just Camelot now."

"But we have been chosen. We found the Grail and must share its blessings with others. It is as Galahad instructed," he implored.

"Galahad is dead."

"No, you know better than that," he argued. "He has experienced the Rapture and has joined God in heaven. We are immortal now, and when our mission is over, we will one day join them."

"You spend your hard-earned immortality your way, and I'll mine. There are more earthbound raptures I plan to experience."

"But what should I tell the others?" he begged, the noble knight Bors now reduced to tears.

"Tell them I went with Galahad, or that I'm in a monastery somewhere, or that I'm dead. Tell them whatever you want . . . or better yet, come with me. Join me in an eternity of experience."

"It would be sinful. This is not why the Grail chose us."

"The Grail did not choose us. We found it. Come with me. We could live like kings."

"Farewell old friend," he said sadly. "Go with God. I shall miss you."

I never saw Bors again. History and legend say that he eventually joined Galahad in the hereafter, or at least so the scholars think.

Bors was pure. His only sin was when he lied to the court about my fate.

I'm sure he was forgiven. He led a good life.

I carry the sins of several lifetimes.

"Moisten his lips. It helps to keep the skin from cracking."

"Jeez, I hope I never get this bad. How old is he?"

"Don't know. He's been on the ward since '88."

"Damn. Five years. I know I couldn't take it. Why doesn't someone just put this withered old husk out of his misery."

"Hush, show some respect. He didn't mean that, Percy."

"For chrissakes, Giles, he can't hear us."

"You don't know that."

Don't be too hard on him, Giles. He's right. This withered old husk would have been better off dead years ago.

Long dead.

But I'm not.

It was about thirty years after parting with Bors that I realized that I wasn't getting any older. The plagues of Europe were claiming young and old. I was immune.

I thought I was lucky.

I made it a habit to move on every ten years or so to avoid making any of the locals suspicious. After all, I didn't want to waste my hard-earned long life finding out what it felt like to be burnt at the stake for witchcraft.

No sense in wasting it.

War was another matter.

I had always been a soldier, a warrior. A warrior has to fight and protect. Normandy, Constantinople, Salzburg, Petersburg. The places all run together.

I took my chances, and I survived.

War brought back that sense of comradeship that had been missing since I left the Round Table.

So many lives, so many deaths.

Mostly war relieved the boredom.

I remember Martin. We fought the Armada together, I think.

We gave each other comfort on those long nights at sea.

"So, my love, what are you going to do when the war's over?"

"What do you mean when the war is over?" he'd say. "It won't be over in our lifetimes, I'll tell you that."

"But what if it was?"

"I don't know, probably go back to my father's farm, marry, and raise a new crop of soldiers for the Queen. What about you?"

"I have no family left."

"Too bad," he offered, and then, smiling, added, "you could come home with me. Father has plenty of land. You could marry my cousin. She's not really that bad off. We could all be one happy family."

He leaned over and kissed me.

"I don't think so. Settling down on a farm is not my cup of grog, if you know what I mean."

"Then I'll join you," he replied. "Two merry gents on the open road. Soldiers for hire for fame and fortune."

I took him in my arms, and as lovers we passed the night away.

He died the following week when we sank the Armada.

He was what we now call an acceptable casualty.

He didn't suffer long.

"Here, let me get that sun out of your eyes. I'll pull down the shade."

Bless you, Giles.

"That new doctor is a real honey. Must be fresh out of med school or something. You notice they keep making them younger and younger."

Youth and appearance aren't all they're cracked up to be.

"I could never have been a doctor. It takes too much time. You could never find me in a classroom when there was a sun to warm my buns or a dancer calling my name. You're only young once. Right, Percy?"

I remember having fun.

"I guess that's why I'm a nurse's aide. It's hard work, but the hours are cool, and besides, where else could I meet interesting guys like you?"

Enjoy while you can, Giles. The clock is ticking for everyone.

"And try not to let Max bother you. He doesn't mean to hurt your feelings. Max is a veteran and his head sort of got messed up during Desert Storm. Takes a lot out of a guy, war does."

That's why I gave it up after a century and a half.

Korea, Vietnam, Palestine. After World War II, I just didn't have the heart anymore. I just gave up soldiering. There had to be better ways to fight boredom.

Maybe I'd just grown too tired of the pain and suffering.

Things began to loosen up a bit too. For a while, I hung with Ginsberg and his crowd, then I ran a club on Bleecker. Dylan played there. Then came Stonewall, liberation and dancing in the streets.

Sex without questions, camaraderie without commitment.

Who needed anything else?

Well . . . Bobby did.

"Now don't take that tone of voice with me."

I had never seen him so angry before. We had been together for nine months and this was our first argument.

"I don't see what the big deal is," he said with that cute little pout that first attracted me to him. "I mean, it's just Sunday Mass."

"You told me you weren't religious."

"But it's a gay church, the Church of the Beloved Disciple."

"I don't have time to just sit around and be called a sinner by some holier-than-thou mama's boy."

"It's not like that. The priest is gay, and he's young, and he's . . ."

"Oh, I see," I answered. "You have the hots for him."

"No, that's not it. I just thought that maybe it was time we sort of got serious about ourselves."

"Serious?"

"You know, maybe get married."

I had been Bobby's first and only live-in lover. He wanted more than I could give him.

"I don't think so," I said, turned and walked out. I didn't come back for a week.

Bobby was gone . . . but that was for the best because I had brought home David. No, not David. He was the one in France, or Germany.

I can't remember anymore.

I thought I loved Bobby, but . . .

What's happening?

Damn this disease. I'm losing it all!

What good is living forever, if I have to live like this?

All of the faces are interchangeable.

There has to be more than this.

"I've got to go, Percy. Max will look in on you after the doctor leaves."

No, Giles, don't leave me, too.

I don't want to forget you.

I want to die!

The room seemed to get brighter. I heard someone's footsteps approaching the bed. It must be the doctor.

Please put me out of my misery.

I couldn't believe it. The doctor was beautiful, full of vigor and health. I didn't even notice that for the first time in four years, I could see.

I recognized him.

He said, "Perceval, it's been a long time. Remember me. I'm Grail. Come home."

I smiled, and felt myself leaving to join Galahad and Bors.

"Shit. Giles leaves, and his favorite old codger dies. Why do I have to be the one to tell him. . . ."

Quest Now

———— ✠ ————

Margo Skinner

For eight hundred years the tale of the Grail
Inflamed the hearts of men
In legends, lays, romances, songs of troubadours,
Some old as Brahma, or the courts of Celtic kings,
Champions congregated at Arthur's table
Perceval, Bors, Galahad, Gawain;
Fair damsels, flaming tapers, feasts and music,
Lapsed champions like Lancelot with his dark-eyed queen,
Who, lost in love and lust, betrayed his king
Yet from his loins bred Galahad,
Untouched by mortal sin, moving through strange dark forests,
Rescuing pure maidens, daunting dragons,
Flame-eyed and fire-breathing in the darkness,
Defeating evil knights, clad in black armor,
Defeating all the forces of the darkness
Until the ultimate blazing victory.

Today there are no knights, not even those
Whom lust and corruption spoiled and soiled.
Vanished now that Luminous Wonder,
A lost legend, hidden in darkness,
Where ragged men sleep in the dirty streets,
The rich stride by them unseeingly,
Their women's rich fragrance taunting raw nostrils,

*To dine in luxe restaurants on fair viands while gaunt children are
     hungry*
And dance in no Grail Castle, but a streamlined mansion,
*Escaping the harsh odor of cheap wine from the man who lies in
     his own vomit,*
The blow on the head, the shot from a stranger,
The lonely death in the dark night.

The rulers are safe from these terrors in barricaded palaces
Or skyborn or seaborne, guarded by security,
Protected by armed men and strong walls,
Drinking the fine wine of luxury,
Embraced in the soft arms of bejeweled women,
Dallying on silk sheets in loveless congress,
Living in a Now world where the soul is dead,
As dead as the vagrant,
Brain-drained by cocaine, staring in the darkness.

Here the Grail is a long-dead dream, the champions vanished.
*Will they return to save the poor, cleanse the loveless grimy chil-
     dren,*
Uproot dead concrete so trees can grow,
Bring forth fruit and flowers once more in the City,
Purify with incense the gas-polluted air,
Bring back the birds to a clean blue sky
In which the Grail shines, radiant forever?

Chivalry

—✠—

Neil Gaiman

Mrs. Whitaker found the Holy Grail; it was under a fur coat.

Every Thursday afternoon Mrs. Whitaker walked down to the post office to collect her pension, even though her legs were no longer what they were, and on the way back home she would stop in at the Oxfam Shop and buy herself a little something.

The Oxfam Shop sold old clothes, knickknacks, oddments, bits and bobs, and large quantities of old paperbacks, all of them donations: second-hand flotsam, often the house clearances of the dead. All the profits went to charity.

The shop was staffed by volunteers. The volunteer on duty this afternoon was Marie, seventeen, slightly overweight, and dressed in a baggy mauve jumper which looked like she had bought it from the shop.

Marie sat by the till with a copy of *Modern Woman* magazine, filling out a Reveal Your Hidden Personality questionnaire. Every now and then she'd flip to the back of the magazine, and check the relative points assigned to an A), B), or C) answer, before making up her mind how she'd respond to the question.

Mrs. Whitaker pottered around the shop.

They still hadn't sold the stuffed cobra, she noted. It had been there for six months now, gathering dust, glass eyes gazing balefully at the clothes racks and the cabinet filled with chipped porcelain and chewed toys.

Mrs. Whitaker patted its head as she went past.

She picked out a couple of Mills & Boon novels from a bookshelf—*Her Thundering Soul* and *Her Turbulent Heart,* a shilling each—and gave careful consideration to the empty bottle of Mateus Rose with a decorative lampshade on it, before deciding she really didn't have anywhere to put it.

She moved a rather threadbare fur coat, which smelled badly of mothballs. Underneath it was a walking stick, and a water-stained copy of *Romance and Legend of Chivalry* by A.R. Hope Moncrieff, priced at five pence. Next to the book, on its side, was the Holy Grail. It had a little round paper sticker on the base, and written on it, in felt pen, was the price: 30p.

Mrs. Whitaker picked up the dusty silver goblet, and appraised it through her thick spectacles.

"This is nice," she called to Marie.

Marie shrugged.

"It'd look nice on the mantelpiece."

Marie shrugged again.

Mrs. Whitaker gave fifty pence to Marie, who gave her ten pence change and a brown paper bag to put the books and the Holy Grail in. Then she went next door to the butcher's and bought herself a nice piece of liver. Then she went home.

The inside of the goblet was thickly coated with a brownish-red dust. Mrs. Whitaker washed it out with great care, then left it to soak for an hour in warm water with a dash of vinegar added.

Then she polished it with metal-polish until it gleamed, and she put it on the mantelpiece in her parlour, where it sat between a small, soulful, china basset hound and a photograph of her late husband Henry on the beach at Frinton in 1953.

She had been right: it did look nice.

For dinner that evening she had the liver fried in breadcrumbs, with onions. It was very nice.

The next morning was Friday; on alternate Fridays Mrs. Whitaker and Mrs. Greenberg would visit each other. Today it was Mrs. Greenberg's turn to visit Mrs. Whitaker. They sat in the parlour and ate macaroons and drank tea. Mrs. Whitaker took one sugar in her tea, but Mrs. Greenberg took sweetener, which she always carried in her handbag in a small plastic container.

"That's nice," said Mrs. Greenberg, pointing to the Grail. "What is it?"

"It's the Holy Grail," said Mrs. Whitaker. "It's the cup that Jesus drunk out of at the Last Supper. Later, at the crucifixion, it caught his precious blood, when the centurion's spear pierced his side."

Mrs. Greenberg sniffed. She was small and Jewish and didn't hold with unsanitary things. "I wouldn't know about that," she said, "but it's very nice. Our Myron got one just like that when he won the swimming tournament, only it's got his name on the side."

"Is he still with that nice girl? The hairdresser?"

"Bernice? Oh yes. They're thinking of getting engaged," said Mrs. Greenberg.

"That's nice," said Mrs. Whitaker. She took another macaroon.

Mrs. Greenberg baked her own macaroons and brought them over every alternate Friday: small sweet light-brown biscuits with almonds on top.

They talked about Myron and Bernice, and Mrs. Whitaker's nephew Ronald (she had had no children), and about their friend Mrs. Perkins who was in hospital with her hip, poor dear.

At midday Mrs. Greenberg went home, and Mrs. Whitaker made herself cheese on toast for lunch, and after lunch Mrs. Whitaker took her pills: the white and the red and two little orange ones.

The doorbell rang.

Mrs. Whitaker answered the door. It was a young man with shoulder-length hair so fair it was almost white, wearing gleaming silver armour, with a white surcoat.

"Hello," he said.

"Hello," said Mrs. Whitaker.

"I'm on a quest," he said.

"That's nice," said Mrs. Whitaker, noncommittally.

"May I come in?" he asked.

Mrs. Whitaker shook her head. "I'm sorry, I don't think so," she said.

"I'm on a quest for the Holy Grail," the young man said. "Is it here?"

"Have you got any identification?" Mrs. Whitaker asked. She knew that it was unwise to let unidentified strangers into your home, when you were elderly and living on your own. Handbags get emptied, and worse than that.

The young man went back down the garden path. His horse, a huge grey charger, big as a shire-horse, its head high and its eyes intelligent, was tethered to Mrs. Whitaker's garden gate. The knight fumbled in the saddlebag, and returned with a scroll.

It was signed by Arthur, King of All Britons, and charged all persons of whatever rank or station to know that here was Galaad, Knight of the Table Round, and that he was on a Right High and Noble Quest. There was a drawing of the young man below that. It wasn't a bad likeness.

Mrs. Whitaker nodded. She had been expecting a little card with a photograph on it, but this was far more impressive.

"I suppose you had better come in," she said.

They went into her kitchen. She made Galaad a cup of tea, then she took him into the parlour.

Galaad saw the Grail on her mantelpiece, and dropped to one knee. He put down the teacup carefully on the russet carpet. A shaft of light came through the net curtains and painted his awed face with golden sunlight and turned his hair into a silver halo.

"It is truly the Sangrail," he said, very quietly. He blinked his pale blue eyes three times, very fast, as if he were blinking back tears.

He lowered his head as if in silent prayer.

Galaad stood up again, and turned to Mrs. Whitaker. "Gracious lady, keeper of the Holy of Holies, let me now depart this place with the Blessed Chalice, that my journeyings may be ended and my geas fulfilled."

"Sorry?" said Mrs. Whitaker.

Galaad walked over to her and took her old hands in his. "My quest is over," he told her. "The Sangrail is finally within my reach."

Mrs. Whitaker pursed her lips. "Can you pick your teacup and saucer up, please?" she said.

Galaad picked up his teacup, apologetically.

"No. I don't think so," said Mrs. Whitaker. "I rather like it there. It's just right, between the dog and the photograph of my Henry."

"Is it gold you need? Is that it? Lady, I can bring you gold. . . ."

"No," said Mrs. Whitaker. "I don't want any gold, thank *you*. I'm simply not interested."

She ushered Galaad to the front door. "Nice to meet you," she said.

His horse was leaning its head over her garden fence, nibbling her gladioli. Several of the neighbourhood children were standing on the pavement watching it.

Galaad took some sugar lumps from the saddlebag, and showed the braver of the children how to feed the horse, their hands held flat. The children giggled. One of the older girls stroked the horse's nose.

Galaad swung himself up onto the horse in one fluid movement. Then the horse and the knight trotted off down Hawthorne Crescent.

Mrs. Whitaker watched them until they were out of sight, then sighed and went back inside.

The weekend was quiet.

On Saturday Mrs. Whitaker took the bus into Maresfield to visit her nephew Ronald, his wife Euphonia, and their daughters, Clarissa and Dillian. She took them a currant cake she had baked herself.

On Sunday morning Mrs. Whitaker went to church. Her local church was St. James the Less, which was a little more "don't think of this as a church, think of it as a place where like-minded friends hang out and are joyful" than Mrs. Whitaker felt entirely comfortable with, but she liked the Vicar, the Reverend Bartholomew, when he wasn't actually playing the guitar.

After the service, she thought about mentioning to him that she had the Holy Grail in her front parlour, but decided against it.

On Monday morning Mrs. Whitaker was working in the back garden. She had a small herb garden she was extremely proud of: dill, vervain, mint, rosemary, thyme, and a wild expanse of parsley. She was down on her knees, wearing thick green gardening gloves, weeding, and picking out slugs and putting them in a plastic bag.

Mrs. Whitaker was very tender-hearted when it came to slugs. She would take them down to the back of her garden, which bordered on the railway line, and throw them over the fence.

She cut some parsley for the salad. There was a cough behind her. Galaad stood there, tall and beautiful, his armour glinting in the morning sun. In his arms he held a long package, wrapped in oiled leather.

"I'm back," he said.

"Hello," said Mrs. Whitaker. She stood up, rather slowly, and took off her gardening gloves. "Well," she said, "now you're here, you might as well make yourself useful."

She gave him the plastic bag full of slugs, and told him to tip the slugs out over the back of the fence.

He did.

Then they went into the kitchen.

"Tea? Or lemonade?" she asked.

"Whatever you're having," Galaad said.

Mrs. Whitaker took a jug of her homemade lemonade from the fridge and sent Galaad outside to pick a sprig of mint. She selected two tall glasses. She washed the mint carefully and put a few leaves in each glass, then poured the lemonade.

"Is your horse outside?" she asked.

"Oh yes. His name is Grizzel."

"And you've come a long way, I suppose."

"A very long way."

"I see," said Mrs. Whitaker. She took a blue plastic basin from under the sink and half-filled it with water. Galaad took it out to

Grizzel. He waited while the horse drank, and brought the empty basin back to Mrs. Whitaker.

"Now," she said. "I suppose you're still after the Grail."

"Aye, still do I seek the Sangrail," he said. He picked up the leather package from the floor, put it down on her tablecloth and unwrapped it. "For it, I offer you this."

It was a sword, its blade almost four feet long. There were words and symbols traced elegantly along the length of the blade. The hilt was worked in silver and gold, and a large jewel was set in the pommel.

"It's very nice," said Mrs. Whitaker, doubtfully.

"This," said Galaad, "is the sword Balmung, forged by Wayland Smith in the dawn times. Its twin is Flamberge. Who wears it is unconquerable in war, and invincible in battle. Who wears it is incapable of a cowardly act or an ignoble one. Set in its pommel is the sardonyx Bircone, which protects its possessor from poison slipped into wine or ale, and from the treachery of friends."

Mrs. Whitaker peered at the sword. "It must be very sharp," she said, after a while.

"It can slice a falling hair in twain. Nay, it could slice a sunbeam," said Galaad, proudly.

"Well, then, maybe you ought to put it away," said Mrs. Whitaker.

"Don't you want it?" Galaad seemed disappointed.

"No, thank you," said Mrs. Whitaker. It occurred to her that her late husband, Henry, would have quite liked it. He would have hung it on the wall in his study next to the stuffed carp he had caught in Scotland, and pointed it out to visitors.

Galaad rewrapped the oiled leather around the sword Balmung, and tied it up with white cord.

He sat there, disconsolate.

Mrs. Whitaker made him some cream-cheese-and-cucumber sandwiches, for the journey back, and wrapped them in greaseproof paper. She gave him an apple for Grizzel. He seemed very pleased with both gifts.

She waved them both good-bye.

That afternoon she took the bus down to the hospital to see Mrs. Perkins, who was still in with her hip, poor love. Mrs. Whitaker took her some homemade fruit cake, although she had left out the walnuts from the recipe, because Mrs. Perkins's teeth weren't what they used to be.

She watched a little television that evening, and had an early night.

On Tuesday, the postman called. Mrs. Whitaker was up in the box-room at the top of the house, doing a spot of tidying, and, taking each step slowly and carefully, she didn't make it downstairs in time. The postman had left her a message which said that he'd tried to deliver a packet, but no one was home.

Mrs. Whitaker sighed.

She put the message into her handbag, and went down to the post office.

The package was from her niece Shirelle in Sydney, Australia. It contained photographs of her husband, Wallace, and her two daughters, Dixie and Violet; and a conch shell packed in cotton wool.

Mrs. Whitaker had a number of ornamental shells in her bedroom. Her favourite had a view of the Bahamas done on it in enamel. It had been a gift from her sister, Ethel, who had died in 1983.

She put the shell and the photographs in her shopping bag. Then, seeing that she was in the area, she stopped in at the Oxfam shop on her way home.

"Hullo, Mrs. W," said Marie.

Mrs. Whitaker stared at her. Marie was wearing lipstick (possibly not the best shade for her, nor particularly expertly applied, but, thought Mrs. Whitaker, that would come with time), and a rather smart skirt. It was a great improvement.

"Oh. Hello, dear," said Mrs. Whitaker.

"There was a man in here last week, asking about that thing you bought. The little metal cup thing. I told him where to find you. You don't mind, do you?"

"No, dear," said Mrs. Whitaker. "He found me."

"He was really dreamy. Really, really dreamy," sighed Marie, wistfully. "I could of gone for him. And he had a big grey horse and all," Marie concluded. She was standing up straighter as well, Mrs. Whitaker noted approvingly.

On the bookshelf Mrs. Whitaker found a new Mills & Boon novel—*Her Majestic Passion*—although she hadn't yet finished the two she had bought on her last visit.

She picked up the copy of *Romance and Legend of Chivalry,* and opened it. It smelled musty. *Ex Libris Fisher,* was neatly handwritten at the top of the first page, in red ink.

She put it down where she had found it.

When she got home, Galaad was waiting for her. He was giving the neighbourhood children rides on Grizzel's back, up and down the street.

"I'm glad you're here," she said. "I've got some cases that need moving."

She showed him up to the box-room in the top of the house. He moved all the old suitcases for her, so she could get to the cupboard at the back.

It was very dusty up there.

She kept him up there most of the afternoon, moving things around while she dusted.

Galaad had a cut on his cheek, and he held one arm a little stiffly.

They talked a little, while she dusted and tidied. Mrs. Whitaker told him about her late husband, Henry; and how the life insurance had paid the house off; and how she had all these things but no one really to leave them to, no one but Ronald really and his wife only liked modern things. She told him how she had met Henry, during the war, when he was in the A.R.P. and she hadn't closed the kitchen blackout curtains all the way; and about the sixpenny dances they went to in the town; and how they'd gone to London when the war had ended, and she'd had her first drink of wine.

Galaad told Mrs. Whitaker about his mother, Elaine, who was flighty and no better than she should have been and something of a witch to boot; and his grandfather, King Pelles, who was well-meaning although at best a little vague; and of his youth in the Castle of Bliant on the Joyous Isle; and his father, whom he knew as "Le Chevalier Mal Fet," who was more or less completely mad, and was in reality Lancelot du Lac, greatest of knights, in disguise and bereft of his wits; and of Galaad's days as a young squire in Camelot.

At five o'clock Mrs. Whitaker surveyed the box-room and decided that it met with her approval; then she opened the window so the room could air, and they went downstairs to the kitchen, where she put on the kettle.

Galaad sat down at the kitchen table.

He opened the leather purse at his waist and took out a round white stone. It was about the size of a cricket ball.

"My lady," he said, "this is for you, an you give me the Sangrail."

Mrs. Whitaker picked up the stone, which was heavier than it looked, and held it up to the light. It was milkily translucent, and deep inside it flecks of silver glittered and glinted in the late afternoon sunlight. It was warm to the touch.

Then, as she held it, a strange feeling crept over her: deep inside she felt stillness and a sort of peace. *Serenity:* that was the word for it; she felt serene.

Reluctantly she put the stone back on the table.

"It's very nice," she said.

"That is the Philosopher's Stone, which our forefather Noah hung in the ark to give light when there was no light; it can transform base metals into gold; and it has certain other properties," Galaad told her, proudly. "And that isn't all. There's more. Here." From the leather bag he took an egg, and handed it to her.

It was the size of a goose egg, and was a shiny black colour, mottled with scarlet and white. When Mrs. Whitaker touched it the hairs on the back of her neck prickled. Her immediate impression was one of incredible heat and freedom. She heard the crackling of distant fires, and for a fraction of a second she seemed to feel herself far above the world, swooping and diving on wings of flame.

She put the egg down on the table, next to the Philosopher's Stone.

"That is the Egg of the Phoenix," said Galaad. "From far Araby it comes. One day it will hatch out into the Phoenix Bird itself; and when its time comes, the bird will build a nest of flame, lay its egg, and die, to be reborn in flame in a later age of the world."

"I thought that was what it was," said Mrs. Whitaker.

"And, last of all, lady," said Galaad, "I have brought you this."

He drew it from his pouch, and gave it to her. It was an apple, apparently carved from a single ruby, on an amber stem.

A little nervously, she picked it up. It was soft to the touch—deceptively so: her fingers bruised it, and ruby-coloured juice from the apple ran down Mrs. Whitaker's hand.

The kitchen filled, almost imperceptibly, magically, with the smell of summer fruit, of raspberries and peaches and strawberries and red-currants. As if from a great way away she heard distant voices raised in song, and far music on the air.

"It is one of the apples of the Hesperides," said Galaad, quietly. "One bite from it will heal any illness or wound, no matter how deep; a second bite restores youth and beauty; and a third bite is said to grant eternal life."

Mrs. Whitaker licked the sticky juice from her hand. It tasted like fine wine.

There was a moment, then, when it all came back to her—how it was to be young: to have a firm, slim body that would do whatever she wanted it to do; to run down a country lane for the simple unladylike joy of running; to have men smile at her just because she was herself and happy about it.

Mrs. Whitaker looked at Sir Galaad, most comely of all knights, sitting fair and noble in her small kitchen.

She caught her breath.

"And that's all I have brought for you," said Galaad. "They weren't easy to get, either."

Mrs. Whitaker put the ruby fruit down on her kitchen table. She looked at the Philosopher's Stone, and the Egg of the Phoenix, and the Apple of Life.

Then she walked into her parlour and looked at the mantel-piece: at the little china basset hound, and the Holy Grail, and the photograph of her late husband, Henry, shirtless, smiling, and eating an ice cream in black and white, almost forty years away.

She went back into the kitchen. The kettle had begun to whistle. She poured a little steaming water into the teapot, swirled it around, and poured it out. Then she added two spoonfuls of tea and one for the pot, and poured in the rest of the water. All this she did in silence.

She turned to Galaad then, and she looked at him.

"Put that apple away," she told Galaad, firmly. "You shouldn't offer things like that to old ladies. It isn't proper."

She paused, then. "But I'll take the other two," she continued, after a moment's thought. "They'll look nice on the mantelpiece. And two for one's fair, or I don't know what is."

Galaad beamed. He put the ruby apple into his leather pouch. Then he went down on one knee, and kissed Mrs. Whitaker's hand.

"Stop that," said Mrs. Whitaker. She poured them both cups of tea, after getting out the very best china, which was only for special occasions.

They sat in silence, drinking their tea.

When they had finished their tea they went into the parlour.

Galaad crossed himself, and picked up the Grail.

Mrs. Whitaker arranged the Egg and the Stone where the Grail had been. The Egg kept tipping on one side, and she propped it up against the little china dog.

"They do look very nice," said Mrs. Whitaker.

"Yes," agreed Galaad. "They look very nice."

"Can I give you anything to eat before you go back?" she asked.

He shook his head.

"Some fruit cake," she said. "You may not think you want any now, but you'll be glad of it in a few hours time. And you should probably use the facilities. Now, give me that, and I'll wrap it up for you."

She directed him to the small toilet at the end of the hall, and went into the kitchen, holding the Grail. She had some old Christmas wrapping paper in the pantry, and she wrapped the Grail in it, and tied the package with twine. Then she cut a large slice of fruit cake, and put it in a brown paper bag, along with a banana and a slice of processed cheese in silver foil.

Galaad came back from the toilet. She gave him the paper bag, and the Holy Grail. Then she went up on tiptoes and kissed him on the cheek.

"You're a nice boy," she said. "You take care of yourself."

He hugged her, and she shooed him out of the kitchen, and out of the back door, and she shut the door behind him. She poured herself another cup of tea, and cried quietly into a Kleenex, while the sound of hoofbeats echoed down Hawthorne Crescent.

On Wednesday Mrs. Whitaker stayed in all day.

On Thursday she went down to the post office to collect her pension. Then she stopped in at the Oxfam Shop.

The woman on the till was new to her. "Where's Marie?" asked Mrs. Whitaker.

The woman on the till, who had blue-rinsed grey hair, and blue spectacles that went up into diamante points, shook her head and shrugged her shoulders. "She went off with a young man," she said. "On a horse. Tch. I ask you. I'm meant to be down in the Heathfield shop this afternoon. I had to get my Johnny to run me up here, while we find someone else."

"Oh," said Mrs. Whitaker. "Well, it's nice that she's found herself a young man."

"Nice for her, maybe," said the lady on the till, "but some of us were meant to be in Heathfield this afternoon."

On a shelf near the back of the shop Mrs. Whitaker found a tarnished old silver container with a long spout. It had been priced at 60 pence, according to the little paper label stuck to the side. It looked a little like a flattened, elongated tea-pot.

She picked out a Mills & Boon novel she hadn't read before. It was called *Her Singular Love.* She took the book and the silver container up to the woman on the till.

"Sixty-five pee, dear," said the woman, picking up the silver object, staring at it. "Funny old thing, isn't it? Came in this morn-ing." It had writing carved along the side in blocky old Chinese characters, and an elegant arching handle. "Some kind of oil can, I suppose."

"No, it's not an oil can," said Mrs. Whitaker, who knew exactly what it was. "It's a lamp."

There was a small metal finger-ring, unornamented, tied to the handle of the Lamp with brown twine.

"Actually," said Mrs. Whitaker, "on second thoughts, I think I'll just have the book."

She paid her five pence for the novel, and put the Lamp back where she had found it, in the back of the shop. After all, Mrs. Whitaker reflected, as she walked home, it wasn't as if she had anywhere to put it.

Falling to the Edge of the End of the World

Bruce D. Arthurs

I bring my own illumination to this dark corner of the tavern, for Captain Silver has no need for such. His head rises up from his nestling arms at the sound of my footsteps, and his blind eyes are a sickly white in the ruin of his face. His skin is deeply wrinkled, darkened and spotted by decades of the intense Quito sunlight.

It is said that Captain Silver has not left the Old Quarter—the cobbled streets, the insane and dangerous-looking vertically oriented buildings—of Quito since it became, by default, the world capital so many years ago. Not since the Turning.

Never has he travelled upsouth, towards the flow of radiant, healing energy that gushes from what was once Antarctica. Never has he basked in the glow of the Turnlight.

All men and women make the great uphill climb, even those crippled and blind, shortly after attaining adulthood. Most travel only one or two hundred miles upsouth, where ills and deformities will be eventually healed, and settle in the new cities there. Some hardier souls are willing to face more of the six-thousand-mile-high mountain beyond the horizon, and go as far as a thousand miles upsouth, where the Turnlight is a glowing fog, blowing with hurricane force.

It is only here, near what had been the equator, that what once was "normal" still holds sway. And it is only here that conception and childbirth can still take place.

But Silver had been one of the ones to go downnorth after the

Turning, farther than any man but one, and the only one to return. And for that returning, he paid with his eyes, and his youth, and his innocence.

The tavern is ancient, a building of dingy stuccoed brick, dating from long before the Turning. Here, each day, Captain Silver waits for those who wish to hear his story.

I sit, placing the required pitcher of thin sour beer on the table, and ask him to begin.

This is what he says.

*   *   *

I can tell from your voice that you are youthful. That is no longer the same as young. Once, I was young.

Before the Turning, men travelled in the sky. Unbelievable, but true. Machines threw themselves through the air, with men wrapped inside their metal skins.

I was one such man. Harralson was another. Our machines were designed and built for intelligence work, crowded with cameras and detectors and radars, with a range of travel that could let us cross continents at undetectable heights. When the Turning occurred, we were high over the central Pacific, searching for the presence of Russian submarines. The flight was a final qualification for Harralson to become an intelligence pilot, and I flew near in my own machine, observing and judging him.

You are silent, youthful man. Most who listen to my story are full of questions by now. What is radar? What are submarines? What are Russians? It is not important that you understand all my words. Radar and submarines are no longer built, and the Russians are all dead.

When the Turning occurred, we were near the equator, and felt only a slight disorientation. Then our radios went mad with cries of confusion and panic and pain. Most transmitters were off the air within seconds. We heard cries of "Earthquake! Earthquake!" from a station in Mexico, then it too ceased.

For moments more, I tried to reach our home base, to reach anyone. I heard Harralson muttering prayers—he was a religious man—in a trembling voice, and I told him to be quiet. Finally, I gave the order to swing back to the north, towards base.

Both of us, I am sure, were thinking that a nuclear war—you do not want to know what that is—had begun. But if so, our instruments should have detected it, and we were high enough that we should have seen the flash of explosions beyond the horizon.

As we went north, we began to encounter difficulty handling the machines. We kept veering to the west, even though the horizon before us told we were straight and level. The attitude indicators refused to agree with what our eyes told us.

There was one station left on the air, broadcasting from the city of Quito, in Ecuador. They knew, no more than we, what disaster was overtaking the rest of the world, but they had been untouched.

I gave the order, and Harralson and I fought our planes around, heading south and east. The handling problems lessened as we neared the equator, but the machines were consuming fuel at a rate much faster than normal. We landed at an Ecuadorian military base with our tanks almost empty.

We were seized and tossed into prison, our machines confiscated. Within a week, however, Harralson and I were on a labor crew, trying to salvage as many crops and foodstuffs as possible, trying to build shelters for the thousands of displaced persons, digging mass graves for the thousands more dead. We fought against hunger and deprivation, trying to survive, trying to let others survive. But mostly we fought against the weather gone mad, the torrential rainstorms, the never-ending winds, the dark ash-clouds that covered the sky and made the rain a slick mud.

Most of the labor crews died, as did many others. Harralson found an English-language Bible on one of the dead, and took it for his own. I raged at his prayers, his acceptance of God's punishment on the world. I raged at our captors, at the loss of our ships, at the loss of our nation. It was my rage that kept me alive while others around me died.

Once, I snatched his Bible from Harralson and threw it into the mud. Then, finally, I saw Harralson's rage, the rage that matched my own, the hidden and denied rage that kept him alive. Others pulled us from where we grappled in the mud. For a time, we did not speak together.

One of the others who did not die was a man named Rivera, a professor of physics who had been in prison for making unwelcome political statements. He had been one of the ones to separate Harralson and me. It was Rivera who listened to what Harralson and I told, who gathered information from other prisoners, from guards, from people encountered in our labors and struggles. And it was he who first theorized the truth of the Turning.

Gravity had twisted, he said.

Near the equator, gravity was still what we thought of as normal; perpendicular to the surface of the Earth. The farther north and south one went, the more gravity twisted away from perpendicular. Westwards became "downhill" as one travelled north; eastwards was "uphill" to the south.

Excepting a narrow band near the equator, perhaps one hundred miles wide, where the tilting effect was slight enough to still be habitable. Elsewhere, civilization had literally been tipped onto its side.

Perhaps ten million people survived the initial Turning. Another seven to eight million died in the flooding and starvation that followed, before the first effects of the Turnlight reached the habitable zone.

Rivera drew a curve in the mud to illustrate his ideas. It began as an almost vertical line that curved over, became momentarily horizontal, then mirrored its curve until it was vertical again. "We're here," he said, pointing at the flat midpoint. "To the north, we fall off a cliff. And to the south, the curve of the world turns into a mountain thousands of miles high."

"That's ridiculous," Harralson said, looking over our shoulders.

I looked at him. "It makes sense. As much as anything makes sense now. Do you have a better explanation?"

"I don't need an explanation," he replied. "I can accept what God has done, without needing to know exactly what it is, without having to draw graphs in the mud. I have a question, however."

"What is it?" Rivera asked.

"If gravity has twisted like you say, shouldn't the oceans all be flowing northwards, toward your new downhill direction? And if so, what happens when all those billions of tons of water accumulate at the top of the world?"

Rivera had an answer for that, too. He drew in the mud again, two half-circles, with a narrow corridor between their facing flat sides. One end of the corridor he marked "N," the other "S."

"Going north," the professor began, switching into his lecturing voice, "gravity twists until it's horizontal to the surface of the earth. As the twisting effect approaches the North Pole, there is a lesser surface area affected. I theorize this results in a 'packing' of gravitational effects. Above a certain point of latitude, gravity increases in force, rather than continuing to twist. And at the Pole itself—gravitational collapse. A black hole."

I stared into his fervent eyes for a moment. "And at the South Pole?"

"A white hole, of course. The other end of the space-time warp, where everything comes out again. Where something comes out."

I couldn't stop from snorting; it was a bit much by this point. "Rivera, what about axial tilt? The Poles wobble, don't they? The magnetic poles, too. How do you fit all that in? And what in Hell caused it to happen?"

"Not Hell," Harralson said. "God." His eyes turned inward.

Rivera ignored the interruption. "I have no way of knowing. I can judge what is, from what I and others have observed and still observe. But I can't judge why. Not yet. I don't have enough hard data." He looked up from the mud, and fixed his gaze on both of us. I should have had a chill run down my back then, but nothing like that happened.

"Someone will have to go look."

The next day Rivera was taken away. It had happened to others. We kept working. Over the next several weeks, the storms lightened in intensity, and one day the clouds broke apart for a short while and let us see how pale and thin we had become.

Soon after, the guards came for us.

We were taken to the military base where we had landed. Rivera was there, in the company of government officials and military men. He was wearing clean clothing, and it took me a moment to recognize him.

"The worst is over," he told us. "The weather is stabilizing, and soon new crops can be planted. The human race will survive, and now we can find what has happened to us."

They wanted Harralson and me to go back up in our machines, to investigate and record whatever was still there to the north and south. Extra fuel pods would be installed wherever weaponry could be removed, extending the machines' range.

Even so, I pointed out, the range was not limitless. But the choice remained the same; go up, or go back to the labor crew.

We spent the next several months getting back into shape, supervising the modifications, waiting for the necessary fuel to be brought along the rain-ravaged, washed-out roads.

Harralson was more the man he had been before the Turning. Although he continued to carry his stained book, his machine was again the most important thing in his life.

Following some short flights to check out the machines' flightworthiness, we lifted into a sky scattered with clouds. Heading north, we climbed to avoid the heavy banks of clouds on the horizon. There were, as always now, constant winds from the east.

We began to feel the Twisting within minutes, our perception of down shifting towards the west. The planes became jittery, harder to control, to keep pointed north.

We flew over what should have been the eastern coast of Mexico. It wasn't there. Our scopes and radars, and breaks in the clouds, showed a huge body of water where land had been. The Gulf of Mexico had tilted onto the land.

The winds were growing in intensity, buffeting our machines. We turned westwards, using the shifting down and the winds to pull and push us towards the southwestern U.S. Our jets were muted to a minimum burn, saving our fuel, using it only for maneuvering and the continuing slide northwards.

Geography, when we found dry land again, was insanely rearranged. Mountain ranges had crumbled and slumped sideways. The hills that remained acted as dams against the debris flooding in from the east. Sometimes we could see different-colored smears against the ground, where a town or city had fallen, scraping into tangled ruins.

The Baja and the west coast of the U.S. were gone, too. California had finally slid into the ocean.

I did not pray for the wife and children I had left there. There was no longer anything to pray for, and there had never been anyone to pray to. Harralson, in his own machine some miles off, was very quiet.

We gained altitude as we crossed what had been the upper Pacific. Now it looked like the mouth of the Mississippi, stained with the billions of tons of soil washed into it. Our perceptions told us we were falling down the face of an endless vast wall.

Russia was flooded, too, being scoured away by the torrents of water futilely seeking an end to their infinite fall. Only isolated mountain peaks still stood erect through the waters around them; eventually, they too would fall.

Our flight plan had us heading southwards again at this point, passing over the Mideast and North Africa before crossing the Atlantic back towards South America.

I signalled Harralson and banked left, southwards across the waters far below us. I was numb with the utterness of the devastation we had seen. That was why, perhaps, several minutes passed before I realized Harralson was not following.

When he failed to answer my radio calls, I fed fuel to the jets and banked around, climbing back to the east. By now, there could be more than a hundred miles between us. Precious seconds, precious gallons of fuel, slipped by before I got his blip, moving northwards, on the screen. He finally responded to my calls.

"Turn around, Captain. This is something I have to do."

"To kill yourself? What good is that supposed to do?"

"I don't think I'll die, Captain Silver. At least, not in the sense you mean. If I do . . . well, that's an end to it."

"Dammit, Harralson, there are still lives, still civilization, back at the equator."

"Not a very civilized civilization, anymore, and it will become worse, despite what Rivera and the government people say. It's all downhill from here, Captain. And I have to take this chance, my last chance, to find an answer."

I paused. "Answer to what?"

"The answer. Do you know why I joined the Air Force, why I wanted to get into intelligence flying? Flying is the nearest I can get to God. I have to fly, Captain. How many more flights will there be after this one? How much more fuel and parts can be salvaged? I think we're the last pilots in the world, Captain, and this is the last flight."

It took me a moment to answer. "Maybe so," I admitted. "But I'd rather live, and remember what I was. I don't want to lose those memories."

"That's where you and I are different, Captain Silver." There was a pause. "I'm going to have to say goodbye. It's getting harder to keep the plane under control."

I felt it, too. A straining on the engines, a heaviness in my arms and shoulders. It was getting difficult to push the air in and out of my lungs.

I tried one last time. "Harralson, turn back."

"Goodbye, Captain."

That was the last I heard from him. I sat unmoving at the controls for several seconds before realizing I might not have seconds to spare.

By now I was above the Arctic Circle, the waters below churning into a maelstrom of unimaginable intensity. The waves I saw below must have been hundreds of feet high, and moving at hundreds of miles per hour.

Going after Harralson had left my fuel margin dangerously thin. I turned towards the west and let gravity add its impetus, using the new rush of speed to lift the machine farther and farther from the surface. Ten miles. Fifteen. Twenty, close to its limit, even under normal conditions.

There was a glow of light at the horizon to my right, a harsh light not of the sun. There was that much of Harralson in me; I had to see. I pushed the plane higher still.

By all the physics and geometry and geography I knew, the sight should have still been beyond the horizon. All that I knew, though, need not still apply to this altered world. Perhaps the sight was bent, like a mirage, around the curve of the world. Perhaps it was not located, truly, at the North Pole. Whatever, I saw it.

There was a pit, a funnel, in the top of the world. Hundreds of miles wide, it went centerwards in a series of steps, of terraces. Eight steps, was it? Or nine? I cannot say, but at the deepest level burned a star, a star that absorbed the waters flashing towards it, emitting the harsh and burning light in return.

I had to turn away from it, my eyes burning, my vision spotted. I turned the controls of the machine, and used the gravity to sling-shot away from the pit's center.

There is little left to tell, youthful man. My fuel margin was almost sufficient. Almost. I had to eject less than a hundred miles from Quito, sending the plane and all its collected data into the ground.

I should have been able to cover that hundred miles in several weeks. But my vision had not fully cleared, and worsened after I reached the ground. The eyeballs coarsened and clouded over, and I went slowly blind. It took months to reach Quito, and finally only by the grace of pilgrims travelling upsouth, following rumors of the Turnlight.

Quito was even emptier than when I had left. Fewer than a thousand people remained. While I had been gone, the first word of the Turnlight and its effects had reached the city. Rivera had gone, and most of the government men, following all the others seeking the luminescent manna.

I remained, and remain, here, a witness to two worlds, one ending, one beginning. I tell my story to those who wish to listen. When there is no one to listen, I pray.

I pray for Harralson's forgiveness.

* * *

The old man falls silent. The pitcher is empty. This is when I should rise and leave, to ponder what I have heard.

I reach out and touch his tumor-scarred face. My illumination flares, cutting through the congealed corneas, into his essence. I enable him to see again, to see beyond sight. I show him my face, and the faces of his wife and children, and the faces of the billions of others within me.

He blinks, then weeps, and kisses my hand.

I lead him outside and present him to the thousands waiting silently in the streets. I remove his clothing and dress him in a cloak of light. "You have told your story for many years," I tell him. "Now you must make a new one. One for all of us."

He takes my hand in one of his. With the other, he points the direction we must go.

Once again, together, with the thousands following, we head north.

Greggie's Cup

✝

Rick Wilber

A small boy imagines being a Knight of the Round Table, and stands atop a low stone wall to hold a mock sword-fight using a slat torn from the old wooden fence that surrounds the vegetable garden. He yells with glee at the imaginary foe that he duels, triumphant in warding off the attack from the lesser knight.

The boy is twelve. And the boy is six, too, in his own way. His eyes are slightly slanted, his face vaguely Asian, rounded like the Mongolians, the nose flattened, the lower jaw pronounced. His movements are a bit clumsy, his dexterity not quite what it should be as he thrusts and parries. He smiles a lot as he plays. He seems happy. He has Down's syndrome.

His swordplay, while clumsy, is effective enough. He knocks away the enemy's weapon, puts his sword to the loser's throat, and listens to an earnest plea for mercy.

Giggling, laughing, happy in his success, he grants the favor, lets the knight rise. And they start again to play.

Greg sits with Tam and Louise at a small table stuck into an alcove in Henderson's vegetarian restaurant on Hanover Street in Edinburgh. They carefully avoid talking about his divorce or the terrible season he had at quarterback for the hapless Buccaneers back in the States. Instead, they toast Louise's reviews and talk about Greg's son's new imaginary friend.

They saw a performance of Louise's play last night at the Tra-

368

verse Theatre. *Rhiannon* is her first to find its way onto a major stage, and has earned raves. She is on her way.

And little Greggie, they all laugh, is just full of new information every day about his make-believe friend, the one he meets each sunny day at the old Roman fort in Cramond, the little fishing village on the edge of the city where Tam and Louise have their refurbished old Victorian home. Greg and his son are staying in the spare bedroom. The house backs up against the ancient stone wall that encircles the ruins, so the place is a perfect playground for the boy, who is, outside of his retardation, as active as any other twelve-year-old.

Tam, who fancies himself quite the expert on Cramond's past, explains how the fort was the farthest extent of the Roman Empire in its glory days in the Second Century.

"Septimius Severus himself paid the place a visit, you know. Imagine that, the Emperor of Imperial Rome traveling all that way to stand in your back yard and look across the water to the kingdom of Fife where those bloody, nasty Picts still roamed the hills."

Tam, a bit of a mystic as well at times, is also convinced the fort has Arthurian associations. "That fort became one of Lancelot's castles, you know," he explains, leaning forward and pointing his pint of Belhaven at Greg for emphasis. "I've read up on this, Greg. It's quite well-documented, mind you. This part of Scotland was Arthur's domain, and Lancelot held this coast for him. Stirling Castle, they reckon, was Camelot."

Greg can only smile as Tam goes on about it. For patriotic Tam everything connects up to Scotland in one way or another, including, of course, King Arthur.

He listens patiently as Tam dives into a long, convoluted explanation of the details of various historical aspects of Arthur, Gawain, Lancelot and Guinevere, and all the rest, until Louise, nearly a Scot herself by now after ten years of marriage to Tam and his gray, old Edinburgh, finally stops him with a smile and says she's been with him to at least fifty ruined Scottish and Welsh castles over the years that all claim connections to the Knights of the

Round Table. It is, she laughs, sort of in league with being the old-est pub in Britain—there are hundreds of bars making the claim.

He is called a strange dreamer, prone to visions and madness. Now, in heavy cloak, wearing his helm and carrying his sword, he adds evidence to such suspicions by mumbling to himself as he walks the courtyard by the kitchen, a private place where all know not to bother him. So many turning points, he mutters, so many poor decisions. And now perhaps a ruined life. No, three ruined lives, a dozen, hundreds. Gods, what tragedy. What can be done to remedy this? How can he explain?

Arthur was right to send them all on this quest, no matter its foolishness. It defuses the tensions and focuses the table on a pur-pose, a reason to go on.

The Holy Grail, indeed. He chuckles. Well, it is certainly not a grail that he will find, not if the tales of purity and devotion hold meaning. It is far too late for that. Gawain, now he might succeed. There is a true-heart if ever there was one, the best, the one true example of what they all had once hoped to be.

Lancelot turns a corner. The thick mist obscures the River Al-mond, emptying into the Frisican Sea on the low ground below. He can barely see the river, and the sea is hidden in gray swirls. In the distance, on a better day, the hills of Fife beckon.

This is his place, this old fortress once Rome's outpost and now his domain. He should stay here, sequester himself, save himself and his King from further pain by absenting himself from it all, the quest, the court, the passion that rules him. He wonders if he will do that, stay and hide. Or will he return to Camelot, return to the King he wronged and try to make it right?

He laughs aloud. A Holy Grail, indeed. For the truest of them. He can only shake his head. He stops, stares into the mist.

And sees a child, a simpleton by the look of him, dressed strangely, walking atop the old, low Roman portion of the wall that still lies in ruin. The boy holds a wooden slat high, laughs and smiles, raises the would-be sword to offer challenge.

The knight accepts, smiling, bowing first, then picking up his

*own wooden slat from the ground to cross swords with the young-
ster.*

*He has never seen this lad before on the grounds, but the boy
seems friendly, eager to please. They duel. The boy has no skills
for this, but enjoys it nonetheless.*

*Such simplicity. An honest, smiling face. Here, Lancelot thinks,
is the purity Arthur seeks, though it comes from addled senses.*

*They duel for long minutes, both laughing and enjoying the play.
As they do, Lancelot, knowing this boy will never pass the tale, be-
gins to speak to the lad, to tell of the woes that face the Kingdom.
Of the tragedies that abound. Of the search for the Grail.*

Greg smiles at Louise's comments. She can always bring Tam
back down to Earth when he wanders off into day-dreamy mysticism like that. As a child, she had years of practice doing just the
same to her little brother, bringing him back from the Wild West or
Sherwood Forest or Camelot—wherever he happened to be when
he was supposed to be doing his household chores.

Now, all grown up in some ways, Greg sits back to sip at his
own Belhaven and thinks about how fortunate he is to have someone as steady and supportive as Louise at a time like this. She is
his good friend as well as his sister. Along with his good-hearted
little son she is the best, most honest person he knows. He trusts
her.

She was wise, he thinks, to tell him to come visit, to check out
the opportunities while he was here. It was the right thing to do after all the hell of the past year. The distance, and difference, from
Tampa washes him clean of the ache, the oppressive gloom, that he
seems unable to shake back home. Here he can get lost in the history, the very age, of the place. Almost nothing in this city is new.
It is all cold, old stone, and he likes it for that, thanks it.

Tam rises to buy the next round and Louise leaves to make a
phone call and check with the sitter on little Greggie and her own
twins. Alone for a few minutes, Greg turns to stare out the window.
There he sees, reflected in the glass, Caroline, the woman from
yesterday, standing over by the bar and smiling at him.

He saw her reflection in much the same way on the train back down from Aberdeen yesterday, where he spent the morning with the owner of the new Scots franchise in the World League. By the end of their meeting the owner told him the job was his if he wanted it, quarterback coach for the Highlanders. Decent pay, a chance for the head job in the future. It was a good offer. New league, new beginnings. In a lot of ways, the deal makes great sense. It would be, he knew, the best thing for Greggie, certainly.

But it means giving up playing the game, and Greg doesn't know if he is ready for that. Last year's debacle, back-up quarterback for a horrible team, might just have been a fluke, a bad season. He is only thirty-seven, and the arm feels good, the left knee is healed from the surgery. He thinks he has one more good season in him, maybe two. If the Bucs don't want him, somebody else will need him, somebody will call.

He told the owner he'd let him know in a day or two, and by half past six he was on the train heading back down to Edinburgh, trying to relax with the local papers, puzzling out the impossible crossword as the train made the run down the coast; Stonehaven, Montrose, past the golf course at Carnoustie, on into Dundee and then across the Tay bridge into Fife—a long line of villages, cliffs, wide strands of cold beach, ruined castles, and cathedrals.

In Arbroath, the train rumbled right through the long shadows thrown by a ruined tower from the abbey and in the brief darkness the scenery disappeared and he saw her face, reflected sharply for that instant, in the window.

The whole ride she'd been sitting across from him and one seat over, paging through a slick women's magazine that hid her. Every now and then he looked out toward the views that passed by and saw a dim, thin version of her in the glass, the angle of reflection getting around the glossy pages. He didn't pay her much attention.

Then came that moment of clarity, of focus. She was perhaps thirty, with Celtic green eyes, soft cheeks, nearly black hair. She wore an old wool sweater and jeans. She smiled as she looked up and caught his eye in the reflection. All this in an instant.

He kept looking toward her in the glass after that, but the image was again indistinct. Later, lulled by the rhythmic train, the sway and occasional jolt from the rails, he drifted away, daydreamed a whole alternate lifetime spent with this apparition.

They met on the train, chatted, began to date, fell in love, married, had three wonderful, normal children. The oldest, a girl, was a doctor. The next, a boy, was a striker for Glasgow Celtic who later coached the national side. The youngest, a bit sickly early on, became a great novelist.

It was a tidy little fantasy, broken up by the memory of Anne's face at the final hearing for the divorce, of her anger, and of the loathing he hadn't known had grown there.

She'd been an hour late meeting him at the airport after the charter home from another loser of a Sunday. Greggie, poor confused little Greggie, was watching from the back seat as Daddy climbed in.

She didn't apologize for being late, didn't say much at all during the thirty minutes home as they careened down the curving, billboarded interstate through the city's new core of reflective downtown glass towers and on into the safe suburbs, waving idly at the guard at the gated entrance to Avalon.

Then, after they pulled into the drive, she stopped short of the garage, shoved the van into park, and said quite calmly: "Greg. I've had it. I'm sorry. I'm leaving."

He tried to say something useful, something to keep her around long enough to talk it out, but there was no overtime here, no two-minute warning.

She dropped them both off, said she simply couldn't spend another day with the two of them, couldn't handle the thought of raising someone else's retarded child for the rest of her life, of being married to one big kid who wouldn't ever grow up and mother to another one that couldn't, and left.

Just like that. Greg stood in the driveway, floppy little Greggie with that goofy grin on his face standing next to him, as she left, taillights flashing in the heat as she rounded the corner from their cul-de-sac and pulled onto the main street. Greggie waved bye-bye.

Later that evening, standing in the kitchen while he talked to

Louise about it, needing a better connection with her than he had, he watched as Greggie struggled with his homework, some exercises in a workbook from his special school. The boy, working hard, had figured out a whole short sentence: "I do not want green eggs and ham." He read that aloud, knew he had it right, and looked up to see his father smile. God, he was finally reading.

Louise had understood why Greg cried as he told her what his son had done, and his wife. Louise, five thousand miles away, had cried with him.

Greg pats his sister's hand. Louise, beautiful Lou. Grown into a stunning woman, tall and blonde, confident, and successful. Gawky and clumsy as a kid, all freckles and teeth and pigtails. Writing those damn stories for as long as he could remember, paying her dues. Suddenly, one friend recommending her to the arts council and another backing that up. There was this chance for a play and she'd taken it, a switch of goals, really. He remembers she worried about it at first.

But the worry faded as she worked on the piece, and now, hard-earned, it is her time for success. On the wall of the stairwell that winds its way up to the wine bar was a poster for her play. Her name was on it, and a picture of her smiling, big as life. She posed next to it, open hands framing her face in mock surprise. He realized only then, seeing her there next to the image of her, how real, how tangible, her success was. It was a long, circuitous path to achievement, but she stuck to it, did it, made it.

There was a boyfriend for Anne, of course, a lawyer. And a settlement, and a nasty enough time of struggling to work things out for Greggie's care and get through all the losses all the way around. The team told him they planned on picking up another back-up quarterback in the supplemental draft, just in case Greg's knee didn't come around like it should. Just in case.

And then, mercifully, slowly, it all eased. The divorce papers signed, the final aching defeat on the field, day-care for Greggie at a place that could handle Down's kids and another place, a good

one, where Greggie could board permanently. That would solve
that problem.

It all took months, but the chaos finally calmed and then he
came here with little Greg to see Louise and settle back from it all,
spend a month or two on healing, to laugh and see the sights with
his happy son, who treated the whole divorce, even Anne's leaving,
as if it were nothing, really, just another bit of confusion in a long
series of incomprehensibles.

When Greg's first wife, Greggie's mom, had left, the boy had
been too young to be affected by it much. Now, when the second
one drifted away, the boy just took it in stride, clung a little tighter
to Daddy, smiled a little harder when they went on their walks.

On the train, Greg shook his head, disappointed at himself for
running through the whole damn thing again. Rain splattered
against the train window, the day's slate tones deepening as they
rumbled through Fife and down toward Edinburgh. He looked out
at the gray, at how it blurred everything around the edges, so different from the hard sun and dark, sharp shadows of Tampa.

And he saw that she was looking at him over the pages of her
magazine, smiling at him in the glass. He smiled back, afraid to
look away from the reflection and directly at her, afraid to ruin
whatever quirky little magic was at work.

They didn't say a word the rest of the ride, only glanced a few
times back and forth, as if sharing a secret. The clouds rose,
thinned, and the sun fought through weakly here and there, improv-
ing the evening. At the end of the ride, at Edinburgh's Waverley
Station, they stepped off the train nearly together and both walked
briskly up the steep walk to the Waverley Bridge. The view there,
of the Castle rising abruptly in the shadowed evening, stopped him
for a moment, splashes of subtle sunset red and pink high cirrus
brushed over the old stone battlements.

"It's quite beautiful, really," he heard her say, and turned to see
her there, smiling at him. "Hello. I'm Caroline, Caroline Forbes,
from the train." And she blushed as she held out her hand.

He blushed back. There hadn't been any women in his life
since Anne. It wasn't like the old days anymore for him, when

there were women everywhere. The easiness of it all had helped ruin his first marriage, and led a few years later to Anne, who'd caught him at the end of that one great year, the playoff year, the Pro Bowl year. Now, burned twice, he had just avoided it, the whole scene, refused to let sex, much less love, slip back into his life. Too much damn disappointment there.

But she was very pretty, and didn't know him as a quarterback, a local hero. Didn't know football, it turned out, from rugby or soccer. Not a fan at all.

So they talked. He had a few hours before he had to pick up Greggie at Louise's place. She had the evening open, had finished her work early in Aberdeen and taken an early train back south.

They took the conversation over to the Red Rose and from there, a couple of hours later, to her place in Marchmont near the university, all of it very natural and comfortable and sexy flirtatious fun.

She liked him, and he needed that, hadn't realized just how much he needed it until she offered it to him. And football, for maybe the first time in his life, had nothing to do with it. She liked him for being him, Greg Fletcher, a guy who read spy novels, who jogged to keep in shape, who liked things from bad pizza to good wine.

Just a guy. Nice enough looking, tall, fit, able to hold a conversation about politics, willing to listen to her opinion.

Damn. He enjoyed himself. Damn near fell in love all at once, started thinking that little daydream on the train was true, was ready to spring the news about his son on her. . . .

When she told him, while sipping on some Aussie wine, that she was married.

"He's an engineer," she said, "petroleum. Works in Oman."

She smiled at Greg, sipped. "Hell of a thing, really. He's gone for months at a time, you see. He knows I date while he's gone, says he doesn't mind."

Greg sat back on her couch, stared out the window to the park below, watched a jogger go by in the evening gloaming, running smoothly down Jawbone Walk toward the university. Damn.

"Look," he said. "I just don't think . . ."

She hushed him. "I know, I know," she said quietly, coming up behind him to rub his shoulders, leaning over to whisper in his ear, say it softly. "We can just share each other, that's all. No commitments. No worry. Just two adults. Enjoyment."

She was, Greg thought, working hard on the profits of her own kind of engineering.

She walked across the room and took a compact disc out of its case, inserted it into the player, hit a button. Van Morrison started singing about enlightenment.

Greg wanted her. Very much.

She turned to face him. Smiled. Held out her arms. "Dance?" she asked. And he rose from the couch.

And thought of Greggie, watching Mommy drive away down the street. Smiling. Waving bye-bye.

The kid was the most innocent, honest, open person there could be. And he trusted Daddy. Completely.

Greg sighed. "Look, you're very lovely, Caroline. And a wonderful person. But, I . . ."

"Just can't do this, right?" she said, dropping her arms. "I know. I know."

She turned away from him, stared out the window. "Damn," she said. "I'm just searching for some comfort, Greg, you know. Mind you, I love my husband, I really do. But months go by." She stopped for a moment, said that again. "Months, Greg."

Van Morrison was talking about the sound of one hand clapping in that song. Greg thought how stupid, how trivial, it was to yank your philosophy from a pop song, but damned if it wasn't spot on. He felt sorry for her. He felt sorry for her husband.

A few minutes later, walking down Jawbone Walk toward the main street where he could hail a taxi, he looked back up to her window. She waved at him, once, and turned away.

What was this miracle? Was the boy an angel? Lancelot, always the dreamer, began to think of this as a spell, something of Merlin's, meant to teach him something. What else could it be?

At noon, he took food from the boy's hands, bread and meat and cheese. Then, later, they sat side by side on the same low wall, a remnant of empire, and Lancelot told the boy of Guinevere, of the miracle of her beauty though she was far older than he, of how he had fallen in love with her despite his great love of his King.

And of how, now, for that King, he sought the Holy Grail.

The boy just smiled to hear this, and then reached out to hug Lancelot, the boy's arms just long enough to barely cross the knight's chest, the cold leather warmed from the embrace. Later, the boy left for a time. When he returned, the two of them, soldier and saint, walked the grounds in the mist, Lancelot telling tales of adventure, the boy, smiling, just listened and held his hand.

Now, in the wine bar, the woman is there, a smiling reflection of her in the glass again. Greg still wants her, of course. He is afraid to turn and see her there, afraid he might walk over and start to talk with her, take things from there to who knows where. He started having second thoughts about walking away from her yesterday the very moment he took the first step out the door.

Then he turns, catches her eye, smiles. And she smiles back, raises her glass in greeting.

He thinks about walking over to her, imagines again what life would be like with her, thinks it might be good, but feels the pain it all would cause, too. And hell, she might not want him, not like that. She seemed interested in a clean little affair, that was all. In and out, as it were. Just Good Fun.

As a kid, playing street football with his neighborhood pals, Greg won a hundred fantasy victories, all last-second come-from-behind wins, long spirals into the darkening evening for touchdowns. He knew then, knew it in his heart, that he was meant for the sport, called to it, would be a star in the NFL, wear a Super Bowl ring, hang his weary arm around the trophy cup after the victory.

It just didn't quite turn out like that, that was all, though he'd made a career of it, a good living really, even at back-up quarterback on a last-place team. He had some moments here and there, golden spirals into outstretched hands, a final-second win over Dallas in eighty-six, that long nine-pass drive against the Falcons the next season. They held promise, those moments, and hope. They kept him going, kept him searching for that ultimate moment, the treasure of success.

And now that search would end, if he let it, and he would have to find a new goal to work toward. Hell, Louise had done it, made that shift, and she seemed happy with it.

Hell, maybe he could even fix his personal life while he was at it. He didn't have much of a track record there, either. Two botched marriages, one flawed son.

But a wonderful kid, really. No question about that. He wouldn't do anything to hurt Greggie, to disappoint him in any damn way. Nothing. Ever. The kid means everything to him.

Greg thinks of all that, of his life and how it's gone, of his son and the boy's future, and looks up to where Caroline stands across the room and smiles at her, waves slightly, and then turns away, his back to her, and waits for his sister to return.

Greggie spent most of the pleasantly warm morning out in the old ruined fort today, clambering around playing gladiator or medieval knight, slaying dragons and rescuing damsels.

At lunch he came in and asked Greg for two sandwiches, one for himself and one for his friend. He asked Greg if he wanted to come out and say hello to the man, a knight, with a sword and everything. Greg, smiling, had declined. Then he took time from his playbook to put some ham and cheese on bread for the boy. Twice. So the friend could have some, too.

Then he watched out the kitchen window as Greggie ran back into the old fort's main yard and pretended to hand one sandwich to his friend before sitting down on a low stone wall to eat the other.

The boy is a charmer. All droopy and loose and painfully slow. But, by God, he is a happy kid, and an energetic, hard-working little guy, full of grins and hugs and love.

On the second day over they went to Tam's centre and watched the kids there play a basketball tournament. Tam ran the place, director of the centre and head coach of a bunch of children in their twenties, thirties, forties, all of them mentally in their early teens at best.

Tam put Greggie on one of the teams, and the kid really played well, considering. He could dribble, and even had a little set shot that went in now and again, and that was unusual in this group.

One of Greggie's teammates, a chubby Down's kid in his forties, maybe, ended one game by dribbling very solemnly down the court, no one bothering him, and then walking in for a lay-up. Dead slow, getting it right, he underhanded the ball toward the rim, where it banged around a bit, rolled around once, and then came back out.

Greggie ran over to the ball, grabbed it, and then instead of shooting it himself rolled it right back to the big kid who picked it up, brought it back to the same spot, and tried the shot again. This time it banged hard off the backboard and settled nicely into the net for a score. Everyone there watching, maybe thirty adults or so, friends and family of the players, applauded for the basket like the kid had just won the NBA.

The whole game stopped for a minute while both sides celebrated. There were happy hugs all around, and clumsy, imitative high fives. Greggie clapped loud and long, hugged the kid who'd scored, was thrilled by all the excitement, glad to be a part of it.

Afterward, everyone on all four teams was given a little plastic winner's cup. Greggie hugged that cup tight all the way home, and put it on the table by his bed, an ultimate place of honor.

Greg had been awfully proud of the boy, for winning the cup, for passing the ball off like that, just for playing hard and being happy.

Sad, too, though. That was his boy's future, that kind of ball, that kind of success. No TV time, no holdouts, no plane flights, no interviews or endorsements.

The boy's world is a foggy one, things half understood, poorly defined. He doesn't understand most of what the knight is saying, catches a word here and there, no more. But he likes listening anyway, hearing the melody of the tales, enjoying the man's smile. The boy can sense a kind of goodness there.

And there is talk of a cup, a winner's cup. Greggie thinks the knight is looking for one. Greggie has something that will help.

Louise is frowning as she walks back into the room.

"Greggie's missing," she tells her brother. "The sitter says he's been out in the fort all evening playing with that imaginary friend, and when she called him to come in he didn't answer. She went out to get him and he wasn't there."

Greggie? Missing? "What?" is all Greg can manage to say.

"She's already called the police, and they'll be there in a few minutes to look for him."

"I'm sure he's right around there somewhere, Greg," Tam adds.

They are there in fifteen minutes, driving up to see the police vehicles, lights flashing, and the sitter, a pleasant older woman who raised four of her own, talking with two officers. It is not long until dark.

The sitter's brave front collapses when she sees Greg. "Ach, the poor wee laddie," she says. "I can't say how sorry I am, Mr. Fletcher. I'm sure he's here somewhere. He came in for supper, and then took that little cup out with him after he'd eaten, said he wanted to show it to his friend. I just thought he was out in the ruins playing, Mr. Fletcher, like he was all the day. I just thought he was there."

Greg hugs her, tells her to go watch the twins, and begins looking for his son.

The police have been walking the beach. Damn, the boy is a good swimmer, but the current here is so damn strong. Would he have waded out into the firth and been carried away?

That doesn't make sense. The water is freezing cold, and Greggie hadn't shown any interest in it before. No, he has to be walking around the town lost, that's all. He'll be fine, just fine.

But the sky slowly deepens into dark blue as the evening wears on and still there is no Greggie.

Greg has walked along the river, hurried along the firth shoreline, checked the four streets of the small town. Nothing. Now he walks through the old Roman fort once again.

Ruins nearly two millennia old throw deep shadows into the corners and he is near tears. This is no sadness like a loss in a football game. This is no career worry, or self-pitying doubt about his damn arm or the season ahead. This is his son.

He hears a rustle in the grass, and Louise and Tam appear around one half-fallen wall some twenty yards away. She waves him over while her husband watches something across the way.

He reaches her, she says softly to him, "Greg. I can't explain this. Please, don't say anything, don't doubt this for a moment, but come."

He goes, and they round that shattered corner of stone, walk through a still functional arch, and there, against a far wall, is a dim figure, medium height, thin, back to them. He is dressed in a long cloak, wears leather over the shoulders and a kind of helmet. There is a long sword at his side. He looks for all the world like some damn Dark Ages knight.

"Who's that? What's he?"

Louise hushes him. Tam adds, "Greg, look closer."

And Greggie is there. Little Greggie, holding the knight's hand, talking to him.

The three of them watch in the deepening shadows as Greggie talks to the man. Finally, Greggie reaches into his jacket pocket and pulls out the plastic winner's cup from the basketball game. He hands it to the man, who shakes his head no and refuses.

But Greggie is nothing if not persistent. He gives it to him again, and, insistent, a third time.

The man takes it. He looks up, sees the three of them watching him, waves his hand in greeting, and turns away to walk through a passage that simply isn't there in the stone wall, to walk right into the stone and disappear.

Greggie, who turned to see them when the man did, waves and runs toward them.

"Hi, Dad. Hi! You see him that time? You see my friend?"

Greg can only smile, and pick his son up to hug him. "I saw him, Greggie, I saw him."

"I give him my cup, Dad. He needed it. He needed it bad."

Greg, just hugs him all the more. Damn kid. Wonderful damn kid.

Later, after Greggie and the twins are asleep, Tam, the would-be mystic, insists it was Lancelot, searching for the Holy Grail, and Greggie gave him one.

Greg just laughs. He's pretty sure it was just some lonely guy who befriended his son and then wandered off. Sweet of the boy to give the guy the winner's cup, just the sort of thing that Greggie would do. And the boy's all right, nothing bad happened. That's all that matters.

And, Greg thinks, maybe it's time to find his own new grail, too. Grow up and take the coaching job with the Highlanders, the best thing all around for Greggie, for the two of them.

Louise, listening to the two of them argue about the guy in the fort, isn't sure what it was and says nothing. She did have a very good view when the guy seemed to walk right through that old stone wall.

Upstairs, in the room that looks out over the fort, little Greggie sleeps soundly. There are dreams of knights and of dragons and of basketball, too. In the morning he will wake and walk into the fort to play, but his friend will be gone.

In the distance, a very great distance, that friend rides toward Stirling, toward Camelot. He mumbles to himself, of Merlin's trickery that brought the strange boy and his message, of the boy's family there by the wall, calling to the lad, ending the vision.

And he mumbles, too, of what he has learned from this, of how he has been touched by that boy's innocence. He has promised himself to at least try to right the wrongs that have happened. There is a great risk here, but one he will take.

He reaches into the inside pocket of his great cloak, and there, next to a piece of the true cross that he won in fair combat in Jerusalem, is Greggie's cup. He touches it, holds it in his large right hand, and pulls it out to see. Such a small thing, really, and of such strange metal. But worth the having, he thinks, well worth the having.

The Grail Legend:

An Afterword

— ✠ —

Fritz Leiber

The Grail is a chalice, the vessel from which Christ drank at the Last Supper. From this vessel He symbolically shared His blood— the blood of the New Testament—with His disciples. An object of great beauty and value, it possesses magical powers of its own, possibly gifts of immortality. Such an object can reside at the magnetic center of an adventure book, say Dashiell Hammett's *The Maltese Falcon,* B. Traven's *The Treasure of the Sierra Madre,* Sir Walter Scott's *The Talisman,* or Portia's casket in William Shakespeare's *The Merchant of Venice.* Sometimes it is a secret weapon, which baffles because of its simplicity, like the AKKA in Jack Williamson's *Legions of Space* novels. Sometimes it functions as a device identifying its wearer, the lens in E. E. Smith's *Lensmen* novels, or it can be an incredibly tiny machine with vast powers, such as the Major and Minor Maintainers in my *The Big Time* stories, which occupy the same space as two fifths of whiskey wrapped in a brown paper bag.

During the four months (November and December of 1936 and the first two months of 1937) when I was in intensive correspondence with H. P. Lovecraft, an astonishing number of experiences were concentrated. I was introduced to Robert Bloch, to Henry Kuttner, and to a New York electrician, who was also a Lovecraft fan. What distinguished the latter was that he had introduced Lovecraft to the supernatural novels of William Hope Hodgson and Charles Williams, including *The Place of the Lion* and *War in*

Heaven. It was a modern mystery novel centering on the Grail, which had been brought to Glastonbury by Joseph of Arimathea.

Opening with a strange murder in a publishing house, the book soon introduces us to the forces of Good and Evil in metropolitan London and the English countryside: urbane diabolists vs. the righteous. Among the latter is a rural archbishop, a man of simplicity, humor, and deep faith, who finds in his church a battered and tarnished silver chalice which possesses remarkable powers. It is stolen by the local landowner, who is also the head of the London publishing firm. He knows it is a thing of power and believes that power can be used for evil in a plot he has hatched involving an innocent child. But the Grail has its own supporters, and in the end, its own victory. Williams' mysticism brings the Grail legend to the England of the 1920's with believable settings, magnificent language, and glowing evocation of the Vessel's past and present reality. These events made the most intense impression on me because of their close proximity to Lovecraft's death in March 1937.

There were the many long letters of Lovecraft's, not only to me but to my wife Jonquil, who had been the first to contact him, and my friend Harry Fischer, the originator of the Gray Mouser. HPL had also read my first-written Fafhrd and the Gray Mouser story, "Adept's Gambit," which he praised generously. I did a series of striking illustrations for his novelette *The Whisper in Darkness,* and gave them to him as a Christmas present.

Before writing this article, I reread Jessie Weston's short book *The Grail Legend,* which in turn was brought to my attention by T. S. Eliot, who said his poem, "The Wasteland," was very much influenced by Weston's book. This is certainly true of the wasteland, for which the poem is named, which surrounds the castle in which Perceval (Parsifal), Lancelot, and Gawain at last had their visions of the Grail. There is a procession led by a youth carrying a lance, from the point of which the Grail-blood drips unceasingly to fall into the Holy Vessel. Another part of the procession is a dead or wounded knight on a litter. There are also several beautiful maidens, some bearing lighted candles in golden candlesticks, while one may be carrying the Grail itself, if not otherwise borne. It is sometimes seen as a chalice, sometimes as a many-jeweled golden object of great beauty, awe-inspiring.

The earliest of the original Grail stories is attributed to Chrétien de Troyes, the latest to Sir Thomas Malory. They were written during the twelfth century and the first half of the thirteenth, and then they die out as though they became very unpopular with the Church. Weston relates this to the persecution of the Albigenses and the Templars at that time. There is a tradition that the Templars had a great treasure that disappeared then, and it is suggested that this might be the Grail itself. *(The Maltese Falcon* is a variant of the same tale.)

Gawain, Perceval, and Lancelot are the chief questers after the Grail. Sometimes in the various stories, the Grail seems to correspond to that of Christian tradition; sometimes it functions more as if it were a magical food source, akin to the myth of Adonis and Cybele, something like the manna that fed the Jews in the desert. But however we look at it, it remains a splendid mystery.